Fairy Tales From The Underworld

Part I

A Bedtime Story

(Beauty Meets the Beast)

L.C. MOON

Copyright 2014 © L.C. Moon

All rights reserved.

License Notes

This is a work of fiction. Names, characters, businesses, places, events, and incidents are either the products of the author's imagination or used in a fictitious manner. Any resemblance to actual persons, living or dead, or actual events is purely coincidental.

ISBN (Print Edition): 979-8-35098-990-8
ISBN (eBook Edition): 979-8-35098-991-5

fairytalesfromtheunderworld.com

Cover Art by Ivanina Elena

*To all whom the darkness coveted,
and to those who loved them nonetheless*

DAY-0

SHE STOOD STILL AMIDST the chaotic music and frantic crowd, holding a Long Island Iced Tea she had been absentmindedly sipping for the past half hour. She had her back to him, and he was silently willing her to turn around. He'd been watching her for two weeks now, keeping track of her routine, habits, and correspondence. She kept to herself. No friends, no pets, and little to no contact with the outside world. She went straight home after her shifts bussing tables at the local deli, where the obese and greasy-haired middle-aged manager seemed to keep her for ulterior motives, considering the number of dishes she broke in those two short weeks.

He liked watching her. She was young, innocent, and pretty. *Very pretty.* She looked even prettier in a grey chiffon cocktail dress and nude stilettos. It was certainly a change from the jeans and hoodies he'd gotten so used to seeing her in. But he wanted to see her face again, to take in her delicate features and stare into those big grey eyes. If he was lucky, he might glimpse one of her scarce but impossibly sweet smiles. He was excited; tonight, he would finally make contact. And yet, he felt slightly nostalgic; tonight, the job was over.

With her back still facing him, she finally turned her head, only her head, as if sensing his stare. Straight chestnut bangs framed her eyes. Her long silky hair, usually in a ponytail, hung loose below her dainty shoulders, brushing against her porcelain skin. She looked sophisticated, far beyond her years. He almost felt reluctant at what was to come. Under different circumstances, his plans for her would have been as sinister, though designed for his own depraved pleasure. *But no, Laura Spencer was a job.* And an important one at that.

★ ★ ★

It was supposed to be fun. The first warm night in early spring had all of Downtown Montreal buzzing with life and excitement. Crescent Street's restaurants and clubs were packed with the overjoyed liberated hibernators. Laura had regretted her decision the moment she'd stepped out her front door. Pamela, the fun and outgoing waitress, had finally worn her down and convinced her to come out. 'It's a new club, classy, you'll love it! Besides, us girls need to stick together! You can't let me meet this guy alone!' Laura rolled her eyes, remembering her coworker's honeyed trap. Pamela seemed awfully fine, flirting up a storm with the handsome customer she had given her number to earlier that day. It didn't take Laura too long to realize she had become the third wheel, and she remorselessly wandered off to get herself another drink. She was tired. She was always tired, and she just wanted to go home. Tomorrow, a new postcard might be in the mail. For the past six months, one postcard was delivered to her mailbox every other week. She lived for these deliveries.

A few men had tried approaching her earlier in the night: a clearly underage charming teen with a presumably fake ID; a pompous, designer-clad entrepreneur who'd addressed her as he would an audience; and finally, a drunken frat boy with an impressively irate girlfriend on his tail. All retreated, unsuccessful.

Suddenly, she felt a prickle down her spine, and turning her head around, she noticed him. He was wearing jeans and a black shirt. He was tall, dark, and handsome. Very much so. She surprised herself by even noticing it. She was seldom aware of her surroundings and often got in trouble at work because of it: daydreaming in the back while clients tapped impatiently on the counter, bumping left and right into staff carrying hot plates—breaking a few too many herself. How she wished to be elegant and graceful. Laura consciously measured her movements in social settings, trying to project empowered femininity she didn't quite possess. Ultimately, she'd resigned herself to looking like a five-year-old covered in bruises and losing a tenth of her paycheck to compensate her employer for her clumsiness.

He was staring at her, his features unexpectedly serious for a man she presumed was out chasing tail. She held his gaze for an instant before her eyes instinctively fell to the ground, and she didn't dare look in his direction again, convinced she would be caught red-handed. She gulped the remainder of her watered-down drink in one shot and headed to the bar for another.

The sultry bartender was evidently more interested in serving the male clientele. And after a few failed attempts at waving her down, Laura was set to accept defeat when a freshly made Long Island Iced Tea miraculously appeared. Her heart skipped a beat in anxious excitement. Could it be the incredibly handsome and slightly unnerving mystery man? She was relieved, if not disappointed, to find out it wasn't. One of those conceited, corporate-looking guys was grinning at her, wearing the typical expression you *would* expect from a man on the prowl.

"So, did I get it right?" He shot her a cocky smile.

"Yes. I mean, no… I'm sorry. I can't take that."

"Ah, c'mon, don't be like that. It's just a drink. I saw you down the last one pretty fast. Sure seemed like you could use another."

She giggled uncomfortably. "Sorry. Really, I can't… I have to find my friend. Thank you, though," she mumbled and quickly turned away, chiding herself for her lack of cool composure. Before she knew it, she ran into a wall of flesh and was about to lose balance when two firm hands caught her on either side.

"Easy there… you okay?"

It was *him.* Laura remained mute, gawking up wide-eyed at the imposing body, which stood too close for comfort. He was taller and better looking than initially assessed, with a light tan, a square jaw, deep brown eyes over plump crimson lips, and dark wavy hair that fell to his chin.

"Are you okay?" he repeated slowly, leaning in and speaking softly in her ear.

Laura could feel his breath on her face and gulped in response. Her heart thumped in her chest, and, for an intangible reason, her instincts threw up red flags all over the place. "Yes… Thank you… I have to go," she managed to blurt out before breaking free of his hold. She fervently looked for Pamela; she wanted to leave. *Now.*

She found her making out in a corner with Mark, because he was just *Mark* now, not the stranger for whom Laura had to play chaperone. Pamela frowned at Laura when she voiced her aggravation at the disappearing act. *She was just with Mark, "It's okay, don't freak out!"* Like she'd known him her whole life. *"Just fifteen more minutes? Please, pretty please?"* she even threw in with eye batting and the whole hoopla. Rolling her eyes, Laura warned her coworker, *not friend*, definitely not at this moment, that she would go outside for a cigarette. Ten more minutes. Not. A. Second. More.

He was already outside by the time she made her way to the street. And he was alone. And he spotted her. She almost turned on her heel but reasoned it would be rude and quite immature. Instead, she smiled politely at him and stood at the opposite side of the door. The mystery man gave a slow nod in acknowledgment, following it with an imperceptible smirk as he took another drag of his cigarette. She waited for him to break the ice and initiate small talk, but he seemed at ease in the ensuing silence.

Feeling self-conscious, Laura's discomfort increased with each drag, and she was halfway through her cigarette when her nerves got the best of her.

"Hey... sorry about earlier. I didn't mean to be rude." She flashed him an honest smile, reminded of the discourteous way she had treated him following their collision. He'd shown concern and was only met with a dismissive brush-off. No wonder he didn't venture again, she surmised.

"It's okay, no harm done." He offered her a disarming, million-dollar smile.

Her heart fluttered, and she couldn't stop grinning herself. "I just... I really suck at these things. And by things, I mean most social interactions," she nervously babbled. Why couldn't she be the composed, self-assured and aloof type? Even her voice went up a few octaves, the sound grating her ears. This man was in his late twenties, at the very least, and there she was, sounding like a high schooler on her way to the prom.

"You're doing all right," he said with an indulgent smile, flicking away his cigarette between thumb and middle finger. "Take care of yourself," he then added on his way back in, brushing her elbow with the tip of his fingers.

Laura felt confused, if not rejected, by his abrupt departure. And yet, she couldn't help softly rubbing the spot where their skin had just made contact. With a telling smile on her face, she gladly welcomed the daydream accompanying her remaining puffs.

Once back inside, she found Pamela in the same corner. Laura tugged at her friend, purposefully looking away in her vain effort to detangle her from Mark. Annoyed, even more so than the last time, Pamela informed her that she would be leaving with him, adding in a gentler tone, "Is it okay?"

"Yeah, don't worry. I'll be fine. I'll just take a cab." *Of course it's not okay. I came here for you.*

"Oh really? Yay! Thanks, you're the best!" Pamela clasped her hands.

"Yeah, you're the best, Lisa!" Mark agreed.

She didn't bother correcting him; she'd be impressed if he remembered Pamela's name come morning. Laura headed outside, relieved to have survived the supposedly fun evening out. And digging through her purse for her cell phone to call a taxi, she realized her wallet was missing. Could this night get any worse? *Emotionally coerced by a friend/coworker to go out? Check. Rejected by the handsome stranger totally rocking mixed signals? Check. Ditched by said friend/coworker for an obvious douchebag? Triple check.* As for the icing on the cake, the case of the missing wallet... Laura would have gotten much more irritated if she hadn't been used to so much worse. As she lit a cigarette to weigh her options, *and walking was not one of them*, he reappeared again.

"You're still here." A pleased and pleasant smile crossed his face.

And just like that, her insides were swarming with butterflies. "Well... I wasn't here the whole time. I went to look for my friend inside... Turns out she's ditched me."

"I meant at the club."

"Oh! Yeah, of course... I mean, no, I'm leaving. Or I'm trying to. Turns out I lost my wallet too." She offered him a self-deprecating grin.

"So, all in all, a great night."

"Yeah, you could say that again." She let out a soft chuckle under his amused gaze.

"I'm Kayne." He offered his hand.

"Laura, nice to meet you." She gave him hers and was reminded of his warmth and firm grasp.

"Do you need money for a cab?"

"Oh no… I couldn't possibly. No, I'll just walk. It's not that far…" she said unconvincingly, her growing smile unconsciously mirroring his.

He gave her a stare, conveying even he knew she didn't mean that for a second. Shaking his head with playful disapproval, he reached into his wallet and pulled out a fifty-dollar bill. "That should cover it," he said, handing it to her.

"No. Seriously. I *can't* take your money," she adamantly refused, bordering on offended. *Why couldn't he just offer her a ride… like normal people?*

"Where you heading?"

"Close to the university. It's not that far. Seriously, I *could* walk…"

"Hmmm…" he uttered, unconvinced and visibly entertained as he put the money back in his wallet. He pressed his car starter and headed toward a charcoal Audi SUV, leaving Laura perplexed on the sidewalk. "You coming?" he finally asked with a smirk, barely turning his head back.

"Are you sure you don't mind?" She caught up to him, smiling away.

With a sly gaze in response, he offered his hand and helped her into the car. He turned on the radio once inside and then lowered the volume as she began to chat away, jittery. Amused by her nervousness, he would turn to her occasionally, the corner of his mouth quirking up.

The car turned off route, and, for the space of a few seconds, he rested his hand very gently on the top of her knee. "Listen, Laura, I have to drop off something. It's literally two blocks down. Do you mind if we make a quick stop?"

"No, of course not. Please, go ahead." Laura was still giddy from his touch, entertaining all sorts of possibilities. She wondered if he would ask for her number and honestly welcomed any opportunity to spend more time with him.

He smiled warmly at her. "Well, it's here. Would you like to come with me, or would you rather wait in the car?"

She looked around warily. The neighborhood wasn't the best, and the street he'd parked on looked even shadier. "I'll go with you. If that's okay?" she asked uncertainly.

He answered with a soft chuckle, and opening the passenger door, he offered his hand again.

★ ★ ★

Kayne had never seen her smile as much as she had that past half hour. It lit up her face, and he'd taken some pride in being both its source and recipient. The charade would unfortunately be over soon. He was walking fast down the long corridor, and she struggled to keep pace. Feeling her furtive eyes burning his back, he could tell she sensed something was amiss. He had felt her tense from the moment they'd entered the building, and he'd understood that, by that point, she had followed him against her better judgment. For starters, he wasn't visibly carrying anything, but she'd made no mention of it.

They got to a double door, and Kayne pushed it open, ushering her inside with a *ladies first* gesture. Laura smiled nervously, but she obeyed.

There were three men already inside the room. A short, stocky one in a pinstripe suit sat behind a massive mahogany desk facing them. He immediately stood up to greet them, an ugly sneer marring his face. The other two could have passed for Secret Service agents, complete with black suits and earpieces, if not for the AK-47s they carried. They stood stoically against the walls on either side.

"What is this? What's happening?" Laura stopped right in her tracks and abruptly turned to Kayne. His expression was detached, his eyes hard and intense, just like the first time she'd noticed him. A shiver ran down her spine.

Kayne didn't answer her. Never breaking eye contact, he slowly shut the door. And with his hands behind him, he leaned back into it, effectively blocking the only exit. He then nudged his head toward the stocky man that was unsuccessfully trying to get her attention.

"Miss Spencer, how lovely to finally meet you. Let me introduce myself. I'm Maxwell Bane. Please, have a seat."

At the mention of her name, Laura snapped her head back toward the man and then right back at Kayne. "What is this? How does he know my name?" she asked in a shocked whisper, her heart pounding furiously.

"He just wants to talk. Have a seat, Laura," he commanded her, his voice devoid of empathy.

"Miss Spencer, would you please have a seat?" Maxwell started again, the gentleness in his tone more forced. "All I am asking for is a friendly little chat. Let's keep things nice, shall we? I would hate to resort to more... persuasive methods."

Laura finally turned to him. "Please... Mr. Bane... I am sure this is a complete misunderstanding!"

"Is it? Are you not Miss Laura Spencer?"

"Yes... but—"

"*Sister* of Peter Spencer?"

Her face instantly paled. Her mouth opened and closed without releasing a sound. So *this* is what it was about. *Oh, Peter, Peter, what have you done?* She knew he had gotten involved with bad things, bad people. He'd been a recreational drug user for as long as she could remember. However, it had all changed in the last years, and he had fallen into the unforgiving clutches of his costly fantasy world. The deceptive Eden he sought bared its claws, and wherever he turned, the snakes it concealed leaped out at him. His paranoia grew unchecked, and she barely saw him anymore.

About eight months ago, she'd found him waiting at her doorstep. In between furtive looks thrown over his shoulders, he'd ushered her inside the moment she'd unlocked the door. Once in her living room, all he'd said was that he had to disappear for a while, *until things blow over*. He'd initially shut down, defensive at her flood of questions. But witnessing her distress, her Peter re-emerged, just long enough to lovingly explain the secret code he'd constructed to ensure *secure communication*. He'd promised: she would always be able to reach him, no matter what.

Two months later, she began receiving his postcards every two weeks, sometimes three, never more than that. She had never truly believed anyone was after him but didn't have it in her to fight his delusions. And so every fortnight, she had gently kissed the latest treasure held in her hands before offering it to the flames, begrudgingly adhering to its originator's instructions.

"What is this about? What do you want with him?" she voiced in a firmer tone.

"Miss Spencer, please have a seat. We just want to ask you a few questions."

"I don't know where he is. I haven't spoken to him in almost a year."

"Oh, come now... We know that's not true. We know *for a fact* that you are well aware of his whereabouts. We just want to talk to him, that's all."

"Bullshit," she mumbled to herself. "You're wrong. I don't know where he is. I'm sorry."

Maxwell squeezed the top of his nose with two stubby fingers, clearly starting to lose patience. "Miss Spencer, I was hoping we could be civil about this. I don't think you understand the severity of your situation. Perhaps my friends can help." He waved his arm toward one of the men by the wall.

Laura shuddered with dread. She did understand. She understood too well. What *they* didn't understand, however, was that she would never, under any circumstance, betray her brother. Peter. Her brother. Her only friend. Her only family. Peter, who'd bandaged her wounds when she was still a child and held her at night when she had nightmares. Peter, who'd taught her how to lie when social services had gotten involved and skipped supper more than once so she could get dessert with her meal. Peter, who'd sacrificed everything, for her. No, she understood. She was not leaving this room alive. A whimper escaped her lips.

She looked at Kayne, the familiar heaviness back in her glistening eyes. "Please… please… I really don't know… You have to believe me," her soft voice wavered.

He remained unmoved, staring her straight in the eye. "I'm not the one you have to convince. My job was to get you here."

She stared at him, feeling hurt and betrayed. "So… that was your plan… the entire evening?"

The faintest smirk crossed his lips, and he reached into his back pocket, pulling out her missing wallet.

Her eyes grew round, and she felt an icy trickle down her spine. "You're a *monster*," she quietly acknowledged to herself, astounded at the realization.

He didn't respond. Instead, he stepped forward and grabbed her firmly by the arm, though not unkindly, and pulled her toward the chair.

Laura didn't resist, allowing her limbs to be dragged. "So that's it? You're just going to leave me here with them?" She looked up, a mix of pleading and panic reflected in her eyes.

If only for an instant, his gaze softened, his tone remained impassive. "You want me to stay?"

She realized the perverse irony. He had brought her here. He was the reason for all of this. But right now, *yes*, she wanted him to stay. Considering the Bane character, she would feel safer with him around, and she shamefully bowed her head, letting out the faintest "Yes."

Kayne slowly nodded, and with the tip of his fingers, he lifted her chin ever so gently, forcing her to look him in the eye. "Okay. I will."

He walked to the back of the room and took a seat facing her, backing the chair against the wall. The two men in black closed in on her and proceeded to handcuff her hands and feet to each side of the chair. Waiting for her to be settled, Maxwell grinned with perverse pleasure.

"Will you be gracing us with your presence, then? Ah… Just like good old times!" He winked at Kayne. "Nostalgic, are we?" he added, letting out a sickening chuckle, to which Kayne responded with a cool smile. Maxwell then turned all his attention back to the helpless girl tied up before him.

"It saddens me, Miss Spencer, to have to resort to such measures. This could have been easily avoided. I do not wish you harm, but let me make myself clear: I will get my answers. One way or another."

"But I swear… I don't know…" Laura quietly sniffled, defeated and hopeless.

"Very well then. If that's how you want to play, have it your way." He motioned to the man identified as Carlo to bring a medieval-looking iron instrument seemingly straight out of the Spanish Inquisition.

Carlo removed her left shoe and inserted her foot into the contraption. He began twisting one of the dials, and a sharp pain shot through Laura's entire body. She screamed in agony as her sobs intensified, repeating over and over again the same few words: *Please, I don't know, I swear.* She thought she might pass out and could barely make sense of what Maxwell was shouting. She looked in Kayne's direction, her vision blurred with tears.

With his legs spread out, he calmly leaned forward in his chair, resting his elbows on his knees. He slowly inhaled a freshly lit cigarette and returned her stare emotionless.

He truly was a monster. How naïve she was to think his presence would benefit her plight. Despair seeped through her thoughts, and she prayed she would soon pass out from the pain.

Without warning, the dials loosened, and just as she began to catch her breath, she felt the sting of cold metal on each side of her little finger. Carlo held garden shears, trapping her left pinky in between the blades. Awaiting Maxwell's instructions, he applied just enough pressure that she made no attempt to move.

Laura's eyes frantically darted about the room, her state of mind reduced to that of a cornered animal. She repeated the same words, even screaming them, her vocabulary dwindling to *please* and *no*. Maxwell's smile was full-on sadistic. There would be no mercy there. *Was there ever?* No, he was taking pleasure in this; it was more than a means to an end. She instinctively fell back on Kayne, pleading with all she had: her words, her eyes, the broken sobs emanating from a body that still unconsciously leaned toward him.

"Enough," Kayne's voice resonated in the room.

In response to Maxwell's inquisitive look, he finally broke eye contact with Laura long enough to demand they be left alone—he wasn't asking. Maxwell seemed incensed at the turn of events, yet he still chose to remain silent. He gestured to his men, and they all quietly left the room.

Kayne got up and unhurriedly made his way over to face Laura. With his arms crossed, he leaned back against the edge of the desk, patiently waiting for her to regain some composure. He only spoke when her breathing slowed, and she finally lifted her head to meet his eyes.

"You love your brother very much." He waited for her to nod in agreement before continuing. "And you are very loyal to him. I respect that. You think there is nothing in the world that could make you talk. That you'd die for him if you had to... But that's not how it goes, Laura. Trust me, *I know*. Everyone has a breaking point. Everyone talks. The only thing that ever changes is the state they're in when they do."

"What do you want with him?"

"Information. Information he stole."

"You're going to kill him... and you'll kill me regardless of what I say," she accused in a jaded whisper.

"Cooperate, and I give you my word. You will leave this room unharmed."

A cynical laugh took over her. "You give me your word? Oh, what a relief!"

"Think about it, Laura. I haven't lied to you once. I don't lie."

"Seriously? You're gonna pull that—"

He raised his brow in silent warning.

"You said you had to drop something off."

"I did." He held her stare, his predatory instinct reflected in his eyes.

Of course, he did. It was her. Laura felt her Long Island Iced Tea coming back up. "I followed you here... You didn't even have to drug me or anything," she murmured to herself, disgusted and incredulous.

"Don't beat yourself up about it. I would have brought you here one way or another. Thought you'd prefer my way," he taunted.

"You really are a monster." She looked him in the eye and felt her voice crack. "Oh God, oh God, please help me."

"You think God is going to help you? No, Laura. God can't help you. I may be a monster, but I'm the only one who can help you right now."

Her heavy lids slowly shut as if to shield her from the inevitability facing her. "But I don't know where he is."

Kayne approached her, kneeling on one leg so he was at eye level with her. "Look at me." He lifted her chin in the same gentle way he had done earlier. "I'm offering you help. I understand you want to protect him. But don't *ever* lie to me," he spat. "Here is what I am offering you, Laura. I don't want you to tell me where he is."

Though a lingering hope flickered in her eyes as he stood back up, she remained quiet, opting for the safety of silence.

"What I want is for you to tell me something, anything, to lead us in his direction. I don't want his exact location. Just the city he's in."

"So you can find him and kill him."

"It could take us over a week to track him. He may very well be gone by then. Don't you see what I'm offering you? It's a chance for you to get out of this alive while still being able to live with yourself."

"But—"

He could see her thinking it over, hundreds of thoughts racing in her mind. "No buts, Laura. It's a good offer. A *very* generous offer. And it will expire soon. I'm counting to five. If I don't have a city by then, I'm walking out of here. And no one, not God, not anyone, will stop what's to come. Do you understand?"

She nodded with anguish. But she stopped him the moment he moved his lips, grasping at straws to bide her time. "I could lie. How would you know?"

From the way his eyes narrowed and his jaw tensed, she instantly regretted her words, and Laura winced when he approached and leaned into her ear.

"You could. But I would *strongly* advise against it," he answered with menacing softness. "I *will* find out. And when I do, I will *personally* continue what they started. Not for answers. Not for the truth. But for the sheer joy of it. I will make a masterpiece out of you. Do you understand me, Laura?"

Her head bobbed up and down in jerky movements, terror ever-present in her eyes.

He grabbed her chin tightly and forced eye contact. "Whatever you do. Never. Lie. To me," he growled, and then he resumed count. "Two, three, four—"

"Boston! He's in Boston." Devastated, she broke down, her body barely supporting her.

Her mascara ran down her cheeks, her face contorted in raw pain. He knew from the torment reflected in her eyes that she told the truth. Still, he asked, "Boston, are you sure?"

"Yes!" she wailed, shaking uncontrollably.

He left her side and stepped out the same door Maxwell and his henchmen had. Laura could hear hushed animated voices on the other side as if caught in an argument. The men eventually reentered the room, with Kayne leading the pack. He walked straight up to her while Maxwell trailed behind, venom dripping from his strained features. He then proceeded to unshackle her, his efficient hands maneuvering swiftly under her baffled gaze. Were they going to kill her now? Then why unshackle her, her tired brain tried to process.

Ignoring Maxwell's presence, Kayne lifted her to her feet with a firm grip. "You're coming with me," he answered her probing eyes, dragging her impatiently out of the room.

"Where are you taking me?" she softly asked, the fight in her long gone.

"To my home. You'll be under my supervision." And irked by her hesitation, he quickly added, "Unless you prefer I leave you with them, of course."

Laura vehemently shook her head in response.

"It's a long drive. I expect you to behave. If you try to reach out to anyone, even just to make eye contact, I *will* kill them. And you will finish the ride in my trunk. Do you understand?"

She nodded, her eyes wide with alarm.

"I want to hear you say it."

"I understand," she quivered.

A half-smile crossed his face, and he brushed her cheek with the back of his fingers. "Good girl."

If this gesture was meant to be soothing, it had the opposite effect. And Laura remained perfectly still, feeling her insides churn with revulsion. To think that not so long ago, a couple of hours at best, the same touch would have had her dreaming for days. That already seemed like so long ago. It was funny, she thought; this should feel surreal, but it didn't. Everything leading up to this ill-fated room was the dream. The nice club, the flirtations with a handsome stranger; those were the borrowed life. The nightmare that followed, that was her reality. Always had been, always would be.

Kayne opened the passenger door for her and helped her in, always the gentleman. The drive was long and quiet, the roads empty. Dawn was creeping in, and though she was exhausted, Laura refused to shut her eyes, wanting to retain some type of control, however small, in her life. About twenty minutes into the drive, as she was losing her battle to fatigue, his voice startled her.

"While you're under my roof, there are three simple rules you need to follow; the first, you've already been advised of. Never lie to me. Never disobey me. Never disrespect me."

The warning snapped her senses fully awake, and she nodded meekly in response.

"Here, wipe your face." He handed her a tissue she tentatively reached for, then placed a call via Bluetooth. A gentle and kind female voice was heard on the car speakers, with the unmistakable patient tone older women adopted when speaking to their offspring.

"Master Kayne."

"Hi, Olga," he responded in a soft voice. "Olga, would you please fully set up the bedroom in the eastern wing? We have a… *guest*… staying with us." He eyed Laura with an indiscernible smile.

"Yes, Master Kayne. Anything else?"

"Yes. Please ask Lucas to set up the B security system."

"Understood. Will that be all?"

"Yes. Thank you, Olga." He smiled. A genuine warm smile, like the million-dollar one he had flashed her at the club earlier. *So it wasn't all an act…? Who was this man? Was she really getting a room?* She assumed that that was a good thing, hopefully with a lock on the inside. It hadn't even crossed her mind to worry about her new living conditions before; she was so glad to flee the men at the interrogation.

Laura looked out the window, pondering about the meaningless life she had led up to this point. Did she ever truly live? And now it was too late. Worse than the fear of what awaited her was the stab of leaving nothing worthy behind, an existence summed up to an unnoticed ripple in the water.

Eventually, she saw a car fast approaching. For the two seconds they were side by side, Laura chanced a side glance and spotted a woman at the wheels. Her heart raced: could she try anything?

"Don't even think about it," his calm voice conveyed the threat.

"Of course I'll think about it!" she snapped back before thinking her response through.

"Careful, Laura…"

"Well… you said to be honest."

He gave her a long and measured look. "I also said to be respectful. Watch your tone," he added, a shadow of a smirk curving his lips.

The sun had risen by the time Kayne finally turned into a long cobblestone driveway with cedars planted on either side. It was an imposing estate in a very secluded area. They passed electronically controlled gates and continued the long drive up to a huge white stone mansion. Above its grand entrance, an imposing family crest proudly displayed an encircled *M* in stylized iron. Men dressed in black, not unlike the ones she had seen earlier, were spread throughout the premises.

"Here it is, home sweet home." Kayne turned to Laura with an inviting smile. He, once again, walked over to her side and offered his hand, but she remained frozen in place. "Get out," he ordered, all traces of gentleness evaporating into thin air.

She gave him a feeble hand. But when her feet hit the ground, they refused to move, unable to take the final steps sealing her fate.

With an impatient huff, he wrapped his right arm around Laura's back, keeping his left firmly gripping her. Kayne dragged the limping mass forward, impassive to the pained yelps it emitted. They climbed the few marble steps as another security team member rushed to hold the massive French doors open for them. They walked into an opulent foyer, halting before imposing double stairs that led to a mezzanine. The whole area was bathed in a golden glow, sunrays bursting through the skylight in the high ceilings. A slightly overweight, older woman in uniform was waiting for them. She had greying hair tied in a low bun, and with a kind smile, she stood with her fingers laced in front of her.

"Master Kayne." She respectfully bowed her head.

"Olga, this is Laura Spencer. She will be staying with us."

"Nice to meet you, Miss Spencer."

Though her warmth seemed genuine, she showed no reaction to Laura's pathetic appearance. She would find no ally in her, Laura concluded, and she nodded with a vacant stare. She replayed the evening in her head, incredulous at the absurdity of it all. A numbing sensation pervaded her being, and she felt herself drift. Slowly, she floated away from her body as though dissociating from the unfortunate fate befalling her host.

"Laura, this is Olga. I trust her with my life. While I am not here, she will see to anything you may need." He looked at his watch. "She'll show you around tomorrow. Please feel free to go wherever you want and use anything at your disposal on the first floor. Just make sure you never go upstairs, downstairs, or outside without my explicit consent. Understood?"

Laura nodded again, her expression blank.

"There is no Internet. The phone lines will connect you to Lucas, my head of security. If there is an emergency, simply dial 9. You will not be able to make any other type of calls. Security is outside the house 'round the clock, and there are cameras pointing in every direction. All the windows and outside doors are equipped with alarms. My men were given my instructions. Please don't try anything stupid… I think that about covers it for now," he paused and surprised her by adding, "Are you hungry?"

She wasn't hungry, just tired, so incredibly tired. All she wanted was to curl into a ball, cry herself asleep, and hopefully never wake up.

DAY-1

OLGA LED HER TO a spacious, elegant, and distinctly feminine room. A woman had definitely lived here, a woman with refined and expensive taste. *Who was this woman? Where was she now?*

Olga inadvertently interrupted Laura's train of thought, politely asking her if she would need anything else before excusing herself. As it turned out, the door did have a lock, but it was the old style with a key, which Laura doubted would ever be given to her. It could have been worse. Though she felt the urge to investigate her new living space, her tiredness took over in one swift wave. She barely had the strength to kick off her heels, and she collapsed in her grey chiffon dress on the spacious bed, its fluffy comforters promising a mind-numbing slumber.

Laura slept profoundly and had many dreams, mostly about her childhood, mostly about Peter. By the time she woke up, the sun was high in the sky, and she blinked a few times, adjusting to the abrasive brightness. She had almost forgotten… but it all came back crashing down, paralyzing any motivation she might have had to get out of bed. Laura decided to stay right in that spot and never move a single muscle again. Caught in the worlds between, she would remain until death graciously lulled her into eternal sleep. The thought had her almost smiling with relief as she shut her eyes, tumbling back into unconsciousness.

Olga came in sometime later, pushing a metal trolley bursting with appetizing smells. "Ah, Miss Spencer, I'm glad to see you're awake. I hope you slept well. I would have knocked, but I didn't want to wake you."

Laura barely moved her head, tucking the sheets up to her neck.

"Well, I don't want to disturb you. Master Kayne will be home for supper. It will be served at seven, but I thought you might be a little hungry."

Laura cringed at the mention of his name. How could this woman seem so casual about the situation? Did she not know what her employer was? He was obviously part of a criminal organization. Did she not care? Was she some mafia-wife-type housemaid willingly turning a blind eye?

"Supper…? What time is it?" she mumbled, her voice raspy from sleep.

"Four-thirty in the afternoon." Olga offered that kind smile of hers.

"Oh, okay, thank you."

"Well, if you won't be needing anything else, I will be in the kitchen. I can come back later if you like and give you the tour?"

"No, thank you. I'd rather stay here… if that's okay?" Laura asked in a cautious tone, resisting the housekeeper's well-meaning attempts at amicability.

"As you wish." Olga courteously bowed her head and turned around, leaving the trolley in the room.

Laura was wary of touching the food. What if it was drugged? But what would be the alternative, starve to death? She considered the option for a moment, but dieting had never been her strong suit, and she seriously questioned her willpower in the face of famine.

She slowly made her way out of bed as if being observed, careful with every move. She hobbled to the trolley, her swollen ankle torturing her at the slightest pressure, and dragged it back to the mattress. The bed was safe; she had claimed it. The rest of the room was still deemed hostile territory.

Opening the metal dome, she found eggs Benedict. She would have usually been thrilled, but her stomach turned at the first bite. It was too heavy, and her fragile nerves were affecting her appetite. Subdued, she pushed the plate away and crawled back under the sheets. She closed her eyes and waited for sleep to come again.

It was six-fifty when Olga came to fetch her. Laura had finally taken notice of the grandfather clock in her bedroom. She had spent the day dry heaving into the toilet, going back and forth between the bed and the luxurious en suite bathroom.

"Miss Spencer?" The housekeeper gently rapped at the door.

"Yes..."

Opening it halfway, she peeked her head through. "I just wanted to remind you that supper will be ready in ten minutes in case you need to prepare. I will come back in a few minutes to take you to the dining area."

"Actually... can I stay here, if that's okay? I'm not really hungry. I don't feel very good. I'd rather stay in bed."

"Oh? Is something wrong? Can I get you anything?"

"No, no, thank you. I would just like to sleep."

"Very well. I'll advise Master Kayne you are feeling ill." Though her words feigned concern, her tone seemed anxious, if not vexed.

★ ★ ★

Olga hurried apprehensively to the Master of the house; you simply did not disobey Kayne Malkin. He had inherited his mother's good looks and wild Italian temper. Thankfully, he also possessed her good humor, some of her kindness, and all of her charm. His father's heritage was more sinister. From him, Kayne got his ability to manipulate, his need to dominate, and his very blurry sense of morality. Lev Malkin was of Russian origin. Born in his homeland, he had left his country at a young age to immigrate to Canada. He'd arrived with nothing but a picture of his family and the clothes on his back, as was most often the case in those days. He was a stern man, cold and calculating, even heartless when needed. And yet, he was fair. He looked after his own, rewarded loyalty generously, and dealt with betrayal swiftly. He followed his own code of ethics and made no exceptions or excuses. For anyone.

He'd soon found out how to put those traits to good use and had risen quickly to high ranks in the Organization. They didn't have a name. Its members referred to it simply as *the Family*. Lev had met and impressed the right people. Though primarily composed of Russian ex-pats, the Organization had seen its members diversify over the years. Its core and highest positions, however, remained exclusively in the grasp of the *true blood*, Russian-born or descendants. In this strange new land, they flocked to each other and looked out for their own. When Lev met Olga, she had nowhere to go. He'd taken her in and given her a job. He had been a fair employer, perhaps too strict and demanding, but he'd never been inappropriate. That alone had earned him her complicit silence.

When he'd met Kayne's mother a few years later, it had been love at first sight. It had taken him months to convince the beautiful Italian student to give him the time of day, but eventually, he succeeded. Lev always got what he wanted. They had a whirlwind romance and were married within the year. A beautiful boy followed. How Olga loved that boy, that quiet boy, so determined even at a young age.

Olga knew; she didn't delude herself about what type of man the boy grew up to be. But she loved him as her own. He was the only son she'd ever have. And she was the only mother he'd ever know. She'd watched him grow up shaped in his father's mold. Lev would have been proud; Kayne was ruthless, calculating, and cautious—never flashy. And yet, he could still show kindness, and that by itself was a miracle. When his mother died, he was still a toddler, and Olga knew right then that she would never leave his side. That she would always love him no matter what. If his father had earned her loyalty to the Organization, the boy had ensured her devotion to the Malkins.

Kayne was already sitting at the dining table, his head tilted back, when Olga walked in.

"Master Kayne."

He opened tired eyes, his stare immediately darkening upon sensing her nervousness. "Where is she?"

"That's the thing... she says she's not feeling well. She asked to stay in her room to rest."

"Did she now..." he responded, absentmindedly tapping the fork against the table.

"You technically haven't requested her presence, and she *did* ask if it was okay."

Kayne looked her straight in the eye. He knew where this was going; she was pleading Laura's case to avoid her any reprisal. Bringing her to the house, he knew Olga would take her under her wing. She had always been the nurturing type, offering kindness to whoever needed it, to men and beasts alike, a source of inexhaustible benevolence. He gave her an indulgent smile. "Fine, let her be."

With relief in her eyes, Olga smiled at him approvingly and excused herself.

Kayne ate alone, going over the events of the past twenty-four hours. He wondered what had made him change his mind. She wasn't the first pretty girl he had delivered to the wolves. What was different this time? He even surprised himself, stepping in on her behalf. Maxwell was not happy about the arrangement at all, but Maxwell was not the one to be worried about. Though he had gained considerable power and prestige in the Organization over the past years, Kayne still outranked him. Dimitri Drugov, the head of *the Family* and the only one above him, was the worrisome one. If he couldn't convince him, it would not end well for Laura.

Why couldn't he just leave her in that room? She would have talked, he had no doubt. He thought back to her supplicating eyes and could feel himself harden. No, he hadn't saved her out of mercy. He'd saved her so he could be the one to make her beg and cry. So he could be the one to break her and savor her broken parts in all the unholy ways he craved. But first, she would have to surrender willingly, and he would have to make her. He wondered if it was even possible at all considering the situation. Kayne had never personally held a woman captive before. But she was attracted to him, he thought with a smile, remembering her bashfulness at the club. He just needed to buy himself some time. But he would have her, he vowed, powerless and at his mercy.

★ ★ ★

It was past one in the morning when Laura woke up with her stomach growling. Hesitantly eyeing the door, she got up and paced in her room. Her ankle was feeling a little better, and she decided to conquer her quarters before venturing further into the house to appease her hunger. The closets and drawers were bursting with all types of clothing, from casual to formal wear, most with the tag still on. The vanity contained all the beauty supplies a girl could ever dream of, and she wondered if they had been purchased for her. But that couldn't be. He never meant to bring her back to his home; he was ready to walk out on her at the interrogation. Would she still be alive if he had? Would she be mutilated? How much pain would she have endured? She shuddered at the thought. Her hands still shaking, she finally reached for comfortable grey sweatpants and a cozy purple hoodie. Her eyes scanned the room again, and she wondered what fate had befallen its mysterious tenant.

Laura lingered behind the closed door, gathering courage before cautiously pulling the handle. It swayed open without a sound. The house seemed deserted, all the lights off. She felt a shiver run down her spine, and on alert for the faintest sound of life, she tiptoed down the hall. The crescent moon cast spectral shadows down her path to the grand entrance, where the twin stairs awaited her, eerily snaking their way up to the ominous upper level.

Anything beyond that point was stepping into new territory. Laura hesitated again, unwilling to take the next step leading her into the unknown. She reassured herself that she wasn't breaking any rules. Her howling stomach strengthening her resolve, she marched on, momentarily regretting her refusal of the house tour. The truth was that she had just been too afraid of running into *him*.

The kitchen was fortunately right behind the wall to what she presumed was the western wing. It was huge, with an open-concept layout and a sumptuous dining area at the front. Even with the spotlights dimmed to a minimum, she could see it was worthy of being displayed in a magazine. An imposing marble island was surrounded by vast and matching countertops. There was a double-door fridge and a floor-to-ceiling wine cellar. Laura rejoiced in her small victory and headed straight to the refrigerator to reap the fruits of her conquest. It was packed full, and she didn't dare move too many things and risk waking someone with the noise. Clumsy as she was, better safe than sorry. She went with the first loaf of bread she saw, carefully taking out a slice from the package, grabbed a piece of ham, and thanked her luck when she found plates in the first cupboard she opened. As silently and swiftly as possible, she slapped the meat on the raw toast and headed out of the kitchen, looking back to ensure she'd left no trace of her nighttime excursion.

The lights suddenly shone to their full brightness, and Laura found herself face-to-face with *him*. A gasp escaped her lips as her startled hands jerked, dropping her hard-earned loot on the floor. The plate shattered at her feet, her nerves crumbling along with it.

"I'm so sorry. You startled me. I'll clean it up."

"Leave it."

She remained still for a moment, her eyes nervously traveling from the floor to his face and back down to the mess she had just created.

Though he didn't seem angry, his expression was hard to read. He looked down at the shattered plate and then back at her in one slow movement. "Of all the choices, you went for a ham sandwich?"

"I didn't want to make noise and disturb anyone."

He nodded, then casually pointed to one of the stools with a tilt of his head. "Have a seat." His walk leisurely, he went to the fridge and considered the available options. "Let's see if we can fix you a little something."

Laura hurried to the assigned seat, keeping her back straight and her hands folded on her lap. *The world is kinder to good girls with proper manners*, she recalled her second-grade teacher's imparted wisdom. She had spent her life enacting that credo, always striving to be the pleasant, helpful, and agreeable good girl. She labored tirelessly to prove her worth to those around her, hoping to believe it herself upon convincing them.

"I see you're feeling better," Kayne said from behind the refrigerator door.

"Yes. Thank you," she sheepishly managed.

He popped his head out and gave her the once-over. "Hmm," he uttered, unconvinced.

She immediately lowered her eyes. Laura would have done anything to avoid his stare. Her heart raced, fraught at being caught red-handed in the kitchen when supposedly sick in bed. She would pull all the *thank yous* and *pleases* necessary and remain on her best behavior facing his suspiciously pleasant mood.

"How about chicken?"

"That would be perfect, thank you."

He proceeded to pull a few things out; chicken, salad, and some rice, and then he heated her meal in the microwave. "What do you want to drink?"

"Oh, I'm okay, thanks."

"I have Diet Pepsi... Don't all girls like Diet Pepsi?" he tempted her, offering an impish smile.

She loved Diet Pepsi. It was, in all truth, the only nonalcoholic beverage she drank. "Hmm, yes. Okay, thank you."

"Ice?"

She felt confused by the considerate host she faced, but she knew better than to let her guard down. "Yes, please."

"Just like Olga. She makes me buy these things in bulk." He indulgently shook his head and put the mouth-watering plate down, setting the glass next to it. "Here, bon appétit."

"Thank you."

Kayne took a broom from the closet and cleaned her mess while she devoured her meal. When she was done, he grabbed her plate. "Was it good?"

"Yes, thank you." She didn't think anyone had ever said these two words as often in such a short time. She felt like a broken record, her vocabulary reduced to *thank you, please... I swear, I don't know*. The last part made her eyes water.

It was a while before anyone spoke. She was tracing circles on the counter with the tip of her fingers. He was leaning back against the closet, where he had just put away the broom, and openly watched her with an amused smile.

The uncomfortable silence was marked by the incessant ticking of the metal-plated clock on the opposing wall. And though Laura could feel Kayne's stare, she refused to return it unless specifically instructed. She thought an eternity passed between each swipe of the pendulum, its swooshing sound increasingly louder in her ears. Unable to bear the heavy silence any longer, she finally spoke up. "May I be excused?" She felt pathetic, like a child requesting permission.

His smirk broke into a full grin. "Yes, Laura. You may be excused."

He had barely finished uttering the words and found her already up on her feet and rushing out of the kitchen. He watched her leave, almost breaking into a run. He would let her run and hide, *for now*.

★ ★ ★

Though this time his face bore that of another, Peter haunted Laura's dreams again. They were alone, surrounded by darkness as violent winds, pulling them apart, roared all around them. Her core recognizing her brother, she gripped desperately to the hands of this beloved stranger. Its source indeterminate, a fluorescent light beamed down on them, exaggerating the hollows in their gaunt faces. Peter called out to her, his face distorted in agony as he struggled to resist the force drawing him into the void. The dark emptiness gradually closed in, engulfing his lower body, and Laura clasped his hand with both of hers, pulling with all her might. Though her body throbbed with pain, she refused to let go. She could feel him slipping away, the resolve in his fingers slowly dissipating, and she shouted for him to hang on, her supplications lost to the howling winds.

Peter lifted his head, looking like himself again. He seemed serene, his face relaxed, and his eyes kind. Tender and comforting, he smiled at her, mouthed *sorry*, and let go. He was immediately sucked into nothingness. Laura stumbled back, falling to the ground. She called for him, crying out his name over and over again, and broke down into incredulous, muted sobs.

Her tears were still fresh on her face when she woke up. She opened her eyes long enough to confirm the nightmare was still real and cried herself back to sleep.

DAY-2

LAURA WOKE UP DRAINED and dispirited, rebuffing Olga's few initiatives to get her out of bed. Not even the appetizing trolley could coax her out of the sheets. The older woman graciously gave her space but emphasized that Master Kayne had explicitly requested she joins him for supper, which would be served at seven.

Laura dismissed her concerned yet subtle warning. She had no intention of leaving her bedroom, come what may. When Olga came knocking at six-fifty sharp, just as the day before, she remained mute, her arms crossed defensively against her chest.

Swaying the door open, Olga's alarm became apparent at finding Laura the way she had left her. "Miss Spencer, please, you must get ready. You must eat something!" she tried to reason with her.

Laura pushed the sheets further up and covered half her face, her eyes carefully monitoring her opponent's response.

"Master will not be happy…"

At the sound of these words, Laura snapped with the fury bubbling underneath her previous apathy. In one movement, she was up on her feet. "Master will not be happy! Master will not be happy?"

"Miss Spencer, please. I beg you, calm yourself."

"No! I will not calm myself! Do you even know why I'm here? Do you even know who you work for? Who you're asking me to have supper with?" her voice faltered, the lump in her throat stripping away the righteous outrage her splintered nerves clung to.

"Oh, Miss Spencer… please," Olga beseeched, her eyes constantly flicking behind her. Her fears materialized as loud steps approaching echoed throughout. While the older woman's chin dropped, Laura kept her posture firm and ready for battle.

"What's with all the commotion?" Kayne slammed the door open and, walking past Olga, faced Laura in a few steps. "Is there a problem, Laura?" he inquired with chilling calm.

"No, Master Kayne, no problem," Olga threw to his back. "I was just about to get Miss Spencer ready…"

Her words lingered in the air as Kayne's eyes bore into Laura's, daring her to defy him.

She gulped but held his stare. "I would prefer staying in my room." Her steady voice did not betray her frantic heartbeats. Though she knew it to be madness, she couldn't fathom spending another supper as his obedient pet.

"You would *prefer* staying in your room?" He sneered at her, and with a wicked gleam in his eyes, he lifted a hand to her face. Laura flinched, but he gently brushed her cheek. "And here I was thinking we were off to such a good start," he mocked.

With no other warning, Laura felt his firm grip on her arm propelling her forward, passing a miserable-looking Olga with her head bowed. They crossed the length of the house in seconds, only stopping when they reached a door at the back of a study located in the furthest section of the western wing.

Laura had maintained her composure until that moment. Even the air felt different upon entering the room, a chill escaping the door Kayne had just pulled open. It revealed a castle-like downward spiral staircase with exposed stones, its steep steps encroaching one another, the black iron ramp cold at their touch.

"Where are you taking me?" she breathed, fear-stricken.

He looked her over very briefly, his eyes cold as ice. "You'll see."

As they reached the sublevel, he pushed her to the left, stopping in front of a metallic door with a keypad. He pressed a few buttons, and offering her a sinister smile, he urged her inside with a sarcastic *ladies first* gesture. Laura shuddered, remembering her last moments of freedom, before following him into the interrogation room.

It was an impossibly claustrophobic, concrete holding cell. It accommodated a toilet bowl, one roll of paper sitting on top of it, a sink, and one plastic cup—not even a dirty mattress on the floor.

Laura blanched and began to shake her head violently. "No! No-no-no… Please! No!" Seeing his stoic face, she grabbed his shirt in anguish. "You don't understand! Anything! But not this, please! I'm sorry, I'm sorry, please!"

"It's a little late for apologies, Laura," he said, coolly unlatching her hands off him.

"You don't understand… please, not the cage! I'll do anything!"

Her desperate pleas fell on deaf ears. His eyes hard, he pushed her in and locked the door.

Kayne could hear relentless banging and despairing sobs as he walked away. He had never utilized the cell in that fashion. Mainly, he'd used it for its intended purpose: bringing in countless men for interrogation and holding them prisoner when necessary. A few times, he had locked away submissives as punishment, but it had always been part of the game. Never had he forced a woman in against her will, let alone one he was intent on seducing. He shook his head, all too aware of how detrimental to his cause his actions had just been.

He couldn't help it. He was still livid—he would not stand for such behavior. She had to pay for her impudence. He did not expect, however, such a violent reaction. Did she just call it a *cage*? Interesting…

Kayne realized the narrowness of the line he wished to tread: to engender fear without triggering trauma. He couldn't soften up. She had to learn that her actions would have consequences. Tonight had not gone according to plan, which alone was a powerful irritant. He did like her spirit, though; he didn't think she had it in her. He smiled to himself: the perfect combination of submissiveness and pride.

★ ★ ★

Laura banged on the doors until her knuckles bled and screamed until her lips moved but emitted no more sound. She let herself fall to the ground, wrapped her arms around her knees, and rocked herself just as she had as a little girl. She cried and cried, pleaded and begged, but Peter couldn't let her out of the cage this time. She called out to him nonetheless, denial tempting its way through her consciousness. He had always come to save her. Regardless of the beatings that followed, he would find a way to set her free once her father's drunken snores reverberated in the small studio apartment. Peter would crouch next to the open door and, holding up the key, would grin from ear to ear. They would silently chuckle with their hands covering their mouths. It was all just a game, the kind little children invented to endure an unbearable reality.

She had lost the notion of time. She'd never been in the cage for so long. With deadened eyes, she cradled herself in the corner, the tip of her fingers forming random patterns on the concrete wall. Thinking back to the interrogation room, she wondered where Peter was. Like so many times before, the manic twinkle returned to her eyes, and with her hands over her mouth, she quietly chuckled by herself. The game was still on: still outwitting, outrunning the villain.

This villain, however, was not as easily fooled. He did not let his guard down, seeking solace in a bottle. A true predator, he was sharp, fit, and merciless. He hunted her savior down while keeping her prisoner. Her thoughts shadowed Peter's footprints; he should be long gone by now. He never stayed in one place for more than two weeks, and his last postcard had reached her close to three weeks ago. She had been expecting one at any given moment. But what if something had gone wrong, derailing his methodical pattern? What if, despite all of Peter's paranoid efforts, the wolf on his trail caught his scent? With only time on her hands, her thoughts quickly turned against her, swaying back and forth from arrogant optimism to utter despair.

DAY-3

OLGA WOULDN'T LET UP. She had pleaded the girl's case incessantly since the previous night. "But she is just a terrified little girl. What did you expect?"

"She is a twenty-three-year-old adult," Kayne responded, refusing to yield.

"Exactly. Twenty-three. Do you remember what you were like at that age?"

He let out a long sigh. "Did you check up on her?"

"Of course I did. I brought her a meal at two, just as you asked. Soup and bread," she pursed her lips, barely masking her disapproval.

"Did she eat?"

"No, Master Kayne. She hasn't moved from the corner since last night. She didn't look well."

"What do you mean?"

The hint of concern in his voice wasn't lost on Olga, an emotion he tried to pass off for irritation. "She seemed… I don't know. Disconnected… like she wasn't there. She was very pale. She hasn't eaten in two days."

"And whose fault is that?"

The scowl she threw him in response hit its mark. His eyes softened. "All right… what time is it?"

"It's almost six."

He exhaled. Without another word, he got up and made his way down to the holding cell.

Olga hadn't exaggerated; the girl looked pitiful, scooped up in the corner. He felt an impulse to pick her up and hold her in his arms and, disconcerted, dismissed it just as quickly.

"Supper will be served at seven. I will expect your company," he announced in a low, stony voice and exited the room, leaving the door wide open behind him.

Olga appeared not long after, rushing to Laura's side. "Oh, Miss Spencer." She shook her head sadly. "Here, let me help you."

With a dejected smile, she strived to communicate her solidarity. She helped the young girl to her feet, gently up the stairs, and into her room.

Laura obediently sat as Olga fixed her hair, picked her clothes, and helped her into a floral dress with a powder blue cardigan. She felt like a puppet on a string, going through the motions unaffected. She did think a shower would have been in order, but as Olga didn't bring it up, she let it be. She barely had the strength to form cohesive thoughts, let alone full-on sentences.

It was five to seven when Olga clasped her hands. "Well, we should get you to the dining room. You look beautiful, Miss Spencer."

Laura dutifully nodded. Feeling lightheaded, she followed Olga down the corridor and into the dining area.

Kayne was already sitting at the table and stared at her, his expression unreadable. "Glad you could finally make it," he said after a while.

Dark spots were beginning to cloud her vision, and caught in a pleasantly disorienting haze, Laura offered him a faint smile.

Her reaction both surprised and concerned him. Her features were too serene when they had no reason to be, her smile similar to those offered by good-hearted people to strangers, sweet and impersonal at the same time. As if sensing danger, Kayne intuitively leaned forward in his chair, seeking to close the distance between them. He barely finished the thought when he saw her eyes slowly roll backward and her muscles going limp. In an instant, he was at her side, catching her frail body as it went slack in his arms.

Calling for Olga, he carried her to the couch in the adjacent living room. He laid her down gently, tucking her under the covers and fluffing the pillow Olga had just brought.

From the La-Z-Boy, Kayne observed his young captive. He scrutinized her relaxed traits, the even rise and fall of her chest, and wondered what dream, if any, had her looking so peaceful. A bead of sweat escaped her humid bangs, slowly dripping down to her moist pink lips, and he restrained an urge to reach out and brush away the errand strands sticking to her flushed face.

She looked so beautiful now, calmly asleep. She had looked irresistible, frightened and supplicating him. She was objectively striking when, furious, she'd stood up to him. He had gotten just a taste the previous night. There would be many more of those to come, he predicted with a devilish grin forming on his lips. His mood shifted at the thought, and long gone were the sweet caresses he had yearned for just a few moments ago. But as enticing as she was, his fantasies were wasted on an unconscious body.

Kayne had never forced himself on a woman. His boundary, however, was not dictated by a moral compass but rather pointed at the arbitrary sexual penchants governing its host. Granted, he understood the exhilaration that came with a beautiful woman's tears, the bliss found in her horror at realizing her powerlessness. But the similarities ended there.

It wasn't physical domination Kayne sought, which was so easily reached by the average man, let alone of an unconscious body. The control he pursued was of a very different nature. It was a battle of the mind and soul, where his ecstasy could only be found at the deliberate and complete surrender of the object of his desire. Her tears would taste sweeter as he pushed her toward climax, the terror in her eyes not directed at him but at her body's reactions to him; her powerlessness only understood after a long lost battle, fought within herself.

They say rape is about power; the truth is all sex is about power.

★ ★ ★

Laura awoke sometime after. Cautiously opening her eyes, she silently looked around, taking in her new environment. She was on a comfortable couch. In the dimmed light, she made out a large rectangular table with a glass top in front of her. A big screen TV hung on the wall, surrounded by a sizable TV stand. She didn't risk moving her head to check out the rest of the room, a splitting headache limiting her range of motion. Her limbs also refused to move, as if weighing a thousand tons each.

Kayne was still on the La-Z-Boy, an open laptop illuminating his face, when he noticed her slight movement. "Good morning, Sleeping Beauty." A cryptic smile formed on his lips.

Laura turned toward him, moving barely an inch, and instantly brought her hand to her forehead, a whimper escaping her lips.

"Don't move." He slowly put the computer on the table and threw her another look before disappearing. He returned with a glass of water and two pills, which he offered her, crouching on the floor by her side. "Here, take this."

"What is it?" she whispered apprehensively.

"Cyanide."

Her eyes instantly shot up to meet his.

He smiled. "It's aspirin, Laura."

Kayne patiently waited out her hesitation. Like a parent caring for a petulant child, he watched as she tentatively reached for the pills and swallowed them, and satisfied, he disappeared again. He returned a few minutes later with a hot bowl of soup and some crackers. "Eat this. It'll help."

She pulled herself up and, resting on her elbows, suspiciously eyed the platter in front of her. She knew she was famished but had no appetite, and a part of her didn't want to eat simply because he had said to.

"If you want to defy me, Laura, at least make it worth your while," he said as if reading her mind, standing with his arms crossed and an amused smile on his face. "Eat," he then added in a commanding tone.

Bringing herself to a sitting position, Laura obeyed with reluctance. With each bite, however, a knot in her head loosened, her headache faded, and her strength slowly returned, she begrudgingly acknowledged.

When she was almost done, Kayne reclaimed his seat. He turned to her and, with a veiled expression, he softly said, "Good girl."

Her stomach turned at the words, at the way they were said, and she blushed. Never once, since that night at the club, had she thought of him as anything but a monster. But he was also a man, she would do well to remember: a dangerous and beguiling man. She could feel his predatory eyes linger on her body, and she shifted uncomfortably in her seat. And even though he went back to his laptop and didn't look her way after that, she remained quietly seated. As desperate as she was to get back to her room, she wondered if that was still a possibility and wasn't keen on bringing his attention back to her. At last, she cleared her throat, her voice tentative, "May I... would it... be okay... if I go to my room?"

Kayne stopped typing and looked at her. "I understand you don't leave your room in the day."

Laura remained silent, dipping her chin with a guilty look.

He sighed. "Have Olga give you the tour tomorrow, okay?"

"Yes… Sir." The word just slipped past her lips. She wasn't sure why she called him that, but calling him casually by his name felt even more bizarre, and *Master Kayne* wasn't even an option.

His expression slightly surprised, he stared at her pensively, and seeming pleased, he nodded. "Good night, Laura."

★ ★ ★

Laura lay awake for a long time, tossing and turning in bed, with his face imprinted on her mind. She had the most peculiar dream.

In the darkest of nights, she ran blindly through a stone labyrinth, desperation propelling her forward. Kayne's Security team was spread throughout, their menacing murmurs heard in echoes as if coming from speakers overhead. With a torch in hand, Laura picked random paths, twisting and turning at the sight of the black silhouettes. In a narrow pathway, a guard almost caught her, pulling his arm to an unnatural length. She kept running ahead, looking over her shoulders, and abruptly found herself at a dead end.

Kayne was already there, also in black and looking strikingly devilish, having materialized as if out of thin air. Smiling seductively, he crooked his finger to beckon her to him. Laura felt her heart sink and stumbled backward before noticing the mass of security men that had caught up and blocked the way out. He seemed to glide toward her, and her eyes rounded when she realized it was she who already walked to meet him as if hypnotized, her feet moving of their own accord. He pulled his arm out and brought her to him, enveloping her with his whole body. She felt a sense of safety washing over her and leaned into the warmth of his embrace.

Everything vanished around them. They were the only two people left in the world. She giggled, finding strange comfort in that idea, and looked up at him. He smiled and lowered his face to hers. "Everything is going to be all right," he huskily whispered in her ear. Her voice throaty, she obediently replied, "Yes, Master."

Laura closed her eyes as he pulled her even closer, holding her so tightly in his arms that she couldn't move. He started kissing down her neck, his hands caressing her arms and lightly trailing down her back. She wanted to tell him something and tried to open her eyes but was unable to. She couldn't move a muscle. She could only feel his hands all over her body, everywhere at once. As if he had a thousand of them, just like the mythical Greek giants. Panic took hold of her. And yet, every sensation was heightened, every caress reverberating throughout her body, and she didn't know if she truly wanted it to end.

She woke up panting, sweaty, and distraught. And much to her dismay, moist in places she shouldn't be. She tried not to analyze what it meant and to block it out completely. Unable to find sleep again, she spent the rest of the night staring out the window until the sun crept up.

DAY-4

WHEN OLGA CAME IN to serve Laura breakfast, she was pleasantly surprised to find her sitting up in bed. "Good morning, Miss Spencer. You're up early this morning. I hope you feel better. You gave us quite a scare last night."

Laura wondered why the housekeeper would bring her breakfast at this time if she thought her asleep, trying to discern any hidden agendas. She thought back to the previous night, to the reason she was up so early, and blushed. She questioned Olga's choice of the word 'us'. Was she expected to believe he worried about her well-being?

"Well, if you're up to it, I can come back after you've finished your breakfast and give you the tour of the house?"

"Yes. Thank you, Olga," Laura answered, attempting a feeble smile.

"Wonderful." Olga clasped her hands together.

When she returned about half an hour later, Laura was dressed and ready. She was anxious to leave her bedroom, eyeing the traitorous bed resentfully. In fact, Laura had thought of escape for the first time since her arrival. She knew it would be near impossible, and she shivered at the consequences she would face in the event of a failure. Even if she succeeded, where would she go? They surely wouldn't have trouble tracking her down. She didn't have Peter's skill, knowledge, or paranoia to survive so long on the run. Still, she needed to maintain the hope that she would one day leave this house. But first, she had to know her enemy.

The Malkin mansion looked very different in the midday light. She noticed the security men roaming on the premises and tensed, feeling thankful not to run into any of them on the inside. She followed Olga around quietly in and out of every room. In the eastern wing, she was shown a cozy room with a fluffy red couch, a small wooden table, and a big-screen TV. Plants amassed from the four corners of the world endowed it with an eclectic charm; there were pots on the ground, one on each side of the window, and quite a few hanging from the ceiling. Laura immediately decided to claim this small haven for her own.

And on they continued with the tour; employees' quarters, more media and living rooms, and there even was a ballroom. Laura recalled *The Sound of Music* and wondered what type of people still hosted balls nowadays.

Noticing the lack of staff in this impressive residence, she questioned Olga about it. The latter pointed out that a cleaning crew came by weekly but advised that it was best to ignore them and that they would do the same. In any case, they were Russian and didn't speak a word of English or French.

In the western wing, Olga opened French double doors to a grandiose library. Endless books from the ground up filled every wall. Crafted within the high ceiling, a stained glass dome imbued the space with a beatific glow, the sunlight shining through it in vibrant hues. The bookshelves were made of intricately carved wood, with inner marble stairs circling around to the higher levels and a finely sculpted ramp guiding the way.

Laura breathed 'wow', rushing inside and looking around excitedly. For a moment, she forgot where she was. She nearly ran to the closest row of books, reading titles while scurrying from one end of a shelf to the other. The books were classified by language. Most were in English, but there was an imposing section in Russian, one in Italian, and a couple of dozens of novels in French. Being a fully bilingual Quebec native, she even recognized a few French classics.

Laura loved books more than anything in the world. She loved the escape they offered, the teachings they generously imparted, and, most of all, the promise each story held of a unique journey. She felt exhilarated and, for the first time in a long time, safe amid old friends and wondrous new suitors.

Beloved novels leaped out at her bearing their leathery spine, and she smiled as she languidly caressed them, elated with each title she recognized. Past lovers she still cherished: Salinger, Dickens, Hugo… Even her first love, Emily Brontë's *Wuthering Heights*, came out to greet her. This was not a man's library, she noted; a woman had undoubtedly contributed to the inventory. She was suddenly flooded with the image of *her*: Kayne's girlfriend, a tall and breathtaking beauty, stylish and sophisticated… The embodiment of everything she yearned so earnestly to be, Laura registered with a twinge in her heart.

A woman he might have loved, who had lived here, in her room, and whose unworn clothes Laura had now inherited. The idea bothered her, and with no further analysis, she quickly dismissed it. She wouldn't let anything taint this magical moment. Who knew when would be the next, if ever.

The moment the thought entered her mind, Laura went on a mission to find it: Hermann Hesse's *Steppenwolf*. Her greatest love, her one true love, the book that had saved her life all these years ago when she was still a teenager. It was after Peter had left, and she was all alone in the world. She wondered if she'd find it here. It wasn't one of those famous classics that mainly attracted pretentious readers wanting to add another notch to their belt. It had, in fact, been met with heavy backlash upon its release, largely due to widespread misinterpretation. Initially considered the author's black sheep, it had gradually garnered a fanbase over time, gathering a select niche of souls that evolved into devout disciples.

Originally written in German, Laura looked for the English translation she had read herself. It was there. Her heart thumping, she retrieved the worn-out copy and held it close to her chest. Somehow this discovery had a significant impact on her. At some point, someone who lived in this very same house bought it, read it, and revisited it enough times to leave wear-and-tear scars. That sole discovery gave humanity to this place. If someone like that could live in this house, then maybe, just maybe, she could survive it.

Slowly, she came back to herself and found that Olga hadn't moved from the doorframe, letting her have her moment though sharing in her joy. Slightly embarrassed, Laura pointed to the book. "I'm so sorry... May I?"

"Of course, Miss Spencer, please go ahead."

"Thank you." For the first time, she said it out of genuine gratitude.

With the house tour completed, Olga advised Laura that supper would be ready at seven, as always, and asked if she would like to be fetched or meet Master Kayne directly in the dining area. "Now that you know how to go about the house," she added with a conspiring smile.

As hard as she fought it, Laura's resistance to this kind woman chipped away little by little.

Laura was a nervous wreck as suppertime approached. She dreaded the thought of spending an entire evening alone with him. One part, intrigued by her recent discoveries, wanted to know more about her captor. Another part, all too aware of her nighttime disgrace, recoiled in horror at the prospect of his stares, the blushing that would incur, and the unreasonable concern that he could actually read her mind. But above all else, it was the *cage*, or the threat of it, that had her show up at seven on the dot to meet him. She chose to wear jeans with the same loose-fitting purple hoodie. She would not play the pale copy of his banished lover. Closets full of clothes were wasted on her, Laura decided, rebelling against the impalpable pressure of just not being *woman enough.*

Kayne looked her up and down, an imperceptible smirk on his face. "Good evening, Laura."

"Good evening," she responded, her voice guarded.

"Take a seat." He pointed to the chair facing him and waited for her to oblige. "Olga tells me you finally ventured out of your room."

"Yes…"

When he realized she would say no more, he leaned back in his chair, considering her with a cunning smile. "No more *Sir* today?"

Laura turned bright red, cursing herself and her explicit dream. "Do you want me to call you that?"

Kayne's lips widened at witnessing her discomfort. His eyes glowing with wickedness, he ignored her question. "Shall we eat?"

He served them generous portions of salmon with a fresh garden salad. They ate quietly, her nerves thankful for the temporary respite. Every now and then, he would look at her with a sly smile, causing her to look down. They kept up the dance the entire meal. Once they were done, he reinitiated the conversation, "Why don't you tell me about yourself."

Laura felt put on the spot and hated that feeling. The question was too broad, and she dreaded the many possible answers she could provide, frozen at the prospect of choosing the wrong one.

"What do you want to know? I'm not sure what to tell you."

He cocked his head. "Whatever worth telling."

"Okay... hmm... I was born here in Montreal. I graduated from Concordia, hmm... I don't know... I like soft music and long walks on the beach," she quipped, throwing him a sarcastic look.

He seemed surprised for a moment, then scowled at her.

Laura fidgeted in her seat. She often fell back on humor when uncomfortable or nervous, frequently putting her foot in her mouth in the process. "I'm sorry. It was just a joke," she added sheepishly, desperately wanting to avoid worsening her already precarious position.

"I don't care about school and jobs. What do you like? *Besides* soft music and long walks on the beach." The corner of his lips curled up.

A sound, somewhere between a chuckle and a sigh of relief, escaped her lips. "Well, reading. I love books. And movies."

"What kind?"

"I don't know... very different genres. Books, mostly fiction. I love Gothic mysteries. I like thrillers. Oh, and like, coming-of-age stories. I love those. ... Do you like reading?"

"Sometimes."

"Your library is amazing," she said in wonder. "Do you speak all these languages?"

He hesitated before answering, as if realizing the conversation was inadvertently turning to him. But deeming it harmless, he allowed it. "My Italian is very basic. But I speak Russian and French fluently." He could sense the questions burning at the tip of her tongue and smiled indulgently. "What else do you want to know?"

Her brows furrowed. So many questions she was dying to ask, where to even begin. She feared bringing up her brother would deteriorate into an interrogation. And her bleak vision of what lay in store for her warned against confirming her worst fears. She opted for the safety of small talk.

"Are you Russian?"

"My father was. I was born here."

"Oh, I see."

"Anything else?" he added, amused.

"Yes… so much," she softly said, more for her benefit.

He smirked. "You get one more question."

"Okay… Did you… have it built? The library, I mean."

"No. It was my mother's," Kayne answered curtly, his eyes darkening.

She thought the topic safe and wondered what triggered his sudden mood change. She couldn't help acknowledging, however, the smallest yet undeniably present relief she felt at the destruction of the pseudo-perfect girlfriend she had conjured up in her mind.

"What about boyfriends? Do you have one?" he asked, though fully aware of the answer following the two-week surveillance.

The question caught her off guard, and she just shook her head in response.

"But you've had boyfriends before…"

"Yes, of course."

"How many?"

"Two," she responded, readjusting herself, her discomfort palpable at the turn the conversation was taking.

"Just two?"

"Well… yes. They were long-term kinda relationships."

"Tell me about them."

"Okay… I met Jarred in school when I was sixteen. We were high school sweethearts. We were together for two years. Then he went off to college, and we broke it off." She shrugged her shoulders.

"Who broke it off?"

"It was mutual."

"It's never mutual."

She took a deep breath. "I did."

"Why?"

"I don't know, we were growing apart… He was a really nice guy. I just… we just grew apart."

"And the other?"

"Eric?" Her jaw tensed.

He nodded.

"Eric, too, was a nice guy," she added hurriedly, hoping to cut his line of questioning short.

"So you like nice guys," he commented, sarcasm tainting his voice.

"Well… yes. That's pretty normal."

"You'd be surprised…" he purred, his eyes dark and his voice silky, and then continued in a more commanding tone, "Go on, what happened with Eric?"

"I met him in college. We were together for three years. It didn't work out." She stuck to the facts, steering clear of the painful emotions associated with his memory.

"How come?" he asked, intrigued by her distress and strangely aggravated that another was the cause.

Laura took a long breath and closed her eyes as if to prep herself. "He proposed."

Kayne's brows shut up in surprise. "So you broke up with him? ... Maybe she doesn't like the nice guys so much after all," he added, with mischief in his emerging smile.

"No. It wasn't like that... I didn't want to break up," she confessed, fiddling nervously with her fingers.

He scrutinized her, his silence expectant, even entitled, to all her secrets.

"He wanted children."

"And you didn't?"

"No... I couldn't. I can't... have children." She looked up at him, her shoulders slumped in defeat. She expected him to badger her further, to laugh and be cruel, but he didn't. He took a sip of his drink, gazing at her with quiet intensity.

No one ever knew. Not even Eric. She had wanted to tell him, but a voice inside of her had warned her against it. He would have stayed. And she would have hated herself for making him give up his dream. Down the road, he, too, would have ended up resenting her just as much for it. So she had remained quiet when, staggered, he had gotten on his knees, vowing eternal love and begging her to see reason. She had kept up the façade, even as his distress came out in accusatory slander raining down on her. She had stayed still and silent as he called her heartless, tossing the ring at her feet before storming off into the moonless night. Alone in her one-bedroom studio, she had picked up the gold band carrying the microscopic diamond and broke down. It had taken him months slaving away to offer her his dreams on a silver platter. With one word, she had smashed them all to smithereens.

Only Peter ever knew. Always, Peter. It was he who had made the appointment and sat by her side at the doctor's office. She was fifteen, and her periods had failed to start. Blurry memories of that day, long tucked away in the recesses of her mind, resurfaced by pieces: a faceless white coat, white hair, white walls; words like primary amenorrhea, congenital defect, and failure of the ovary to receive or maintain eggs. They didn't mean anything to her back then. If anything, she remembered her relief at never having to go through painful menstrual cramps like so many girls her age.

She recalled Peter's shattered face. His voice, wanting to be comforting, barely masked the pain. "Oh, Laura, I'm sorry, I'm so sorry…" he had kept repeating as if he was the cause of it. She couldn't understand his sorrow. It would only be years later, clutching the discarded engagement ring and its dissolving promises, that she understood the magnitude of it.

Kayne examined the introspective beauty facing him. Laura seemed so far away, as if she had forgotten about him. It should have aggravated him, but instead, he felt like a privileged spectator, peering through the looking glass. "You never told anyone," he guessed, a softness creeping into his voice.

Laura slowly shook her head.

For an instant, he felt for her and wanted to comfort her. Watching her head bent sideways, the errand strand of hair covering her face, he almost reached over.

"Have you been with anyone else since?"

She looked up, peeking through heavy lids. "What do you mean?"

"Casual dates, one-night stands… a friend with benefits perhaps?" he asked with playful wickedness.

Her eyes widened with surprise. "No," she asserted, reinforcing her negation with a vehement head shake.

"Such a good girl," he teased.

Laura blushed. "Do you… have a girlfriend?" she asked tentatively, trying to divert the attention away.

He scoffed. "No, Laura. In case you missed it, I'm not really the relationship type."

"Oh. I just thought… with the bedroom you set me in… and the clothes and all…"

"The clothes were brought for you. The room was my mother's. Does this satisfy your little curiosity?" he answered, slightly irritated.

Laura felt frustrated at his double standard and lack of fairness. He had coerced her into answering intimate questions all evening, forcing her to scratch old wounds not yet fully healed. Still, she noticed his mood change coincided with the mention of his mother again. She would try to steer clear of that topic, although she knew her curiosity would eventually get the best of her. But then another thought came creeping, and her face fell. If he'd already bought the clothes for her… Wouldn't that imply that he had always meant to take her back with him, regardless of her answers and the levels of betrayal she was ready to sink to? Her fate had been sealed before she had even set foot into that cursed room. She was not spared Maxwell's sadism. Kayne did not take pity on her; he had meticulously planned her abduction for weeks.

"What's wrong?" he asked, still in a tempestuous mood.

Her voice was strangled, and she swallowed before meeting his gaze. "You knew all along… from the first night. Even before you brought me into that room. You knew you would bring me back here. You even had clothes brought… You said if I cooperated, I could leave… You… lied."

His eyes narrowed in quiet fury, and though his voice remained calm, it dripped venom. "And you've come to this conclusion because… I was kind enough to make sure you'd be comfortable? If I remember correctly, I promised that you would get out unharmed, which you have. The clothes were brought on that same night. Don't you think I have the resources to get you a few pieces of clothing? I have contacts everywhere, Laura. And that's not a lie, either. You would do well to remember that in case you get other brilliant ideas."

Laura ardently shook her head, attempting to retract her accusations and damage control.

"Never. Call me. A liar," he hissed.

Before he even knew it, she had dropped to his feet, with her hands grabbing his jeans at the knees and her eyes glistening with unshed tears.

"Please, please, forgive me. I made a mistake… I mean… Stores are closed at this time… and there was just so much stuff. Please forgive me… I don't want to go to the cage."

Kayne felt confused and conflicted. A part of him, still seething with anger, wanted to leave her on the floor, drag her by her hair, and punish her for her careless words. Another part, however, even stronger than before, wanted to comfort and reassure her. He felt the urge to take her in his arms and hold her until her fluttering heart quieted against his chest, becoming both her poison and its sole antidote.

He was thrown off by his reaction and the emotion she stirred in him. His comfort had always been provided as a reward well earned. Even then, only given so he could further savor the fruits of his victory, basking in the euphoria reached through absolute control. Genuine compassion was a foreign concept to him and, most likely, a major factor in his success in the Organization. It was not a desired trait in his world, and he ground his teeth, irked at his passing weakness. Quickly collecting himself, he grabbed her chin between his fingers and raised her head to face his. When he spoke to her, his voice reflected the iciness in his stare. Never could she have suspected the thoughts that just ran through his mind.

"You will mind what you say and how you say it. Anything you do or say has consequences. Do we have an understanding?"

"Yes…Sir," she sniffled.

His eyes gleamed with an indiscernible emotion, between annoyance and excitement, at the sound of the word that came to her lips more naturally this time. He nodded his head. "Go to your room… before I change my mind."

★ ★ ★

He watched as she made her exit, much like the first night, rushing to leave his side. With a long sigh, he raised his hands and rubbed his face. He thought back to that first night. What had he gotten himself into? The girl was an enigma. He wanted to know so much more about her. He'd gotten some information over dinner. Most, he could have guessed. So she was infertile. That, he did not expect. He wondered if it was that fact alone that troubled her so or the loss of Eric because of it.

She wouldn't have to worry about that with him, he thought with a cynical smile. The situation suited him just fine. He had never wanted children, or a wife for that matter. What he wanted from her, he wouldn't get by offering a ring.

Clearly, she wasn't very experienced. He wasn't surprised that she'd only been with the two boyfriends she mentioned. He wondered if she'd ever had an orgasm and deemed it unlikely with the nice guys she thought she liked so much. She definitely had a submissive streak, calling him *Sir* twice without his prompt. She'd instinctively known what to say to appease him, even falling to his feet in a manipulative bid to pacify him and appeal to his mercy. It had slightly annoyed him, but it worked nonetheless. She craved the kind of power and control that didn't come from nice guys. It was written all over her. He had sensed it in her self-conscious flirtation from that first night at the club. A half-smile, akin to tender, crossed his lips.

She was submissive, but she wasn't aware of it yet. He would awaken the inclination he knew lay dormant within her, and he reveled at the delectable rewards his pursuit offered. A self-proclaimed submissive lost her appeal to him. He'd usually leave them, bored to tears, by the time they were all but too eager to please. *How delicious was the path to depravity*, how he would love to show her.

But there were other things that intrigued him about her. For one, her trauma with the *cage*, as she called it. He guessed that she was abused. But how and by whom? Clearly, not one of the boyfriends or her brother. Her father, perhaps? He had to know.

Methodically, he would study her and extract her deepest fears down to her darkest desires. And only then, once she had willingly handed him the key to her innermost secrets, would he use them to his advantage.

DAY-5

IT WAS PAST ONE in the afternoon when Laura heard a knock on her door.

"Sorry to disturb you, Miss Spencer. Master Kayne would like you to meet him in the living room," the housekeeper advised.

"Oh? Did he say why?" Laura's heart skipped a beat and then pounded frantically in her chest. She had hoped against hope the incident would be forgotten and had spent the day hiding out in her room, trying to remain under the radar.

"No. He just asked me to fetch you. He's waiting for you."

"Like now? ... *NOW*, now?" her tone raised a few octaves, panic permeating her entire being.

"Yes, Miss Spencer."

Laura looked around longingly at her room, dismayed at having to abandon the trusted cocoon she had been so cautiously building. "Okay," she conceded, downcast.

★ ★ ★

Kayne was sitting on the same couch she had fallen asleep on, his legs open wide and his head thrown back. His expression impervious, he motioned with a cigarette in his hand toward the available spaces on the couch and adjacent La-Z-Boy, inviting her to sit down.

Opting for the furthest distance from him, Laura sat at the edge of the La-Z-Boy, her eyes fixed on a loose thread she nervously played with on her jeans.

Kayne took his time, slowly inhaling and exhaling his last few puffs before putting out his cigarette. "Can I get you anything to drink?"

Laura cleared her throat, her mouth dry from her faltering nerves. "A glass of water?"

He nodded and got up, returning with a bottle of cold water and a beer for himself.

"Laura, I have to ask you something," Kayne said with a grave expression.

"Okay..." She had initially feared reprisal over her rash and false accusation. Now, she understood: it was about Peter. For how much longer did she hope to dodge further interrogation?

"Were you ever abused?"

"What?" Of all directions this conversation could have taken, she did not expect this.

"Answer me."

"I don't understand... like... *sexually*?" She hated having to pronounce any word containing these three letters in front of him.

"Were you?"

"No!" Her answer was unequivocal.

He closed his eyes as relief washed over him. He hadn't realized his hands were balled up in fists so tight blood had drained from them, and he wondered what made him feel so strongly about the issue. Granted, abuse victims didn't make ideal lovers considering his peculiar taste; so many triggers. He had neither the patience nor the mildest inclination even to hope to make it work had it been the case. But it was more than that. Sheer rage blinded him at the thought of her being abused. The emotion was too strong to be explained away by his hope for sexual compatibility. Had she said yes, had she given a name, that name would have been carved on a tombstone not long after. He was surprised at how fast he had claimed her as his. He had always been the possessive type. He'd never shared a submissive with another man. This time, however, he recognized a strange feeling that went far deeper than male territoriality. It was one he hadn't often felt: protectiveness.

"Have you ever been abused any other way?" he pressed on.

"What do you mean?" she asked, bewildered at his line of questioning. What possible link could her traumatic childhood experiences have with Peter's whereabouts? What was his angle? She couldn't fathom his motivations for asking such questions.

"Mistreated… Physically? Emotionally? Perhaps… locked in a *cage*?"

As expected, her face instantly paled.

"Yes," she breathed through thinned lips.

"Your father?"

Her eyes shot up, round with surprise.

It wasn't such a difficult assumption to make from what she had told him. "Did he ever lay his hands on you?"

"Why are you asking me all these questions?" she inquired, her distraught voice barely above a whisper.

"Just answer me, Laura."

"I just don't understand—"

"I didn't ask you to understand," he sharply interrupted.

She was beginning to know his moods, to know how far she could push before hitting the wall and facing its thunderous response. "No, he never laid his hands on me."

He nodded. "But he locked you… in a cage?"

"Yes."

"How long did this go on for?"

"The cage?" Her face twisted with repulsion as she uttered the word. "I don't know, years… Since I was a child. I don't remember exactly when… for as long as I can remember."

She sounded detached, almost robotic, and he could feel her retreat somewhere deep within herself. "What about your mother?"

"She wasn't around."

"Tell me about it."

Laura let out an exhausted sigh. "My father was a drunk. My mother, too, I suspect, but she left when I was still a baby. We lived in a dump. Peter…" Her voice faltered. She glanced back at Kayne uncertainly, as if the mere enunciation of his name would suddenly remind him of why she was there. And that jumping at the realization, he would begin torturing her on the spot for more information.

When he didn't react, she continued. "Peter said that Dad wasn't so bad when she was still around. He still drank then… but I don't think he put me in the cage when she was there. I mean, she wouldn't have let him put her baby in a cage…" She looked up at him, her eyes seeking reassurance in her shaky faith.

Kayne didn't nod. Instead, he slid the cigarette pack over to her end of the table. She took one, grateful though surprised by this unexpected and subtle display of empathy.

He held up the lighter but didn't hand it to her, forcing her to lean in and close her hand right above his to catch the flame. "Go on," he finally said after giving her the time to enjoy a few puffs.

"Not much to say. Dad drank every day. But if you caught him sober, he was actually kinda sweet. He used to buy me this chocolate cake I liked that was only sold in a shop on the other side of town. We didn't have a car, so he'd walk all the way there just to get it for me." She smiled tenderly at the memory, then quickly shook it off. "But most of the time, he was just upset with me. The worst time was when I got suspended." She smiled grimly. "I got in a fight with this girl at school who kept picking on me. He had to miss work and everything to stay home with me. I think it was the longest time I ever spent in the cage… It was just a stupid dog crate, you know?" She let out a bitter laugh. "One of those big plastic ones for large-size breeds…" her voice broke, her eyes gleaming with raw hurt. "He had a lock on it and kept the key on him. But Peter would always find a way. I just had to wait. I'd count up as high as I could, and then Peter would magically appear with the key and sneak me out once Dad fell asleep. It was the only time he'd ever get in trouble. Because of me. *For* me. Dad always beat him afterward. You know, it's funny. We never once thought of sneaking me back in before he woke up… We were just kids, I guess…" She shrugged her shoulders.

He watched her, engrossed and studying her every move. She relived every moment as she recounted it, tensing up at some memories, her eyes softening at others, her tears flowing down her cheeks without her consent or acknowledgment. She had no poker face.

"When I was ten, I don't remember why, but my father got really, like really, mad at me. I think he saw me holding hands with the neighbor's kid or something. Anyway, he reached for his belt. He'd never hit me before… I was terrified. Peter freaked out. He jumped in. Got the beating of his life. He left that same day. He didn't come home for three whole days. Longest days of my life. He was sixteen then. I just couldn't believe he'd leave me like that, you know? But he came back for me. In the middle of the night. Had packed my bags and everything. He snuck me out. I was still half asleep. He had gone out and bought a car. This old beat-up Tercel, you should've seen it..."

She softly chuckled, wiping her tears away dismissively with the back of her hand. "It made this horrible sound every time you started it... And that was it. I never saw my father again after that." She sighed, her emotions settling as she slowly returned to the present.

Kayne had lit another cigarette, and, for the first time, he offered her a kind and sincere smile. Without saying a word, he put it out halfway through and went over to the bar again. He returned with a glass of whiskey in each hand and put one down in front of her before reclaiming his seat. He raised his own, a shadow of compassion softening his face. "Cheers."

"Cheers."

At this moment, she almost forgot he was her captor. She had shared things with him that she never had with anyone else, not even her boyfriends. But then again, they had never locked her in a cage and forced her to open up about it afterward. They hadn't even suspected what lay buried deep beneath. She had made it a point to play the *girl next door*, bubbly and carefree. They all fell for it. Even Eric. He'd never called her out once. Not even when her stories were off and her responses suspiciously evasive, especially when it came to her family and her irrational fear of small, enclosed spaces. He hadn't wanted to scratch the surface. Even he hadn't wanted to expose the ugliness underneath and risk breaking the beloved illusion.

Some part of her had resented him for it, for his willful blindness that had enabled her to save face at such costly silence. No one besides Peter ever knew her, ever fully knew her, until now. She didn't feel vulnerable and exposed as she had thought she would. She felt relieved, like a huge weight had been lifted off her shoulders, and she was almost thankful for the coerced confession.

She looked at her unlikely confidant and considered this fragile bubble of intimacy they had just formed. Maybe because of it, she found the courage to voice the question tormenting her. Her fingers tracing the rim of the glass, she cleared her throat. "Can I ask you something?"

He nodded, his expression somber.

"Did they find Peter?" she rushed through the words, her eyes fixing a scratch in the hardwood floor.

He remained quiet for a while, gazing at her before answering. "No."

Laura let out the breath she'd been holding in and couldn't help smiling at him, half expecting him to share her joy.

"They did trace him back to Boston," he added, impassive.

She mouthed *Oh*. Her relief was short-lived.

Kayne leaned forward in his seat conspiringly, causing her to unconsciously mirror his movement. "Want to know what I think, Laura? I don't think he's in Boston. I think he's already far, far away…" He leaned back, spreading his arms over the couch. "But don't worry, your secret is safe with me," he said with a dark twinkle in his eyes.

Dread swiftly shot through her nervous system and invaded each limb, all the way to the tip of her extremities. She remained as still as a deer in the headlights, powerlessly waiting for the blow to strike. It didn't. Smiling knowingly at her panicked stare, he leisurely took another sip from his drink.

Unsure how to respond, Laura blinked a few times, shifting uncomfortably in her seat. "I didn't lie to you."

"I know."

She breathed a little easier. How she regretted bringing it up. "Are you going to kill me?" she blurted impulsively.

He stared her in the eye, his voice betraying no emotion. "Only if you make me... But don't worry, I won't let you."

Her eyes watered with both terror and relief at the conviction that he was telling the truth. She felt exhausted. Though the sun still shone brightly in the sky, Laura just wanted her bed. "May I be excused?" she asked at last.

Upon his nodded consent, she got up, her movements slow and pained, and left his side.

★ ★ ★

Kayne spent the day thinking of her. Time was running out. He received a call that evening from Dimitri. The big boss wanted an update on the progress. Peter had betrayed them. Not only was he seen talking with federal agents, but he'd also stolen a file with very damning information, presumably, to negotiate a better deal. It was the highest possible offense. This act alone had earned him a high priority on Dimitri's hit list. Dimitri would not rest until he had his head. It was more than getting the file back; it was a matter of principle. He had to die. Traitors could not be allowed to live. Kayne knew there would be no price too great for Dimitri to ensure Peter got his comeuppance. He would spend all the resources necessary. He would never forget, never move on, until justice was served.

The Peter he had met was very different from the one Laura described. Did she have any inkling as to what her brother had become? She idolized him, however destructive he had been. Laura had remained forever faithful to the beloved version she clung to, regardless of the heartaches brought on by the others. Her only knowledge of love, Kayne pondered, seemed to have always been intricately enmeshed with grief.

She was unlike any other girl or woman that had crossed his path in his twenty-nine years. They had more similarities than he cared to admit: both motherless, with all its implications. And though he'd never been abused, his father, too, had had a creative idea or two when it came to disciplining him. His father was a peculiar man. He'd made Kayne the man he now was. From him, Kayne had learned the value of words and the importance of choosing them carefully; that any man worth his salt did not demand respect—he commanded it. Lev Malkin laughed at clowns in flashy cars making ruckus whenever possible, desperate to impress and be seen, to reassure their fragile egos. *Know who you are, and they will, too*, was Lev's golden motto. As a true disciple, Kayne steered clear of red convertibles and extravagant clothes. He appreciated beauty in its simplest form, always opting for understated elegance.

He remembered his tenth birthday. He had asked for a toy gun he had seen on TV. He'd received a real one. His father had led him down to the holding cell where a man was tied up on a chair, beaten to a bloody pulp. It was his first kill. He remembered how nauseated he had felt and the taste of bile rising in his mouth. When it was all over and done, however, and his father had patted him on the back as he seldom did, he had felt a sense of well-being wash over him. He knew then that he had done the right thing.

Kayne looked back at the postcard he was holding in his hands, feeling conflicted. He had Lucas go through Laura's mail and clear her apartment. It had taken them over six months before even uncovering her existence. Peter had never mentioned a sister, *smart move*. In the two weeks he'd watched her, he hadn't noticed anyone close to her. He doubted anyone would raise too many questions about her disappearance. Her few acquaintances would assume she'd taken off. What a shame, he thought; she was definitely worth looking for. He hadn't mentioned the postcard to Dimitri. Looking at the jumble of random characters and scribbles, he knew he'd keep it that way.

DAY-6

THE DAY WAS RELATIVELY uneventful. Laura made sure and asked Olga whether *Master Kayne* was around before she ventured out of her room. She went to the library, picked up a few books, made herself a sandwich, and settled in her living room, now baptized as her reading room. It was a somewhat pleasant day, all things considered. Olga came in only once to check in on her and, as always, to confirm that supper would be served at seven. But she was otherwise left to her own devices. Laura even found a sealed pack of cigarettes on the table in the living room and wondered if Kayne had left it for her on purpose. She smoked one or two, remaining in the same area as she was unsure whether it was allowed anywhere else in the house.

    Laura's nerves ebbed and flowed as the clock hands moved toward the dreaded hour. Since the moment they had tipped their glasses to one another, an infinitesimal shift had also followed in their relationship. For the first time, he had almost felt like an ally in the dark. And Laura was tired of fighting the darkness alone. But Kayne Malkin was a friend of the night, and she knew that the hand he offered shouldn't be so quickly trusted. It was a volatile and mercurial hand that could just as easily crush as it could rescue. Her fear of reaching for it was only matched by the intoxicating desire to, and the conquering pull alternated by the minute. In the end, when Olga came to fetch her for supper that evening, she was dressed and ready, with her hair down, wearing jeans and a cute sleeveless pink top.

As usual, Kayne was already seated at the table, this time in jeans and a grey sweater. He seemed amused, noticing her different look, and she blushed, cursing herself for straying from her drab attire.

"Good evening, Laura."

"Good evening." She kept her head up as if unaware of the smoldering stare he threw her way.

"How was your day?" he added in a jovial tone.

"It was good, thank you."

"Olga tells me you borrowed a book from the library yesterday... *Yes, I ask about you*," he teased in a mock romantic confession.

"She said it was okay. I asked…"

"Relax. I told you. As long as you obey my rules, make yourself at home."

Laura wondered if he saw the paradox in his statement.

"I just wanted to ask you which one."

"Oh. It's just this book… by Hesse… *Steppenwolf*. I read it a long time ago." He kept surprising her with his unpredictable conversation twists.

"You like Hesse? Well, aren't you full of surprises, Miss Spencer," he teased. *And she was*. Although he could better understand her fondness for such an author with everything he now knew about her.

Steppenwolf followed the story of a tragic character, Harry Haller, a man torn from within. With two dominant and opposite natures, Harry constantly felt at war with himself. His wolf-self was merciless to the part of him that craved the comforts of domestication and a sense of belonging. Harry despaired and, believing he would never reconcile his inner duality, decided to end his life. His mysterious journey leads him to the iconic *Magic Theater*, instead, where the lines between fantasy and reality blur.

It was an unusual and surreal story, unafraid to sink into the darkest pits of the human soul yet still land in a place of hope.

"You've read it?" Laura almost screamed with excitement.

He nodded. "My mother loved that book. It was hers." Though his eyes darkened at her mention as the few times before, he forced a comforting smile.

"I see." She smiled back feebly. "Are your parents... still around?" she asked, treading uneasily on dangerous ground.

"No."

"I'm sorry." She meant it.

"Don't be."

She wanted to ask more but knew instinctively she had reached the limit. They both remained quiet for a moment: her, waiting for his lead, him, to confirm the end of her probing questions. Satisfied, his face brightened again. He pulled out a small box, beautifully gift-wrapped with ribbon, and handed it to her.

"What is this?" she asked, eyeing it suspiciously.

"A gift. Open it."

"Oh... thanks?" she replied, her tone suggesting uncertainty. Carefully, she unboxed her present, making sure not to tear the wrapping. It was a book, *The Kite Runner*, by Khaled Hosseini.

"Wow... Thank you," she said, the feeling sincere.

He smiled at her. "Have you read it?"

"No, actually. I've been meaning to. Just never got around to it. Have you?"

"Yes."

"Thank you, really." She held the book lovingly and looked him straight in the eye, wonder and gratitude in hers.

With a gracious nod, he gently commanded, "Let's eat."

Supper went relatively smoothly, discussing books and movies. It turned out they both shared a passion for film though their tastes varied considerably. Laura bowed in awe at Peter Jackson's masterpiece, *The Lord of the Rings*, and rambled endlessly on the many levels *Harry Potter* could be understood and appreciated. Kayne preferred Korean action thrillers and Scorsese films. They both agreed, however, smiling at each other as if on a first date, *The Shawshank Redemption* was possibly the best stand-alone movie ever made.

After they both finished eating, he cleared their plates, refusing her offer to help. "I'm staying in tonight. Would you like to watch a movie with me?"

She hadn't realized he'd gone out the previous nights. She was caught off guard and was unsure how to respond. Was it a genuine question or a subtle command?

"I'll let you choose which one," he cajolingly added.

A part of her was enjoying the company, having spent most of the last few days by herself. She craved human interaction, she realized, even if it was with a monster. But was he? She wasn't so sure anymore. What kind of monster could appreciate Hesse, grasp the beauty of *Shawshank*, and admit his favorite novel to be Saint-Exupery's *The Little Prince*? She was intrigued by this unusual brand of monster. Partly in fear of his reaction to rejection, partly out of the troubling desire to spend more time with him, she accepted his offer.

With a pleased smile, Kayne pointed to the couch and handed her the remote. As she scanned the options on the menu, Laura began to feel chilly and cursed, once again, the cute but sleeveless top. Noticing her rubbing her arms, Kayne offered her a throw.

"No, I'm okay, thank you."

"Don't lie to me, Laura. Even out of politeness."

Her body immediately tensed. "A blanket would be great. Thank you."

He nodded, satisfied, and left to fetch it for her. She scrolled up and down, trying to find a movie they could both enjoy. Her eyes fell on *The Usual Suspects*. She had read many positive reviews about it but had never given it a chance, deeming it a gangster flick.

"Have you seen it? It's really good, apparently."

"Your choice," he answered pleasantly as he handed her the blanket and sat beside her.

The movie started. They had never been so physically close for such a long period. Laura cuddled up on the couch, trying to maintain space between their bodies. Placing the cushion on the arm of the sofa, she pulled the cover over her shoulders and leaned away from him. Kayne sat with his legs spread apart, his arms wrapping the back of the couch, and his knee brushing her feet. She could feel his warmth and was troubled by it, getting distracted from an otherwise captivating movie.

Halfway through the film, his cell phone rang. Kayne picked it off the table and read the caller ID. "I have to take this," he excused himself, resting his hand lightly on her leg, and walked out of the room.

Through the thick cloth, she could feel the imprint of his touch, and she felt her stomach knot remembering her dream; *Yes, Master*... Laura squeezed her legs tighter in response to the feeling it triggered, mortified and thankful for the cover.

Kayne returned with a pleasant smile but a disappointed look. "I'm sorry, Laura. I have to get going."

"Oh?" She had paused the movie for him and was about to stop it completely.

"No. Please, continue without me. I'll catch up later, okay?"

She was never sure when he seemed so benevolent if he was giving her an order. And just as before, she decided against finding it out for herself. "Are you sure?"

He nodded. "I'll be home late... Don't wait up," he added, his eyes and tone filled with mischief.

DAY-7

LAURA SLEPT DEEPLY AND woke up rested, grateful for a dreamless night. She headed straight to her reading room, looking forward to exploring her gift. Why had he selected this specific book, she wondered; a narrative centered on regret and redemption. Was it the Monster's way of showing his humanity, subtly delivering clues through the story's protagonist?

She settled on the couch and, lost in her thoughts, looked out the window at the sunny day. Seeing the security men guarding the premises, she pondered again about a possible escape. If she ever tried, it would have to be planned. She would have to earn his trust enough so he would let her go outside. Even then, she couldn't hope to outrun the gunmen to the front gates.

She tried picturing the life that could follow a successful venture. What would she do? Where would she go? But the bitter answer came too fast: Nothing. Nowhere. Only more of the same would follow; a life half-lived, mechanically going through similar days blending into one another, with nothing to look forward to and nothing left to hold on to.

Laura imagined the security guards tracking her down and delivering her to Maxwell and his henchmen, and she shuddered at the thought. She then realized, against all logic and reason, that she felt safer with the Monster than she would on her own. She recalled a quote from *Gangs of New York*, one of her Scorsese favorites, where Leonardo DiCaprio's character befriends his father's killer, hoping to eventually exact revenge.

In one scene, he describes their complex relationship: *"It's a funny feeling being taken under the wing of a dragon. It's warmer than you'd think."*

She shook her head as if trying to shake her thoughts off. She didn't have the strength to strategize or analyze. For now, her main goal was to get through the day, survive until the next, and, if possible, maintain her sanity throughout.

She opened the book decisively, opting for the safest escape: within her mind. The story mesmerized her from the first line, and she didn't notice the hours go by. Sometime in the afternoon, Olga gently confirmed the usual suppertime.

When Laura looked at the clock, she realized with shock that she had less than fifteen minutes to prepare. She decided on slim jeans in a darker hue and paired them with a beige long-sleeve fitted sweater. Her hair up in a high ponytail, she decided to forgo makeup once again. With a twist in her gut, she realized that she *was* trying to look pretty for him, but in a manner that wouldn't betray her desire.

Laura showed up at seven sharp and found him sitting on a high stool by the kitchen island. Kayne was in grey sweatpants and a loose white T-shirt, his hair in a low ponytail with loose strands tucked behind his ears. He looked weary and offered her a mirthless smile as she took a stool next to him. It made her uneasy, and she wondered if his somber mood had anything to do with her.

"Olga left early. I ordered us some Chinese." He pointed to the bagged cartons on the counter in explanation, a forced breeziness in his voice. Supper was unusually quiet. Laura kept her eyes on her plate, throwing furtive glances when she thought he wouldn't be looking. But Kayne caught her gaze every time.

"How was the movie?" he eventually asked in a visible effort to lighten the mood.

That was all it took. She dropped her fork and clasped her hands. "It. Was. Crazy! Wow! I can't believe I waited so long to watch it!" Laura gestured with excitement. Discussing books or movies that captured her heart or blew her mind had always been among the rare instances where her features came to life.

"That good, huh?" Kayne entertained her with a soft chuckle.

"Yes! You definitely have to finish it!"

"Why don't you just tell me what happens?" He grabbed another bite, amused by her childlike enthusiasm.

"No way! I'm not telling you. Are you crazy?"

His brow shot up as if he was taken aback, and he calmly put his fork down on the table.

Laura immediately regretted her candor and rushed to justify her words. "No, no, no… I didn't mean it like that. I just meant that… I mean…" she frantically searched for words. "I just didn't want to ruin it for you… I wasn't trying to disobey or disrespect you. I swear! I can tell you if you want me to… do you want me to? Please don't be mad…"

Kayne crossed his arms, patiently waiting for her nervous ramble to end. "Are you done?"

"Yes… Please, Sir," she implored again, her voice cracking.

"Come here."

Laura hesitantly got up and took his offered hand. While still sitting on the stool, Kayne pulled her between his legs. They met at eye level, her frantic heart searching for any indication of what was to come in the pools of darkness facing her.

"Breathe, Laura… Breathe…" He placed his hands on her waist, his soothing voice coming through a roguish grin. He softly stroked her arms, forcibly calming her down. "Don't you think I can tell the difference?"

"Yes… I don't know. Please, Sir…"

She flinched when he brought his hand to her face, but he caressed her cheek with the pad of his thumb. There was a certain pleasure at the feel of his rough skin touching her ever so lightly. Bringing her even closer, he leaned his face to the side of hers.

"Tell me, Laura," he whispered huskily in her ear, "Why is it you always call me 'Sir' when you feel afraid?"

"I don't know," she bit her lip.

"You do know… tell me."

"I don't know… it just… comes naturally, I guess. Please, Sir… I don't want to go back… there."

He pulled back so he could face her. "You think I would lock you up just for that?"

"I don't know…"

"You really think I'm a monster, don't you?"

Her eyes glistened.

"Answer me," he ordered. "And remember… no lies," he warned, toying with her with devilish pleasure.

Laura dipped her chin, unsuccessfully concealing the tears streaming down her face.

Kayne sighed and, standing up lazily, pulled her to him. He brushed the tips of his fingers up and down her back, comforting her with one hand. With the other, he softly brushed her hair away from her face.

He knew she thought of him as a monster. How right she was, he smiled. He looked at her with fondness as she closed her eyes, unconsciously, ever so lightly, leaning into his embrace. She *was* innocent, though not naïve. Life had not afforded her such privilege. He began to understand that was precisely the key to her charm.

He was a monster indeed, the truest kind of monster. He would not be satisfied with only making her cower in fear; he would also make her crave his comfort and render her desperate for his touch. Kayne held her until her sobs died down and her breathing slowly returned to normal. Grabbing her by the shoulders, he gently nudged her back and stared into her eyes.

"Better?" he asked with a restrained smirk.

She sheepishly nodded.

"Good." Then, as if remembering something unpleasant, his mood shifted again. "Go to bed. It's been a long day."

Though she staggered out of the kitchen, Laura turned to face him as she was about to round the corner. "Good night…" She wasn't sure if she was supposed to call him 'Sir' at all times, but she sensed he liked it.

"Good night, Laura." He sounded pleasantly surprised at her initiative.

She hesitated a little. "Should I always call you … Sir?" she asked, avoiding his eyes and with a faint blush coloring her face.

With a wicked smile, he quoted back her words in response, "Whatever… comes naturally, I guess."

★ ★ ★

Kayne lay wide awake in his bed. He had received another call from Dimitri. The big boss was throwing a party the next day and wanted Kayne to bring the girl. He was curious and wanted to see her for himself. Kayne's words carried weight in the Organization. No one would contradict him or disobey him openly. Those who had were no more. But even he couldn't go head-to-head against Dimitri. He had explained his position as clearly and truthfully as he could. He wanted the girl for himself and to be given the discretion to deal with the situation however he saw fit. He would get the information out of her, he assured the old man. Dimitri had consented because he could understand his motives. Pretty women who unfortunately got caught in their world were often used to various ends. Just like in the days of old, the victors claimed the spoils of war. They were turned into personal whores, shared as sex slaves, or sold according to the whims of their holders. Laura was his to claim, and he had. But this time, it was different. She still had a purpose to serve. Dimitri was a reasonable man. He'd allowed Kayne to have his way provided he got what he wanted. But Kayne knew he was treading a thin line; vices were never put before business. What if Dimitri wished to have the girl interrogated again?

Kayne was apprehensive about how things would unfold. He would try to talk to him and buy himself and the girl a little more time. It was his only option. He knew Dimitri held a certain fondness for him, having been close to his father and even acting as a second mentor. If it came to it, Kayne would speak on her behalf, ensuring she remained under his care. He felt the same surge of animalistic protectiveness as he had when questioning her on whether she'd been abused. She was his, to do with as he pleased. He would not stand by and watch someone else have their way with her.

Kayne tried to convince himself that nothing drastic would ensue. He would reason with Dimitri and have his way, as always. He was earning the girl's trust. Soon, if he played his hand well, she would tell him of her own accord. He knew he could make her. Dimitri would have Peter's head, he would get Laura, and they would all live happily ever after. *Well, except for Peter.* He laughed sardonically in the dark at the fantasy and derided himself; maybe he *was* in love with the girl. After all, for all his stoic appearance, it had taken just one look for Lev Malkin to fall helplessly in love with Elena Galiano.

He had first noticed her sitting on a bench by a willow tree in the dying summer, her brows furrowed over a novel. Before even hearing her voice, for the space of the three minutes he'd watched her from across the street, Lev Malkin had understood he had just met *The One*.

He had approached the beautiful reader, but she hadn't even lifted her nose to rebuff his attempted courtship. He'd processed her response as a mild inconvenience. Lev Malkin wasn't a man easily deterred. With confidence and dedication, he had returned to the park daily; until the weather would no longer permit it, and the object of his affection sought refuge in the coffee shop nearby. Unbothered by her unwavering rejection, he had followed her inside and tried every machination that came to mind to woe the studious beauty: from flowers and chocolate to perfume and jewelry, appearing as a confident contender or playing the devoted suitor. He had spared no trick from the playbook as he pursued her relentlessly. But the young student wouldn't budge, dismissing his every initiative with the same amused headshake.

The barista had finally taken pity on the spurned lover and pointed out the obvious: *what* was she passionate about? Lev had then disappeared for over a week. By the second or third day, Elena Galiano had finally lifted her head to confirm the time on the clock above the counter. Following the military precision with which he had conducted his daily advances, she had registered with a surprise, a tinge in her heart at his absence.

When Lev Malkin finally reappeared, the very air about him was different. He had approached her table with a triumphant gait and, without a word, produced a signed first edition of her favorite novel. Their first date had lasted over forty-eight hours, and within the month, he had proposed—not with a ring, but by presenting her with the library he had built for her.

What was it with women and books? Kayne wondered, then corrected himself; not all women, just the ones the Malkin men seemed unable to resist.

DAY-8

LAURA WAS CUDDLED ON the couch in her reading room with *The Kite Runner* pointlessly opened on her lap. She couldn't quite get into it, catching herself reading the same lines over and over again. She had an uneasy feeling replaying the scene from the previous night. Kayne had seemed tired, burdened even; his gentler approach more of an effect of his weariness. She thought back to his embrace, her skin remembering the feel of his caresses. Lost in the moment, she could hear his soft and reassuring voice again. Shameful, she chided herself and resumed the fruitless analysis of her captor's frame of mind.

Her entire day was spent in this fashion, her eyes either staring off into the distance or distractedly resting on the pages in her hands, the blots of ink losing all meaning the longer she stared. It was almost five in the afternoon when Olga tapped at the door. Though surprised at the random visit, Laura welcomed the interruption.

"Sorry to disturb you, Miss Spencer. Master Kayne wanted me to inform you to meet him at seven in the living room… He said to… fix your hair and makeup," she finished, slightly uncomfortable delivering such instructions. "I can help if you like," she added with a warm smile.

"Okay… so no supper tonight?"

"I'm not sure what Master Kayne planned for dinner. He didn't ask me to prepare anything."

"I see. Thank you, Olga."

"Well, please let me know if I can be of any assistance," she offered again before leaving.

Laura was unsure what to make of this. Why would he make such a demand? He had never done so before. Were they going somewhere? But then again, he didn't allow her out in the gated front yard; she highly doubted he was taking her to a five-star restaurant. She kept speculating, unable to come up with any logical explanation.

A thousand questions accompanied Laura back to her room, each muffled by an unbidden and even more unsettling answer. She drew a bath, hoping to drown them all in vanilla-scented water. Her body easing into its lulling warmth, her hand unconsciously grabbed a blade, and she began to shave before stopping at the realization. It was such a meaningless action, yet it carried so many implications.

She did her legs and armpits, those were innocent enough, and then lingered with the blade resting below her belly button. The question begging to be asked: Did she, somehow, hope he would see her there? Her inner voice responded with an emphatic *NO*, making her jump up and step out of the bathtub as if snapping out of a haze. On her way out of the bathroom, however, she couldn't help sneaking a quick peek in the mirror. The regrowth was still minor, she noted with suppressed relief.

She rummaged through the walk-in closet indecisively, considering all the choices at her disposal. Wardrobe was a tricky issue; it was not directly addressed in his request. She didn't want to seem too eager to please, going above and beyond the call of duty. But she was in no position to give him cause to feel slighted either.

After selecting seamless pink panties and a matching push-up bra, she finally settled on a loose-fitting beige silk camisole over skinny black trousers, matching them with a fitted black blazer. She found some black stilettos at the back of the walk-in and threw them on. Unsure, she considered herself in the mirror for a moment. She was no fashion expert by any means, but judging the result satisfactory enough, she turned her attention to the vanity. She straightened her hair and, opting for a more natural look, stuck to earthy tones for eye shadow.

By six-thirty, she was ready and pacing around her room, a mixture of apprehension and excitement sweeping over her. She waited for the last minute before the clock struck seven, took a big breath, and walked out her bedroom door. Her heartbeat increasing with each step, Laura realized she was anxious to see his reaction; beyond the captive seeking to please, the woman in her wanted to know. He had never seen her dressed up... not since that first night, she reminded herself with a tightening in her chest.

Donning a formal black suit with his hair slicked back, Kayne sat on the couch with a glass of whiskey in hand. He stared at an invisible spot on the wall, consumed with thought, and didn't notice her come in. On the table by his side was a large, fancy-looking gift box in a deep black velvet finish. It was wrapped with a lustrous gold ribbon, its elegant design leaving no doubt as to the worth it housed.

Laura eyed the mysterious package. And standing in the corner, she softly cleared her throat, politely requesting his attention.

Only his eyes moved to find her, and his brows shot up upon seeing her. He bobbed his head as if impressed with what he saw.

Her relief mixed with a trickle of pleasure, and Laura blushed, turning her luminous eyes away.

"Come closer," Kayne commanded in a husky voice.

She took a few hesitant steps and stopped at the corner of the couch, just a few inches within his reach.

"It's for you." He pushed the box toward her with a somber expression.

"Thank you…" This had nothing to do with when he offered her the book; his strange mood disquieted her. She reached for it uncertainly, almost expecting a bomb to explode.

It contained a backless, dark purple silk gown. She pulled the dress from the box, the rich material gently flowing to her feet. It was her turn to lift her brows, awestruck. "Wow… it's beautiful! I don't think I've ever owned anything this beautiful. Like *anything*. Not just clothes…" Laura smiled brightly at him, barely aware she hoped it would be returned.

His face still serious, Kayne nodded. "Try it on."

The trepidation she felt became increasingly difficult to ignore, and all the warmth that had filled her features deserted them. She was heading out of the living room with her new gift in hand when his voice stopped her.

"Where are you going?"

She spun back around. "You said to try it on…"

"I did." His eyes glinted with a predator's thrill.

"I don't understand…" Laura murmured uncomfortably.

"Of course you do. Take off your clothes, Laura." His wolfish expression cushioned the callous command.

She remained still, her breathing growing louder. "Sir?"

"Sir me all you like; you will still do as I say."

Her eyes watered, and she nervously played with the dress in her hands. "Please, Sir. Please don't do this…" She recalled her earlier hesitation in the tub and berated herself for being so naïve. Why wouldn't he abuse her? What made her think he would be above it? The memory of their first night came to her. How he had earned her trust only to betray it right after. How he had remorselessly owned up to it, staring her in the eye unblinking as Maxwell shackled and hurt her. A shiver ran down her spine.

"Do what, Laura?" He leaned forward, his eyes boring into hers.

"Please… don't rape me," she answered, her voice thick with emotion.

"You think I'm going to fuck you?" he sneered at her. "Don't worry, Laura. I won't. Not until you ask…" he added with a seductive smile.

Her initial relief slowly turned to disbelief and, replaying his words, morphed into outrage. Was he so conceited that he thought she would want that, *ask for it*? She opened her mouth but, upon a second glance in his direction, closed it right back, swallowing the affront.

"Laura. Take off your clothes," he reiterated, losing patience.

Her gaze fell to the floor. Slumped in defeat, she looked for a place to set the dress, trying to delay the inevitable. Kayne took another sip from his drink and lit a cigarette, watching her nervously twist the material in her hands.

Upon catching his stare, Laura hurriedly placed it on the arm of the La-Z-Boy. Dejected, she first removed her shoes. On to her blazer, she fumbled nervously with the sleeves and then reached her arm out to set it next to the dress.

"Leave it."

She flinched at the sound of his voice and let it immediately drop to the floor. She then hesitated between moving on to her top or the pants first, her hands undecidedly going from one piece to the other. Unable to make the call herself, she looked toward him for guidance.

"Your shirt," he directed, his eyes burning into her.

She slid off her camisole, almost thankful to have the burden of decision removed. She then lingered for a few moments, still unwilling to take the next step unprompted, and played with the band of her trousers.

"And now your pants."

He understood her, her brain process. She would await his spoken instruction before removing each item. Her pride wouldn't allow her to take any initiative and participate on her own. Her submissiveness, however, had her abiding hastily to his every command, albeit with clumsy and jerky moves.

"Good girl."

Laura instantly blushed at his words, her intimate parts contracting despite herself.

Kayne smiled wickedly at her, conscious of her conflicting emotions. "Remove your bra."

Her eyes darted up to meet his and silently pleaded. Restraining a smirk, he nodded in affirmation and saw her eyes water again. Though she obeyed, she tried to cover herself with her arms.

"Put your arms down, Laura." He exhaled with mild annoyance.

She did, slowly, fidgeting with her hands as if not knowing what to do with them.

Kayne enjoyed a few more sips of his drink, shamelessly leering at her exposed, squirming body. She looked up at the ceiling, blinking tears away, and he marveled at her raw beauty, her discomfort only adding to his thrill.

"Don't, Laura. You'll only ruin your makeup. Why do you want to cry?"

"Isn't it obvious?"

"Not from what I see," he answered with a sneer, his eyes on her panties.

She followed his gaze to the source and, mortified, instinctively covered the dampened spot with her hands.

A chuckle escaped his lips. He finished his drink and languidly walked up to her, grabbing the dress on his way. He stood in front of her, without touching, just close enough so she could feel his warmth on her bare skin.

"Are you upset with me?"

"Yes," she hissed through gritted teeth.

"Hmm… You'll have to get over it. Get dressed. Lucas will be here any moment now."

She reached for the dress, trying to snatch it from his hands, but Kayne held it back.

"Easy now…"

Laura recoiled at the implied threat, all bravado leaving her.

How he loved toying with her: so easily riled up, just as easily calmed down. He loosened his hold and watched as she poured the silky material over her curves.

"Sit."

Kayne held her stare as she lowered herself onto the chair. Then kneeling in front of her, he grabbed her stilettos. And though remnants of mischief still lingered in his eyes, he offered Laura a warm smile. He gently held her leg in his hand, his warm skin radiating against hers, and slid one shoe after the other on her feet. He was all business by the time he stood up.

"We're going out tonight. Lucas will drive us. I don't believe I've introduced you. I expect you won't try anything stupid."

"May I ask where we're going?"

For barely a flash, she could see the apprehension on his face. But in an instant, it was gone, replaced by his usual phlegmatic expression.

Her question remained unanswered, her words lingering in the air as his attention turned to his vibrating mobile.

"He's outside. Let's go." He offered her his arm.

Walking out of the house, he leaned into her ear and whispered, "You looked beautiful."

Looked... not look, and Laura turned bright red at the insinuation.

Kayne quietly chuckled as they caught up with the head of security. Lucas Belfort was a handsome and refined man of biracial background. He was tall with a muscular build, his pale green eyes even more striking against his dark skin, his hair shaved in a buzz cut. He carried himself with dignity, his laughing eyes sparkling with intelligence. His deceivingly boyish good looks were reinforced with his deadliest weapon: a smile designed to instill trust. Both magnetic and familiar, it enabled its caster to easily penetrate any defensive walls erected by its recipient.

Kayne had met Lucas in elementary school. He had first noticed him in his ragged clothes, standing up to the school bully and his two faithful trolls. The brainless sadist that tormented all the outcasts had picked the young Belfort as his newest target. Lucas had stared him straight in the eye, unflinching, and threw the first punch. He got beaten to a pulp. A week later, his face still bruised, Kayne had seen the shame in Lucas's eyes as he faced the cafeteria lady, counting the spare change in the palm of his hand. He'd seemed more defeated standing in front of her than he'd been lying on the ground. Without a word, Kayne had crept to his side. Under the counter, he'd covertly slipped him the twenty-dollar bill his father had given him earlier that morning.

An alliance was formed then. One that strengthened over the years, deepened over shared experiences and solidified over crimes perpetrated together. Lucas had been spending his days at the Malkin residence since early adolescence. His mother had never asked questions. His father, he'd never met. By the age of sixteen, he'd permanently moved in, staying in the employees' quarters in the western wing. After they graduated high school, Lev Malkin had covered all the expenses for his higher education. They were twenty when Lev finally lost his battle with cancer. After his passing, Kayne followed in his father's footsteps, stepping in as the Master of the house. Lucas began addressing him as 'Sir' and took over the security detail. He'd rallied all those remaining loyal to the Malkins and ensured his closest friend's ascent and control in the Organization.

"Good evening, Sir."

"Evening, Lucas. I don't believe you've met Laura."

"Ah, Miss Spencer, no. What a pleasure." He respectfully bowed his head and then turned back to Kayne. "We should get going."

They embarked in the Audi, sitting in the back with Lucas at the wheel. Laura remembered the first time she'd gotten in this car, how it had changed her life, and she considered with a gulp what could possibly lie ahead. Kayne seemed preoccupied during the ride, withdrawn, and her nervousness rose as the car sped away. Where was he taking her? It couldn't be anywhere good if it had even him rattled.

"Sir..."

Kayne absentmindedly turned to her, still absorbed in thought.

"Are you taking me to an interrogation?" she asked in a whisper.

That got his attention. *No*, definitely not naïve, Kayne thought to himself. He sighed and looked away, staring out the window. "We're going to a party... I suspect it's not your typical scene."

"Why not? What's at the party? Please tell me."

He faced her again. "My boss wanted me to bring you. He's the one hosting."

She paled. "So you *are* taking me to an interrogation..."

He hesitated. "I don't know, Laura," he finally admitted, irritation tainting his voice.

He was nervous. That didn't happen very often to Kayne Malkin. The entire way, he tried to reassure himself. He would talk to Dimitri. It would all work out. It had to; there was no other viable option. He could not openly defy Dimitri, yet he would not let him harm the girl. *His* girl.

Laura couldn't have suspected his inner turmoil. She only heard his fatalistic answer, the crushing response thrown callously at her. She wanted to jump out of the moving car. But they were going over a hundred kilometers per hour on the freeway, the doors locked under the driver's control. Reverting to self-soothing methods learned long ago, she began rocking herself back and forth, her jumbled thoughts seeing only danger with no escape. She felt a firm but gentle hand grab her arm and, with calm assurance, steady her movement.

"Laura. Look at me." He waited until she did. "Do as I say, and you will be fine. Okay?" His eyes burned into hers, and he felt her muscles relax. Kayne realized his commitment to the statement uttered as it came out of his lips. He would not stand by and watch as they had their way with her. She was his and his alone. He had found and claimed her. And Kayne always protected what was rightfully his.

Laura nodded, her eyes vacant.

"Do you trust me?"

A bitter laugh resonated in her soul and, dying out, revealed a darker truth. She did. Her sharpened survival instinct, perfected over the years, had still conceded enough safe space for her to hesitate in the bathtub—and now acquiesced with quiet relief to his question. She met his gaze and nodded again, this time slowly and deliberately.

Kayne gently squeezed her arm with a brittle smile and then turned away.

* * *

The SUV finally entered a driveway not unlike Kayne's, though the mansion it led to was twice the size. Security was all over the premises. There was valet service and even a doorman. Right before exiting the car, Kayne turned to Laura with fire in his eyes; his mood entirely changed. "Ready?"

"Ready," a subdued voice answered back.

He led her to the entrance with his hand on the small of her back, the material of her dress cascading in graceful folds.

Laura tried to walk ahead, ignoring the knot in her stomach at the feel of his palm on her skin.

As they got to the door, he leaned into her ear and instructed her in a hushed tone, "Stay close to me. Don't speak to anyone. And keep your eyes on the ground… Last part shouldn't be too hard," he teased.

Laura nodded, too nervous to be offended or embarrassed.

Words could barely express the sickening spectacle awaiting her. She froze in the doorway, refusing to take another step. There were hundreds of people. The men were dressed formally in fancy black suits, much like Kayne's. As for the women… she was shell-shocked. Some, which she assumed were strippers, were dancing in metal cages dangling from the high ceilings. Others donned black latex outfits and six-inch heels. Some were completely naked. Most of them had collars. Some even had leashes and were being dragged around on the floor. Only a very select few wore dark gowns like herself. Laura felt nauseated.

"I told you you wouldn't like it," Kayne whispered with devilish amusement in her ear before dragging her forward.

As they moved into the house, more explicit scenes befell her eyes. Orgies were breaking throughout wherever she turned. In one room, a group of men casually conversed with drinks in their hands while naked women serviced them, one of them even acting as a footrest. In another, five men were huddled by a woman splayed flat on a table. One of them was carelessly thrusting himself in her mouth while another put her other orifices to good use. With her hands, she pleasured others gathered around her as they fondled her generous breasts.

She looked around, both repulsed and disbelieving. It reminded her of the sex scene in the movie *Eyes Wide Shut*, except there was no pretense to this, no need for ceremonies and occult hocus-pocus. It was pure, unapologetic debauchery in its most perverse form.

"You… you go to these things?" she asked, her hushed tone barely masking her disgust.

"Yes."

Laura let go of his arm and took a step back.

Kayne didn't reach out to pull her back to him. He remained in his spot, his stare brimming with sinful intent. As if on cue, a man drunkenly stumbled toward them, undressing her with his eyes.

"Well, well… what do we have here?" he slurred, raising a hand to touch her hair.

In an instant, she was back at Kayne's side. Half-hiding behind him, she fiercely gripped his arm, her nails digging into his jacket.

"She's with me," Kayne coolly warned the man.

"Mr. Malkin. I'm so sorry, I didn't know." And just as fast, the man scurried out of sight.

Kayne waited a few moments, then turned to Laura with a smirk. "So we're friends again."

Laura, still terrified, mutely clung to his arm. Walking around the premises, Kayne ran into many acquaintances. They ogled her shamelessly and made lewd comments. He dismissed most of them with a dry smile, holding her closer when sensing her rising panic.

A shiver ran through her spine at every degrading word and lingering stare. The thought of these men touching her made her feel sick. They conversed about her as if she wasn't there. From the unpalatable bits of conversations, she understood that they thought she was his whore, and that Kayne didn't share his whores with other men. But sometimes, he let them watch… Appalled, she wondered if he'd do this to her. Would he make her remove her clothes in front of them as he had her do earlier that night? She prayed he would remain the only one to violate her intimacy.

Her frightful speculations were suddenly interrupted by a very present and tangible terror. Maxwell Bane stood across the room from them, caught up in a lively conversation with another man and a woman wearing a black velvet gown. "Kayne…" Laura's face blanched, her voice coming out in a strangled cry.

Kayne was caught unaware hearing his name from her lips. He was even more surprised at how much he liked it. She hadn't called him by his name since the night of their meeting, when he'd revealed the Monster in him.

He'd never allowed his submissives to address him so informally. They referred to him as *Sir* or *Master*, conveying the respect they owed him. But she wasn't his… yet, and he questioned if that was still his sole objective. Granted, he wanted her in all the twisted ways he always wanted beautiful women. But he was at a loss explaining the emerging feelings she stirred in him, the protective way he looked at her, the slow seduction he'd instinctively opted for. Never before had he felt such pleasure hearing his name uttered. Never before was it spoken with such intimate urgency. He wondered if the bond he'd inadvertently created was the price to pay for holding her captive: the responsibility he now felt toward a woman he would have otherwise just seduced and discarded without a second thought.

His gaze followed hers as she nudged her head toward a trio conversing at the back of the room.

The group immediately noticed Kayne and Laura's presence. Maxwell acknowledged them with a toothy sneer. The woman at his side turned their way, playful curiosity animating her features, and smiled brightly upon recognizing Kayne. She was tall, slender, and strikingly beautiful. Her red mane, slicked into a stylish side ponytail, contoured her delicate face and feline green eyes. Taking Maxwell's offered arm, she abandoned the conversation she was engaged in with no further warning, and with effortless grace, she glided toward them.

Kayne's eyes narrowed, landing on the source of Laura's distress. His attention fell back on her, and feeling her quickened breaths, he pulled her to him. "Laura... Laura. Look at me," he patiently commanded her attention, pulling her out of the swirl of terror ensnaring her.

She raised her chin, her eyes filled with dread.

"Don't worry about him."

Still not fully appeased, she gave the faintest nod in acknowledgment.

"I won't let him hurt you." With his hand on her shoulder, his thumb softly caressed her skin.

At his touch, the blast of the blaring alarm receded a little. His soothing words found hidden paths into her turbulent thoughts and, with calm authority, quieted her fears.

"Kayne! How are you? I see you brought the ever-so-lovely Miss Spencer." Maxwell turned to Laura with a reptilian smile plastered on his face.

"Oh my... she's a shy one," the pretty redhead said in a cutesy voice.

"Maxwell, Tanya… How have you been?" Kayne replied, a hint of impatience perceptible in his voice. He then wrapped his arm around Laura's waist, pulling her protectively to him.

"Good… good. I see you didn't waste your time with her. Can't say I blame you… She sure is a delectable little thing." Maxwell licked his lips as Kayne's stare turned icy.

Laura couldn't help noticing the antagonism between the two. Maxwell's convivial attitude seemed affected. Kayne barely bothered trying to hide his hostility. There was definitely bad blood there. As for the woman smiling with such familiarity at Kayne… *Tanya*, was that her name? There was no doubt in Laura's mind; from the first glance they exchanged, she knew the animosity she felt was reciprocated.

"So, Kayne… How long 'til we can play a little with her, huh? It's so unfair, really. You're no team player!" Maxwell chortled.

"Oh, come now, Maxwell. You know Kayne doesn't like to share his toys…" Tanya added in a singsong tone. "My guess is… hmm… two months? Maybe three… She looks *special*. But tell me, Kayne, if I promise not to break her, can *I* play with her?" She batted her eyes coyly at him, her fingers reaching for Laura's face.

As Laura shrunk back, Kayne caught Tanya's arm in midair. "Don't," he warned.

She glared at him but quickly fell back on a honeyed tone, mocking a hurt look. "Not even me?" She pouted her mouth. "My my… Guess she *is* special after all."

"Bah… no matter." Maxwell shrugged his shoulders. "They're even better when he's done with them." He winked at Tanya.

Throwing her head back coquettishly, she let out a strident laugh. But her eyes, if only for a fraction of a second, betrayed the hurt the remark had just inflicted on her. And with that, they walked away,

Tanya's chuckle still chiming, Maxwell, with his hand wrapped around her waist, his head barely reaching her shoulders.

The whole time, Laura had kept her eyes down and tried to focus on breathing and the calm Kayne's hand steadily provided, gently rubbing her back up and down. She tried to resist, with increasing difficulty, the compulsion to shriek at the top of her lungs before stumbling into complete insanity.

With his hand still on her back, Kayne leaned closer once they were alone. "Are you okay?"

With her eyes glistening, she shook her head. "Can we leave now?"

"Not yet… Not yet," he repeated, brushing her cheek. "Come."

He led her to the back and out double doors giving way to a gorgeous terrace. Waiters in black tuxedos went about a dozen satin cloth-covered tables, offering extravagant hors-d'oeuvres and drinks served in crystal glassware. An illuminated water fountain stood in the middle, surrounded by a magnificent, minutely well-tended garden. Laura couldn't help but take in all the beauty and thought, with bitter irony, how enchanting the place must appear looking in from the outside.

Kayne pulled her into a corner and offered her a cigarette, holding both in his mouth to light them before handing her one.

Laura took it with shaky fingers. "You do this…"

"Do what?"

"*This*… to women…"

"Do you really want to have this conversation now, Laura?" he gently cautioned in the form of a question, the wise voice steering the fool away from danger.

She heeded the advice. What good could come out of exposing the beast and confirming which atrocities, in this godforsaken place, was her only protection capable of?

One of the doormen approached them and, bowing his head with deference, addressed Kayne. "Mr. Malkin. Mr. Drugov is ready for you."

Kayne nodded, and the doorman left. He looked back at Laura. "Ready?"

"No?" She offered a weak smile.

He gave her an indulgent look and, grabbing her hand, led the way.

They went back in and got into a glass elevator that took them to the third floor. Dimitri Drugov was in his office waiting for them at his desk. Laura guessed he was in his sixties, with a full head of white hair and an imposing belly that he divulged when standing up to meet them. He had a large nose, no facial hair, and light blue eyes. His expression, though severe, softened considerably when he smiled.

"Ah, Kayne, my boy! How are you?" He affectionately embraced him and smiled as kindly to her. "I presume this is the lovely Miss Spencer?"

Laura remained in the doorway, looking down as instructed.

"Please, Laura. May I call you Laura? Come closer so I may have a look at you."

"Come, Laura," Kayne quickly interceded, seeing her hesitation.

Her eyes still glued to the floor, she cautiously approached the desk.

"Hmm… I see. Very lovely indeed." He winked at Kayne. "Please, sit down. Are you enjoying the party?" Dimitri then asked Laura.

She remained quiet, her shocked nerves zoning out most of her environment. In this state, only Kayne could reach her. Only his voice and touch were able to retrieve her, however lost she was in her mind, nightmarish visions lapping at her heels.

"It's her first time, Dimitri," Kayne responded for her.

"Yes, of course. You'll see. It's an acquired taste…" he added playfully. "So, Laura. Kayne tells me that you've been cooperative. I like that. I like reasonable people. Suicidal heroics, what are they good for, huh? Only wasted blood…" He gestured his hand disdainfully at the notion. "I just wanted to ensure that we do have your full cooperation. Not that I don't trust Kayne's judgment. I just wanted to see for myself. I'm sure you can understand. I want to ask you one simple question. Have you answered all of Kayne's questions truthfully?"

"Answer him," Kayne gently ordered the rigid beauty at his side.

Laura's eyes snapped up and then back down, remembering her instructions. "Yes, Sir. I have."

"Hmm…" Dimitri considered her some more.

"May I have a word with you in private?" Kayne asked him. The patriarch nodded, waving his arm in consent, and Kayne lightly tapped Laura's elbow. "Wait outside by the door for me."

She nodded but didn't move, her eyes imploring him not to make her. She dreaded the thought of being alone in this place, even for a moment, even on the third floor, where none of the obscene party guests were present.

"Go," he reiterated through gritted teeth.

She flinched at the severity in his tone and rushed to the door. Patiently, she waited, every second seeming an eternity. When he finally came out to meet her, he flashed her a radiant smile, his demeanor more relaxed than it had been the past few days.

"Is it okay? Can we go now?"

"Soon," he answered, gently brushing her face with the back of his fingers.

Laura closed her eyes at his touch, drinking in the reassurance and tenderness she so desperately craved.

Kayne led her back downstairs, where most guests had gathered in the grand reception hall. A stage had been built in the middle. Tables, couches, and even beds were spread all around it. While the men sat comfortably, most women crouched at their feet as obedient pets, a majority being put to good use. Only the handful of women in gowns sat on chairs at the tables.

In the center stage, a naked woman, bound with an iron collar, was shackled to a Dark Ages-looking pranger. She dangled helplessly from a metal chain to which she was tied at the wrists. Forced up on her toes, she struggled to keep her balance. A shirtless man in a black mask and leather pants whipped her mercilessly, drawing blood with every stroke. The audience perversely cheered with every blow that landed on her, their excitement invigorated with each pained scream as her skin ripped.

"What is this?" Laura's eyes darted around like a trapped wild animal, ready to strike at the slightest movement.

Kayne didn't let her see his own sadistic smile. They could've left after meeting with Dimitri. They didn't have to stay for the show. He wanted to. He had wrecked his nerves the past few days over her, for her. She would now return the favor. He wanted to see her reaction to it, test her boundaries. He knew very well she would be frightened and repulsed. But would any part of her, however small, also be intrigued?

Ignoring her question, he picked a couch in a hidden corner and led her to it. Just far enough from the crowd, she could feel a safe distance from her environment. Just close enough from the stage, she couldn't entirely disconnect, forced to witness the scandalous fetishes out in plain sight. Kayne sat her next to him, wrapping his arm around her.

"What's going on?" she asked, panic seeping through her hushed voice. Her eyes were glued to the horrid scene.

Kayne's were on her. "Relax, it's just a show." He gently rubbed her shoulder.

"It's *not* just a show." Though her voice remained low, it rose a few octaves. "Kayne… Please… I don't want to be here."

He took her face in both hands, forcing her to stare at him. "Laura. Calm down. It's just a show."

By now, the masked man had abandoned his whip, and another had joined him on stage. One of them began penetrating the woman forcefully from behind. The other forced her mouth around his length, her gagging sounds echoing throughout the room.

Though her face was still trapped in Kayne's hands, Laura's eyes reverted to the stage. "They're raping her," she whispered in agony.

"They're not raping her," he dismissively assured her.

"They are! They're raping her!" she insisted, her voice growing erratic.

Kayne let out a long sigh, his nostrils flaring. "Come with me."

He pulled her off the couch and dragged her out of the room, taking long strides as she struggled to keep up with him.

He turned a few corners and abruptly stopped in a deserted corridor. Pinning her wrists to the wall, he leaned in close, his mouth barely a few inches from hers.

They stared at one another, both panting. Kayne, with a mix of aggravation and arousal, Laura from fear and the knot in her gut. His breathing slowed back to normal, and he pulled back, maintaining his firm grip on her wrists.

"There. Out of the room. Better?"

Holding back tears, she slowly shook her head.

Kayne sighed again, though this time his features softened. Leaning his forehead against hers, he briefly closed his eyes. He then let go of her, his stare somewhere between amused and fascinated.

"What am I going to do with you?" He shook his head. "You're really convinced she is being raped."

"Yes." Her answer was emphatic, though spoken in a soft voice.

He shook his head again. "And what makes you so sure?"

"Seriously?"

"Tell me." He crossed his arms, entertained at her stubbornness.

"You want me to believe that *this* was consensual? Listen, I know all about S&M and bondage and stuff—"

His brow shot up with surprise, then smiling seductively, he interrupted her, "Do you now?"

Laura turned beet red and, unable to hold his stare, stammered. "Well… I mean… like… not firsthand…" Then with more conviction, she met his eyes again. "But yes, I do know about it. And this, *this*, was not role play. It was real. It was *very* real."

"Which still doesn't make it rape," he flatly concluded.

"This was NOT consensual!"

"And you know that… how exactly?" he asked patronizingly.

"You want me to believe she *wants this*?"

"What if I told you that I knew *for a fact* that she was into *this*," he mimicked her disdain at the word.

"You can't possibly know that…"

Kayne didn't answer, lifting his brows instead in silent innuendo.

"You've done this to her..." Laura's voice dripped with dread. She backed away from him, every inch of her body pressing against the wall behind her.

He leaned forward, caging her within his arms, "Don't ask questions you don't want answered, baby girl," he wolfishly whispered in her ear.

She gulped, the rest of her body remaining very still. "Will this happen to me?" Laura asked, her eyes filled with pain and her voice so soft it was barely audible.

"What?" Genuine surprise marked his voice.

"You send girls here... when you're done with them. Is that what will happen to me? If you never find Peter... it's not like you'll keep me in your house forever. And if you do..." Her voice cracked with pain. "It's not like you'll let me go. Is this where you'll send me?"

"No, Laura. I will not send you here," he answered, his expression inscrutable.

She dropped her head, shutting her eyes with relief. When she reopened them, they glistened with all the emotions she couldn't process.

Kayne cocked his head, watching her beautiful features looking almost sultry in their haze, her soft pink lips moist and quivering. He languidly grabbed her by the front of her dress, pulling her unresisting body into his.

Laura looked up at him, her eyes filled with questions.

He met her gaze. Slowly, he leaned in. And he kissed her softly on her lips.

★ ★ ★

Laura lay in bed, replaying the night in her head over and over again. She had never felt as confused in her life. She still shivered, remembering the *show* and how the women at the party were treated. Then the image of

Kayne would appear, overpowering all others. Kayne pulling her close protectively, Kayne whispering scary and seductive things in her ear, Kayne shamelessly leering at her naked body...

She squeezed her legs in an effort to both appease and banish the feeling. Her body reacted in so many ways when it came to him. Too often, in ways she couldn't control or understand. But even her heart proved itself unreliable when she recalled his kiss. His luscious, gentle kiss. It had her in a daze, realizing she was leaning into it when he broke it off. She remembered the sweet way he had looked at her afterward. He'd held her hand and pulled her out of that nightmarish place. In the car, he was silent, almost distant. She had glanced at him a few times hoping to catch his stare, but he never looked her way.

When they'd finally reached home, he had caressed her cheek as he had so many times that night and sent her off to bed while still standing in the doorway. He had somewhere else to go, it seemed. She wondered if he was returning to the party. Tanya's image flashed in her mind. She could picture her greeting him on his own, flirting and making snide comments as she led him somewhere dark and private. Laura chose not to pursue this line of thought, surprised at how fast her stomach turned with the vivid images taking shape in her mind, her teeth clenched so hard her jaw hurt.

She couldn't understand the intense and opposite feelings he triggered in her. She couldn't reconcile the Kayne that had kissed her so softly, protected her, and even comforted her with the Kayne who participated in these sordid parties. The Kayne who admitted unblinkingly to the monstrous things he would do there... The same Kayne, she recalled with her chest tightening, who had brought her into an interrogation room and had, by his own confession, interrogated countless others. And yet, he had stepped in and rescued her from the wolves he had delivered her to. What kind of monster was he? What kind of monster kisses like this? She caught herself imagining what being intimate with him would be like. Would he be gentle? Would he be cruel? Or perhaps, just a little of both…

She felt the urge to touch herself down there and soothe the building ache between her thighs. She resisted, unable to accept the effect he had on her. She had touched herself before. But never with anyone specific in mind, especially not a man, a monster, like him.

DAY-9

LAURA SLEPT IN THE next day. She was just waking up when Olga came sometime in the afternoon to take back the untouched breakfast.

"Ah, you're finally up. Should I bring you a new plate? This won't do." She pointed to the cold food on the trolley, her smile as warm as ever.

"Hmm… It's okay. I think I'll just have coffee for now. Thank you, Olga."

"As you wish." She was about to head out, then added almost as an afterthought, "Master Kayne won't be home for supper tonight. Would you still like to eat at seven?"

"He won't?" Laura asked a little too loudly.

"No, Miss Spencer."

"Oh… Yes, seven will be fine, thank you."

Laura could barely disguise her disappointment. He'd never missed their nightly rendezvous since bringing her to the house. She used to dread it. She was even locked in a cage barely a week ago for refusing his company. His sudden and unexpected absence stung, waking in her a feminine unease. Was he avoiding her? She couldn't help but wonder.

She fended off this new breed of vulnerability. Considering the increasingly complex feelings he sparked within her, Laura willfully suppressed this newly added layer. Every so often, she caught her thoughts treading the forbidden path, a path he had led her into and now left her alone in.

DAY-10

LAURA WOKE UP PANTING for the second night in a row, her panties betraying the nature of her dreams. She got off to an early start that morning, her racing thoughts forcing her out of bed. Would Kayne meet her for dinner tonight? She watched the sunrise with this one question on her mind. Hoping to retrieve the answer from the unsuspecting housekeeper, she impatiently awaited her arrival.

When Olga came in at nine to bring her breakfast, Laura forced herself to get through at least half her plate.

"Thank you, Olga. It was delicious."

"It's my pleasure, Miss Spencer."

"Olga… Can you just call me Laura, if that's okay?" She smiled sincerely at her.

"Of course, Miss Laura, if you prefer."

"You can just call me Laura…"

"No, no, Miss Laura. That wouldn't be proper." Olga adamantly refused, waving both her hands in front of her. The older housemaid was excessively traditional and perceived good manners as far more than good etiquette: they were lifelines. She had suffered too much at the hands of predatory men before being taken into the household. Once upon a time, she had been young and thought herself invincible. She had learned the hard way that she wasn't. Life wasn't a big adventure. It was a realm ruled by a mad king. His arbitrary judgments were handed down with no rhyme or reason, and it was best to stay humble and out of his line of sight.

"Oh… Okay." Though taken aback, Laura didn't insist.

"Well, will you be needing anything else?" Olga asked, serene again.

"Hmm… Actually, I was just wondering… Can I have supper in my reading room tonight?" Laura subtly inquired about *Master Kayne*'s whereabouts.

"Yes, of course. Wherever you like, Miss Laura. Any special requests?"

Her face dropped. *He was avoiding her*. An old thorn dug anew at her side. Was she being abandoned again? What did she do wrong this time?

"Hmm… Nope, carte blanche." Laura aimed for a warm smile.

"Very well then." Olga nodded, pleased with the vote of confidence.

Laura was grateful for her companion. Olga's reassuring warmth was a welcome and soothing respite, providing Laura temporary shelter as she navigated her way through the Monster's lair.

She thought back to her old day-to-day routine, blurry flashes appearing before her eyes as if echoed from another lifetime. Would anyone be looking for her? Was there anyone left that cared enough to dig deeper? Her throat choked with emotion, confirming the hollow answer she feared.

★ ★ ★

It was late into the night when Laura awoke and sat up on the red sofa. Rubbing puffy eyes, she read the time off the TV clock; it was past one in the morning. Still half asleep, she dragged herself out of the room, her sore neck yearning for the comfort of her bed.

Once engaged in the hallway, she heard the TV and noticed the shadows it cast on the opposite wall. He was there. An adrenaline rush coursed through her, and feeling hesitant, she remained in place. To her right awaited the safety of her bedroom. To the left, him, and all the implications that only word contained. With her heartbeat quickening, her gaze turned to the dancing images on the wall. She wanted to see him, to know how he would react to her. What would ensue following their last encounter?

Laura had always had a morbid curiosity that pushed her forward to meet the storm head-on and open Pandora's box, come what may. Taking a few steps, she stopped short of rounding the corner and lingered at the edge of the wall, her impulses finally confronted with reason. Shouldn't she just wait? He couldn't possibly avoid her within his own house forever. It was madness to seek his company alone and in the middle of the night.

"Laura." His voice resounded crisp through the distance.

Her heart sank.

"You should really work on your stealth mode if you don't want to be heard," he said playfully into the dark.

She readjusted the dipping V-neck of her fitted white T and subconsciously dusted off her granite-colored leggings. "Hi..." She appeared from behind the wall with childlike embarrassment at being caught.

Kayne was on the couch in his usual spot, in jeans and a white shirt, the top buttons left open. He looked her up and down sensually and reached for the whiskey bottle on the table.

"You're up late," he observed, pouring himself another glass.

"Yeah... well, no. I was passed out in the reading room. I mean, that room with the red couch? I just call it the reading room," she rambled. And catching herself, she took a measured breath and smiled. "I was on my way back to my bedroom," she finished with more self-assurance.

"Wrong way," he pointed out with a smirk.

"Yes... I heard noise," she explained. "Well, I don't want to bother you."

"You're not. Have a seat."

Her heart fluttering, Laura took a few unsure steps and settled on the La-Z-Boy.

"Are you enjoying the book I gave you?"

"Yes, very much."

He smiled. "How far along are you?"

"Oh, not that much."

"How come?" Witnessing the blushing his innocuous question caused her, a knowing grin flashed on his lips.

"Nothing. I guess I've just been a little… distracted."

"I see. With what?"

"Everything…"

He stayed quiet. The silence hanging between them felt heavy and expectant, pressuring her to break it. "I don't know… everything. The party…" She looked away with the admission.

"What about it?" Kayne asked, a dark gleam burning in his eyes.

"May I ask you a question?" she ventured hesitantly, throwing furtive looks his way.

He waited for her to gather the courage to meet his gaze. "Ask."

"The women there. Were they… sex slaves?" she asked uneasily.

He remained silent, examining her with a curious stare. And as if satisfied with the conclusion reached, he gave the faintest smile. He stood up to fetch a glass and, filling it halfway, set it down next to his—not at her end of the table, his eyes silently communicating the directive.

She understood. With cautious moves, she lowered herself on the cushion next to him. She brought her feet up and pushed herself to the furthest side of the couch, wrapping her arms around her legs.

"Some, not all," he finally answered. "Drink."

Laura took a sip and felt the burn numbing her bubbling nerves. "Do you... Do you do that?" she asked. She needed to know to which extent her beguiling captor could cross the lines of right and wrong. How profound was darkness's hold on him? How intricate was the bond they shared? He, who in turn, bound her with similar threads, pulling her irreversibly into his web.

"Do what? Deal in sex trafficking?"

She nodded, apprehension holding her breath.

He leaned forward and, resting his elbows on his knees, turned her way. "Not personally."

She sighed with the slight relief that came with his answer but persisted, needing her suspicions confirmed. "But the people you work with do."

"Yes," he confirmed, his face betraying no emotion.

"You don't... care?"

"No, Laura. I don't."

"But... how can you stand for it?"

"I don't *stand* for it. I don't stand *against* it," he corrected her. "I'm not out to save the world, Laura." He leaned back in his seat, his eyes boring into hers. "Just protect what is mine."

Her stomach churned, and she attempted to sway the conversation back to the other women. "Don't you worry about catching anything?"

"The girls are closely supervised and regularly tested. They're clean."

"And... the others... were there by choice?" she asked, still doubtful.

"The others were there because their Masters wanted them there. And they want to please their Masters," he explained, his voice gruff.

It sent shivers down her spine. She recalled the haunting stories of star-crossed lovers she had read in adolescence. Dark tales of forbidden romances with anti-heroes cursed to destroy whomever they coveted. The tragic plight of their willing prey had rung an uncanny bell buried deep within her subconscious.

Kayne had claimed he'd never been in a relationship, and she wondered about the women in his life. What were they to him? Who was he to them? Who were they? A colorful and highly abrasive image materialized in response. The *Redhead*.

"What about that woman… *Tanya*, I think?" Laura tried to conceal her antagonism, turning her eyes away.

"What about her?" Kayne asked, the corner of his mouth quirking up.

"She wasn't like the others. She doesn't have a… *Master*?" she uttered, repulsed by the word.

"She belongs to Dimitri."

"Oh… I just thought… I thought you were together," she admitted, her eyes rising from the floor to meet his.

"She was mine. A long time ago."

"Oh."

Kayne indulged her curiosity with amusement. He'd never let other women interrogate him like that. But her candid questions alone were more revealing to him than any answer she sought. So he let her ask away, divulging her fascination with the sinister world he had just introduced her to, even betraying a pang of jealousy she could barely disguise.

A silence followed, which she tried to fill by taking small consecutive sips, with the one question she'd been holding back burning at the tip of her tongue. Then tipping her glass back, she took a big gulp. Liquid courage, they called it. It did the trick.

"Are you a sadist?" she blurted, surprised at her boldness.

He lifted a brow, seemingly taken aback as well, and offered his most devilish smile. "What's your question, Laura? You want to know what I'm like in bed?"

Blood rushed to her cheeks. She realized too late she had crossed the line. It wasn't about sex slaves, abuse, and female solidarity anymore. It was about *him*, and he very well knew it.

"No." She shook her head. "No. I just… I don't understand. How could any woman want this… consent to it. That woman on stage, it was horrible. And you said… you did things like that to her too…" her voice trailed off.

"Hmm…" Kayne leaned on his elbow, and with his other arm, he languorously reached for her foot.

With her nerves on high alert, Laura instinctively tried to pull away.

A mischievous smile crossed his lips, and he swiftly grasped her ankle. He felt her entire body stiffen, and with patient eyes, he silently guided her through her panicked breathing. Only once he could feel her loosen in his grip did he release his hold.

He brushed the tips of his fingers against her bare skin, drawing little shapes on the arch of her foot. "Sometimes, what you think you want, and what your body wants, are very different." His gaze followed the little patterns he traced. Lifting his eyes to meet hers, he added with a smoldering stare, "I think you can understand that."

Bewildered, she shook her head in denial.

"No?" he taunted her, "Then tell me, Laura. Why did you get so wet when I made you strip for me?"

She opened her mouth and closed it right back in the face of the seductive smirk daring her to deny it.

With his hand still on her foot, Kayne softly chuckled at her unvoiced indignation. In a flash, he grabbed both ankles and pulled her to him, and towering over her, he pinned her wrists over her head. He smiled wickedly at the subdued body at his disposal. "So many things I can do to you right now…"

Laura's frantic breaths further awoke the insatiable beast within him. He lowered his face, his mouth hovering over hers, and licked his lips. With a smirk, he confirmed she expected their feel, seeing her features relax as she closed her eyes. He didn't kiss her.

Instead, Laura felt his lips trace the lines of her jawbone, and panted with the sensations assailing her body.

"Would you stop me, Laura? Would you *consent*?" he huskily whispered in her ear, his breathing growing louder with arousal.

With her hands still pinned down, she felt her stomach knot, her body's reaction so familiar now. Lust mixed with fear, the two primal drives bleeding into one another. "Please… Please, Sir… I just want to go back to my room."

Kayne pulled back and slowly shook his head.

"Liar," he accused in a hungry whisper.

He locked both her wrists in one hand and brought the other to her face, feeling himself harden with the mayhem forming in her eyes. His fingers grazed her cheek in an indiscernible caress and softly roamed down her neck. He glided them over her collarbone, all the way down the middle and over her chest, his eyes following the intimate path. He lingered around her belly button and crooked his finger over her waistband. With a devilish grin, he softly stroked her skin with the back of his finger, and applying the slightest pressure, he teasingly pulled the material downward.

Raging emotions clashed within Laura, the soreness between her legs intensifying at his every touch.

Abandoning the waistband, his index joined his middle finger, and they traveled further down her body, hovering over her pants at a maddeningly slow pace. When he finally reached her core, he didn't touch her there, on the sensitive spot that both dreaded and arched toward his touch. His fingers circled around it a few times. He then delicately rested them in the middle. And he stopped moving.

Laura unconsciously whimpered at the contact, desperate for him to press harder and for his fingers to offer her the release she wouldn't allow herself. She blushed with shame at her animalistic thoughts, deeply disconcerted at her responses to his sordid ministrations. With incoherent thoughts rushing in her head, she pleaded again, "Please..."

His fingers gave the faintest twitch. At an unnervingly slow pace, he started applying the softest pressure and moving in a circular motion. He would increase the speed and then unexpectedly hold back, giving just enough pleasure to push her toward the edge without allowing for her capitulation.

"Please what, Laura? Please... stop? Please... continue? Please... *make me come*?"

Without will or awareness, Laura's muscles contracted and quivered against his fingers, the building storm within her finding release with a soft and surprised "Oh" escaping her lips.

Kayne wore a triumphant smile as her horrified eyes turned hazy with pleasure, and her body slackened underneath his. Then freeing her wrists, he felt an even bigger high at her mortified expression, her abandoned senses repossessing her in the wake of her dissipating bliss.

"You may be excused," leaning in, he teasingly whispered.

Laura carefully avoided meeting his gaze, and he watched with open amusement as she staggered to her feet, flushed and flustered. He caught her by the waist when, her eyes roaming in every direction, she took a false step and lost her balance.

She blushed and muttered, "Thank you," then rushed out of the room without turning back.

"You're welcome," he called out after her, his troublesome snicker underlining what he was referring to.

★ ★ ★

Kayne poured himself another drink staring blankly at the TV. He could still feel the physical effects she had on him and even considered making a call to appease his frustrated desires. He decided against it, feeling lazy and pensive. The girl surprised him. She was gutsier than he had given her credit for. He still couldn't believe she had come to meet him on her own. *Crazy girl*, he shook his head with an amused smile.

Though terrified, she had still spoken her mind and ventured down paths he had expected her to shy away from. Had she revealed a jealous streak? He smirked. It seemed the young Miss Spencer was not too keen on sharing either.

I thought you were together... He recalled Laura's comment and laughed inwardly. That's one way to put it.

His mind revisited his time with Tanya, back when he still held the key to her body. He could still see her defiant eyes as she unblinkingly obeyed his most degrading demands, crawling on all fours with her head held high. She was something else, bringing out his most sadistic side. He felt himself stiffen. How he had loved to hurt and humiliate her, constantly pushing her further. What he had wanted from her, above all else, was to make her bow her head, to feel her break in his hands and crumble at his feet.

He remembered when it had finally happened. It was neither whips nor canes that had ended the long duel. It was cruel words softly whispered in her ears that had sealed her fate. As shameless and thick-skinned as she was, her guarded heart had ultimately spelled her demise. He remembered how she had crawled to him and latched on to his foot, kissing it again and again. "Please, Master… I love you…" she had finally confessed in a whimper. He had stood over her and looked down with disdain at the dewy-eyed creature he could barely recognize. He knew it was over right then and there.

"How incredibly disappointing of you," he had callously answered before shaking his foot free from her clutching hands. Then he'd walked away, leaving her sobbing on the floor. Before exiting the room, he had turned his head back. "You're free. Find another Master."

He had received the courtesy call from Dimitri barely two weeks later. That was three years ago. She had come a long way since, even becoming one of Dimitri's favorites, her status further cemented upon being granted permanent quarters in his second mansion. It was where he hosted all his parties, where Kayne had brought Laura barely two nights ago.

Then his mind went back to his young captive. She would have let him inside of her earlier, he had no doubt. But he wanted more, so much more. He wanted to turn her against herself, at the mercy of the sinful and dark pleasures he'd introduced her to. Kayne felt that same unwholesome urge to dominate, conquer, and destroy. And yet the girl stirred something else in him.

Unlike Tanya, she easily cowered and bent to his will. Unlike all the others, she managed to hold on to herself, guarding an uncorrupted version safely tucked away deep within her soul. It was specifically that pure light within her that the Monster yearned to devour. He wanted to get inside her head and invade her every-waking thought, leaving no space unconquered: within her body, mind, and soul.

★ ★ ★

Reliving the play-by-play of their evening, Laura curled in a little ball under the sheets, feeling shame mixing with anguish. How could this monstrous man elicit such dubious responses from her? The man holding her captive and hunting her brother down. A man who killed and tortured in cold blood and idly stood by as women were being sold and abused. This was the man she knew would eventually have her. Had he tried tonight, could she have cried rape?

She mourned the life he took from her and the dream of ever improving her lot. She thought of Peter. No longer able to retrieve his postcards, she wondered if one awaited her in the mailbox. Wouldn't they have sent someone to go through her stuff by now? If they had found a postcard, wouldn't she have been interrogated?

Was Peter still in Boston? Was he still alive, riding a convertible into the sunset? Or was he huddled by a gutter, looking for his next fix? Would they get to him first, or would life simply catch up with him? How long did addicts really live?

Questions flooded her thoughts, her heart breaking when confronted with the reality of what he had become. She mourned the Peter she loved. The one that had already died long, long ago.

DAY-11

LAURA TOSSED AND TURNED all night, disparate scenes and images superposing one another in a never-ending nightmarish streak. In a dark forest, a crone digs into her black cloak and presents her with an orb of light. Twisting, intertwining stairs dangle in midair, with no beginning or end in sight. A decadent feast with Kayne at the head of the table. Lifting beastly golden eyes, he shows her a jewel-incrusted dagger and, with it, stabs a single red apple on his plate. Purple butterflies flutter, trapped within satin crème sheets, their muffled wing flaps increasingly deafening.

Though the sun was shining bright outside and the weather was fit for a beach day, when Olga came in with breakfast, she found Laura in a warm grey sweater, dark circles framing her vacant look.

Concerned, Olga badgered her with well-meaning questions while checking the thermostat, rushing to the bathroom and back with a thermometer.

With a kind smile, Laura gently pushed away the device Olga had stuck in her face. She confirmed, absentmindedly reassuring her, that she would attend supper at seven.

Laura spent the day in her room just looking out the window, trapped in her mind.

★ ★ ★

Kayne was already seated when Laura arrived for dinner. He had been looking forward to her choice of attire. What message would her clothes convey this time?

Would she, feeling embarrassed, hide her femininity in her trusted hoodie? Or, in abject denial, feign innocence in a demure outfit? Or perhaps, her inner Lolita would come out to play, showing just a little more skin than usual.

His mischievous smile immediately dropped upon seeing her dejected expression. "What's wrong?"

Laura moved slowly, taking the seat facing him. "I would rather not talk about it, if it's okay."

His jaw tensed. "What's wrong."

"Have you found Peter?" she asked in a strained voice.

Kayne bobbed his head a few times with understanding. "No, Laura. We haven't."

She breathed with relief. "Will you ever let me go?" she inquired, her directness not emanating from courage but with the carelessness of those with nothing left to lose.

This was not the evening he had in mind. Kayne had anticipated the various reactions Laura could have in the aftermath of their encounter. A shy and sweet Laura would have earned a more playful supper. A defiant one would have granted him one. He hoped to meet the version from last night, daring yet still pure. He would have gladly welcomed any response from the woman in her. He did not expect the sister to emerge, her face haggard, looking through and past him to her one true desire. There was an acute sting to the feeling beyond the blow to the ego.

"I don't know," he finally answered, his voice cold.

Laura bowed her head. "What about my stuff? My apartment, my job…"

"It's been taken care of."

She nodded, her eyes fixed on the untouched meal before her.

"Eat," he commanded.

Playing with her food with no appetite, she tentatively brought a spoon to her mouth. "Will you let me go outside?"

Her soft voice reached into his turbulent thoughts. "What?"

"Just out in the backyard. I just thought I could read there…"

"No."

"May I ask why?" she asked, her voice cracking with emotion.

"So I won't have to hurt you when you try something stupid."

"I won't. I swear… I mean, how could I even? There are guards everywhere."

"You think you won't, now. But you will. Believe me, Laura, you will."

"No… I swear. I just wanted to read. You can't lock me in here forever…" her voice quivered, her anger imploding as a knot in her throat.

"Try me."

An oppressing silence marked the rest of supper. Laura waited until Kayne finished his plate and asked to be excused.

He nodded, his expression inscrutable.

"Leave it," he barked as she picked up her plate.

She jerked at the command and, under his unnerving gaze, quietly exited the room.

★ ★ ★

Mentally drained, Laura collapsed on her bed. But even in her sleep, her tormented conscience stalked and tortured her.

The setting sun colored the sky over a fully packed Roman arena. She sat beside a faceless king with a heavy crown on her head and an uneasy feeling in her gut. She wore a long-sleeved, white lace dress, its skirt dragging on the floor and the high turtleneck suffocating her.

The crowd cheered and roared dementedly as a scraggly gladiator faced a lion, shakily holding his blade up. The pitiful man kept turning around on himself, trying desperately to keep in view the beast circling in on him.

The king raised his arm in front of him and, pointing straight forward, mumbled a phrase Laura didn't understand. She turned to him, still unable to register his facial features.

"Father!" he then yelled, still staring ahead.

A cardinal in a red robe leaned into her ear and, in a solemn tone, whispered to her, "The lion begets the wolf."

Disquieted, she looked down and was surprised to notice red slippers peeking from under the dress. She could hear her name being shouted over and over again, but transfixed, she could not stop staring at the shoes.

"Laura! Why won't you help me?"

She finally lifted her head and recognized Peter. Having thrown his blade down, he had run to her in a last-ditch effort. The lion had quickly followed suit and, breaking into a run, leaped out at him.

She yelled her brother's name.

She woke up still screaming, her face wet with sweat and tears. Someone was shaking her awake.

"Laura… Laura. Wake up." Kayne was sitting on the bed by her side, the darkness in his eyes contrasting the softness in his voice.

She blinked a few times, slowly coming out of her dream-induced haze.

"You had a nightmare. You were shouting in your sleep."

She brought herself up to a seated position, her eyes looking deep into his. "But it wasn't just a nightmare... Peter..." her voice cracked.

Though he remained quiet, he held her gaze.

"Peter..." she repeated, tears streaming down her face.

Kayne pulled her to him carefully, as if afraid he might break her. Burying her head in the nook of his neck, he ran his fingers through her hair and made shushing sounds.

Laura collapsed against his strong chest, allowing herself to be caressed and comforted. "I don't want him to die," she whimpered in his arms.

"I know," he responded in a hushed tone, a hint of affection softening its inflection.

She leaned back. "Help me..." she implored, the last shred of hope threatening to abandon her big grey eyes never to return.

They remained in this loose embrace for what seemed like an eternity, locked in the darkness that swirled within and all around them. They had both been so intimately acquainted with the Dark Mistress since childhood. It now surrounded her pupils, both inhabiting and uniting them.

His eyes boring into hers, Kayne slowly nodded his head. Without another word, he got up and walked away.

DAY-12

KAYNE WOKE UP EARLY and came home late that night, heading straight to the office across from his bedroom on the second floor. He reached for the drawer and pulled out the postcard, turning it over pensively. *He was already helping her.*

The ghost with the deadened eyes that had greeted him for supper the previous night reappeared at the front of his mind. Laura's aloofness had felt like a slap in the face, goading the beast within him. Licking the wounds her snub had inflicted, he had growled at her in response.

He'd risked a lot for her, too much, to justify it as a capricious fancy. It was a price too high to pay for flesh. He acknowledged that his investment in the girl was more than skin-deep. Laura Spencer had somehow ventured behind enemy lines and slipped right under his shield. He began to understand that she would remain there. Regardless of the outcome of his seduction schemes, he would keep her safe.

His talk with Dimitri had been tense but successful. Dimitri had immediately detected that the girl knew more than she let on. He had questioned him about it, displeased. The old man felt the need to remind him what they stood for; it was far more than getting the information back. If Peter wanted to use it, he would have. It was about righting the wrong. Betrayal cannot go unpunished, he'd reiterated. He'd reminded him of his father's teachings. Kayne did not take kindly to being lectured but forced his lips shut. Dimitri wanted to take the girl back and have her interrogated right there and then. He had assured him she would be returned to him still attractive, *still useful*.

Kayne had stood his ground then. It was about much more than the girl; it would undermine his position. If they took her from him, Dimitri would openly disgrace him, deeming him incompetent in the eyes of all. He would not tolerate such an insult. The mood got tense.

Kayne made his arguments, carefully choosing his words. Peter had been on the run for over eight months now. He would be found, and his head, along with the information, would be brought to him, he had assured Dimitri. He had never failed him before. Was Dimitri ready to jeopardize a lifelong relationship to gain a few days? If betrayal could not be forgiven, disrespect would not be tolerated, Kayne had asserted. He drew the line in the sand and hoped for the best. Dimitri had finally broken the strenuous silence that followed and, chuckling, waved him into an embrace, "*So proud, just like your father, you are.*" He'd given him one more week. That was four days ago.

Kayne thought back to their kiss, the night he opened the door separating their worlds. He knew she would come to him, that her body would answer his call. He remembered her meeting him in the living room at night with cautious but expectant steps. Lying on her back, she had quivered at his slightest touch, with terror, pleasure, and shame in her eyes mixing into an unholy trinity. Then a new Laura revealed herself to him, trusting and open. She had shattered in his arms, looking up at him as a savior. *Help me.*

How desperate she must be, he considered, to place her hopes in a monster. Hunt, track, destroy. Those were his talents, his very identity. He'd never been the person you turned to for help. Something in her had resonated in him, something he had never encountered in eyes that returned his gaze: faith. It had triggered something in him, and he had acquiesced.

And yet, he still needed to find Peter. Within the next three days, he would need to find a way inside her mind and convince her to cooperate.

Her attitude tonight was not promising. He shook his head, tired and irritated. He put the postcard back on the desk and, leaning back in his chair, reached for the phone.

A female voice answered, "Master…"

"Hello, Pet." A sadistic smile covered his restlessness, the worst in him coming out in a silky and tempting voice. "You have twenty minutes."

"Yes, Master."

★ ★ ★

Laura was informed early on in the afternoon that Kayne would not make it home for supper. She had paced all day, unable to set her mind to anything but awaiting his return. Had she dreamt it all? Had he really walked into her room last night and consented to help her? Had she imagined all of this?

She spent the evening in the living room, wanting to ensure she wouldn't miss him walking in. She'd finally retreated to her bedroom around midnight and woke up sometime later to clicking sounds coming from down the hall. Intrigued, she picked up a pair of jeans she found by her chair, threw a T-shirt over them, and tiptoed out of her room. But the sound was gone by the time she made it into the main parlor. She wondered what it could have been. It made her think of the clacking of high heels. Could there be another woman in the house? *With Kayne?*

An alarm went off in her gut, striking a deeply anchored and primitive emotion. Rattled, she sought out this intruder, going in and out of every room. The mysterious visitor seemed to have vanished into thin air. Furrowing her brows, she plopped on the sofa in the living room, *their* living room. On the very cushion he had laid her barely forty-eight hours ago. *How could he bring another woman here?*

The very idea of the house welcoming this other guest set her ablaze. She acknowledged that the appropriate reaction would be to feel relief, perhaps even worry for her kin—not the betrayal she felt. He had agreed to help her and didn't ask for anything in return, sparing her his sordid sexual penchants. Wasn't that the best-case scenario she could have hoped for? And yet, the unrelenting twist in her gut disproved her efforts at reason. *Kayne was with another woman.*

Metallic doors came to mind as if to pull her back into her perilous quest. In the basement. That's where they were. She had a vision of the intriguing visitor: slim-toned legs in nude stockings, her delicate feet in sexy black stilettos rounding the corner before disappearing behind the wall.

Laura stood up with determination and retraced the steps that had taken her down to the enclosed nightmare. The back door easily gave way, creaking as the spiraling staircase came into view. She unconsciously rubbed her fists, her skin remembering her first time in the basement, the night spent in hell, hammering at its locked gates.

As if in a trance, her feet took her down the steps, her hands gripping the cold rails. Walt Disney's *Sleeping Beauty* came to her mind, a scene that had marked her younger self: Aurora, under the spell of the wicked witch, climbing the winding stairs alone in the dark tower. To the hypnotizing music of Tchaikovsky, she follows the green light, which turns into the very spinning wheel meant to destroy her. The powerful enchantment turning her against herself, she pricks her own finger on the spindle, bringing the dark prophecy to fruition. What had struck Laura, she later understood, was how inevitable the scene had framed Aurora's demise to be. Was the evil green light just a cover for the destructive impulse the lost princess couldn't control either?

Reaching the lower ground, she shuddered as the holding cell emerged to her left. She quickly looked away, turning to the corridor concealing the intruder. She wasn't sure what she hoped to achieve beyond putting a face to the feeling.

The long narrow hall was filled with similar-looking locked doors. A female moan escaped one of them, rushing to Laura's ears and trickling down her spine, and she set forward to reach its source. A loud cracking sound followed, then a whimper, a whisper, and finally, a low and manly grunt.

A metallic door had been left ajar at the very end of the corridor. Through it, she saw a half-naked woman hog-tied on a metal table facing away from her. Her long black hair cascading down, she writhed as harsh whips fell unto her back, behind, and thighs.

Laura's blood curdled, and yet she couldn't look away. *Yes, Master… Thank you, Master… Please… More…* The words uttered in a throaty voice warmed the air, setting Laura's cheeks on fire. Though he was hidden from view and his words veiled by a low and gruff tone, she knew it was Kayne. She could recognize his voice anywhere, his own brand of brutish force and sensual persuasion. He stepped toward the woman, and she could finally see him.

He was topless, with his hair tied back, wearing crisp black dress pants and spotless shoes. His raw strength on display contrasted with the polished finish, enhancing the air of power and danger about him. He leaned over the powerless body, reminding Laura of a beast readying for the kill, and she unconsciously gulped.

The faint sound was enough to get his attention, and while still bent down, Kayne lifted his head in Laura's direction. His eyes rounded with surprise upon finding her, then narrowed with fury at the realization, and he slowly brought himself up to his full height.

Horrified, Laura took a few steps back, mouthing *No* as she shook her head. She ran up the stairs and all the way to the front doors. With growing panic, she turned and shook the electronically locked handle, banging on the door with frustrated despair. Her only reward was attracting the attention of the closest security guard, who turned around with both hands on his weapon at the ruckus. She fell to her knees, resigned. There was no way out. Any moment now, Kayne would come. God only knew what he had in store for her. There was nothing else for her to do but to get back to her room and powerlessly await the ramifications of her impulsive actions.

★ ★ ★

Kayne was livid. He almost chased her up the stairs but talked himself out of it. He would have to reign in the beast before finding her, or else he didn't know what he could do. He unceremoniously dismissed his guest and returned to his room for a shower to help collect himself. For all the anger that surged through his body, he recognized the intoxicating thrill tingling his senses, the smell of fresh blood calling out to him. He threw on a pair of blue jeans and a white shirt, went to his office, and picked up the postcard. Carefully folding it, he put it in his back pocket, took a deep breath, and headed to Laura's room.

He turned the knob without knocking, slowly pushing the door open, and found her crouching on the bed. Her back against the headboard, she hugged her knees, nervously biting her cuticles. Kayne didn't walk straight toward her. He looked around, familiarizing himself with her environment. He had always avoided this room—his mother's room. Too many emotions attached to too few memories.

He lingered by the vanity, picking up and inspecting some items with curious casualness. He then turned to Laura, his expression contained, almost threatening in its quietness. Grabbing the chair facing the mirror, he moved it close to the bed before taking a seat. With his legs spread, he leaned back with acerbic eyes. "Speak."

She began rocking back and forth, further cocooning within herself.

Kayne leaned forward and rested his elbows on his knees, his soft voice dripping with threat. "You have disrespected and disobeyed me.

In my own house. I am being kind enough to give you a chance to explain yourself. You would be wise to use it."

"No... no, no, no..." she repeated, shaking her head. "Please... please. I swear... I didn't mean to... I didn't mean to disrespect or disobey. Please..."

He stood up, impassive. "I will count to five. If you don't start talking by then, I guarantee you will wish you had."

She wanted to speak and explain, but she barely understood her own behavior. She threw herself at his feet. "Please, Sir. Please... Please forgive me. I didn't mean to."

"Get up," Kayne said with irritation.

He remained stoic as she finally climbed to a full standing position, keeping her head bowed.

"Look at me, Laura."

Her chest rose with every breath, her lips parting with each gasp of air. She lifted swollen eyes to his.

He grabbed both her arms and, pushing back her frail body, pinned her against the wall. "Why did you go downstairs?"

"I don't know... please. I'm sorry..."

He kept one hand firmly grabbing her arm, and the other, he slowly brought up and closed around her neck. She gasped, but he didn't apply pressure. He just left it there, the threat hanging, and leaned in. "You don't know?" Cold rage filled his voice, and his hand tightened just a little on her throat.

"I don't know... I heard her come in... I don't know why I went... I'm sorry! Oh god, I'm so sorry..." she sobbed against his cheek.

"Yes. You will be sorry," he whispered menacingly, then let go, turning away from her.

She grabbed his arm with both of hers, clenching with desperate urgency. "I was jealous!" she almost screamed in agony, aware his window of mercy would seal shut within his first step away from her. "I was jealous," she softly repeated, the realization dawning on her.

Kayne lowered a stern gaze to her grip, and Laura immediately let go of his arm. "Why were you jealous?"

She looked down, remaining quiet.

He let out an exasperated sigh, his frustration quickly mounting.

"You know why." Bitterness bled through her hushed tone.

His lips quirked up, playful wickedness shifting his mood. "Tell me."

"Please don't." She gazed up. "Don't make me say it."

He sneered and stepped forward, towering over her as their bodies stood at an unsettling closeness. "Tell me," he commanded in a gruff voice, his face so close she could feel his breath on her skin.

"I want you." She sheepishly looked up at him.

He exhaled, his expression as veiled as ever. Wrapping his arm around her back, his fingers gently worked their way up, through her nape, and into her hair. Laura sighed in relief, and closing her eyes, she leaned into his caresses. But Kayne suddenly fisted her hair with his palm at her nape, and he slowly tugged, forcing her head backward and up toward his. She whimpered, opening her eyes with surprise.

"Do you want me to fuck you, Laura?" he huskily whispered, leaning close.

An incoherent sound, between a moan and a cry, escaped her lips.

He pulled her head further back, arching her body into his, and admired his view. Using his free hand, he caressed the outer side of her breast and felt her breaths quickening against his chest. "Answer me."

"Yes…" she breathed.

"Yes. What?"

"Yes… I want you… to fuck me," Laura conceded at last, caught in a merciless battle between lust and guilt.

Kayne emitted a low guttural sound, feeling himself harden. Loosening his grip, he cautioned her with a devilish smile, "You must still be punished."

"Sir, please, *no*…"

"Hold your arms up," he ignored her plea.

She obeyed. With gentle fingers, he lifted her T-shirt over her head and threw it to the floor. She watched it fall, her bare breasts exposed, then looked back at him. "Please…"

Kayne unbuttoned her jeans while looking her in the eye, and with a wolfish grin, he pulled down her zipper.

Laura's heart pounded in her chest as she quietly continued her plea.

Unaffected, he bent down to lower her jeans. Then kneeling on the floor, he directed her to raise one leg after the other to remove them.

"Sir?"

Still kneeling on the floor, Kayne looked up at her inquisitively.

"Please… don't hurt me."

He gave a soft chuckle and stood back up.

"Are you going to hurt me?" she softly asked.

An amused smile crossed his lips. He caressed her cheek with the back of his fingers and, dragging them down, wrapped them around her neck. He leaned in and, with hungry eyes, kissed her gently on the lips.

"You will do what I say, as I say it, without question, hesitation, or delay. Is that understood?" he cautioned, leaving his hand on her throat.

"Yes, Sir."

Kayne grabbed her by the waist and pulled her to him. He kissed her again, this time more deeply. And with his lips still pressed against hers, he commanded her to open her mouth. His tongue invaded her, demanding, unavoidable, and lascivious. He brought her arms up and wrapped them around his neck. His hands traced along her spine down to her bottom.

Laura surrendered to him, her body both melting and tensing at his touch, her eyes hazy with desire. He grabbed her behind and, picking her up, wrapped her legs around him. He carried her to the bed without breaking their kiss and, kneeling on the mattress, gently laid her on her back. Her eyes filled with excitement and apprehension, seeking answers and reassurance in his.

His body over hers, Kayne gave her an indulgent smile, directing her to grab the posts on the headboard. "Keep your hands there, no matter what."

"Okay…" she hesitated but quickly caught herself. "Yes, Sir."

He loved how alert she became when on edge, how her heightened senses played so easily into his hands. Still kneeling between her legs, his fingers traveled the length of her body, and lingering on her breasts, they circled her hardened nipples. He lowered her underwear, tracing the outlines of her thighs.

Her panting increased as he gently pulled her panties off, resting the palms of his hands on her knees to wedge them apart. Laura resisted the pressure with quickening breaths.

He smirked. "Open your legs."

She felt a jolt resonating deep in her gut, and she blushed, self-conscious at exposing her moistened private parts.

Kayne remained still, savoring the moment: his willing prey, irrevocably his for the taking. He let his fingers glide across her soft skin, up and down her outer thighs. His shirt came off, joining Laura's on the floor, and he moved over her naked body with feline grace.

His fingers then dipped down her belly and touched her wetness, his middle finger pressing at her entrance. He circled and teased, torturing her with the promised pleasure he wouldn't give. His mouth replicated the ache, brushing her lips without touching them. He kept at it until he could feel her shame evaporating, her parting lips gasp and moan, and her core accommodating his touch. Only then did he kiss her, his tongue hungrily penetrating her mouth as he slowly pushed his finger inside her. With his palm pressed against her, he slightly rubbed, intensifying her building ache.

"I know you want to come," he whispered in her ear. "Don't."

A strangled cry escaped her lips, her eyes shooting open.

"You need my permission for that." He smirked.

Kissing her neck, he moved down her body and took her breast in his mouth. His tongue swirled on her nipple, his thumb reproducing the motion on her sensitive spot while his middle finger exerted his power over her from within.

She moaned louder and louder, her breaths ragged.

Kayne brought his face close to hers. "Do you understand?"

"Yes... yes, Sir."

"Good girl."

His fingers abandoned her, and with a playful smile, he moved back and bent down. He brought his mouth to her, his tongue continuing the sweet torture his fingers had initiated. He could feel her tension building up, her wetness on his lips. Laura squirmed under him, and he steadied her limbs, firmly pinning her hips on the mattress.

"Sir...Sir, please," she cried out.

Kayne didn't respond. He decided that would be punishment enough, making her say the words and confronting her to her baser, darker urges.

"Sir… please… can I… come?" she panted.

"Come." He crooked his middle finger inside of her. Her whole body spasmed then went lax, her muscles clamping down on him as she screamed her release. He licked his lips, hungrily staring at her as he removed his jeans and laid his body over hers.

She could feel his erection and panicked for a second at the thought of him crossing the last frontier. But he didn't enter her immediately. He rubbed himself against her over and over, taking his time, until her ache came back, deeper and harder. Off the first high, her body demanded more. She felt a visceral need to feel him inside and all around her, to drown in him, filled to the brink in his essence.

"Ask me," he commanded, his hips grinding against her.

She blushed, her eyes watering with shame. "Please… fuck me."

He grunted and, bringing his hand to her face, pressed his thumb down her bottom lip. His first thrust was slow, entering her inch by inch, slowly pulling out and reentering her, his rhythm picking up with each stroke.

Laura could feel a second orgasm building up and closed her eyes. She had never shared that experience with anyone, never felt that level of vulnerability before a man.

"Look at me."

Landing on his inviting smile and enveloping gaze, Laura wished she hadn't. It cut right through her. She could barely accept the effect he had on her body. She couldn't tolerate the seeds he had planted in her shattered heart. The rapture found in the transgressions of their merging bodies pushed her ever so closer to the edge, and she panicked at the prospect of disobeying him. "Sir! Sir, please…"

"Again?" he taunted her, his smile devilish.

"Yes...yes..." She conceded, lost in a state where only hedonistic pleasure existed.

"Come for me, Laura."

Her moan was low and long, immediately followed by his growl as he found his release. He collapsed on top of her, both panting against each other. Raising himself on his elbows, he cocked his head to the side and, eying her playfully, kissed her forehead.

Laura was still catching her breath, looking at him through a haze of confusion, when he rolled off her. He turned on his side and brought her to him, spooning her affectionately. With her body sweetly nestled against him, he kissed the back of her head and caressed her arm. "Laura..."

His voice came to her disembodied. She was still lost in the moment, trying to make sense of everything that had just happened. "Hmm?" came her absentminded answer.

"Laura." His tone was stricter, demanding her immediate attention as his caresses ceased.

The slight shift in his mood was enough to snap her back to reality. "Yes, Sir."

"You asked me to help you."

"Yes..." she answered warily. She didn't expect him to bring this up as she lay in his arms, naked and spent.

Kayne moved behind her and placed a very familiar-looking postcard in front of her. Her chest tightening, she jumped out of his embrace and reached for it.

"Where did you get this!" Laura almost screamed, sitting up nervously as she awaited his explanation.

He leaned on his elbow. "Where is he, Laura?" he softly asked, ignoring her question.

Her heart dropped to her stomach. So it was all just another of his twisted games. The seduction, his supposed kindness, the thoughtful gifted book and pleasant movie night, the caresses and comforting embraces; were all meticulously planned to strategically earn her trust and usurp Peter's whereabouts.

"You used me," she said, her face expressing her repulsion toward him. "You really are a monster."

Kayne sprung up, pinning her back to the mattress. "Am I?" he growled. "Who do you think has been protecting you all along? Huh? Who do you think stopped them from interrogating you at the party? Your guardian angels?" His voice was low and jerky. "No, Laura… It's a monster that's been keeping you all safe and warm in your ivory tower," he snarled. "I could've left you. Dimitri wants you. Maxwell wants you. Do you think they would have shown you the patience I have?" He laughed sardonically at his rhetorical question. Then his tone softened, his hold on her wrists following suit. "I am helping you. Can't you see that?"

Silent tears slid down the sides of her face, little drops forming on the pillow. She remained quiet, turning her gaze away from him.

"Look at me, Laura."

She did, her eyes holding a resigned intensity. Kayne rested his forehead against hers, letting out a long sigh before meeting her gaze again.

"They will find him… soon. We tracked him down to Chicago. It won't be long now," he broke the bad news in a gentle voice.

Laura closed her eyes to the flood of tears rushing down her cheeks.

"Trust me. You would rather I find him first. I will go alone."

"To kill him."

"To retrieve the information he stole. I'll make sure he doesn't suffer. Believe me, Laura, it's the best option you have."

"No! No!" she howled. "You can't kill him!"

"I can't let him walk," Kayne admitted, his face grave.

"No…" she repeated in broken sobs.

"It will be quick and painless. I give you my word."

"No! I can't… Please…" she gasped for air.

"Even if I could, Laura, it would just delay the inevitable. When they find him, it won't be quick. They will torture him. He will beg for death. Do you understand what I'm telling you?"

"No… no… But he would still have a chance… They've been hunting him for eight months. He's good. They won't catch him…" she pleaded desperately. "Please… Kayne… Please…"

He considered her for a moment. "Okay."

"Okay?" she asked, disbelieving, waiting for the confirmation that she had finally lost touch with reality.

"Tell me where he is. I won't kill him," he asserted, his eyes locked on hers.

He reached for the postcard and handed it back to her. Laura pushed herself up, leaning her back against the headboard. Her fingers lovingly traced the little scribbles. "Promise me." She finally looked up at him.

"I promise." He nodded, his eyes solemn.

She gazed at the card, the fatality of it dawning on her. She was numb and, feeling herself going out of her body, witnessed a stranger dictate the address down to the street and apartment number.

"How do you know?"

Laura explained the juvenile yet complex coding system her brother had invented, interchanging letters and numbers following math equations to determine the city and state, their arrangement dictating which characters stood for which. A square meant a residential building, a rectangle, a motel, symbols within a circle determined a room or apartment number, and so forth…

Kayne breathed out slowly, mentally readying himself for the steps to come. With unhurried moves, he got off the bed and reached for his shirt.

"Are you leaving? Now?" she asked, her voice growing shrill with panic.

He bent down and, with inscrutable eyes, kissed her forehead in response.

"Wait… wait!"

"Try to get some rest. I'll be back as soon as I can." He offered her a weary smile, and just like that, he was gone.

★ ★ ★

Laura watched Kayne leave in disbelief. Had she just delivered her brother's location? Had she just turned Peter's unconditional love for her against him? *You will always be able to reach me, I promise.* He had created the diligent system solely to reassure his hysterical sister; was she its only flaw, Peter's one fatal miscalculation?

Had she just succumbed to her brother's hunter? She remained still, poisonous thoughts spreading like cancerous lesions in her mind. So much, too much, had happened in one short night. She looked back at the card and kissed it over and over again. The tears landing on the thick paper diluted the blue ink, concealing its secrets far too late.

But Kayne promised, he promised, he wouldn't kill him. She clung to this one hope founded on a monster's code of ethics. She slid under the covers and, bringing them over her head, stared into nothingness, disconnecting from her splintering mind.

DAY-13

KAYNE HAD DRIVEN ALL day, going on almost forty-eight hours without sleep, his fatigue and hunger yielding only to his willpower. The neighborhoods steadily worsened as he neared his destination; the hard times reflected, giving way to despair. He dove deeper into this display of human misery, entering lands where no children ever played. He finally parked a non-descript vehicle by a decrepit three-story building. Its walls were covered with graffiti and rusty staircases hung by loosening screws, its windows either broken or filled with plywood.

He turned a shaky doorknob with a black leather-gloved hand, finding the door unlocked. Old pizza boxes and milk jugs littered the room. A patchy yellowed carpet was barely visible under stacks of books, newspapers, and all sorts of bric-a-brac, from pens and candles to used lighters and syringes. Kayne took cautious steps, staring back at the printed faces taped to the walls. Stars of a bygone era peered out at him from their black and white headshots, their plastic smiles almost identical. He removed a heap of dirty clothes from a beat-up armchair, dusting off the cushion before taking a seat. With a silencer on his lap, he patiently waited.

A disheveled, scraggly-looking man walked in at last. With nervous tics, he carefully pushed away the junk on the one table to create space for his white plastic grocery bag.

Kayne remained silent, waiting to be noticed. Kayne always waited for the perfect opportunity to strike. Regardless of the target or aim, he knew patience to be a predator's most faithful ally.

The man finally turned around, his look of shock quickly dissipating into resignation. "I should've known it would be you." Peter smiled bitterly.

"It's been a long time," Kayne conceded, feeling somewhat sorry to witness what the man he once called a friend had been reduced to.

"Yeah... How did you find me?"

"Take a seat, Peter." Kayne waved the gun toward the sofa.

Peter's eyes darted back to the door as if making a quick calculation. Still, he only sighed, his shoulders slumping as he obliged.

"Laura," Kayne explained with this one word.

Peter instantly snapped back up, his eyes full of venom. "What have you done to her?"

"Sit down, Peter."

"Answer me, you son of a bitch!"

"She's fine," Kayne raised his voice. "Sit down."

Peter hesitated. Kayne's word was bankable currency. It was a well-known fact throughout the underworld. For the first time in a long time, Peter felt shame. He'd given it up long ago, along with his principles, the lines he was willing to cross moving forward on a one-way track. He had first resorted to store theft and other impersonal so-called victimless crimes. When that alone could no longer sustain his habit, he began breaking and entering, even mugging, rationalizing this new low as his needs being greater. He hadn't even realized it when he'd hit rock bottom. Going through trash and begging on street corners, he'd abdicated his dignity for the next hit. He wasn't even sad to part ways with it; he had had a good morning that day, having gathered enough spare change to meet his usual dealer. But now, hearing his sister's name from the Russian grim reaper's mouth and knowing he was the cause, he realized the scum he was.

"She's fine, Peter. No harm has come to her," Kayne reassured him, his tone softer.

"She gave me up that easy, huh? Good on her." He smiled sadly as he reclaimed his seat.

"No. She hasn't."

"Okay…" Peter added, confused.

"I gave her my word I wouldn't kill you."

"Then why are you here?"

"The case file."

Peter nodded and went rummaging through a heap of broken things and dirty laundry, pulling out a USB key.

"Here, it's all there. I destroyed the folder. I transferred it onto this key." He handed it to Kayne. "Where is she?"

"She's at my house, under my protection."

Peter exhaled the breath he'd been holding, relief washing over his face. "So that's it? You're just going to let me walk?" He laughed, disbelieving.

"You know I can't do that."

"Yeah… Dimitri can sure hold a grudge, can't he?" He chuckled bitterly, his eyes defeated. "I just couldn't, Kayne. I mean, I know I'm no fuckin' Captain America. But the women trafficking… I just couldn't…" He shook his head. "I kept thinking of Laura, you know? What if someone did that to her?"

Kayne gave a slight nod.

"What about Laura? Dimitri will want you to get rid of her… a *liability*," he uttered, disgusted.

"I won't. I'll keep her safe."

Peter considered him a moment. "You… care about her," he voiced his incredible realization, returning his old friend's cool stare with a tender smile. *Did Kayne Malkin even know he had a heart?*

"You promised her you wouldn't kill me?"

Kayne nodded again, this time the move more deliberate.

"But you have to."

Kayne reached inside his pocket and brought out aluminum foil and a syringe. He placed them on the table. "It's good stuff."

Peter laughed, his face surly. "And if I don't… You let me walk?"

"If you don't, Dimitri will have her interrogated. In two days. That's all the time I could get."

Peter's face dropped. He understood; Kayne meant to keep his word. He wouldn't kill him. Peter would have to do it all by himself, or Laura would pay the price. The two men stared at each other in silence. Peter finally nodded, his face somber. His body relaxed, finally accepting his fate, and he reached for the package.

"You know… I was trying to quit. Shit is bad for you," he joked, disheartened. They quietly chuckled together. "What about Dimitri? Doubt he'll be too pleased with an overdose…"

Kayne simply waved the gun in response.

"You thought of everything, huh? Well… can you wait 'til after the high?"

The unusually morbid conversation, undertaken with such calm pleasantries, was telling of its participants—both too familiar with loss and grief, whether on the giving or receiving end.

"I'll wait until it's all over. The gun's just for the pictures. For Dimitri's benefit."

Peter threw his head back, smiling tight-lipped with understanding. "Can I write her?"

Kayne closed his eyes in acknowledgment, and Peter went scavenging for a pen and paper. He began cooking the heroin, scribbling away on the loose leaf before handing it to Kayne and then went back to filling the syringe.

"You will take care of her...?" Peter's last wish landed as a question.

"You have my word," Kayne reassured him and saw his features relax, a glimpse of the old Peter filled with gratitude.

The sweet moment passed. Fate was already knocking at the door. They nodded at each other, their eyes grim.

"Well... Cheers, mate!" Peter raised the syringe.

Kayne smiled back at his old friend one last time.

DAY-16

IN THE TWO DAYS that followed Kayne's departure, Laura tasted every possible emotion, her mind turning into a stage for her sweetest reveries and worst nightmares to unfold. Her feverish heart could visualize their return home, both men walking side-by-side as they made their way back to her. Her fears would then swiftly invade the fantasy with the sounds of bullets popping and blood spattering on walls, pulling her into a bottomless hell. *What was taking Kayne so long?* Caught in the limbo of uncertainty, she badgered Olga ceaselessly for news of the Master's whereabouts.

The concerned housekeeper could offer her no response or respite, being in the dark as well. She fretted over her young charge, pretending to busy herself with other things as she watched over her. It was late in the evening, and Laura sat cross-legged in bed, chewing her cuticles as she blankly stared at the bedroom door. Olga was in a chair by her side, reading a magazine in-between worried glances thrown at her young companion.

The lethargic silence came to an abrupt end. Noise emanating from the entrance made both women jump to their feet.

"Kayne!" Laura exclaimed, rushing to the door. As she reached for the handle, it swayed open. "Kayne…" She smiled at him with fragile hope.

With an inscrutable expression, he turned to Olga. "Could you give us a moment?"

"Of course, Master Kayne. I'll boil some tea." Though happy to see him, Olga tensed at his demeanor. She knew him far too well not to recognize the dark omens his eyes had turned to.

"Kayne?" Laura asked, her voice thinning. "He's okay? He's okay, isn't he?"

She already knew the answer. She had felt it the instant they locked eyes. At her core, she'd known it even before then. Still, her heart had refused to listen to either pragmatism or intuition, blocking off all paths enabling the dreaded outcome.

Kayne shut the door behind him and, leading her gently to the bed, made her sit down. He knelt in front of her and slowly shook his head.

"No. No. You promised. You promised!" she cried out, her tone growing erratic as her mind processed the immeasurable impact of his small movement.

"He overdosed. Intentionally."

"No… I don't believe you. Peter would never. NEVER!"

He closed his eyes, nodding in acknowledgment. Standing up, he handed her a folded note tucked in his front pocket.

"What is this?"

"Read it."

She grabbed the paper from his hand, eyeing it suspiciously. Upon opening it, she immediately recognized the handwriting.

My Sweet Laura,

It's been so long since we last played together. Do you remember all the stories we made up? All the worlds we created? Remember the one with the boat that always flipped over? Or the one about the house with no doors or windows? Did we ever figure out what was inside? I can't remember... Never thought those days would be the happiest of my life. They seem to be all I think about lately.

I had so many plans for us. I'm so sorry, Laura. I was unworthy. Please forgive me.

I must ask you for one last favor. Remember when Hansel used to set Gretel free from the sorcerer's cage? Your turn has come. You must let me go, Laura. You will be safe now. This gives me peace.

Here's looking at you, Kid

"No..." She shook her head. "NO!" she shrieked, falling to the ground and folding over her knees, the prolonged sound almost inhuman.

Though he had remained true to his word, Kayne couldn't silence the inkling of remorse that crept under his skin, leaving an atypical unease in its host. He hovered over her, unsure what to do in the face of all this pain. He bent down, reaching for her shoulder in a comforting gesture.

"Don't you fucking touch me! Do you hear me? Don't you fuckin' dare!" she bellowed hysterically.

Kayne moved back slowly, his surprise barely visible as Laura returned to her grief, wailing her agony on the floor.

"You did it... I know you did. It was *you*," she suddenly accused with eerie softness, her hidden face peeking through her hair. In an instant, she was up on her feet and staring him down with a demented gleam in her eyes. "Tell me. Tell me to my face you didn't kill him."

"I didn't kill him."

She could see pity in his eyes. The very monster who pushed her into the abyss, feeling sorry for her. She snapped. Raising her arm to slap him, she called out, "LIAR!"

Kayne caught her hand midair, holding her wrist so tight he made her wince. "I know you're upset, but I didn't kill him. I have a picture with the needle still in his arm if you would like to see it. Don't you fucking call me a liar," he growled. Then raising his voice, he added, "And don't you *EVER* raise your hand at me."

Peter's blood was on his hands. Nothing he could say would convince her otherwise. This time, she wouldn't fall prey to his manipulative schemes. With utter disgust, Laura spat in his face.

His hand twisted her wrist even harder, his eyes narrowing with silent fury. But she held his gaze defiantly, challenging him with the courage granted to those who've lost reason. Kayne didn't bother wiping his face. He lifted his other hand and, while still holding her wrist, struck her across the face.

Her entire body quivered on impact, collapsing to the ground the instant he let go. Her eyes round with shock, she crawled back and away from him until she hit the wall. With her arms wrapped around her knees, she started rocking herself.

Within seconds, he wanted to go to her, to make it better somehow. Kayne hadn't often felt the impulse to see to another's needs, to have his mood impacted by another's well-being. He snuffed it out, coolly staring her down as he wiped his face.

"When you're ready to talk about it, you can come to me." He then walked out, leaving her behind, shattered on the floor.

DAY-24

EIGHT LONG DAYS HAD elapsed since Kayne's return. Olga still seethed, remembering the bruise he'd left on the girl's face that night. She had chased him down the hall to the bar where he stood, knocking back shots of whiskey. He was in one of those stormy moods, and she could see his father staring out of his eyes. He had snapped at her to leave it alone, but she wouldn't let up.

Ever since that night, Olga had stayed by Laura's side and lovingly tended to her wounds, more deeply concerned about the ones reflected in her eyes. She prepared her favorite meals, but Miss Laura wouldn't eat. She wouldn't get out of bed. She wouldn't even cry. Day and night, she just stared ahead, her blank expression unchanging. Olga bathed and dressed her, brushing her hair as she hummed melancholic tunes. Olga's heart broke for the young girl. She would tell Master Kayne about it at supper. He would listen attentively then shrug it off, as if irritated with his momentary lapse.

Laura had yet to emit a sound, and Olga racked her brain, trying to find a way to snap her out of her catatonic state. Putting her to bed one night, she had a hunch to tell her a story, an old fairy tale from childhood. She dragged a chair by Laura's bed and, blowing over a mug of steaming black tea, repeated what she had seen her mother do countless times.

Laura's eyes barely moved, her irises turning toward the storyteller with piqued interest. Olga rejoiced in the small victory; the anchor had landed. She told her a different story every night. Laura's presence gradually returned to the hollow shell she had left behind. She sometimes closed her eyes as if imagining the tale but remained quiet.

It was on a sweltering evening that broke into a thunderous summer storm when Laura first spoke again. Olga was shutting the windows in the young mistress's bedroom. Looking up at the angry skies and back at the grieving sister, she knew exactly which story to tell her. She retrieved the English translation she used to read to Kayne as a young boy and settled in the chair with renewed optimism.

"I think you will love this one." She smiled and, opening the book, turned to the first page.

THE TALE OF ALEXEI AND ANISKA

Once upon a time, in a land far and away, lived a set of twins, orphaned on their birth day; Alexei, a boy, and Aniska, his sister, had not a thing in the world but their love for one another. Whatever the blessing or cause for despair, what life handed to one was always shared between the pair.

The lone siblings never deplored their plight, and whenever possible always looked for the light. For they knew bitterness was to a heart but a righteous traitor, and that counting misfortunes only ever hurt the counter. They learned how to cook, they learned how to clean, they even tried their hand at tending to a flock of sheep. Every night in the village, they went about the same routine, knocking on every door, offering hard honest work for board and keep.

But these were hard times where nothing ever grew, where the cursed winter had come, leaving everything blue. Farmers and woodsmen alike came home daily empty-handed. And without a second thought shut their doors, leaving the poor twins stranded.

Rumors spread like wildfire among the townspeople. What could have brought upon this unimaginable evil?

"'Tis the work of the Winter Witch!" cried the baker.

"The White Wolf's prints are all over this!" shouted the butcher.

"We have incurred their wrath, our wrongdoings must be paid. So they may forgive the past, a sacrifice must be made," declared at last the shopkeeper.

Terrified families huddled closer, parents and children holding on to one another. All eyes soon turned to the lone siblings. With no one to their defense, they made for easy pickings. They were given a single loaf of bread and one bottle of milk, and through the front gates were pushed out with bony fingers and sticks.

"Go into the woods. Do what must be done," commanded the villagers, "And don't you dare come back, before your work is done. As long as the moon shines blue and snow covers your tracks; know that a fruitless return will be welcomed with an axe."

Alexei and Aniska walked and walked with naught to guide their way, and rationed their lean supplies to one gulp and bite a day. To forget their empty stomachs, they recounted beloved stories, and sang the most cheerful songs to help assuage their worries.

On the very first night, while lying under a full moon, they heard a wolf cry a pained and sorrowful tune. "The White Wolf!" the children exclaimed. They ran back to the village as fast as they could, but were greeted with pitchforks and tossed right back into the woods.

They retraced their steps, cold, hungry, and afraid, and on that second night huddled closer as the wolf's moan replayed. They climbed a tree and slept on the thickest branch they could find. All night long they held hands to drive away the shadows in their minds.

Perched high above in the mountains, an old owl watched the young orphans. In this land of dying hope, he'd been drawn to their resilient spark, and had vowed to safeguard it, sending them light in the dark. The Eye of the Sky, or so they called him, flew down to the dreamers, and in their sleep tried to warn them:

"In the deep, deep, forest that whispers her name,
That knows her every secret and calls out her shame,
The Queen shattered her mirror to forget whom to blame,
And now seeks redemption with the help of a blade.

"Leave tonight, my children, the battle ahead is already lost,
For there is no greater menace than a guilty heart turned to frost.
Deal with the devil, and you'll wager your soul and your head,
And if you let the dead keep you, you may just as well be dead."

Alexei and Aniska did not understand the strange message, and the next morning carried on through the frozen foliage. On the third night, as they neared exhaustion, they met a beautiful woman who appeared as a vision. She had silver-blue hair that fell to her knees, lips the color of sapphire; and wore a pearlescent gown that lit the ground beneath, and was crowned with rings of fire. With a beatific smile, her pale skin translucent in the snow, she embraced the young travelers, promising them a better 'morrow.

She took one of their hands in each of hers, and they no longer felt the cold. She then placed a kiss on their forehead, and their fears could no longer take hold. She blew into their mouth, and they lost the need to feed. And when she covered their skin with ice, they could no longer bleed.

Days turned to months, and months turned to years. The siblings were all but lost, numb under their lustrous veneer. They forgot how to speak, they forgot to think; they forgot how to feel, worst of all, they forgot how to sing. They were never happy, they were never sad—they could not feel a thing, not even when things got really bad.

Night after night, they sleepwalked to the Glass Tower, joined by hundreds of other children under the witch's power. The Winter Witch would greet them with biscuits and hot tea; brewed with her special crystal, for the lost infants she claimed as family.

Tentacles of liquid silver sprouted from the Queen's regal dress, and locking around each child, tethered them to the enchantress. Every night, they set out into the endless darkness, hundreds of floating lights hostage to the Queen's madness. The White Witch would sneak up behind tree after tree, and as if playing hide and seek, would replicate her plea:

"Little Mishka! Little Mishka! Come out, come out and play! Little Mishka, I promise: Mummy's here to stay."

But only the wounded wolf ever responded, its long howl reverberating in the forest. From dusk 'til dawn, the captives followed the sorceress, searching endlessly for the pup in the frozen wilderness. Whatever route they took, whatever echo they followed, always led them back to the same stone altar in a hollow. The pale lady would sigh but turn to the brood smiling, and choose the poor lamb just ripe for the offering. Every night, a storm gathered filled with the sparks of pain. Every night, the lot returned with one less thread on their glowing chain.

On one of the darkest and coldest nights, Alexei's turn came to perish at the site. The Winter Witch made Aniska surround the base with a golden rope, and with a sorry smile explained she was down to her last hope. From her dress, the enchantress pulled a chipped wooden toy: a small white wolf, a remnant of her lost joy. She bent down and, whispering into the brother's ear, showed him the figurine. Alexei nodded and fell into a deep sleep upon hearing the words of the Queen. She brought the toy to her blue lips and laid it gently on the boy's chest. Four white candles appeared at the corners of his deadly nest: One to undo the unforgivable past; One to bring anew the lost, recast; One to deny the debt to be paid; And one to conceal the innocence betrayed.

With one breath, the White Queen lit up their indigo flames. Under her incantations, they grew taller and connected, as she kept repeating the same name. A gust of wind picked up speed, and a storm gathered all around them. Above Alexei's heart, a sword of ice and lightning formed, glowing as a gem.

Acting on pure instinct, from intent formulated so often it became second nature, Aniska threw her body over that of her brother's. The falling blade exploded on impact into meteor showers, shattering the silver bonds holding the children prisoners. The damaged toy had vanished, realized the witch with dread, for a Great White Wolf now appeared in its stead. He bared his long fangs standing over the siblings, and taking a step forward, growled his final warning.

The vanquished Queen clutched at her breast, feeling her thawing heart break in her chest. The spell at last broken, the fatal wounds were revealed, with one so raw and deep, it could never be healed. She looked enviously at the sleeping boy, so peaceful, so calm. How lucky he must be, she thought, to be loved away from harm. She turned to the unconscious girl and her unlikely new guardian, and with wisdom grasped too late, left her with this confession.

"Once upon a time, my heart beat true like yours,
But all hardens and darkens, that which must endure.
Beware, child of light, even ghouls were born with their slate clean,
'Tis but a series of choices that turns the lamb into a fiend.

"Heed the words of the penitent, they are often the wisest,
For no lesson is better learned, than that which hits the hardest.

No sinner is too far gone, who is willing to face his greatest failure,
Meet your demons head-on, lest you become the dreaded monster,
The tyrant that sheds innocent blood
and blinds himself to the horror,
For both heaven and hell may await you, when you look into the mirror."

The fair witch then collapsed on the heavy snow, warm blood pooling around her as she lost her glow. Little by little, the ice began to melt, dashes of color reemerging along the coastal belt. The long-awaited spring eventually returned, bringing back with it the sweet life and its inevitable trivial concerns.

Alexei and Aniska were never heard of or ever seen again. Some believed they followed the defeated witch back to her realm. Others claimed they had been named King and Queen, the first to be deemed worthy of the lands of stolen dreams. There were always those who pointed up above, and said they were turned to stars through the sheer power of their love. But every now and then, rumors of sightings circulated at the village tavern. Though some details changed, the accounts always followed the same pattern; Under a blue moon, the pale silhouettes appeared in the night, Alexei carrying a shield of fire, Aniska with a blade of light. And the Great White Wolf, always at their side.

The End

"I love wolves. I always have." Laura closed her eyes with a faint smile on her face, succumbing at last to drowsiness. She slept through until the following evening, waking to a silver moon accompanied by two particularly bright stars. Could it be a sign from a benevolent higher power that she would be reunited with Peter one day? When Olga walked in with the teapot that evening, she asked her for Alexei and Aniska's story again.

Olga established their new routine. Every morning, she would drag Laura out of bed and bring her to the solarium. Olga had barely mentioned it to her on the house tour, walking past it without stopping. The ill-fated sunroom paled in comparison to what it had been in its glory day. It had been Elena Galiano's domain, falling from grace alongside its mistress. As all other traces of her, it had been forsaken, shut out, and actively forgotten. In so many ways, history seemed to be repeating itself, and Olga frowned at the thought.

The two women would have their breakfast together there. Olga hoped the sunrays, reading nooks, and gorgeous views would help Laura enjoy, despite herself, the good things life still had to offer. Laura would barely nibble on her food, shivering away under the comforters, regardless of the warm weather and layers of clothes. Olga would spend the day doing crochet while telling her quiet companion funny anecdotes she remembered from childhood, back in her homeland. Though Laura offered polite smiles and nods, her gaunt eyes foretold the long battle ahead to recovery.

Sometimes they would just sit together silently, comfortable and comforted by each other. After a few days of one-sided chatter, Laura began throwing tentative sentences here and there. Olga was sharing fond memories involving a mischievous dog the family had when Laura commented, "We had one when I was really young. But my father got rid of him after my mom left. He didn't like dogs."

Laura didn't mention that the dog crate, however, remained. She wondered if Kayne had told Olga about it and gathered from her reaction that he hadn't. He'd remained discreet, once again surprising her with unexpected tact.

She had gone over that night in her head until she couldn't think straight. She wanted to believe him—he had given his word. He had never lied before, not when he easily could have. Kayne had proven over and over again that his word could be trusted, for better or worse. Perhaps, she thought, Peter had noticed the men who'd tracked him down to Chicago. The men she had led to him. Who would truly be the one to blame, then? Or perhaps, he'd simply surrendered to the call of the abyss, going gently into the good night. She unconsciously rubbed a faded scar on her wrist. Maybe it was just the Spencer curse, she thought. The darkness that had always gnawed at her had greedily swallowed him whole. The Spencers, they would be no more. Peter's death ensured it.

She recalled her father's reaction when finding out about her infertility. *Good. Spencers... rotten blood. My father before me and his father before that. What makes you think you would have been any better? We should have aborted you. That would have been the kind thing to do.* She had thought her father cruel at the time, but she forgave him. She always did. She knew of his own difficult childhood, of the abuse he survived, denounced, and so unwittingly reproduced. The Spencers, the cursed. For the first time, she understood her father and felt relief knowing her family line would die out with her.

For her part, Olga obviously treasured her family and, to this day, fought back tears when reminiscing about her time in Russia. For all the heartfelt memories she willingly shared of her childhood, she remained suspiciously evasive about all that followed once she reached Canada as a young teenager.

Though she avoided venturing into any delicate details, she did admit to being with the family long before Kayne's birth. She conceded she was well aware of the family business, confirming Laura's suspicions. But light and darkness existed in all of us, she was quick to add. And to explain her stance, she shared a deeply personal confession with Laura. Though ruthless as they come, the Malkins looked after their own.

Olga had been young and beautiful and, as too often was the case, defenseless in the hands of men who preyed on the innocent. She had been homeless when Lev Malkin found her. He had taken pity on his fellow countrywoman and took her under his wing, offering her shelter and employment. She had initially met his generosity with suspicion, but Master Malkin was of a different kind. Not once had he crossed a boundary, treated her with condescension, or lacked respect. For that alone, he had earned her grateful loyalty.

She had been with the family for nearly two decades, her tumultuous past long behind her, when an unfamiliar guest had come to the house on business one evening. Master Malkin avoided mixing the affairs of the organization with family. But it was an emergency, and this man had been sent instead of the usual pick-up guy. He'd leered at her all night, making vulgar comments out of earshot. Olga had ground her teeth and smiled, sighing with relief when Master Malkin had finally asked her to see the messenger out after business was concluded. But the man had shoved her into a corner the moment they were alone, forcing her mouth shut and her legs open. Master Kayne had witnessed the scene. He was only sixteen then. He came at him like a madman, stopping in no uncertain way the lecherous man.

When Master Malkin was made aware of the situation, he'd given his son a nod of approval. With no other words spoken on the matter, they'd disposed of the body.

DAY-26

KAYNE SAT AT HIS office desk late into the night, a half-empty glass sitting next to a golden ashtray with a lion stamp. Regardless of how he occupied his days, he inevitably caught himself thinking of Laura, the forbidden white bird healing in its cage. How can you possess what you are doomed to crush? Their story had swerved yet again on a darker path still.

Olga met him at the dining table every evening to give him daily updates. He drank her every word, wanting to know the smallest details about his captive: the color of her shirt, how she wore her hair, and what was it that finally made her smile. He was passing by the solarium one day and heard her laughter, that soft, throaty chuckle of hers, almost apologetic for even existing. How he had envied Olga at that moment.

Thankfully others existed, others as twisted as him. An entire world where he was celebrated for the Monster he was. That night he made another call. He whipped and caned mercilessly. Another night, another pet. He made them cry. He made them beg. He made them moan and made them come. He came too but found no release.

DAY-30

LAURA HAD HEARD, NIGHT after night, the clicking of heels. Though she couldn't fathom being intimate with him again, she couldn't bear the thought of Kayne's hunger consumed by another. She had wept bitterly in her pillows, feeling the powerlessness of her circumstances seeping into her heart and soul. By the third night, she had no tears left, blinking cool eyes at the dreaded sound. She had felt the shift in her, however subtle. From the shadows, she never reemerged fully the same. Since she was a little girl, from the cage to Peter's drug abuse, darkness would claim her but never keep her, even when she went willingly. Every time she returned, a little part of her remained trapped beyond the veil.

She wondered how many pieces of broken souls had been lost to the void. She wondered how many belonged to Kayne. A man who hurt women for pleasure and killed and tortured for a living. And yet, a man capable of loyalty and kindness, showing, even at a young age, a protective instinct. He'd stepped in on Laura's behalf as well, keeping her safe by holding her captive. And though fully aware of his reciprocated desire, he'd made no demands from his prisoner in exchange for his favors.

Kayne Malkin. Her captor and tormentor. Her guardian. Her lover. She'd yet to lay eyes on him since the night of his cursed return, when all light faded from the world in a matter of one sorry headshake. From the first time they'd exchanged looks, her life was never the same again. He'd taken her freedom first, then her body, then her brother. Did she even have anything left worth taking, Laura wondered.

The time had come to face him. Laura asked Olga whether Kayne would be home for supper tonight and whether it was okay if she joined him. He would be, and it most certainly was, Olga assured her happily.

* * *

In jeans and a dark olive green top, Laura took a few breaths, purposefully slowing her pace as she walked down the hall to meet him. He was already seated and stared at her, his expression unreadable.

"Hi..." She hesitantly pulled the chair facing him.

Kayne nodded in response, his sealed lips intimating his murky mood as he reached over and served them.

"I believe you," she broke the ice in the softest voice.

He remained silent, scrutinizing her.

"What happened... to his body?" She looked up to meet his gaze.

"The state provided for the funeral."

"Oh... I was just hoping to say goodbye," her voice cracked.

Kayne kept looking at her, his eyes softening though he wouldn't offer any words of comfort.

Her voice went steady then, and she stared far ahead into a nonexistent distance.

"I often thought about it. When I was younger. I even wrote a suicide note once. Peter found it. I had left it out... Guess I wanted someone to find it. I think I was really hoping my dad would. Anyway, he went out to the store, got me all my favorite snacks, and rented *Casablanca*. He said old, black-and-white movies were the best cure on earth. Apparently, our mom was obsessed with old Hollywood and gummy bears. And whenever they had a bad day, they snuggled on the couch with old movies and treats. Whatever the problem was, it always made it better. He tried to take care of me like she would have. He always tried to take care of me. He was all I ever had.

"I did end up trying it once. For real. No notes. No cry for help. I was sixteen. He'd started doing the harsher stuff. Sometimes he'd be gone for days. This one time, he didn't return for two weeks. I was going out of my mind. I wouldn't leave the house. I was so scared I'd miss him when he came back that I stopped going to work. I didn't go to school anymore. I'd literally run to the store when I needed something and run back home. I just couldn't believe he'd abandon me, you know?" She shook her head, melancholy in her eyes.

"He had to come back. At least for my birthday... he'd never missed a birthday, no matter what. I baked a cake and everything," she chuckled bitterly. "I waited until midnight. And when he didn't come home... I slit my wrist. On my sweet sixteen." She finally looked up at him, offering a beaten smile that didn't belong to a twenty-three-year-old. "But he did come back for me. He found me. He saved me... And I didn't. I didn't save him... I didn't... I failed him," she choked, tears running down her cheeks.

Before she knew it, Kayne was by her side, pulling her up into his embrace and holding her close. He didn't do anything else. He just held her tight as she sobbed uncontrollably against his strong, comforting chest. Laura could feel him all around her, an immovable fortress, and she sought refuge in its warmth and safety. The last time they had been this close seemed like a lifetime ago, and her eyes closed, remembering the exhilarating calm she felt in his arms. She wished she could disappear completely into him, merge into one and have him help carry the burden of being Laura Spencer.

Kayne waited for her sobs to fade and her breathing to slow, and then pulled away just a little. He gently lifted her wrist and tilted its palm upward where a little faded scar could still be seen. "You will never try this again."

She returned his gaze, studying his expression. After a moment, she slowly nodded her head.

"Good." A faint smile crossed his face. He leaned in and placed a soft kiss on her scarred wrist.

DAY-31

"**GOOD MORNING, MISS LAURA.** How about breakfast outside today?" Olga entered the room with a picnic basket on her arm, grinning from ear to ear.

"Outside?" Laura asked disbelievingly, still half asleep.

"Yes, out in the yard. It was Master Kayne's idea," the kind housekeeper affirmed with the sparkling eyes of a proud mother.

Laura remained hesitant. She had learned long ago the truth behind the old adage *If it's too good to be true*... Even if *too good* meant taking fifty steps out the front door.

It disheartened Olga to witness Laura's distrust of having such a modest wish granted. Had life taught her to expect so little? Olga shook her head. "Come on, let's get you dressed. It's a beautiful day," she smiled encouragingly.

The guards kept a respectful distance as the two women headed out, fully equipped for a day at the beach. They settled on a spot by an old weeping willow, its majestic branches swooshing with elegance. That willow tree had been among the first Malkin residents, brought in by Lev Malkin for his beloved. It had been a fixture in some of the happiest memories the Malkin house would ever provide. And yet, it had also provided the backdrop to the madness and tragedy that had plagued the family, a witness to intimate wounds no living soul would ever see.

Laura sat down in the grass, leaning back against the large trunk of the tree. There was a distinctive feeling in the air, as if the nature surrounding her whispered soft lullabies. The radiant sun pleasantly toasted her exposed skin, a gentle gust of wind lifting her hair into a playful dance. She took off her shoes and rubbed her bare feet in the soil, and she smiled with innocent glee at the simple pleasure. A feeling of guilt swiftly interjected. What gave her the right to keep grasping at happiness now that Peter had forfeited? A voice, so small she barely even heard it, answered her. Nothing—no right was needed.

Sometimes, particularly in those times, a spec of clarity would come to her. Past the pain, past the despair, she would reach a place where nothing could hurt her anymore. Become so broken she would lose her sense of self, her secret hopes dissolving along her deepest regrets. She would let go of it all, releasing herself from the shackles in her mind. Unencumbered with her heavy baggage, she could connect with the world around her, fully present in the moment. This time, it came in the shape of a green leaf, carried by a warm breeze, falling gracefully to the earth as the sun shone behind it. The same warm breeze that played with her hair, that made her shirt flutter against her skin and the grass wiggle wildly under her feet.

Laura smiled and reached for *The Kite Runner*, intent on finishing it. Olga had her crochet, weaving an impossibly intricate design she'd been working on for as long as Laura could remember. She constantly undid whatever advancement she had just achieved, muttering through gritted teeth in Russian. But she was a stubborn woman, waving Laura off dismissively when she had suggested choosing another pattern.

They stayed the whole day outside, watching the sunset with glasses of red wine under warm blankets. It was well past seven when they headed back inside and crossed paths with Kayne. He was deep in conversation with Lucas on their way up the stairs, hushed murmurs echoing in the great hall. Lucas seemed agitated, waving his hands about with irritation. Atop the stairs, Kayne stopped, turning to Laura without saying a word. She held his stare, a modest smile on her lips as she mouthed *Thank you*. Without openly smiling back, he slowly nodded, the world fading around their locked gaze.

DAY-37

LAURA MADE THE MOST of her new privilege, spending her days outdoors regardless of the weather. The land was much bigger than she had initially thought, extending way beyond the gated backyard. Far ahead of the spacious in-ground pool and manicured lawn lay a path leading through private woods to a charming pond, the whole under surveillance.

On the bad days, when the finality of Peter's absence left her feeling too disconnected from the civilized world around her, she sought refuge in the woods. She would read by the lake, finding comfort and strength in the simple marvels of nature interacting with itself. On better days, she could find that connectedness from under the Weeping Willow, the security men mentally erased from her field of vision. The lost hours in between, when her mind was blank and her senses numb, were spent by the pool. She never went in. She would just lay there, staring up at the skies or contemplating the tiny ripples on the surface of the water.

She would head back in long past sunset, sometimes with dirt all over her, one time dripping from head to toe. She had run out of the house in yellow rain boots and a matching trench coat under pouring rain, splashing away in the puddles, her timid smile breaking free. Olga hadn't complained about the mess. The sparkle in Miss Laura's eyes was well worth the trouble.

A heat wave was sweeping Montreal, and Laura was lying by the pool, pleasantly drowsy under the warm rays, when Olga blocked her sun, apologizing politely. Master Kayne wanted to see her. Laura's heart skipped a beat, and all her senses came alive at the mention of his name. They hadn't spent any time together since their last supper. When she had melted so willingly into his body, feeling his eyes burning into hers and his soft lips against the scar on her wrist. He had then walked away, leaving the room without saying another word while she still processed the promise she had just agreed to.

Since her sixteenth birthday, she had combatted the unending waves of nostalgia just to maintain that status quo, vowing never to put Peter through such heartache again. She no longer owed anyone the will to wake up another day in vain, only to face the same darkness all over again. Was there a sadder liberation than having no one to leave behind? She bowed her head.

And then Kayne made her promise, bonding her to him once more. Why? What more could he want from her when he'd already gotten everything? Regardless of his reasons, she smiled from the comforting warmth she felt in her chest. There was still someone to hold her back from the brink, someone whose pull was greater than the abyss itself. Even if he was a monster.

She followed Olga back into the living room, where Kayne sat on their sofa, looking dashing in a silver suit. Laura pulled at her shorts and purple tank, suddenly self-conscious in her summery attire. Her attention was quickly diverted, however, by a familiar-looking black box with a gold ribbon on the table, and her mouth instantly dried at the memories associated with it. Was that the price to pay for his recent kindness? Her heart raced. Was he taking her back to that unholy place?

"Hey..." Kayne leered at her exposed skin.

"Hi," she nervously replied, her eyes on the gift box.

"How are you?" he asked, an amused grin forming on his face.

"I'm okay... you?"

He smiled in response and motioned for her to sit down, tapping the arm of the La-Z-Boy.

Laura took deliberate slow steps, trying to keep her cool. But her eyes betrayed her internal agitation, reverting too often to the table.

"Laura." Kayne waited for her gaze to settle on him before he went on. "Would you like to accompany me to a wedding?"

She was stunned. "I don't understand. You're not… taking me to a… *party*?"

He shook his head, an indulgent fondness in his eyes softening his smirk.

"So… like, leave the house to go to a wedding with you. And that's it?" she repeated with skepticism.

He nodded.

She clasped her hands, her eyes bright with excitement at the mere thought of leaving the premises. "Yes. Definitely yes," she beamed.

It had been so long since he had seen her look so alive, her lips widening with such ease. Kayne lingered in the moment for a fraction of a second before picking up the package and handing it to her.

Laura slightly blushed, remembering what had ensued the first time. This time was entirely different, she thought, and she felt a rush at the prospect of being his date for what she imagined to be an idyllic wedding. Opening it, she found a strapless ocean-blue chiffon gown with a sweetheart neckline.

"It's beautiful. Thank you." She held it close to her chest.

Kayne watched her silently. Though they shared the same space, she seemed so out of reach. As if a bubble surrounded her, holding her separate from the corrupt world around her.

He had kidnapped and terrorized her, openly savoring every moment. She had seen the Monster in him and had recoiled. Most women who'd met him had blissfully fallen under his sadistic thumb, looking up with blind adulation. Others had walked away without ever looking back, recognizing the Monster for what he truly was.

Never had eyes that understood his darkness hold such pure warmth toward him. Whom was she smiling at, Kayne wondered. What more was there to him? He'd worn his darker traits as a badge of honor his entire life. But now, watching her smile so unabashedly in his presence, knowing himself to be the reason and recipient, he knew the high he felt was unprecedented. He'd been well acquainted with the cool satisfaction of controlling another's pleasure. He'd never been called upon or thought of as a source of happiness. Never had he felt joy, creating another's.

"Be ready for three." With a tender smile, he gently pinched her knee and exited the room.

Laura stayed in her seat long after he left, feeling perplexed. Was she secretly hoping for a repeat of the last unboxing and more indecent instructions from him? Why did their absence unnerve her so? She fretted, confused by her sudden mood swing.

She put in an inordinate amount of effort getting ready that day and showed up at three sharp. With her hair up in an elegant bun, she donned drop diamond earrings and silver sandals, her plump lips glossy in a soft pink shade.

"Come here," Kayne called out in a low growl, with his hands in his pockets and his eyes on her.

Her heart drummed in her chest, a shy smile crossing her face as she looked down and approached him. He stood still, watching her until she finally raised inquisitive eyes to his. With a grin on his face, he took her hand and pulled out a jewelry box, placing it in her open palm.

Laura lifted a brow in question and only received a nudge of his head toward his latest gift for an answer. It contained an incredibly expensive-looking platinum diamond bracelet. And yet, its design, where elegance met with simplicity, appealed to her modest taste.

"Thank you…" she breathed, mesmerized.

Kayne smirked and, turning it around, showed her the engraving: *From Your Monster.*

Her heart sank, and she lifted her head. For the first time, her eyes unapologetically probed his. *Her* Monster. He was so close. She could just lean in. Would he kiss her? She couldn't muster the courage to find out. So she stayed put, silently willing him to close the gap.

He didn't. Instead, he half grinned as if reading her mind and proceeded to secure the bracelet on her wrist. "There. Now you can't take it off. Even if you want to," he cautioned teasingly.

★ ★ ★

They took a private jet there, Kayne acting the perfect gentleman the whole way. Another surreal experience to add to their frenzied history, Laura thought, taking in the breathtaking views. And yet, more spellbinding than anything out her window was the man sitting across from her. *Who was this man who held her fate in his hands?*

Laura kept glancing back at him, her eyes openly seeking him, trying to decipher the puzzle that was Kayne Malkin. Every now and then, he would catch her stare. He would shake his head at her as if in answer to her unvoiced question, a knowing smile advising her to give up the futile quest.

Once they landed, they were driven in a limousine to a castle for the wedding. The ceremony was set outside with the blue sea as a backdrop. There was security everywhere, international celebrities and influential figures, from A-List actors to Nobel Prize winners, old money and self-made millionaires mixed in one lavish event, all guests dressed as royalty.

Kayne introduced Laura as his date, holding her close with intimate ease. *A little over a month*, he'd boldly answered a sweet older woman who had asked *how long*, pointing back and forth between the two of them.

He reluctantly let her go when Mrs. Drugova offered to introduce her to some of the female guests. She had shown interest in the girl—and nothing is refused to Dimitri Drugov's Missus. More so, Kayne accounted for how a good first impression could possibly lead to a very powerful ally.

Natasha Drugova was the matriarch and left no doubt about it. She had maintained her beauty, her distinction shining through her posture and elegance, her piercing gaze only contrasted by her indulgent but reserved smiles. Laura didn't want to leave Kayne, feeling nervous in the company of so many strangers. But Mrs. Drugova had a reassuring authority about her, and Laura followed her obediently to a group of women chatting by the bar.

The beautiful hyenas immediately swarmed around her, badgering Laura with sensitive questions, their curiosity bordering on aggression. She felt uneasy and, constantly looking back at Kayne for reassurance, found him staring back at her every time. She would smile at him, appeased by his enveloping gaze, and turn back to the group with more confidence. Keeping her answers vague, she practiced the art of half-truths she had just witnessed Kayne apply moments before.

Mrs. Drugova gave Laura a complicit smile before pulling her away. "Shall we take a walk," she politely instructed under the guise of a suggestion and stepped away before Laura even answered.

"Don't worry, child. He feels the same."

"Excuse me?" Laura uttered nervously.

"It's quite obvious. He's been watching you like a hawk from the moment you left his side."

Laura wondered what Mrs. Drugova would think if she only knew why she held his undivided attention. It wasn't sweet young love: it was a captor supervising his prisoner. Knowing that at this very moment, she contemplated walking out of the place. As simple as that. *Keep walking, never turning back. Walk past the fancy garden, past the unsuspecting security guards. Or were they?* But Laura knew she wouldn't even try.

It was more than fear of reprisal that kept her locked in his world. More than conditioning to feel safe in her captivity. More than Stockholm syndrome. Laura looked out the open gated entrance and considered the scary and beautiful world awaiting her past these doors, and she knew she wouldn't walk out. Out there was only a life where she had no one left. No one to love, no one to fear, no one to hurt her, or help her heal. A world she was cursed to roam alone, dying quietly a little more every day.

"Blathering fools," Mrs. Drugova proclaimed once they were at a safe distance from the pack. "But you're not, are you? You speak so little." She looked at Laura and smiled before pursuing, "*Those who speak do not know, those who know...* You know exactly the kind of man he is." She waited for Laura to concede, nodding her head uncertainly.

"It's a gift and a curse to be born a woman. You're neither his date nor his girlfriend," she remarked.

Laura's eyes widened at the shock of hearing her reality spoken so casually.

"But you want to be."

Alert and defensive, her head gave an imperceptible shake in denial.

Mrs. Drugova smiled. "I know Kayne. I've known him since he was a little boy. He cares for you. If he didn't, you would already be dead, my dear child. Or worse..." Mrs. Drugova gave her the once-over, sizing her up. "Men like Kayne..." She shook her head with resigned disapproval. "When I met Dimitri, I immediately fell in love with him. But I wasn't a fool about it. I did what I had to do to be with him, in a way that was tolerable for me. Do you understand what I'm telling you?"

"No..." Laura breathed.

"Don't be naive and dream up romance. I see in your eyes how you feel about him. When you give yourself to a man like that, they will take everything from you. It's just their nature. It seems you haven't given him everything just yet. Now I can see *that* from the way *he* looks at you. Negotiate your terms to make the arrangement bearable for you. That's the best advice I can give you."

"No... It's not like that."

"Set your boundaries while you still hold some semblance of power. Negotiating terms before giving in to a man is of vital importance to a woman. I would say that's especially true in your case, where your very life hangs on his affections."

Laura remained silent, looking slightly down as her heart thumped in her chest.

"Kayne is willing to fight for you. He sees in you someone worth fighting for. Kayne will also be the one to drive the dagger into your heart deeper than you ever thought possible. How you respond will determine how you will be treated. Take it lying down, and he will never let you up again. Most sensible women walk away from a man like that. You don't have that option. And yet, I sincerely doubt you would take it given the chance. You'll have to be strong, Laura, stronger than your heart, to be with a man like Kayne."

Laura nodded blankly, still processing the conversation. Everything felt surreal: the beautiful sunny day at the castle by the beach; Kayne, her date, watching her with his unique smile; this unusual and intimidating woman who seemed to understand her better than herself.

Her words still replayed in Laura's head when they rejoined the others. Mrs. Drugova smiled at her and, nudging her head, indicated to Laura to turn around. Kayne was already heading their way, embracing Laura from behind as he exchanged a few pleasantries with Natasha.

"She's a special girl. Hold on to her," Mrs. Drugova finally said, gently squeezing Laura's forearm before excusing herself. A slow song was playing, and Mr. Drugov, grinning from ear to ear, approached them to steal his wife away onto the dance floor.

"Don't worry, she's not going anywhere," Kayne replied in a silky voice, his breath on Laura's neck.

A shiver ran down her spine. She turned her head sideways toward him, landing on laughing eyes.

Kayne stepped back and took her hand, leading her to the dance floor as well. With a cryptic smile, he grabbed her waist and wrapped her arms around his neck.

"Why are you being so nice to me?" Laura asked, looking up at him as they gently swayed to the romantic music.

"I'm always nice to you." He flashed her a mischievous grin.

She snorted humorlessly. "I thought you never lied…"

He answered with a devilish stare and pulled her even closer. "Believe me, Laura. I've been nice to you," he whispered in her ear, his tone surprisingly serious.

Their eyes locked for what seemed an eternity, his powerful gaze meeting her quiet intensity. They remained like this for the remainder of the song, until she laid her head on his shoulder and, closing her eyes, inched her face into the nook of his neck.

"Have you thought of running away?" he asked in a gentle tone.

"Yes," she conceded without shame.

"Is this what you truly want?"

He thought he felt her grip on him tighten for an instant. She didn't answer. He didn't insist.

Her head buried in his chest, she felt his hand reach up and caress her back, all through the song that played, and the next, and the one after that.

"What will happen to me?" Laura eventually asked, her voice barely above a whisper.

She felt him pull her closer. He didn't answer. She didn't insist.

DAY-40

SCENES FROM THE DAY of the wedding kept invading Laura's thoughts. She'd roam the house with a dreamy air and a renegade smile or anxiously biting her cuticles, overanalyze every word and stare. *He feels the same.* She repeated Natasha's words, exhaling softly to quiet her racing mind. And yet, he hadn't tried anything. Not since he'd returned from his morbid mission. Was that the reason he'd acted the perfect gentleman instead of the lustful and self-serving predator she knew him to be? Was Peter's death lingering between them, like poisonous gas dampening the air and suffocating any possible spark? Or was his withdrawal inevitable after she'd finally revealed herself bare, reaffirming her childhood phobia: she was not good enough. Looking down at the bracelet, her heart would swell with emotion, her fingers grazing its engraving. Her Monster. He'd seen her at her worst and bonded himself to her in response.

To ward off her impending insanity, she decided to rearrange her bedroom, going through every drawer and cabinet. She felt the urge to leave an imprint, however small, of her presence at the Malkin Mansion. She emptied out entire wardrobes, arranging and rearranging their content.

It was in a top drawer that she found the picture. Laura sat on the floor, gazing at the smile of a beautiful brunette, her hair styled as they did back in the day, her vibrant hazel eyes gleaming with mischief. Laura stared, mesmerized by the familiar traits of the charismatic young woman, recognizing Kayne's smile in hers. *Kayne's mother.*

Who was she, and what happened to her, Laura wondered. What kind of woman gives birth to this kind of man? Was she like Mrs. Drugova, cold and pragmatic, a force to be reckoned with? Like Olga, a beacon of light to souls lost at sea? Or was she perhaps another comrade, also seeking refuge in fantasy from a world she wasn't armed to face?

"Master Kayne will be home for supper tonight, usual time." Olga smiled as she stepped through the open door to advise Miss Laura.

Startled, Laura quickly hid the picture as if caught with contraband goods. "Yes. Okay, sure... Hmm... Olga? Would you please close the door on your way out? Thanks," she added uncomfortably with a smile, brushing her hair away from her face.

The moment she was alone, she pulled the photograph back out. *Supper with Kayne tonight*, she thought, exhaling deeply to calm her nerves.

It had taken her all afternoon to meticulously select her carefree look. She checked herself in the mirror one last time: casual blue jeans and a loose mustard cotton top, her hair down in soft waves. She reapplied her lip gloss, and satisfied, she headed toward the dining room, the picture tucked into her back pocket.

Kayne was not there, and she double-checked the time, stunned at finding his seat empty. He'd never been late before. She sat down, unease slightly affecting her mood.

She was lost in thought and jerked when two big hands gently grabbed her shoulders.

Kayne chuckled behind her. "What's going on in that head of yours?" he asked, pulling out his chair.

Laura pulled out the photo and handed it to him without saying a word.

He reached for it with curiosity, his eyes instantly narrowing, recognizing the subject. "Where did you get this?"

"In my room."

Kayne looked at her and then back at the picture.

"Is this... your mother?"

He didn't respond right away, his eyes glued to the image. "Yes."

"You look like her..."

"I am nothing like her," he growled, thunderous eyes lifting to Laura's.

"Why are you upset?" she softly asked, almost in a whisper.

"Don't worry about it," he reassured her, his tone still hard, and set the picture facing down on the table, far and out of sight.

"I don't understand... Do you hate her?"

"Drop it," he answered in a cool warning.

Laura held his stare for a moment, then broke away with an imperceptible headshake, unable to link such a violent reaction to the sweet face she had looked at all day.

They finished supper with a heavy silence weighing on them, Laura tracking Kayne's restrained rage in the pools of darkness facing her.

The longer he felt her scanning his every move, the more his anger dissipated, the fire in his heart morphing into a different type of burning. He wanted her. He wanted her smiling or sad, inquisitive or cautious, daring or innocent. It didn't matter. He'd yet to see a facet of Laura that didn't trigger his hunger. He inhaled, slowly closing his eyes and willing his warm blood to cool, then got up and went digging for something in his jacket.

Laura observed Kayne, trying to anticipate his ever-shifting mood. He returned to the dining room and leaned back against the island counter. "Come here," he commanded her with a half-grin.

She turned to him, further assessing the situation, and with unsure steps, she slowly approached him.

Kayne patiently waited, with an amused expression and his arms crossed. At this moment, he knew her apprehension overrode any other emotion she might feel toward him. The instant she was within reach, he grabbed her wrist and pulled her to him. He could sense her maddened pulse and reveled at the chaos he could so easily create within her. He pulled out an envelope and handed it to her.

"What is it?" she asked, her voice low and raspy.

He leaned into her ear, his luscious whisper coming through a concealed smirk. "Happy birthday."

She seemed confused at first, then closed her eyes, the fact dawning on her. It was her birthday. She was turning twenty-four.

"Do you want me to open it now?" she asked, still prudent.

"It's yours. You do what you want."

Laura gave him a playfully suspicious look but opened the envelope with a genuine smile. She found two tickets to the *Swan Lake* premiere by Les Grands Ballets Canadiens for the following evening. Her eyes rounded with surprise.

"You're taking me to *Swan Lake*? How did you even know?" she gasped.

"Happy?" He smiled.

"More than you can imagine. Thank you." She stared at him with wonder.

She could feel the pull toward him, the magnetic power his proximity exerted on her. Against reason and self-preservation, she closed her eyes, and raising herself on her toes, she closed the small distance separating them. Her mouth barely grazed his, and for the length of a second, her sweet lips tasted the saltiness of his. She quickly pulled back and, avoiding his gaze, turned to walk away. Laura felt his hand on her arm, slowly turning her around and pulling her back to him. Her heart sank, and already regretting her impulsivity, she kept her eyes on the ground, unable to meet his piercing gaze.

Kayne brought a hand to her shoulder, letting his fingers run the length of her arm, and feeling her nervous shiver, he sighed. He leaned in and brought his mouth to her ear. "Don't play with fire, little girl," he whispered.

Her face flushed, and she quickly nodded. Without ever looking at him, she rushed out of his embrace and away from him.

★ ★ ★

That night Kayne didn't make any calls nor went out to seek fresh female company. His mind was fixated on his captive, on the soft kiss he could still feel on his lips as he ran his thumb over them. How could anything so sweet and innocent turn him on to such an extent, he wondered.

She had stood still, ripe for his taking, yet he had held back. Had he led her to the bedroom, he knew she would have followed him willingly. And yet, something in her eyes and fluttery kiss had stopped him from abusing his hold over her. Her pure desire was far removed from the twisted fantasies that consumed him. He would spare her the cost of playing with monsters. It was her birthday, after all. Next time, there would be no mercy.

DAY-41

LAURA HAD BARELY GOTTEN any sleep, tossing and turning all night from excitement. The *Swan Lake*. Not just any ballet. She was going to *Swan Lake*. She wondered how Kayne even knew and remembered mentioning something about it to Olga.

She had spent a good part of her childhood viewing and reviewing the famous ballet on an old VHS tape her mother had left behind. Performed by a world-renowned Russian troupe at the time, it had captured a young Laura's heart and imagination, and she would twirl in the living room, mimicking the graceful prima ballerina. Vases and picture frames were among many to fall prey to her clumsy limbs. Her infuriated father's loud steps would be heard, Peter would run to get the dustpan, and she would preemptively crawl into the cage, her head bowed.

None of it mattered now. She was going to attend the ballet in person. No more blurry lines running through the screen against colors faded to different shades of grey. She closed her eyes and allowed herself the most extravagant fantasies, falling asleep with a smile from the images playing in her head. A red carpet, a white limousine, cameras everywhere. Kayne would see in her the woman she'd become and ignore all others, entranced by her feminine guile. He would hold her hand under the envious stares of faceless competitors, leading her inside while whispering sweet nothings in her ear. He would act protective of her as he always did, playful and lighthearted, as he was at the wedding, seductive and dangerous, as he was at the party. *Her Monster*.

The following morning greeted her with clear blue skies and a pleasant breeze. It seemed as if the entire universe conspired with her, smiling down upon her unspoken desires. She spent the day under a glorious sun and finished *The Kite Runner* in one sitting. *For you, a thousand times over*. Another one of Kayne's gifts. She hugged it and kissed the cover, her lips recalling the feel of his. Though she couldn't say what madness came over her, she didn't feel an ounce of regret. His wolfish warning came to mind, one feigning to push away while designed to draw her in. She had felt his pulsating desire and half-hoped that whatever mercy keeping his lust at bay would evaporate. She did want to play with fire. She'd grown dependent on it, yearning for its warmth and relying on its sole source of light in a world of never-ending obscurity. She would withstand its inevitable burns.

She glided back to her room in a dreamy bubble, hours ahead of time, wanting to savor each step of her preparation for a night she would forever remember. She found another familiar-looking gift box on her bed and rushed to it, her heart leaping with excitement. A black satin gown awaited her, majestic as the night.

★ ★ ★

She entered the living room that evening with a radiant smile matching her glow, her hair in a stylish half updo, silky loose curls brushing her shoulders. Kayne was in a black suit, his back turned to her as he stared out the window, and she timidly cleared her throat.

He turned around and, giving her a cryptic smile, caught up to her in a few steps. He pulled her hand and cocked his head, lifting her arm open wide as his eyes rested on her every nook and curve. "You look stunning."

"Thank you," she beamed, lowering her gaze.

"I can't make it tonight," he softly said.

"Oh?" She felt her chest tighten, his words landing as punches to the gut. The fantasized scenes that had her heart soaring the previous night came back to haunt her, coiling around her lungs.

"Something's come up," he explained, a certain melancholy creeping into his eyes. "Lucas will take you."

"Okay." She smiled feebly. She wanted to say more, to project breezy indifference, but the lump forming in her throat suggested otherwise. She tried to focus on the silver lining; she would still get to fulfill a childhood dream. And though she was filled with gratitude, her staggering disappointment unveiled her heart's true desires.

He brushed her cheek with the back of his hand. "He's waiting for you at the front door."

"Okay," she repeated, struggling to regain composure. And turning away, she quickly headed for the entrance, her eyes threatening to betray her.

Kayne watched her leave reluctantly. He had meant to go with her. But Tanya called. She had an update on the Maxwell situation, and that took precedence over anything else.

Tanya and Kayne had maintained a very peculiar relationship. Her heart couldn't move past the injury of his rejection. Her ego couldn't forgive the insult. She'd ensured she remained in his entourage, using whatever opportunity to remind him of what he had foolishly lost, having willingly given it up. And though she sought the feel of his touch in the arms of all others, she never allowed herself to feel it again.

Kayne appreciated their little games. Never had a woman challenged and entertained his depravity as expertly as she had. She'd offer him others and watch with hunger as their fantasies played out, positioning herself as the forbidden fruit.

But all her bids for attention were not gone unnoticed, and Kayne understood he could still use her unresolved feelings to his advantage. Dimitri, unlike himself, had no qualms about sharing his women, and Kayne had asked her to get close to Maxwell and report back to him, dangling the lure of his affections for a reward.

Kayne had felt nothing but disdain and repulsion toward Maxwell from the moment they had met. It was unrelated to his off-putting appearance. It was in his uneven voice and slithery demeanor, in his stooped posture and furtive glances. It was in the euphoria in his eyes when performing deeds others would have deemed necessary evils. Kayne didn't trust him and was convinced Maxwell was pulling dark strings behind his duplicitous smile. He'd been acting a tad too friendly as of late.

Tanya had called in the early evening, her voice victorious. Months of sharing his bed had finally paid off. She wanted to meet with Kayne as soon as possible and refused to reveal anything further on the phone.

★ ★ ★

Lucas was dressed for the occasion, smiling lightheartedly at Laura as he offered his arm and helped her into the car. The entire night he was attentive, ensuring she was comfortable and enjoying herself. Once over her initial deception, Laura appreciated his pleasant company. He was refined and cultured, his wit and charm winning her over despite the uphill battle. She felt like she'd known him her whole life, an old friend whose spot-on observations never failed to amuse her.

The lights dimmed, and the curtains opened to fading murmurs. Tchaikovsky's memorized beginning notes resounded in the plaza, and Laura leaned over the balcony, peeking with glee at the live orchestra; the ballet started.

For the following hours, Laura was transported to another world. She barely dared to blink, entranced by the beautiful tragedy of the star-crossed lovers. How could the prince mistake Odette for her pure opposite? What did it say about his love? Odile twirled onstage, mesmerizing both the unfortunate prince and the audience. Laura's heart swelled, and she couldn't help counting as the ballerina performed the famed thirty-two fouettés. Then the Swan Queen returned, dancing away her torment, her lover's actions having sealed her fate. Laura thought of how particularly cruel it was to have to bear the weight of your own betrayal. As the ballet neared the end, Odette leaped to her death, followed by her beloved prince, now aware of the treachery. But a note of hope lingers, and the doomed lovers are reunited at last, rising into the air as united orbs of light. Would they have been better off not meeting? Was it truly better to have loved and lost? Laura believed so. She was among the first to stand, clapping long past the curtain call.

She smiled through the ride home, thinking of the magical night she was just gifted, and blushed, thinking of the gifter.

Stepping excitedly through the front door, her eyes scanned the house for Kayne. Laura wanted to thank him for possibly the best night in her miserable, short life.

She ran into the kitchen and living room, trying the usual rooms with no success, and shrugged her shoulders. He must still be out, she thought, defeated, and wondered what could have come up. *Work?* Was he out interrogating someone, this very instant, with blood on his hands and fire in his eyes? While she looked for him in an empty house, still high off tutus, sorcerers, and spellbound princesses?

A shrill laughter pierced through the air and into Laura's skull. Though having heard it only once at the party, she could recognize the high-pitched voice anywhere. Her face dropped. Was he *here* with Tanya? Is that why he couldn't go with her? Her heart sank, the acute stabbing sensation incomparable to the vague sense of dread the earlier violent image had conjured.

With a fastening heartbeat, she followed the echoes of the grating sound down the west corridor and into the reception hall, and she slowly lowered the right handle of the double white doors.

Kayne was sitting on a massive couch, the top of his shirt unbuttoned and his hair messy. A woman in a black thong and heels knelt on the floor between his legs. Her head bobbing up and down sensually, she took him in her mouth, her face hidden by a curtain of dark curly hair. Empty glasses of alcohol littered the table nearby. With smoky eyes and in a body-hugging mini-black dress, Tanya sat at Kayne's side, her whole body turned toward him. Her legs, slightly apart, caused her skirt to lift even further up her thighs. Her dainty fingers were intertwined on his shoulder, her chin resting on them as she whispered in his ear. Kayne smirked, looking straight ahead with one hand at his side, holding the whiskey bottle by its neck, the other resting on her inner thigh with intimate familiarity.

Laura gasped and, horrified, brought her hand to her mouth as the two touching faces simultaneously turned her way; Tanya's almond green eyes alight with carnivorous thrill, Kayne's alcohol-induced state reflected in his dark and engulfing stare.

Laura shook her head, her fingers hanging on her lips, then taking a step back, she exited the room. It was all a dream, a nightmare where the earth beneath her feet had opened and swallowed her whole. Her heart pounded furiously, her mind racing with incoherent thoughts. Worse than the woman performing the sexual act on him was the display of his closeness with Tanya. It kept the constant pain shooting in her chest. He'd abandoned her for Tanya. Was that why he'd passed over the opportunity the night before when he could've so easily had her? For a rendezvous with the one who could truly satisfy his appetite? She remembered the kiss she gave him, the fantasies she entertained. *Don't be naive and dream up romance*, Mrs. Drugova's words came back to her. Laura felt her heart shatter, the pain physical. How many times could a soul break apart before it ceased being itself? What fills the holes left behind beyond darkness?

She walked to the main entrance, her feet carrying her of their own accord, and heard voices calling out to her. They seemed to be coming from another world. She kept walking, out the front door and onto the paved lane. The front gates, which had been constantly shut since her arrival, were open, as if quietly egging her on forward. She kept walking, past the iron gates and security men. Though looking at her, none tried to stop her. She walked into the street. The moonlight was shining brightly, illuminating her way. She removed her heels and carried them in her hands. She kept walking, in her evening gown, her feet bare on the asphalt. Cars passed by, honking. She didn't register them. She kept walking.

★ ★ ★

Kayne's cell phone rang.

"Sir, Miss Spencer is heading toward the front gate." Lucas waited for instructions.

"Is she still wearing the bracelet?"

"Yes, Sir."

"Good. Let her." Kayne hung up and pushed the woman off him as he got off the couch.

"Oh, what's wrong? Did the little bird fly away?" Tanya offered him a delighted smirk as she feigned concern.

He shot her a cool warning stare, then turned around and walked away. "You know the way out," he threw back, his voice hard.

He headed for the stairs, frustration quickening his steps. It was what he wanted. He had meticulously calculated the pros and cons of this collision. Why, then, had he felt such irritation toward Tanya?

After business had been discussed, she'd opened a bottle to celebrate. Within the first couple of shots, she brought up Laura. Since their separation, Tanya had taken to asking him to share intimate details of his latest conquests. Kayne was never one to enjoy disclosing private matters. But with Tanya, when he needed special favors, sometimes, he obliged. He understood that his willingness to insert her into his latest formed duo was how Tanya tested his loyalty. A way he could show her that regardless of the women that came and went, she would never be dethroned. He had reassured her many times over the years, providing salacious details in a husky voice and, in doing so, used the opportunity to remind her what she, in turn, willingly forbid herself.

This time, he wouldn't. She'd laughed it off playfully but had taken her phone out in response, sending for the new girl with a devilish smirk. She was giving him a second chance to prove he would still betray all others for her, with her, one way or another. With Tanya's latest recruit between his legs, he'd still refused to answer her probing questions, smirking as he shook his head, staring straight ahead with his fingers grazing her inner thigh.

Part of him had wanted Laura to see, intent on showing her how deeply into him went the Monster's reach. If she wouldn't join his demons, could she at least withstand their cruelty?

He hoped she would. He'd stared her in the eye with no shame or remorse. *Jump into the abyss*, he'd silently willed her. *I'll catch you.*

★ ★ ★

Laura kept walking. Pebbles cut her feet. Angry drivers cursed at her through lowered windows. She kept walking, her mind numb. She didn't know for how long she walked. She didn't know where she was going.

★ ★ ★

"Where is she headed?" Kayne asked Lucas, stepping through his office door.

"Nowhere in particular, I think. She seems to be just walking along the highway. Could be dangerous, Sir. Are you sure you don't want me to retrieve her?" Lucas asked, his face behind the screen on which he tracked Laura's movements, her chip-encrusted bracelet popping up as a little red spot on their monitoring system.

"No." Kayne's reply was instant. "I want to see where she goes. Have Kiev follow her. Only intervene if she gets close to a police station."

"Yes, Sir."

Kiev, a slim, dark-eyed man with a crooked nose, was also part of the security team. Proud and patriotic, he'd taken the name of his home city for his own when he'd left the motherland. Though he was well into his fifties now, he was fit and strong, his erect posture still reflecting the military training received in his early years. He specialized in interrogation techniques and executions no one else wanted to perform. Kiev wasn't a sadist. He'd just seen too much, too early on in life, to feel the sting of right and wrong anymore. In the world he knew, ethics were a luxury; as in the face of necessity, all other values failed. Loyalty, however, he understood. For even in hell, alliances had to be made. He'd been with the family long before Kayne's birth, being one of Lev's first soldiers and most trusted allies. Kiev had served Kayne as faithfully, helping the family rise and maintain its position within the Organization.

★ ★ ★

Laura saw the flashing red neon of the open sign and headed straight toward a seedy bar in the middle of nowhere. *Le Rendez-vous du Chat Noir*, it said in black iron cursive letters above the heavy wooden front doors. Inside were dark blue walls with the paint chipping off, old chairs and tables of various shapes and sizes spaced out haphazardly. There were men engaged in a card game at the back and a few waitresses past their prime, donning outfits suggesting they refused to acknowledge it. They all stared at her in an awkward silence.

Laura walked straight to the counter on her bloodied bare feet, her expensive gown torn and dusty. "A whiskey. Straight up, please."

The barman lifted his brow, checking her out with open curiosity as he kept playing with the dirty towel on his shoulder. At last, he obliged, pouring a glass he set in front of her.

She downed it in one shot and smiled, feeling a head rush, the burn in her throat, and the slow numbing of her senses. "Can I have another, please?" she asked, smacking the glass back on the counter.

"Sure thing, Doll. Four dollars for the first, unless you wanna open a tab?" He eyed her suspiciously.

"Oh..." She had no money. It hadn't even crossed her mind; such a mundane everyday worry. When was she last confronted with one of those?

"May I?" A man approached, offering her a toothy smile. He didn't wait for her answer and gave the barman his credit card. "Two more, please."

She kept staring ahead, refusing to acknowledge him. When their drinks arrived, he reached for both glasses before she could take hers. He handed her one, forcing interaction, and raised his own to clink it with hers.

"To beautiful, mysterious ladies appearing out of nowhere."

Laura cocked her head, sizing him up. He was attractive. Brown silky hair and deep green eyes, but something in his smile kept her on guard. She thought of Kayne's, of all the warmth she'd feel in response. Then Tanya's flashed in her mind, and she swallowed the drink in one shot. Feeling light-headed, she gripped the counter and grinned at the spinning sensation.

"And she smiles…" he teased.

* * *

"She's at a bar, Sir. Kiev is in the parking lot. She's been inside for over twenty minutes."

"A bar…" Kayne licked his lips, pensive. "Okay. Let's go."

* * *

Laura was a little more than tipsy, and she complied with a giggle when her drinking companion led her out of the bar. He'd been talking about himself incessantly, bragging about his career and ambitions in between rounds of shots he kept coming. He'd then suggested they go out for a smoke and some fresh air.

She tried to enjoy the offered cigarette, but he kept invading her space, his sense of entitlement coming through in increasingly aggressive advances. He'd pushed her against the brick wall of the back alley, inching forward to kiss her. She'd turned her face away, her soft chuckle dying down. He'd leaned even closer, and though she could feel her skin crawl, imagining Kayne and Tanya, she'd allowed it. She could feel him kissing down her neck, his hands reaching for her breast. And in an attempt to stop him, she'd lifted her arms, trying feebly to push him off.

He flew away, landing on the ground a few feet behind. And Kayne, appearing as if out of nowhere, now faced her instead, his eyes open slits of fury.

"What the f—" The man dusted himself off as he stumbled to his feet.

Staring at Laura, Kayne pulled out a gun and pointed it at him. "Stay down."

"Hey! Easy—" The man raised his hands, remaining on his knees.

"Shut up," Kayne interrupted without even looking at him.

Laura could see two black SUVs blocking each side of the back alley, Lucas at one end and a man she'd noticed around the house at the other.

"Has he touched you?" Kayne's eyes bore into hers.

"No, man, I didn't! I swear! Listen, I don't want any trouble..." the kneeling man mumbled, panicking.

"Be quiet," Kayne hissed, throwing a quick glance that had him cowering further down on his knees and crooking his arms behind his head. Turning back to Laura, Kayne addressed her with deceptive calm, "Laura, have you let this man touch you? In any way?"

She shook her head, dumbstruck with disbelief. Everything felt surreal: Kayne, here, with Lucas, on whose arm she had just attended the ballet; her overbearing companion now begging on his knees.

"Don't lie," Kayne reminded her in a sinister tone.

"He... he kissed my neck—" she stammered, interrupted by a deafening popping sound. Warm liquid spurted on her. She understood what it was, recognizing the red splatter on Kayne's face and all over his white shirt. In shock, she remained still, looking in denial at the limp body on the ground.

Kayne's eyes remained locked on her, venom seeping through them as he pulled out a handkerchief and slowly wiped his face. Laura felt herself shiver, her teeth chattering uncontrollably. Kiev approached them and dragged the body, rolling it up in plastic. *This isn't real. This can't be real*. She gasped for air, watching Kayne calmly turn away and walk back to the car.

"Miss Spencer." Lucas gingerly pulled on her arm. "Miss Spencer, we have to go," he softly said, leading her to the approaching SUV.

"Lucas... no. Please, no," she pleaded, shaking her head.

"We have to go, Miss Spencer." He gently but forcibly pushed her into the backseat of the car.

Kayne was already seated and looked straight ahead, his eyes cold as stone. She pulled her feet up on the seat and hugged them, her entire body shaking with convulsions.

"Do this again, and I will kill you," he finally said without looking at her.

Laura began rocking herself, chewing her cuticles bloody. Was a man really dead because of her? How did Kayne find her? What reprisal had he in store for her? Could he so easily take her life while she struggled to resist giving him her heart? The entire way home, her mind flitted from one morbid thought to another.

"Get out," he hissed, waiting by the open car door, his harsh voice snapping her back to reality.

"No... wait, please. You don't understand," she tried to explain.

He roughly pulled her out, unresponsive to her desperate pleas, and dragged her into the house. Olga, who was waiting inside, instantly paled at their sight. Both covered in blood, Kayne shoved a terrified Laura, making her tumble forward and fall sideways on the floor.

"Master Kayne—" Olga began in a shaky voice.

"Leave us," he warned in a low growl.

"Master, I beg of you—" She used her remaining courage to face his wrath.

"Now!"

Olga looked down at Laura, attempting to offer a reassuring smile. Her eyes, however, conveyed the shame she felt as she obediently retreated to her bedroom, closing the door behind her.

With her hands behind her, Laura crawled backward until her spine hit the wall, and there was nowhere further to seek refuge. She panted like a cornered animal, turning at the slightest sound or movement.

"Is this how you repay me?" Kayne controlled his tone between ragged breaths, his eyes blackening with rage.

Laura shook her head in panic.

"Do you have any, *ANY*, idea what I've been through for you?" His voice was sharp, growing louder with his faltering self-control. Then he paused as if to regain composure and started again. "Dimitri... wants you dead. Maxwell... wants to sell you. Had I known you were just dying to whore yourself, I wouldn't have busted my balls over you."

"No... No. Master, please..." she pained to get each word out.

"Oh? It's *Master* now? Quite the manipulative little thing, aren't we? Well... Master is not happy, *Pet*." A sadistic gleam merged with the residing rage in his eyes.

"No! It wasn't like that." She shook her head with despair.

"No? What *were* you doing in a back alley, drunk and alone, with a man you didn't know? Please, do enlighten me."

"You were with your whores!" she wailed, shouting at the top of her lungs. "What do you want from me?" Her voice broke.

He grunted, a diabolic smile matching his menacing eyes, and answered with hair-rising softness. "Don't worry, Pet. I'll show you."

Her eyes snapped up to meet his, but he was at her side in an instant, pulling her roughly by the arm off the floor. He dragged her, kicking and screaming, all along the hall, down the stairs, and into the dungeon.

Once they'd reached the bed, he let go, and Laura fell to her knees, sobbing as her upper body landed on the soft mattress. He lifted her up by her hair and, bringing the side of her face to his lips, asked with thunderous calm. "How many times have I spared you?"

She ignored his question, thrashing her arms about as she tried in vain to free herself from the painful hold.

With his free hand, he pulled her back against him. He then brought his fingers down and inside her thighs, stopping right at the edge of their intersection. "I know you want it." He softly bit her ear, his other hand still fisting her hair, and watched her pant in response. "Did you want him?"

"No…" she sniffled.

"Then why do it, Laura? Were you that desperate for my attention? Well… you have it now."

He pushed her down on the mattress and climbed over her. Kneeling with one leg on each side of her body, he ripped her dress off her back. She gasped, and he felt her body tighten under him. Her distress somewhat pacified him, and he trailed his fingers on her exposed skin in a soft caress. He reached for her arms and, bringing them to the bedposts where handcuffs awaited, locked both wrists.

"Please… please…" she implored, out of breath, her voice throaty with emotion.

Kayne leaned in close and made shushing sounds. "Want to know what I do with my whores, is that it?" he whispered huskily, kissing her earlobe.

"No! Please… I don't know why I did it… I just… I saw you with her—"

"So you whore yourself to a stranger?"

"No, I didn't! I was just... jealous," she admitted, her emotions settling with defeat.

"Whores don't get to be jealous," he callously threw at her. "Let that be your first lesson."

Laura's eyes flashed with a deep-rooted anger she hadn't felt in so long. It was the agony of remaining silent when facing injustice only the powerless could truly understand. It was the type of outrage that never saw the light of day and, turning on its host, insidiously poisoned its home. She lay her head down on the pillow, filled with bitter surrender. "I didn't whore myself. Believe what you want."

A sardonic chuckle escaped his lips. "I *believe* I've been too soft with you." Kayne left her side, returning with a whip he cracked on the floor.

Laura jerked and shouted from the imagined pain, hearing his derisive snort in response. She'd barely composed herself when the whip came down on her. It cut her breath, the long-lasting sting unbearable, and she was in shock, rendered mute with the overwhelming sensation. It sank down on her again. This time, she bellowed with all she had, her scream lingering in the air. He struck her again, again, and again. She hollered and shrieked at every strike. She thought she would pass out from the pain, convinced he'd drawn blood and scarred her for life.

He hadn't. Kayne had been careful not to break her skin. He liked her pristine skin and kept the intensity at a minimum, controlling the impact of each strike.

"Do you think being jealous gives you the right to openly disrespect me? When I've put my neck out for you. Protected you. From everyone. Even myself. Is this how you repay me?"

"No. I'm sorry. Forgive me, Master."

A guttural sound escaped his lips. "You'll have to earn that, baby girl."

He caressed her, his hand trailing down her back, and he reached between her legs, growing hard at finding her wet. He spread her wetness through her slit and back to the darker tight little circle, spreading her round cheeks apart. He pressed with the pad of his thumb, applying pressure in a circular motion.

Laura could feel his finger triggering new sensations in her, slowly loosening her despite herself. But the pressure became evermore intrusive, his thumb pushing his way into her to penetrate her from behind. She gasped, contracting her muscles at the unpleasant feeling.

"Relax."

"I can't," she panted, lifting her head in panic.

He smiled. "You can. Trust Master." His free fingers found her core, and while he kept pushing his thumb into her tense opening, his fingers teased her pulsating nerves, adapting the pressure and rhythm to her reactions.

He kept at it patiently, subduing through pleasure the body he sought to dominate. He waited for her to acclimate to the new sensation, enmeshing it with the bliss he'd trained her to crave. After some time, he felt her muscles around his thumb loosen and smirked, hearing her moan. Her hips rocked against his fingers, and he reveled at feeling her desperation to maintain the contact he'd withhold when she'd near climax.

"Just like a bitch in heat." He chuckled sadistically, knowing how deep his words cut her.

A whimper escaped Laura's lips, her eyes tearing at the sting of his words. And yet, the pleasure she felt from his touch quashed any other emotion. And the realization of her vulnerability in the face of his immense power acted as an incredibly potent aphrodisiac.

Kayne pulled out his finger and laid his body on top of hers. Laura could feel his erection rubbing against her, lingering at the entrance his thumb had just violated. Tense and on edge, she wanted to beg him to spare her one more time. But he continued to play with her pulsating nerves, his body surrounding her and his fingers driving her mad. She understood, at that moment, just how deep his hold over her truly went. With his touch alone, he could cast aside all the values and principles she had clung to her entire life.

"Beg me," he commanded, his voice wolfish in her ear.

She whimpered.

He grabbed her hair, tilting her head back to his. "Beg me to make you my whore."

"Make me your whore… I beg you, Master." Laura closed her eyes, unable to face the humiliation of uttering these words.

Kayne thrust very slowly inside her and heard her cry out. Once fully inside, he stayed still, nibbling on her shoulder while his fingers continued their torture. He waited to feel her body relax under his. And only then did he begin moving in and out of her, pulling out completely before reentering her at a leisurely pace.

Laura was caught in a foggy haze where pleasure, pain, and shame coexisted, and her blood and tears paved the way to her haven. She was no longer herself, just a feral animal reacting to primal sensations.

It hurt to admit to herself the distress she had felt facing another man. She had recoiled from someone she had deemed attractive, her every cell resounding with a visceral *no*. How different her resistance was when it came to Kayne, how cerebral and toothless. It was a lie. Meant only to soothe her conscience and simultaneously deny her innermost desires. What did it say about her?

A man was murdered, in front of her, because of her. And all she could feel in this moment was the sweet numbing relief of belonging to him, her Monster, surrendering to this unavoidable and irrepressible force. Kayne... Kayne... Kayne... She repeated his name over and over again in her head. She came, submerged in the intensity of feeling the assertion of his ownership over her body. He came not long after in a low growl. And after unshackling her, he got off without saying another word.

Emptiness filled Laura's heart as the chill air replaced his body's warmth. Kayne had threatened her life, killed a man, and twisted her desires to degrade her. He'd whipped her and used her as a whore, mercilessly taking the only thing she had left: her dignity. And now, after he'd gotten his release, he left her to deal with the aftermath alone. Naked, lost, and ashamed. She brought her knees to her chest and stared vacantly into the open space.

Kayne opened the door, ready to exit the room, but stopped at the last second. He looked back at the broken body he just left behind. Pure, fragile, and beautiful. He didn't want to go back to her; she had run away and deserved any punishment he saw fit. Worse than that, he'd found her in the arms of another. He could've massacred an entire village. But he understood, looking at her, that if he walked out on her now, the Laura Spencer he knew would be no more.

He got irritated and, feeling trapped, slammed his fist on the wall, yelling out "Fuck!" in frustration. Her frail body jerked at the sound, and he slowly exhaled, lowering his head as he closed his eyes. His walk resolute, Kayne returned to her and scooped her in his arms. He smiled kindly to reassure her terrified eyes, sadness buried underneath his. Still holding her, he grabbed a blanket and covered her body. He then carried her to her bedroom, laying her gently on the bed and under the covers. And after removing his clothes, he climbed in next to her.

Laura stared at him, her eyes carrying the weight of the world. She kept her arms protectively closed over her chest, her hands in tight fists under her chin. Kayne rubbed them soothingly, stroking her arms and shoulders. Then wrapping his arm around her, he brought her into his embrace. He could feel her little heart pounding furiously against his chest, and for the first time, he bore sorrow.

"Laura…" he softly said, caressing the face still covered in blood. "Do you want to tell me off? … Curse me? … Hit me?"

She remained silent, her broken expression unchanging.

"Want to spit on me? … *Again?*" He chuckled softly at the memory.

A lonely tear rolled down her face.

"Laura…" He didn't know what to do. He'd only ever been taught how to break, never how to mend. At this moment, he would have given the world for that power; to have her lean in and kiss him softly again, her eyes sparkling with innocent expectation.

"Anything. Ask me anything," he commanded, his tone gruff and solemn.

Laura fought hard. Darkness, her old friend, had come knocking on her door again. It was a toxic parasite, feeding off its host while simultaneously devastating it. It feigned usefulness, pointing out all that was wrong with her, presenting gut-wrenching memories it distorted even further as proof. Laura had no strength left in her to defend herself. How do you fight an enemy that knows everything about you? And used your deepest regrets, worst fears, and repressed desires to destroy you from within? You set a bigger monster against it.

She lowered her gaze. "Make love to me."

Her voice was so soft that Kayne wasn't even sure he'd heard her correctly. He closed his eyes and, leaning on top of her, rested his forehead against hers. With the utmost care, he caressed the dried blood on her face and pulled her arms apart, lifting them over her head.

She felt his hands reaching for her wrists, beginning to pin them down on the mattress, then pull further, his fingers intertwining with hers. He kissed the wet path of her tears, rubbing himself against her. Every time, his caresses would start out soft. Every time, they grew possessive, ending on a tender note.

Laura could feel him restraining the urge to dominate her and forcing his moves to be gentle. Drained from her extreme and contradicting emotions, she let them all go, surrendering completely to her Monster. No more anguish. No more guilt. She had opened Pandora's box and now faced the evil she had unleashed.

Kayne passionately kissed her, swallowing all her pain and despair, her broken dreams and abandoned hopes. With every inch of their bodies intertwined, he penetrated her slowly and felt her moan into his mouth. And as he continued thrusting sensually inside her, he brought his mouth to her ear. "I may be a monster. But I'd fight for you. I'd kill for you. Go to war for you. If you only knew… what your Monster would do for you."

She squeezed his hands, her eyes lost in his, hazy and intense at the same time. His words felt like medicine on her wounds, his touch, the only anchor left in her godforsaken world, the last barrier keeping the darkness at bay.

Her body shattered underneath his. He kissed her again, swirling his tongue against hers, and picking up the pace, he reached his own release. He came in a grunt, collapsing on top of her, then kissed her temple before turning on his back. Staring up at the ceiling, he pulled her to him so she lay against his chest and absentmindedly ran his fingers through her hair.

Laura curled up against him, into him. She would've slit his chest open and crawled into it if she could. Her Monster. Never had she felt so bare, so raw, her most reviled parts exposed so mercilessly. Never had she imagined it would lead her home in her Monster's embrace, where for the first time, she felt seen and accepted for all of her; *The good, the bad and the ugly*. It is a very unique bond, one that is formed in hell.

Her Monster. Her Master. Her mystery. She would gladly dedicate the rest of her life to studying every inch of him. If only he could see that she wanted nothing more than to offer him the same liberation. *Show me your wounds. Let me see the broken boy behind the Monster, and trust that I will stay.*

"Kayne… What happened to your mother?" she tentatively asked, knowing instinctively to reach for the source.

Kayne could feel her little fingers trail his chest and slowly exhaled. "She betrayed my father," he softly answered as he guarded her in his embrace, his hurt coming through for the first time for what it was, and not the cold rage it had festered into over the years.

"With… another man?"

"No." He took a long pause before exposing his old wound. "Because of me. After I was born. It fucked with her head. She turned on him."

"Oh…"

"She went to the cops, Laura. Agreed to help them put him behind bars. He'd only ever loved and cherished her. Can you think of a worse betrayal?"

"But… she did it for you. Out of love… for you."

"That's not love. She would have deprived me of my father and betrayed a man who loved her beyond measure. My father was loyal to her, to a fault if you believe Dimitri. He never lied to her. She knew the life he was offering her, and she chose to marry him and carry his child. And then she betrayed him, although he'd never wronged her. My father took good care of me. He was there for me, always. She didn't even give him a chance. She just turned on him. For no reason. It was all in her head."

"Is that why she died?"

"Yes."

It was tragic and horrible. Kayne didn't blame his father for the murder of his mother; he held it against her. Laura's heart broke for the beautiful brunette who had given her life for her son; for the motherless babe taught to hate his bearer; for herself, for Peter, for the children they had been, worshipping the traces of the mother who left them behind. Her heart broke for all the suffering that had happened between these walls. She understood the message in the cautionary tale of Mrs. Malkin's life and death, grasping the deadly warning given to her earlier in the car. "I wasn't going to the cops. That's not why I left…"

"I know." Kayne kissed her forehead.

With their voices soft and their wounds bare, they opened up to each other under a silvery moonlight.

"My father… he told me he loved me… all the time. He would pull me onto his lap and watch the same Disney movies with me over and over again. I think I made him watch *Beauty and the Beast* every Sunday for a whole year." She chuckled softly, Kayne responding with a similar smile to the one he had given her earlier, filled with warmth and heartache. "Sometimes, I thought it just made it worse, you know? Sometimes, I wished he could just… *be* a monster. Not make me forget and trust him again. The pain would be so much worse… *every time*," her voice quavered.

He considered her, realizing the depth from which this cry came and the world of hurt Laura kept buried deep within. He'd never known another woman to such an extent, never knew any other person so deeply. He understood the plea in her confession: her plea to *him*.

They fell asleep with their bodies intertwined, Kayne spending the first night of his life in the arms of another.

DAY-42

KAYNE WAS ALREADY GONE by the time she awoke. Olga came in to greet her, looking sheepish, and Laura smiled kindly at her, trying to reassure her that there were no hard feelings. Of all people, she could understand the terror of facing Kayne Malkin's wrath.

The previous night still felt like a blur, and various moments resurfaced randomly all day, keeping her locked in her mind.

Kayne did not come home that evening, and Laura wondered if she was on his mind as well.

★ ★ ★

Kayne was with Tanya. They were going over the details for the following night. Dimitri was throwing another party, and Maxwell was going to use this occasion to touch base with possible detractors. Tanya was to remain by his side and give Kayne the names of all the men Maxwell would interact with.

Kayne was almost at the door when Tanya threw to his back, almost as an afterthought, "Oh… will our little bird be joining us?" She flashed him a devilish grin, following him close behind.

Kayne smirked, shaking his head. He would not play this game with her. Not when it came to Laura; she was off-limits. Instead, he leaned in and kissed her goodbye on the cheek, his lips grazing the corners of hers. He surmised she would accept the consolation prize.

"I'll see you tomorrow," he said, turning to the door.

"So… no, then?" she insisted playfully and heard him chuckle.

It was already late when he left her quarters. On the ride home, he thought of the night he brought Laura to the party and felt both amused and aroused by his memories of that evening. His thoughts shifted to the previous night, to her naked, sweaty body against his, to her soft pleas and ragged moans. *Make love to me*, he heard her frail voice again. He considered the unique way she had of reaching into him and bringing out something he didn't even know was there.

DAY-43

LAURA HADN'T SEEN KAYNE since the night she had spent in his arms. Olga had advised her early on that he wouldn't be home for supper again, and she had spent the day lounging lazily by the pool. She was on her way back inside when she unexpectedly ran into him on his way out, looking sharp in formal attire.

"Hi…" she shyly greeted him, her face bright with the happy surprise.

"Hey…" he smiled somewhat tenderly.

She lowered her gaze with modesty, and he pulled her to him, caressing her cheek with the back of his hand. Laura blushed and raised her eyes to his, looking both bashful and decadently sensual in a way that was entirely hers.

Her fingers lingered on his arms, and she looked down again, recognizing his black suit. She'd seen it on the first night he'd given her a glimpse of what was to come: from the party and the whips, to his protection and his kiss. Her face dropped.

"What's wrong?" Kayne softly asked, the slightest variation in her demeanor or shift in energy never going unnoticed.

Laura shook her head slowly. She didn't want to ask. She wasn't even sure she wanted to know.

"Laura, what's wrong," he inquired again, irritation quickly replacing concern.

"You're going to a party," she whispered.

He sighed. "Yes, I am."

She closed her eyes from the pain his response caused her, and she took a step back, turning her face away from him. After everything they'd just been through, the bond they forged with pain, blood, and tears, how could he do this to her? More excruciatingly, how could she be so naïve to think otherwise?

Kayne grabbed her arms, gently pulling her back against the wall by the front door. "Look at me," he commanded.

She shook her head, a single teardrop running down her exposed cheek.

"What am I going to do with you…" He watched her with a discouraged smile.

Still refusing to meet his gaze, Laura shrugged her shoulders.

He grabbed her chin, forcing eye contact. "Don't get jealous. It always ends badly when you do," he cautioned her. Then leaning in, he licked his lips, grinned, and walked out.

★ ★ ★

Laura spent all evening in her bed. Hours passed as she lay looking out the window. The moon was particularly bright, reminiscent of their night together. He had held her all night long, and Laura, who always froze in such intimate moments, had felt at home in his arms. Closing her eyes, she could still feel Kayne's embrace. With her head on the pillow, she stared at the bracelet he had given her, *From Your Monster*.

Was he, at this very moment, doing to another what he had just done to her in the dungeon? Was he laughing with Tanya in a dark corner, holding her by the waist? With the knife twisting in her heart, Laura understood he wasn't hers. And he never would be.

It was late at night when her door cracked open, letting in the light from the hallway. She closed her eyes, feigning sleep, as she heard him walk in and move about.

Kayne removed his clothes down to his boxers and climbed into bed by her side, wrapping his arm around her.

Laura remained very still, holding her breath as he leaned close.

"I know you're awake," he said, with a smirk on his face.

"I know," she responded in a subdued voice.

He sighed and pulled her even closer to him. "I didn't fuck anyone," he softly reassured her.

"More blow jobs, then?" she spat with bitterness, trying to ignore his comforting warmth, her mind stuck on the visuals of his past indiscretions.

Kayne flipped her on her back, pinning her down by the wrists. They stared at each other, her eyes filled with righteous indignation, his conveying exasperation.

What did she want from him? What did she expect? He'd kept to himself and stayed away from his usual vices. *For her.* Did she also expect him to openly rebuff the escort making rounds as he sat with his associates? Politely decline because of the lover he was supposed to dispose of? Show any sign of weakness, and it would be the last thing you do. Did she still not understand his world?

Her juvenile expectations aggravated him to no end. And yet, Kayne delighted in her jealousy and her desire to possess him. No woman had ever made such demands, holding him to such standards. Tanya had rejoiced in his debauchery, hunting prey along his side, eager to outperform and impress. His submissives accepted his terms without question, never demanding, never complaining. And there she was, Laura Spencer. Calling him by his name, digging into his deepest wounds, and though unable to resist him, still walking away when he'd crossed the line. His Laura. She wasn't made for his world. For this reason, he knew they could never be together. For this very same reason, he knew he would never want anyone as much as he wanted her.

"You really can't help it, can you…" He shook his head, his frustration at their impasse coming out spiteful. "What did you think would happen exactly…? That I would turn into Prince Charming overnight after a good fuck? Do you think I can just walk away from this life? What did you imagine…? We'd drive into the sunset? That I'd propose in Italy… or France? How fucking naïve are you?"

Laura's eyes widened, shocked by his gratuitous cruelty, then narrowed with burning intensity. "Fuck you."

Kayne softly chuckled, lowering his face and breathing down her neck.

"Get off me!" she barked, wiggling wildly under him. "Get off me!" she screamed again, fighting him off with all her strength.

He subdued her with ease, pulsing with animalistic excitement. "What am I going to do with you…" Kayne smirked at the helpless prey panting under his body, her face flushed and her lips moist. Pinning both her arms with one hand, he reached between her thighs with the other and bit his lower lip at finding her wet.

"Missed me?" he taunted her.

"I hate you," she breathed through clenched teeth.

He grinned with wickedness, moving his fingers around her wetness. "Do you…" He kept stroking her, watching her anger dissipate and transform, her head lolling back as she gave in to the pleasure he offered her. "That's what I thought."

Leaning in, he wolfishly whispered, "How long will you keep fighting me, Laura? Don't you know you're going to lose?" He slowly penetrated her with his middle finger. "Every. Time."

A soft cry escaped her lips. "Fuck you."

He smirked. "Not unless you beg…"

"Fuck you."

His brow shot up. He released her wrists and, with a sinful smirk, wrapped his hand around her throat and began applying pressure.

Laura's eyes snapped open with terror, and she reached for his arm with her newly freed hands. His hold tightened under her fingers, and though she struggled to breathe, she could feel her panic give way to an increasingly pleasant light-headedness. Kayne kept fingering her, rubbing her with the palm of his hand, and Laura gasped for air that never came. Only more pleasure, mind-numbing waves of an overwhelming tingling sensation. Her entire body was reduced to the sensitive spot he kept stroking and the muscles clamping uncontrollably around his finger. Her eyes rolled back, her whole body stiffening.

Sensing she was on the brink, Kayne let go of his grip. Her entire body convulsed in a sustained orgasm, and she gasped loudly as air rushed back into her. He lay back down by her side and, leaning lazily on his elbow, watched as she came down from her high.

"What the *fuck*?" Laura asked in a raspy voice, turning to him.

He kept staring at her, the corner of his lips quirking up. "Thought you might like that."

"You could have killed me," she softly reproached, defensively reaching for her throat.

Kayne half rolled his eyes, amused by her perceived affront, and languidly pulled her to him.

She didn't resist, breathing in his scent as her body molded to his. "Kayne…?"

Her voice reached him, so fragile and small, he wanted to pull her even closer, beyond any physical embrace. He could've split his ribs open to hide her within him, to hold and protect her, keeping her safe forevermore.

"Yes, Laura?" His voice, however, came out amused, even mockingly patient.

"Was she there?"

"Who?"

She didn't answer.

"Tanya?" he guessed and felt her body tense at the mention of the name.

"Yes."

He smiled behind her. But this time, he didn't want to toy with her emotions. Not while she lay so sweetly against his chest, her naked body rising with her soft breaths.

"I'm not fucking her," he gently reassured her. Then before she could twist his words, he added, "Nothing is going on between us."

"Okay…" she responded hesitantly, barely relieved.

Kayne turned her around to face him, trying to read into the pools of sadness that wearily returned his gaze. "What is it?" he asked her, caressing the side of her face with the tip of his index finger.

Laura shook her head.

"Tell me."

She took a beat longer, gathering courage. "I hate… that you bring her here." She closed her eyes, bracing herself for another vicious response.

Would he mock her for this too? Dismissing it as a childish tantrum over an ex?

He remained silent for a while, gazing at her. Kayne couldn't understand why she fixated on Tanya. She'd walked in on him with a woman in the dungeon and seen another perform oral sex on him barely two days ago. Yet it was Tanya she despised.

Another part of him, however, understood very well. He gently lifted her chin and nodded. With a tender smile, he leaned in and kissed her softly on the lips. "Okay. I won't bring her here anymore."

Laura exhaled with relief and impulsively pushed herself up, her lips meeting his with desperate passion, her whole body openly seeking his with urgency.

Kayne was taken aback by her ardor for a second but quickly recovered, opening his mouth to receive and guide her ravenous, swirling tongue.

He kissed her back and, sitting up on the mattress, helped her up on top of him. Never breaking the kiss, Laura lifted herself to straddle him, her hands combing through and pulling his hair, her nails digging into his shoulders.

He grabbed her wrists and, bringing them around her back, held them together.

"Fuck me... I beg you, Master," she panted on his lips, grinding against his growing erection.

Kayne fisted her hair, pulling her back and admiring her raw beauty, and gave her a lustful smile.

Laura resisted the pressure at her scalp, pushing forward to seek his lips with wanton desire. He'd let her mouth graze his but wouldn't allow contact and smirked at her growing frustration. She would rock her hips with renewed fervor, trying to find release however she could.

"You want it, baby girl?" He pulled on her hair even harder and heard her gasp, somewhere between a moan and a cry. "How bad do you want it?" He licked his lips, his stare voracious.

"Bad. I want it bad. Please, Master. Fuck me," she answered with no shame or modesty, her eyelids heavy with carnal desire.

Kayne grunted and, tilting his hips, placed himself at her opening. Still, he wouldn't penetrate her, sliding his middle finger down her behind and lingering at the entrance between her cheeks. He pulled back every time she brought her hips down to take him in, grinning at her cries of protest.

He slowly entered the tip of his finger, moving it in and out as he continued rubbing himself on her.

The intrusion was oddly pleasurable, and she met his movements, rocking against him in synch. Laura felt the length of his finger inside of her simultaneously as he penetrated her. It was overwhelming, feeling him inside of her in two separate orifices. Then his tongue invaded her with the same passion with which she'd kissed him, and she no longer knew where she ended, and he began. She moaned in his mouth, panting *fuck* over and over again.

Kayne struggled to resist his building orgasm from the first thrust. He pulled her head back again, hypnotized by the woman facing him. She was a far cry from the scared little girl he had brought to his house. He pulled her hair further down her back, exposing her delicate neck. Leaning in, he bit the hollow of soft skin above her shoulder. She cried out, in pain or pleasure; he wasn't sure anymore.

"Come for me, Laura."

She gasped, her cry long and loud, her body automatically responding to his command. Her Master. Her Monster. Her Man.

Kayne came in a growl and kept thrusting slowly afterward, still pulsating inside her. They stayed as one long after they had both settled. Laura kept straddling him, her back straight and her head held high. No one uttered a word. They remained as they were with their eyes locked on each other, a wicked smile on both their lips.

DAY-44

KAYNE FACED TANYA.

"Everything is set then?" he asked.

"Yes. In the black Lexus. Just like you said." She half rolled her eyes.

"*Where* in the black Lexus?" he insisted, his patience forced through gritted teeth.

She exhaled, just as aggravated. "I slid it in that little gap near the gear stick. Then I made a huge scene the next day about losing it," she added, somewhat proudly. "*If* he ever finds it, he'll just be happy to give me back my earring."

"Good. And these are all the names?" Kayne lifted the folded paper in his hands.

"Yes," she huffed impatiently. Then her energy shifted, her eyes gleaming with mischief. "I could come over tonight… I think he's meeting someone. I'd bet good money it's someone on the list. We could test my little tracker earrings. Have *supper* at Tiffany's?" She grinned at her own joke. "Besides, there's this adorable little blonde I just found…" She smiled wickedly. "Perhaps you could return the favor and test *her* for me before I present her to Dimitri?"

He considered her for a second. "Lucas will track him. No need to come over."

"Oh?" She sounded surprised, if not peeved, by his response.

"I'll come to you from now on."

"What?" she snapped. "Why?"

"Good night, Tanya." Kayne smirked and turned around.

"Is it because of her? That new whore of yours?" she accused, her eyes ablaze.

She got the reaction she wanted, the hooks in her words stopping him in his tracks. "It is!" She let out a sardonic chuckle.

Kayne hesitated at the door. He had nothing to gain by taking her bait. And yet, such was the power the scarlet siren held over him. Regardless of the countless times he'd beat her at her own game, Kayne remained unable to turn down the lure of another round. He walked back to her and, leaning in, answered with a seductive smile, "Have to keep the vultures away from the little bird."

Tanya laughed. "Then *you* should stay away."

She then raised her eyes to his, her entire being pulsating with sexual energy. "You and me. We're the same. The same poison runs through our veins. Do you really think that scared little puppy can survive you? Can even begin to understand you?" she paused, moving back to face him. "Why play the fool in love when we both know you'll just break her, leave her, and come back to me. You always do," she added with a defiant smile.

"Do I? Or are you just always there, waiting with open arms. You don't know shit, Tanya."

His pointed words hit their mark, bruising her where it hurt the most: her pride. "I know that when you'll finally get bored of playing house with that woman-child and come to your senses, I won't be… what was it? Oh yes, *waiting with open arms*." She shook her head, mimicking playful disapproval. "Is it worth it? Is it really worth throwing away your only friend?"

Kayne brought his hand to her neck, his thumb turning her face to his. "*Friend*? We're not friends," he gave her the most devilish smile.

Tanya smirked in response, her breathing ragged with arousal. "Do you really think that yelping little puppy could ever satisfy you? Even now, you still can't help it. It's me you want. I can read you, Kayne. Do you forget how well I know you? I can read through your every move, your every stare and smile. I know when you want to hurt me. I know when you want to fuck me. I know when it's both at the same time. Like now..." She held his stare, dripping with sensual promise. It was her favorite game, pulling out his inner beast and turning his chaos into lust.

She waited until she felt his animalistic urges rise and then continued, choosing each word carefully. "You used to be so fun. Is that why you were being such a *good boy* at the party yesterday, to please that toothless little puppy? Kayne, how could you allow your own *Pet* to keep *you* on such a short leash?" she added with the perfect sprinkle of disdain.

He knew she willfully provoked him. He knew her little games all too well. But they worked nonetheless, and he slowly exhaled, flaring his nostrils. Kayne wanted to choke the life out of her, fuck her senseless, and wipe that smirk off her face.

With one hand still on her neck, he grabbed her hip and pulled her to him, hunger mixing with his irritation. "It must sting, doesn't it? Knowing that I prefer that *little puppy* to you? Tell me, Tanya... do you still think of me whenever Dimitri whores you around? Still wish it was me every time you feel the touch of a man? When was the last time you came...? Was I on your mind? And you think you punish *me* by holding out?" He chuckled. "Is that why you're being such a cunt? Because she's getting hers, and you can't?"

Tanya closed her eyes and remained very still, only her loud breathing betraying her emotions.

Two can play that little game, he thought; she should have known he was better at it. He let her go and turned around, heading for the exit.

"Since she's so fucking great. Have *her* fuck Maxwell for you then!" she screamed behind him, hot rage burning in her feline eyes.

He was already at the door and slowly turned his head back. His expression grave, he nodded only once, acknowledging the alliance that had just crumbled.

Kayne and Tanya stared defiantly at one another, willing to meet in a battle neither truly wanted and neither would back out of.

DAY-50

KAYNE HAD SPENT THE rest of the week with rage boiling under the surface, snapping even at Olga a few times, then reaching gently for her elbow with an apologetic smile. He'd tried avoiding Laura altogether, knowing he would only worsen things. And though unfair and vindictive, he couldn't help resenting her for the unraveling of his relationship with Tanya.

He needed Tanya. She was an invaluable ally: loyal, fearless, and entirely without scruples. He'd expected some backlash but never the speed at which things degenerated. Walking into Tanya's room, he could not have imagined that this uneventful meeting would spell out their end.

With Maxwell seeming on the move, the timing could not have been worse to lose his cunning accomplice. Kayne seethed every time he thought about it.

It was on his mind the first time he had run into Laura, and he'd coolly nodded her way, his expression impassive. He could tell how it hurt her; her eyes widened, and her smile froze, incredulous, as he walked past. After that, she'd also given him the cold shoulder, returning his icy indifference the few times they'd crossed paths. He'd berated himself; he was alienating the one person he'd pushed Tanya, and her resources, away for.

He received a call that evening from Natasha Drugova. She was hosting a brunch in a few days and wished to personally extend the invitation to Laura. He smiled inwardly, feeling somewhat proud at how easily she had won over the underworld's First Lady. Tanya was wrong, he thought. There was way more to Laura Spencer than meets the eye. Never underestimate a survivor.

DAY-53

OLGA HAD ADVISED LAURA the previous evening that Master Kayne had requested she meets him in the living room at nine in the morning, dressed and ready.

She'd considered missing the rendezvous and had delved into elaborate fantasies about what would ensue, from the exciting to the scary, to the downright heartbreaking. Kayne Malkin was a riddle, an intoxicating game of the highest stakes. The losses were devastating, the rewards core-shattering. The rules were unknown, ever-changing, and always favored the house. And yet, you played. All you wanted was to keep playing, forever and ever, on the merry-go-round.

Laura's heart tightened, reminiscing how things had been barely seventy-two hours ago. His warm chest and strong arms wrapped around her. She'd woken up late that morning, elated at feeling him behind her still. She'd turned around, admiring her sleeping Adonis. She could have watched him all day.

He'd lazily smirked at her, his eyes half closed, then abruptly grabbed her, flipping her on her back. He was in one of his playful moods, and she had giggled under him, thrilled and terrified. She was happy then.

The next time she met him, he was entirely different, colder than ever. His indifference had cut deeper than any punishment he'd put her through. But she didn't cry. She didn't crumble. She could handle the burn. She'd been forged in fire.

Laura appeared in a white sleeveless silk shirt and beige linen pants, sexy nude stilettos peeping out the front. She felt feminine and elegant. Her walk confident, she approached him with cool eyes. "Morning."

He was leaning against the wall, in jeans and a white polo shirt with his hair tied back, and smirked upon seeing her. He didn't answer.

Laura held her head straight, meeting his gaze as he closed the distance between them. Kayne took her hand and, bringing it to his lips, left a soft kiss.

"Ready?" he asked with mischief in his eyes.

She would've expected anything from him, not this simple sweet gesture. Though she could still feel its imprint tingle on her skin, she calmly nodded.

Lucas met them outside, waving the SUV down while still on a call. Though he hung up aggravated, he greeted them with a radiant smile as he got behind the wheel. Kayne helped Laura into the car and then got comfortable beside her, his eyes unabashedly devouring her. Sensing the weight of his desire, she purposely looked out the window, keeping her back straight and her hands crossed on her lap. And though desperate to know where they were going, Laura tried avoiding all forms of interaction, feeling her outrage dissipate with each contact. She could feel his eyes undressing her and, catching his wolfish grin in the rearview mirror, would look away, forcing her breathing even.

Lucas pulled into a mansion almost identical to the one where the party was hosted. Where was Kayne taking her, Laura wondered, tensing at the memories. Though her heart raced, she reached for the handle immediately after the vehicle immobilized and got off on her own. The moment Kayne came into view, she stepped forward, trying to walk ahead and maintain a distance.

Kayne watched her, amused by her bid for independence. He wanted to kiss and spank her at the same time. His Laura. He wanted her so much. In this instant, he didn't regret anything. Let Tanya bring all she had. He could handle her. And Maxwell too.

In one continuous movement, he reached for Laura's arm and brought her to him, his lips meeting hers with ferocious hunger. He felt her resistance, her open palms on his chest trying to push him away. He pulled her further in, deepening his kiss until she opened her mouth and let him in, her entire body giving in and melting into his.

She felt him pull away and opened her eyes. Catching his grin, she blushed. She then furrowed her brows and sighed, somewhat exasperated. And though her expression softened for a moment, she didn't say anything, turned around, and kept walking.

Kayne softly chuckled and, reaching for her hand, forced her to walk with him. "Natasha is hosting a brunch. She specifically asked that I bring you," he added with a proud grin.

Laura offered a restrained smile and continued to look straight ahead. Her heart beat frantically, feeling his hand holding hers and claiming her in one of the purest ways. In this instant, she could have sworn she was the happiest girl in the world. But that was the thing with monsters, wasn't it? Everything was amplified, the pain abominable, the high unmatched, the simplest gesture, thrusting you into unquantifiable bliss.

Once inside, she could notice how different the two mansions were. While the other projected lustful opulence, this was the good twin. Straight, sturdy, airy, and minimalist; she would not offer dark hallways for secret rendezvous with beautiful strangers.

The doorman led them up to the top terrace, where a crowd was already gathered. The men were on one side, the women giggling away on the other. Kayne and Laura exchanged a glance, and she finally gave him a genuine smile before they separated.

Mrs. Drugova stood up, waving Laura over to her table. She brought her affectionately in her arms and introduced her to the circle before pointing to the empty seat next to hers. "I saved it for you," she said invitingly.

Laura listened absentmindedly to the conversations, nodding her head with an empathetic smile when expected.

"We should go for a walk after lunch. It is such a lovely day." Natasha squeezed her hand.

"I'd love that," she responded brightly, turning to her.

They finished their meal, leaving the women in a heated conversation about the latest trends. Walking away, Mrs. Drugova shook her head with amused disapproval and then turned to Laura with a pleasant expression. "How have you been, my dear?"

Laura nodded, returning her warmth. "Thank you for inviting me, Mrs. Drugova."

"Of course. Please, call me Natasha. All my friends do. I'm glad to see you followed my advice. You look positively radiant."

Laura cocked her head to the side. "Oh... I don't know that I have. Natasha... can I speak candidly with you?" Laura stared her right in the eye, her face somber.

"You already do."

Laura smiled. She liked Natasha. She seemed larger than life, perceptive, calm, and in control. She was powerful and yet, delicate, refined but ruthless, and somehow still capable of kindness.

"Mr. Drugov... Dimitri... wants me dead." Laura's voice came out low and grave.

"Yes. So would Kayne if he wasn't infatuated with you. You're a loose end, Laura. The point of the matter is: it would just be simpler to be rid of you."

Laura's eyes grew round, shocked and hurt by the casualness with which Natasha discussed her life.

"Which is how I know you've taken my advice. Kayne's gone to great lengths for you. To ensure your safety, to ensure you'd stay with him. That your fate and body remain out of their reach. Dimitri came to me. He was very displeased. It's bad for business," she explained.

Kayne's gone to great lengths for you. Laura replayed the words in her mind and heard his voice again. *I'd fight for you. I'd kill for you. Go to war for you.* Laura closed her eyes, her heart swelling with emotion. Regardless of parties and other women, her Monster would stand by her side. "Natasha... may I ask you something... personal?"

She nodded.

"Last time. You were telling me about... being with Dimitri.... in a way that was tolerable for you? I don't think I can," she confessed, remembering her scorched heart from images of Kayne with other women.

"You don't have a choice. It's that simple. Most people lie to themselves. They know very well who their mate is. They've seen their darkness but blind themselves to it. They are then shocked, absolutely distraught when the troublesome reality they ignored catches up and stabs them in the back. That's why you never turn your back on the truth. You face the dagger. Perhaps you will block or dodge it, or perhaps not. Either way, it will be less likely to destroy you.

"You remind me of myself when I was younger. It's no way to live, Laura. You will suffer tremendously. My husband has whores. And that's all they'll ever be. There is only one Mrs. Drugova. He can use any woman of his choosing to his heart's delight. But at the drop of a pin, he would dispose of any of them at my behest.

"I've seen so many men betray their wives in hundreds of different ways and present the faithfulness they achieved through lack of options as the ultimate redeeming quality. Given the opportunity, these same men would be the first to follow temptation. What you have, my dear, is far more important. You have his loyalty.

"Just make sure you keep the one you want the furthest from him, closest to you."

Natasha imparted to Laura what her life had taught her. She liked the girl and had leaned in Kayne's favor when her husband was still on the fence. Dimitri couldn't afford to alienate the both of them, so the girl remained with Kayne. Natasha could see herself looking into Laura's eyes, reminiscing about the dreamy, kind girl she had once been. All the good values her parents had dutifully imparted to her were of no help in the world she was thrust into. Just like she did decades ago, Laura would have to destroy this version of herself, thought Natasha, before life did it for her. *Kill your weaker self.* It was the surest way to rise from your ashes.

Laura was deep in thought. Could she ever become this way? The image of another woman touching Kayne sickened her. A part of her envied Natasha; using pragmatism in the face of a seemingly impossible situation, she managed to come out on top. *Keep Kayne's whores around?* They wouldn't survive the day. She'd gladly ship them back to whatever hell they came from. She remembered when she'd seen them as victims not too long ago. Her heart had gone out to the poor souls she'd seen at the party. Kayne was the Monster then, an abuser of the innocent and helpless. She wondered what changed. The answer came back quickly, resonating deeply within her. It was just a word, a mere preposition, but it had changed everything. He went from the Monster to *Her* Monster.

Natasha pulled her out of her thoughts, gently squeezing her arm. A woman anxiously waved her down from the terrace, pointing at an empty silver tray. "If you'll excuse me, dear, there must be an appetizer crisis, given her state of panic…" she said with a grin and left her companion to her introspection.

Laura remained by herself for a while, processing everything. The difference was that Natasha had a choice and had willingly picked this life. Laura didn't have the luxury to hold on to her values and walk away from Kayne. She would remain his prisoner, willing or not. Bitterly, she realized that no matter what path of action she'd settle on, no matter how hard she'd resist—should he try, she would end up in his arms, drained and docile, somewhere in an abyss of pleasure and pain.

"Morning!" A singsong, gratingly familiar voice snuck up behind her.

Laura snapped around. "What are you doing here?"

"Natasha invited me, *Silly*," Tanya responded with condescending sweetness and a saccharine smile on her face.

Keep your friends close… Laura quoted *The Godfather* in her mind and couldn't help admiring Natasha even more. She shook her head, her lips quirking up.

Tanya lifted a brow in mild surprise at Laura's composure but shook it off instantly. "I saw you talking with her earlier. Don't you just love her?"

Laura didn't respond. She barely dared to move for a second, feeling as though she was walking into a trap. She considered her opponent and accounted for her disadvantage, but she stood her ground and raised her chin. "I do."

"Well, she really likes you," Tanya added in a convivial tone. "I know she does, she told me."

"Did she now…" Laura forced her voice even.

"Of course. We're quite close, actually. She talks about you. *A lot.*" She smiled, her expression carefree.

"Cool," Laura said nonchalantly though her heart raced. "Well… she never mentioned you. In any case, *Kayne* is waiting for me," she excused herself. "See you around," she threw back with forced casualness.

She couldn't repress her smile as she turned her back to Tanya. She'd caught the flash of anger that had crossed the redhead's face and knew she had hit the mark.

Tanya held her arm. "Wait… Listen… I know we got off on the wrong foot. I guess… I just wanted to apologize… I don't want you to hate me." She looked her in the eye and seemed sincere.

"Okay," Laura conceded though suspicious, trying to cut the conversation short.

"I just… I would like it if we got along." Tanya offered her a tentative smile.

Laura lifted her brows in response. Even she wasn't that naïve.

"For Kayne," Tanya explained, picking up the weapon Laura unsheathed. "I care about him a lot. I mean, we've been through *so much* together. And he cares about you… so…" She half-shrugged her shoulders with a pleasant smile.

This was a woman's war. And Laura, already seething with jealousy, cursed herself for playing so easily into the fiery seductress' hand.

"I don't think he's ever cared about anyone like he does about you." Tanya's eyes darkened for an instant, but her composure quickly returned, as it always did. "Honestly, I'm happy for him. Kayne and me… we were something else." She shook her head, a devilish grin on her face. "But you two go well together. You obviously love him very much."

Laura wanted to skin her alive. Cocking her head to the side, she offered her a thin-lipped smile, then turned around, ready to walk away.

"I mean… that you can just forgive him like that. I don't think *I* could have…" Tanya added, smirking at Laura's back.

Laura instantly felt it in her chest. This was the moment, her last chance to walk away somewhat unscathed. What ace did Tanya hold up her sleeve, dangling it like a sword over her head? Had he slept with her? Kayne swore nothing was going on. More women at parties, then? What else could it be?

She stayed; she always did. She would open Pandora's box yet again. Laura steadied herself, covering her heart with stone, and waited. She crossed her arms, her hostility bleeding through her feigned boredom.

"I mean… your own *brother*." Tanya shook her head with disbelief, her whole demeanor theatrical.

"*What?* What are you talking about?" Laura's heart pounded furiously in her chest, sensing the imminent danger, far, far too late.

"I mean… when I saw the pictures… with his head blown off? To know *Kayne* did this… How could you even look at him? Weren't you, like, very close with your brother too? Peter? Was that his name?" she asked, her brows furrowing. "He had it coming, mind you… Anyway, guess love does conquer all, huh?" She sneered, victorious.

Laura understood then just how fatal her miscalculation was. She never stood a chance. She had already lost the moment she'd decided to face the scarlet siren. She stared at her and felt strangely calm, like she was leaving her body, rising above, far above everything. Tanya was saying it all to hurt her, just to hurt her… And yet, she knew it to be the truth. Hadn't she known it all along? Hadn't her heart instinctively understood the grim outcome? The timing was too coincidental, the suicide too convenient… Hadn't she known deep down inside that the man she had sent to her brother had caused his death?

She left Tanya and her triumph without saying a word. She focused on breathing, fearing her shaky legs would give out any moment. Her face drained of color, she stumbled forward in the blur of sunshine and greenery, walking past everyone on the terrace to the driveway. Lucas was leaning against the car, bathing in the sun with his face turned up and a cigarette in his mouth.

"Lucas… Lucas… take me home."

"Are you okay, Miss Spencer? Should I get Mr. Malkin?" He seemed concerned.

"No!" she replied instantly. "Please… please, Lucas… take me home," she pleaded, shivering in the sun, and climbed in the car before the answer.

Lucas hesitated for a second. Though he took his instructions directly from Kayne, he could sense the urgency in Laura's demeanor and acquiesced. The entire drive, his eyes reverted to the rearview mirror, worried by the reflection he saw. She had never looked like this. Not even on the night they had fetched her from the bar.

Laura walked into the house with deadened eyes and a heavy step, ignoring Olga on her way to the bedroom. It was the calm before the storm. The perfect storm brewing in her blood, poisoning every cell, membrane, and nerve in her body. She paced in circles, suffocating. She wanted to pull her hair out, to find a way, any way, to get the venom out.

In the kitchen, Olga heard a chilling scream echo throughout the house. It didn't sound human. She was drying the dishes and felt a shiver run down her spine, dropping the plate she held. Then she heard glass shattering and furniture breaking. Panicked, she rushed to Miss Spencer's bedroom.

Everything was destroyed. Laura stood in the middle of the mayhem, holding the foot of a broken chair with a demented gleam in her eye. She screamed at Olga to leave and threw the wooden piece in her direction. The worried housekeeper rushed out of the room, picked up the phone, and reached the head of security.

* * *

Lucas was already parking the car back at the Drugov mansion when he received Olga's frantic call. He went inside and approached Kayne discreetly. "Sir. There's a problem at the house."

Kayne turned his head, his eyes instantly darkening in response.

"It's Miss Spencer. She wasn't feeling well. She asked me to bring her back—"

"*What*," Kayne hissed, barely controlling his temper.

"She didn't look well, Sir. I thought it was wiser to bring her back straight away. I thought you'd approve."

"And what's the problem now?"

"I'm not really sure. Olga called in panic. Said Miss Spencer had gone... mad... she apparently destroyed her room."

Kayne rushed behind the wheel with Lucas in the passenger seat. He was livid. It seemed no one had any idea what triggered Laura's meltdown. Grinding his teeth and breaking every speed limit, Kayne screeched the car to a complete stop before walking in and slamming the door open.

The house was quiet. Olga was sitting on the tip of the couch, nervously twisting the towel she had been using to dry the dishes.

"Where is she?" Kayne asked.

"Still in her room.... She's quiet now."

He nodded, his eyes ablaze, and with determined steps, he went to her bedroom. It was completely trashed. There was broken glass everywhere, the furniture either turned over or in pieces, but no Laura in sight.

His gaze turned to the closed bathroom door. He tried the handle. "Laura. Open the door."

Nothing.

"Laura. Open this fucking door before I do it for you," he threatened, his façade of coolness long gone.

Nothing.

A sadistic smile crossed his lips, and he kicked the door in.

Laura lay unconscious in the bathtub, the water surrounding her an unwholesome tint.

His eyes widened, his anger evaporating instantly. He was at her side within seconds, reaching for her wrist as he covered the gash with his hand, blood seeping through his fingers.

"Lucas! Get Iman! Now!" he shouted. He picked up the limp body and laid Laura carefully on the bed. Then he removed his shirt, bandaging the wound as best as possible.

"Laura! What the fuck!" he screamed to himself, all too aware his words couldn't reach her. He understood that, at this moment, he had no control: over her, over himself, over anything. For the first time in his life, Kayne Malkin felt the stab of powerlessness.

He paced around like a madman waiting for Iman's arrival. Iman, a slim brunette with olive skin, was in her late thirties. She had been a surgeon back in the Middle East. Like her father before her, she was fascinated with medicine and had felt a calling to save lives, regardless of what God they bowed to. But that was until she saw her world come crashing down, her entire family annihilated before her eyes. Iman, whose name meant "faith" in her mother tongue, understood that day there was no greater good. Or God. Only monsters fighting for power. She left her country, her life, and her memories.

Upon arriving in Quebec, she worked as a cleaning lady at a hotel downtown, pretending not to speak French or English. Shutting herself off from the world had been cathartic. Then as fate would have it, she walked in on Lucas one night, bleeding from a gunshot. Without saying a word, she had removed the bullet and stitched him back together. She'd been with the Organization ever since. Only a scar on the left side of her face kept her linked to the hopeful hazel-eyed beauty she had once been. Iman now accepted the world for what it was and who populated it; she would at least decide which monsters got her help.

DAY-55

IT HAD BEEN TWO days. Iman had assured Kayne the girl would live. She had given him pills and advised him to let her get as much rest as possible. She returned daily to check up on her.

Kayne had not left Laura's side. For two days and two nights, he'd kept watch from the La-Z-Boy he had dragged to the side of her bed.

He'd wiped the sweat off her forehead and dabbed wet washcloths on her cracking lips. He'd heard her cry in her sleep, uttering his name as she tossed and turned, and he'd cringed, understanding he was the Monster in her nightmares.

He couldn't know Laura hopelessly called for him, lost in a foggy labyrinth. Where was her Monster, now that she needed him more than ever? Laura stumbled blindly into the mist.

DAY-56

LAURA'S EYES OPENED TO the setting sun. Her hollow stare landed on Kayne, and she slowly turned away, staring out the window. "You should have left me."

He immediately put the laptop away and stood up. "Laura… why? You *promised*," he asked, approaching her, his voice raw with emotion.

An embittered snort escaped her lips. "And you promised you wouldn't kill Peter. Guess we're both liars."

"*What?*" he snapped, both enraged and incredulous.

She stared at him silently, with nothing but boundless grief inhabiting her haunting grey eyes. They contained no more light, no more flame, no aggression behind the blame.

"What the fuck are you talking about?" he asked again, his voice gruff.

"You shot him."

Kayne slowly exhaled. "And where did you get that piece of information?"

"*Tanya*," she answered with a spiteful smile.

"Are you fucking kidding me? And that's it? You just took her word for it? A goddamn whore… who hates you."

"But *it is* the truth…" Laura remained calm, lifting jaded eyes to his.

"It's not. I had given you my word," he responded, a flicker of hurt flashing in his scornful look.

"Right... Mr. Honesty incarnate," she derided. "So you just *happened* to find him dead from an overdose... the *moment* I sent you to him... and I suppose he shot himself afterward?"

"No," he conceded, his expression unreadable.

Laura closed her eyes, bracing herself for the last missing piece of the puzzle, both dreading and relieved at finally laying her brother to rest.

"He was alive. But I didn't kill him. I waited for him in his apartment. He wasn't that surprised to see me. I explained the situation to him... It was you or him, Laura. Dimitri had given me another week that night at the party. He wanted to interrogate you right then. But he gave me another week. I offered Peter the drugs, the choice was his. I would have let him walk, but he understood what that meant for you. I only shot him after. *With* his prior knowledge. For Dimitri's benefit. He was already gone."

"You used me as a pawn in making my brother take his own life. And you think that's a good thing. Even when you try... you're just a monster." Laura didn't know if she meant those hurtful words. She just felt the need to hurt him, to bring him into her pain and hold him prisoner, just as he'd done to her.

"You should have left me. Let me go, Kayne... or let me die," she pleaded, all malice gone.

He remained quiet, taking in her words. In the oppressing silence that followed, he turned around and left her room.

DAY-58

KAYNE HAD GONE TO Dimitri, requesting approval to deal with Tanya as he saw fit. Dimitri had listened quietly, his face dripping venom. His official favorite, on whom he'd bestowed status and privilege, had publicly humiliated him. She'd betrayed a confidence shared on a pillow and revealed that information to the very loose end he already wanted to be rid of. What sealed Tanya's fate, however, was the reason for her betrayal. Had it been over Dimitri himself, her jealousy would have been severely reprimanded but more likely forgiven. It was over another man.

The old patriarch was well aware of her ongoing infatuation with his subordinate. At times, he'd even caught himself resenting his former protégé over the unacknowledged slight. He'd openly shared her in retaliation, to leave no doubt as to his absolute control over her. Dimitri enjoyed nothing more than displaying his power over his subjects: whether by sharing women he'd claimed, shaming soldiers that failed, or torturing enemies that fell.

Only Natasha had ever been able to keep him in check, her eyes piercing into his soul. She'd understood him. And she'd faced him as would a lion tamer, never showing her back. Not once had she exposed her underbelly in the decades they've shared a life. And though she read him like a book, she'd remained a mystery to him.

She'd once again sided with Kayne, irking him furthermore, though he suspected personal biases had come into play. All this commotion over an outsider Kayne refused to let go of, thought Dimitri, and seethed. He still remembered the many nights spent counseling a distraught Lev over Kayne's mother. *Another outsider.* The Malkin men picked the worst women, he condemned with irritation.

His bruised ego still reeling, Dimitri had given Kayne his consent. He'd even bedded the scarlet vixen afterward without giving her wind of any trouble ahead.

* * *

Tanya Malone. Kayne reminisced about their first encounter. A party, very similar to the one he had taken Laura to. Tanya, however, was all smiles, clearly in her element. She had come willingly, unclaimed, and actively looking. He had spotted her amidst a circle of admirers, her demeanor closer to Scarlett O'Hara at the fancy picnic than a woman surrounded by predators, criminals, and psychopaths.

She looked magnificent, dressed in a royal blue gown with crystal embellishments. Tilting her head back in a burst of perfectly choreographed laughter, she flirted with the men of power. Tanya Malone was no prey; she baited solicitors and would only go to the highest bidder.

He had crept up behind her and, wrapping his arm around her, pulled her to him. He'd left his hand on her stomach, and leaning in, he'd whispered in a silky voice, "I can play, or I can fight… whichever you prefer."

She'd turned her face back, coquettish and daring. "Aren't they the same?"

"Only to the winner."

Her eyes bore into his as if recognizing her kin. Her smile devilish, she nodded; the challenge had been accepted.

Kayne shook his head, remembering their torrid affair, their toxic journey to its bitter end. Tanya had brought out the worst in him, perhaps had even loved him because of it. She'd been the first person to ever tell him. His father had loved him his own way, dedicating his time and dispensing hard-learned lessons. Olga, though unconditionally devoted, had always maintained a respectful distance. Tanya was the only person to ever look him in the eye and unapologetically profess her love.

He remembered his disappointment, the moment so anticlimactic. He had felt nothing. He hadn't wanted her love and didn't know what to do with it. When she'd finally bowed in defeat, he'd only felt contempt.

He wondered if she had ever meant it. A woman like Tanya couldn't love, he thought, though she could feel. The only thing Tanya ever loved was power, even when used against her. A subdued grin crossed his face, his fondness, if not repressed admiration, ever-present for the fiery seductress.

With his head back, he sat on a loveseat in a small private living room when he heard her heels clicking toward him. Kayne opened his eyes to find her in a fancy green cocktail dress, her silky curls tied in a high ponytail. Regardless of the occasion, Tanya would always be red-carpet-ready. She sat in the adjacent chair and, with a guarded smile, studied his features.

"I told you you'd come back to me," she joked half-heartedly, testing her audience.

Kayne gave her a crestfallen smile. "You know why I'm here."

Her eyes glittered with bitter understanding. "Little puppy couldn't handle the truth?"

His face weary, he leaned on his elbows. "What did you think would happen, Tanya?"

She chuckled humorlessly. She had expected retaliation from Kayne. She'd imagined him storming in with fire in his eyes, his body lashing at her. She would have gladly welcomed it. His grave attitude, however, deeply unnerved her, and her perfectly manicured mask cracked at last.

"That you'd wake up and find your way back to me?" She offered a heartbroken smile. "I just… never truly believed we were over. The fights, the separation… it just always felt like it was part of the game. All the others… They were just *pawns* in our game. *Our* sick and twisted game. I was there, Kayne. You loved *every second* of it. We could have been King and Queen of the underworld. How could you not see it?" she asked, both hurt and reproachful.

He bobbed his head in understanding. With a somber face, he reached for her knee and gently brushed his thumb against her skin.

Kayne had never been delicate with her. Never had he shown her tenderness, concern, or compassion. She understood then, from his sweet caress and the truce he offered her so freely, that the battle was over. She closed her eyes and felt a shiver run down her spine. When she reopened them, there was no trace of malice or wicked playfulness. For the first time in his life, Kayne faced the unguarded, uncensored Tanya Malone.

"Dimitri gave you the okay?" she asked, her voice low though unwavering.

He nodded.

She inhaled deeply. "Did it come from him? … Or you?"

"Me," Kayne admitted, holding her gaze.

She snorted bitterly. "Lil' pup has bite…"

A half-smirk crossed his lips. "Was it worth it? Was it worth throwing away your only friend?" he quoted back her words.

She grinned under heavy eyes, playing along one last time. "Friend? We're not friends."

They stared at each other in silence, subdued smiles mirroring one another.

"How do you want it?"

She took a deep breath. "With your hands on my body."

He nodded solemnly and got off the couch. He made his way to her and brushed her cheek with the back of his fingers.

Tanya looked up at him. "I never stopped loving you. Even now..." her voice cracked, "I still love you."

Kayne nodded again, his eyes burning with restrained emotion. He knelt in between her legs and, with their body itching closer, wrapped both his hands around her little neck.

She closed her eyes and raised her chin, maintaining her body as still as possible.

Kayne could feel her heart beating frantically and felt his own twist and tighten in its guarded fortress. It didn't stop him. He'd learned long ago to live with the dreaded feeling. As a child, he'd called it *Monster fuel*.

Like his father before him, Kayne kept applying pressure, extinguishing the light of the woman who had loved him and, ultimately, betrayed him.

DAY-61

KAYNE STOOD IN THE doorway of the solarium, watching Laura. Lying back on the couch, she was looking out the window, her bandaged arm resting lifelessly in her lap. He walked in slowly and took the seat facing her.

Laura turned a gaunt face toward him. "What do you want?"

His expression somber, he pulled out a small jewelry box and set it on the table before her.

Her eyes followed his movements, lingering on the velvety blue case before returning to his, silently awaiting the explanation.

"You asked me to let you go. You know that's impossible. That's the best I can do." His eyes bore into hers. He then got up and left the room with no other words.

Laura observed the box for a long time before her fingers finally reached for it. It held an exquisite engagement ring; an oval sapphire stood on a platinum band surrounded by a thin layer of diamonds.

She remembered the modest yellow-gold pear-shaped diamond Eric had picked for her. How different the two rings were, how different, the men. Eric, who wanted to offer her the world on a platter, had never really known her. She'd gotten a sense of it in the yellow gold he'd opted for, oblivious to her modest yet exclusively white gold jewelry. It was also often apparent when smitten, he would gush over her, bestowing on her flattering traits she did not possess. Not once had she corrected him. She liked the Laura he saw and had worked tirelessly to maintain the illusion. She had held his ring with tenderness, aware of all the extra shifts and sacrifices that had gone into acquiring it.

Then her eyes reverted to Kayne's ring. His was its complete opposite; elegant, simple, and chic, almost off-putting in its cool perfection. It was selected by a man who clearly knew her taste. A man who'd proven again and again just how deep his knowledge of her truly went.

With a tightening in her chest, Laura realized that the only man that had ever loved her had fallen for an illusion. The one that had seen past it, right down to her core, would never give her his heart. Kayne's ring, unlike Eric's, didn't come with promises of happy memories and hopes for a family. His was a calculated offer, albeit a generous one. It was a consolation prize for the life he took from her, *the best he could do*.

Kayne offered her lifelong protection, permanently removing the target on her back. She'd understood from his wording that it was all it was meant to be. She spent the afternoon staring down the open jewelry case in her hands. Within it, Laura saw reflected her most repressed desires involving the man linked to her brother's death.

★ ★ ★

Laura met Kayne for supper in drab attire, wearing no makeup to conceal the dark circles under her eyes and no ring on her finger.

Though he immediately noticed her bare hand, Kayne didn't say anything. He watched as she sat down, holding his stare and silence, and served herself.

"Where's your ring?" he coolly inquired.

"In my room... Didn't really match my outfit," she added, offering a thin-lipped smile. What could she tell him? It burned every time she tried putting it on, her heart yearning for his love, her thoughts crucifying her for it.

Kayne smirked, threat creeping under his calm. "Go get it."

"Why? Why should I wear it? What do you care?" she asked with more intensity than she wanted to show him.

"I'm baffled as to why you think you have a say in the matter, Laura. Did you somehow think that this was a *proposal*?"

She feigned a gasp, childlike petulance masking her pain. "But it was oh-so-romantic!"

His lips quirked up under serious eyes. He got up and went to her in slow, measured moves, towering over her chair. "As of this moment, I will expect you to wear your ring at all times. Tomorrow you will meet with Natasha. She will help with the preparations. In two weeks, we will be married."

Laura stood up to face him. "Why are you doing this? You don't want to marry me… Just to keep me safe?" she asked, her voice quieting to a murmur.

Kayne held her gaze, a shadow of tenderness softening his features.

Laura found comfort in his silence. Had the answer been so simple, he wouldn't have hesitated to deliver the heartbreaking truth, most likely in a monosyllabic response. Could their marriage ever be real, she wondered with a kindling of hope. But even in her split second of reverie, the Spencer curse awaited her, pulling her back to grim reality. "I could never… give you children," she reminded him in a whisper, her chin dipping away from him.

"No matter how close you get, never tell Natasha."

It would be the only answer she would get. She watched him leave, retreating to the upper level of the house.

He didn't want children or a real marriage, Laura thought with a twist in the gut. Their union would only be a means to an end, a sham to uphold for the benefit of others. No one was to know the sole Malkin heir had selected a barren bride. It would further jeopardize her precarious position with Dimitri, which was why Natasha should never find out.

His sole concern was to protect her from the Organization. Unlike her, she thought with a stab, he didn't have visions of the little boy that would never be; handsome and mischievous, with her eyes and his smile, running around the house and filling its halls with laughter.

★ ★ ★

Kayne lay awake in bed. In two weeks, he would marry Laura Spencer. Dimitri was not happy at all about his decision, questioning him relentlessly. *Keep her on the side. We can even settle her in Tanya's old quarters. But marry true blood, Kayne. Remember what happened with your father… Not all women are made for this life. Not all can handle it.* Dimitri had tried to reason with him.

Kayne had reiterated his unchanging position with no further clarification: He wanted to marry Laura Spencer—no one else. How could he explain to Dimitri that he would risk it all to keep her safe, the lengths he could go to, to keep her at his side?

Kayne would never let Laura go. Even if he trusted that she wouldn't go to the police—and he didn't, he knew Dimitri would never stand for it. He would have her taken out the moment she stepped off Kayne's residence and protection. And even if Dimitri agreed to stand down, law and order would remain a threat. Should things ever go south, she could be forced to testify, even against her will, unless she was his wife.

Laura Spencer was a liability. Mrs. Kayne Malkin, however, would be regarded as royalty. He'd thought it through. Marriage was the only freedom he could ever offer her. After recruiting Natasha to his cause, he'd even asked Dimitri to walk Laura down the aisle, ensuring a public display of support he would be forced to uphold.

It would just be a cover, he told himself and sighed. Fate did not seem to fortune the young lovers. The first time she'd surrendered to him, he'd returned with the morbid news. Kayne had played the long game, then, in order to regain her trust. He'd continually adjust to her body language, gauging when to push and when to hold back. He'd shown patience and persistence, dispensing small gestures as breadcrumbs to lead her back to him. With one deadly strike, Tanya Malone had smashed their fragile bubble to smithereens.

He'd seen the damage inflicted, and he'd made sure she knew he had no intention of exploiting her in any way. Her Monster would keep her safe, for better or worse.

DAY-75

LAURA LOOKED IN THE mirror, bathed in the rays of a rising sun. Her hair had grown in the past months and was styled, for the occasion, into soft waves flowing down her back. Her bangs now reached her chin, framing a slimmer face with defined cheekbones, her dramatic eye shadow enhancing her delicate features.

In true princess fashion, her wedding dress had a sweetheart neckline with straps that draped around the shoulders and crystal embellishments embroidered in the tulle skirt. She kept staring at her reflection, unable to find herself in the mysterious bride. Laura wanted to reach out beyond the mirror and embrace this melancholic princess. But she had been threatened by an unusually intimidating makeup artist not to cry; she hadn't.

She was now alone in her room and thought back to everything leading her to this day. Back to the very first night at the club, to the night he pinned her down on the couch… The night he made her ask for it… The night he dragged her to the dungeon covered in blood… then carried her to bed and avowed his fealty as would a knight to his queen… The night she told him about her sweet sixteen. The night he returned from Peter's. The day she broke her promise.

She had barely seen Kayne in the past two weeks. Lucas would drive her to meet with Natasha at the crack of dawn. The Organization's First Lady had taken over planning the young couple's wedding and barely looked to the bride-to-be for input. From the endless hours she wholeheartedly poured into it, Laura understood that Natasha fulfilled a maternal longing for the daughter she never had. Laura wondered about the cause. Had nature robbed her of her birthright as well? A choice made in inconsequential youth and regretted far too late? Or a compromise for love, requiring the lover to destroy the mother?

Laura was glad for Natasha. She doubted she would have survived the ordeal without her taking charge as she had: with an iron fist, and always, in a velvet glove. For the past two weeks, Laura would come home exhausted late at night. And though she only dreamed of her bed, she did not have the heart to let down an expectant Olga. They'd sit outside, and Laura would smoke a cigarette as Olga sipped her tea, making her recount in detail the programming of the day. She'd stay up way past her bedtime and wake the following day even more fatigued, only to go through it all over again.

Laura had begun wearing the ring following her supper with Kayne. She could feel its weight on her hand and, in turn, heaviness in her chest. So many hours had been spent contemplating it, trying to unlock its mystery. Could it possibly conceal, deep within the cool blue sapphire, a piece of Kayne Malkin's heart? But the ring remained silent, loyal to her one true Master.

Her one encounter with him leading up to the big day had been tense. He'd smiled at first upon noticing the ring on her hand, but things quickly turned sour when he informed her Dimitri would be walking her down the aisle. She'd pled with him, begged him even, for the man who wanted her dead not to be the one escorting her to the altar. But even that simple request was rejected in a tone that left no room for negotiation nor the slightest compassion.

The wedding ceremony would be held according to their tradition, Natasha had explained. Kayne and Laura would be betrothed at the Orthodox Church, where the rings would be exchanged. A crowning ceremony would follow. No vows would be made, no promises to uphold *until death do us part*. Marriage was a solemn commitment made before God, a union even the underworld was powerless to break.

The reception would be held at the Drugov residence, and a team had worked around the clock to prepare the premises. White lanterns and veils had been hung up on trees and statues, fairy lights draped between them. The fountains and water gardens were lit up, and white rose petals spread out on the walkways.

In the frantic days leading up to the big event, Laura had maintained her calm, feeling as though she had walked into a hazy fantasy where only she was aware of the illusion. Everyone else just wanted to play along. Natasha fussed over her. Olga had even shed a few tears when she had finally stepped out in her gown. Only she would not get caught in the spell.

Dimitri interrupted her musings, quietly closing the door behind him after entering the room. He opened his arms, pulling a reticent Laura into his embrace.

"Laura, you look stunning! Never has a bride looked so beautiful. Now don't go telling Natasha I said that." He winked playfully at her.

She smiled politely in response.

"What's the matter? You should be happy! Has anyone troubled you?" he asked with concern.

He seemed genuine at this moment, an involved father figure, but Laura remained guarded. "I'm fine. Thank you, Mr. Drugov."

"Dimitri. We've gone through that already," he corrected her. "Laura, my dear, if something is wrong, you must tell me."

"I feel so alone," she admitted, for lack of better words.

His expression changed, and he sounded sincere. "You have no family left, no friends present. But you're not alone. I was against this marriage, I know you know. You're no fool. It was nothing personal, my dear. Just call me a pessimistic old geezer." He smiled. "I'd rather be safe than sorry. Sometimes that means there are casualties. When Kayne came to me, asking for my blessing, I understood the repercussions of standing in his way. *Not a good business move.* You are not alone, Laura. Not when Kayne Malkin stands at your side."

Kayne Malkin at her side. Laura's heart swelled, an image of the Great White Wolf standing defensively over Aniska materializing in her mind.

"Natasha, too, stepped in," Dimitri went on. "She is tremendously fond of you. How you managed to earn her affection so easily is a feat in itself. Forty years later, and I'm still slaving away!" he chuckled.

"You have a new family now, Laura. And family is everything, especially to those who lost the one they were born into. Let go of the past. Leave Laura Spencer to her ghosts. There is a bright future for Mrs. Kayne Malkin."

Laura remained quiet for a moment, taking in his words and drinking in their temptation. The Scorsese quote came back to mind. To be taken *under the wing of a dragon*, how warm it would be. For once, not being the lone warrior facing the army, but instead, a cohort of dragons riding by her side. The comforting thought rocked her in a calming daze.

Staring into his eyes, she gave the faintest nod, a nascent smile on her lips. Laura looked in the mirror, and she understood she would never see the reflection of that person again. She felt a little pinch in her chest, an indistinct heartache. Laura Spencer shouted silently from the other side of the looking glass, trapped by the mysterious princess who had emerged and claimed her body.

Dimitri nodded back to her, satisfied with the mature stare that replaced the innocent sparkle. He folded the veil over her face, offered her his arm, and led her out of the room and into the first limousine in a black procession.

A BEDTIME STORY (BEAUTY MEETS THE BEAST)

* * *

Kayne looked dashing in a black suit, with Lucas as the best man at his side. He awaited his future bride at the church entrance. Laura's heart skipped a beat as she stepped off the black steel horse, taking the final steps to tie her fate to the Prince of Darkness. She felt a shiver run down her spine and looked at the crowded streets. Curious bystanders gathered nearby, smiling pleasantly at the grandiose ceremony. For the briefest of instants, she thought of breaking into a run, to just keep running and never look back. But even with her face turned away, she could feel his smoldering eyes fixed on her exercising their influence. They silently summoned her to him, their pull, magnetic, their power over her, absolute.

She climbed the few steps under his piercing gaze, her limbs being pulled forward as if by puppet strings. A priest met them and blessed the young couple. He recited a few prayers and then took the rings, exchanging them on their fingers three times in symbolic homage to the Holy Trinity. Laura went along as a passive participant, lost in a dream or nightmare; she could no longer tell.

They were each given a candle to light each other's paths in the hour of darkness. They were then led to the center of the church, representing their new journey from flawed fractions to a complete, perfect whole. Laura hung to Kayne's enveloping gaze and found solace in the flames dancing in his eyes, mirroring the ones burning within her.

The priest recited more prayers in Russian, and she felt her heart flutter when he joined her right hand to Kayne's. And when the crowns were placed on their heads, Laura sensed her inner transmutation nearing completion. Mrs. Kayne Malkin stood beside her king, proud and willing to rule with him whatever kingdom he offered.

They still hadn't exchanged a single word when instructed to drink wine from the common cup: a symbol to illustrate their commitment to sharing all of themselves, all burdens, and all treasures equally. Laura squeezed Kayne's hand, attempting a smile as they went around the sacramental table. He quickly looked her way, an indiscernible expression on his face, then faced forward again.

The final blessing was uttered, the crowns removed, and they headed back to the waiting limousine. They made their way in, holding hands and smiling emptily at the showers of rice and congratulations.

"Don't worry, Mrs. Malkin," Kayne told Laura in a deadened voice the moment they were inside. "I've arranged a separate room for you."

Her husband's first words cut through her like a knife. She recoiled from him and didn't look his way again. They spent the entire ride staring out the window with their backs to one another, in an oppressing silence neither acknowledged.

Kayne understood their wedding to be the furthest-possible scenario she could have ever dreamed of: forced to marry a deviant criminal who'd kidnapped her and orchestrated her brother's death. He felt a pang, knowing he'd even managed to betray a young Laura. A Laura he'd never met, who fantasized about Prince Charming and romantic happily ever afters; a young girl who should have never been introduced to his world.

He knew she deserved far more than he could ever offer her, far less than he would inflict upon her. In that isolated selfless impulse, he had vowed not to drag her down to his level of debauchery. He would not take what he manipulated her into offering willingly. Kayne resisted the urge to reach for her, to take her into his arms and kiss her with desperate passion until nothing was left of her.

★ ★ ★

Hundreds of guests cheerfully greeted the newlyweds that had just arrived in the gardens for the reception. Both offered plastic smiles to the sea of faces smothering them in unwanted embraces. Separated by the anonymous arms reaching out, they went their separate ways, neither looking for the other.

The celebrations began with an orchestra playing traditional Russian music. A beautiful singer offered a haunting rendition of "Oy da ne Vecher". It was a popular folk song, Olga explained to Laura, about a famous soldier who foresaw his own death in sleep. In a premonitory dream, he envisioned a dark omen, his horse going wild and then losing his head. That soldier, who had truly existed, was later decapitated in battle.

"What's the point of the story?" Laura asked.

Having had a few drinks, Olga shrugged her shoulders with a hearty chuckle, holding Laura affectionately.

Laura was enraptured by the melancholic song. She felt she'd known it all her life, somehow feeling the tragedy behind the lyrics without understanding a single word. What was the point of the story? Why the premonition if the future is non-negotiable? If not to alter it, to better prepare for it, then? Was she predestined for this life? Did any of her choices matter? Laura pondered. Did other paths exist that had she followed, would have saved her brother?

Olga pulled on Laura's arm; the couple was being called to the banquet. According to tradition, they had to down a shot of vodka and wash away its bitterness with a lingering kiss. Kayne awaited her, his eyes burning with intensity. Without a word, he handed her the glass and clinked his to it. They threw their heads back, casting the wedding guests into a collective frenzy. Blowing whistles and clapping their hands, families joyously cheered on the groom and bride, yelling out "Gorko", meaning *bitter* in Russian, to egg on the much-awaited first kiss.

His eyes smoldering, Kayne pulled her possessively to him. His mouth crushed hers, his tongue prying her lips open. And Laura's heart beat madly in her chest, her senses numbed and awakened simultaneously. Things were moving so fast. She barely had time to collect herself from the kiss that a second toast was already being given. Usually reserved for the parents, it was made to the Drugovs. Kayne then took Laura's hand and pulled her to the center of the illuminated garden, where they opened the dance floor under a setting sun.

They quietly stared at each other as the string quartet interpreted instrumental renditions of popular love songs. Oblivious to the world around them, they swayed in unison, their bodies shouting the truth their mouths were unable to speak.

Loud applause finally reached into their haze. They had not heard the music stop, still facing each other in complete silence. A live band had taken over, belting out the latest hits while inviting guests to the dance floor. With a solemn face, Kayne nodded to Laura and excused himself. His hand abandoned hers, and he disappeared into the crowd.

The moon had long reclaimed its throne. Some of the men had retreated to a private party. A few had remained at the reception with their pleasantly inebriated women and sugar-high children. They danced, they drank, and always, they laughed. Toddlers' cries and screams were heard under their parents' watchful, loving eyes. A chaotic bursting of life. It was uniquely alluring and contagious to all but Laura and Lucas, whom she found while trailing off on her own.

He was hanging far from the rest by the side of the house, smoking nonchalantly with a knee folded against the wall, when Laura approached him.

"Would you have an extra one of those?" she asked with a despondent smile, tilting her head toward the cigarette.

He smirked and pulled his pack out. With his thumb, he lifted one for her to grab.

"How are you holding up?" he asked in a kind tone, flicking his lighter and covering the flame as she bent over his cupped hands.

She shook her head with an indulgent smile, a gentle request to avoid her being the subject of conversation. There was something about Lucas that brought out honesty. Somehow, revealing your true self felt safe in the company of Lucas Belfort. And exposing her wounds was the last thing Laura wanted to do.

He chuckled. "Frankly, I think it was a beautiful wedding. Though you just might be the saddest-looking bride I've ever seen."

"You've been to many weddings?" she asked with honest curiosity.

"No," he conceded. And they both chuckled, the way children did at a silly joke.

"Were you ever in love, Lucas?" Laura asked, still watching ahead the celebrations raging on. The groom was long gone, the bride was nowhere to be seen, but no one asked. With good music, alcohol, and food, the feast would never end.

Lucas considered her for a moment. "Yes. I believe so."

"What happened?"

"Nothing. Nothing happened," he answered with a subdued smile.

She nodded. So he, too, understood the distinctive torture of unrequited love. "Kayne doesn't love me." Laura bowed her head, her feelings boiling to the surface despite her wishes.

Lucas lifted his brows, contemplating her statement. She appreciated the weight he gave to her confession. Lucas Belfort did not fall on easy and dishonest reassurance as most confidants when facing unpleasant truths. With every interaction, her fondness and respect for him grew. "Do you know Tanya?" she asked, staring into the distance.

He snorted. "Yeah… I knew her."

"I think he loves her." Laura felt a stab in her chest pronouncing the words but somehow felt immune to the pain.

Lucas's expression betrayed his surprise. "*Tanya?* I highly doubt that."

"I hate her."

"I could see why," he answered with good-humored sympathy. "But... you know... she's gone. Kayne took care of her."

"What do you mean?" In a second, he commanded her full attention.

"He didn't tell you, did he?" He shook his head with indulgent disapproval of his friend. "Yeah... you were still bedridden."

"He... killed her?" Laura reiterated, still processing the information. It was the third death her relationship with Kayne was linked to. The first had left her in despair and crippled with guilt; the second, horrified and dissociating. Facing the demise of her nemesis, however, Laura felt a vague sense of triumph, her victory over her rival overpowering whatever decent reaction she had expected of herself.

Lucas nodded, his gaze meeting Laura's.

"Because... of what she said to me?"

"Maybe you should ask your husband that, Mrs. Malkin," he grinned.

Her lips responded unconsciously to the label, spreading wide with pleasure. But Mr. Malkin was currently at a private party, partaking in perversion and depravity. Her eyes hardened. "How come you're not at the party with him?"

"Not really my scene." Lucas shrugged his shoulders. "I'm no angel," he quickly added, "That's just not my poison. The real question is, how come *you're* not with him?"

She shot him daggers for an answer.

He chuckled softly. "It's none of my business. But... if I were you, of all nights, I wouldn't want to spend my wedding night chatting it up with the head of security."

"The best man," she corrected.

Lucas cocked his head in a grateful nod to Laura's acknowledgment, charming and dignified as ever with the simple gesture. His expression then changed, his tone serious. "I think Kayne believes he is doing the right thing by you. By staying away. He is putting your interest ahead of his. Isn't that the purest form of love? Now if you disagree with his belief, you should go to him."

She considered his words. How could a being so good and wise flourish in Kayne's world? And yet, he seemed to fit seamlessly. Was that the key to their success: the two opposite forces complementing one another into a perfect whole? Lucas and Kayne, the Yin and the Yang.

"You know I can't go in there," Laura admitted sheepishly.

"You're *Mrs. Kayne Malkin*. Who would stop you?"

She nodded slowly, a sad smile on her face. She had no intent on following his advice. Her heart couldn't bear rejection. Or another punishment.

It was already past midnight when they parted ways. She withdrew to her room and sat on the couch in her wedding dress, watching the hypnotic fireplace. With an open bottle of red wine at her side, she drank alone, replaying the entire day. It all still felt so surreal. Moments reappeared in flashes, as if in a montage. Then came the memory of his kiss, slowing the entire universe to a halt. She could still taste his lips and feel the passion with which they crushed hers. She watched the flames, feeling the fire burning brighter within her with each sip. She would not spend her wedding night alone. Lucas was right. She would go to him, in hell if necessary, and bring him back to her.

Despite her frantic heart, Laura walked resolutely toward the forbidden section of the mansion.

The doormen eyed her apprehensively. "Mrs. Malkin. It's a private party," one of them stuttered uncomfortably.

"Step away."

"Mrs. Malkin, I'm really sorry about this. Our instructions are clear—"

"I need to speak with my husband. Move… or answer to him."

They looked at each other, disconcerted.

"Maybe we can get him for you?" the other offered, his uncertain tone betraying his weak stand.

"Move!" she raised her voice, her eyes cold as stone.

They stepped aside, each pulling open a door as she walked past them, her head held high. The party was held in one of the lower levels where a vast reception hall with many corridors led to smaller private rooms. The entire floor was lit with thousands of red candles spread throughout. Everyone was dressed in black, most wearing capes. Men and women, bonded in the same lustful opulence, swayed their bodies to Khachaturian's spectral masquerade waltz. All wore masks, some held in place with a stick, others secured with an elastic band.

It was very different from the party Kayne had brought her to. There was no established hierarchy, no organized sexual abuse and degradation. This was pure chaos, with men and women equally partaking in hedonistic decadence. A voluptuous blonde rode a middle-aged man on the floor who neighed wildly like a pony. A dominatrix dripped wax on the chest of blindfolded men and women strapped naked to a table. A brunette with cascading long hair was being showered with champagne, men in black capes leaning over her like vampires to drink it off her body.

Orgies broke out everywhere she turned, and masked faces looked her way, cackling at her horrified face. She thought she could handle it, but her head began to spin. Everywhere, masked faces. Everywhere, madness, and no Kayne to be found. With every step, her white dress separated the human black sea, and it gathered right back behind her like a drop of oil seeking itself. She stumbled forward, wanting to scream his name. Couldn't he sense her presence? *Kayne, come to me*, she silently prayed, leaning on a wall for support. She felt uncomfortably hot and light-headed, gasping for air that made itself scarce. She'd come all this way, crossed the River Styx, and paid the ferryman, only to land in a Kayne-less hell, her one true torment.

Just as she felt her knees giving out on her, she was pulled backward by a strong arm hooking around her waist. Rendered mute with panic, she wrestled vainly out of the firm hold.

"Laura. It's me."

His voice was hoarse, vibrating so close into her ear. In an instant, her whole body relaxed against his, air finally reaching her lungs. She could feel his heat radiating behind her. Everything was going to be okay. *Master was here*. She could finally see the shore and closed her eyes with relief, knowing she would reach it safely.

"What are you doing here?" Kayne's voice was calm and, though intense, did not threaten.

She had no words. At this moment, she even doubted she had a voice. Turning in his embrace, Laura was met by the mask of the Beast. A mask that revealed his true nature far more than his spellbinding features ever would. She was ready to face her beautiful Monster, not the beast she knew lurked underneath, and she covered her eyes with her hands in a childlike gesture.

Kayne exhaled slowly. He lifted his mask, letting it rest on the top of his head, and gently nudged her hands away.

His beautiful bride, in his cruel world. Tanya was right, he thought; she would not survive him. Maybe he needed someone like Tanya, who gladly accompanied him to parties, offered him women and watched with animalistic hunger as he subjugated them to his baser instincts. Tanya would've whipped a woman bloody at his single command. She tyrannized others with a delirious smile, avenging her own treatment at his hands.

Laura... his beautiful bride, his innocent girl. He had stolen her. She was only ever meant to be a job. But he'd taken her prisoner instead. From that very first night, he realized, Laura had changed the course of his life. He'd fought for her. He'd killed for her. When facing Dimitri, he'd understood he'd wage war for her. He wondered how she did it. The more he took from her, the more power she held over him. His little white lamb, who'd willingly penetrated the lions' den. *For him.* He would slaughter them all for her. He would paint the world red and lay its carcass at her feet.

She looked up at him and smiled feebly at finding the familiar face. Kayne took her hand and, without a word, led her away from his world of depravity.

They walked in silence. Even in the elevator, they quietly faced each other, the charged air around them a flicker away from combustion.

"Take me to your room," she whispered as they reached the third floor.

He remained quiet, assessing her for a moment, then slowly nodded. With a wolfish grin, he held the metal door open, inviting her to take the lead with his *ladies first* gesture. Her heart sunk remembering the previous times he'd done it: once leading her to an interrogation, the second time to his own version of the cage. This time was different, she reminded herself, trying to calm her frantic pulse.

She stepped into the hall, feeling his stare trickle down her nape. Once they'd reached the door, he stopped and turned to her, as if giving her a last opportunity to walk away. But Laura lifted resolute eyes to his in answer and landed on an amused yet tender smile.

Once in the room, she stopped in the middle, between the couch and the burning fireplace, and stood still as Kayne walked past her, heading straight to the bar. He poured two whiskeys and handed her one. With their eyes fixed on one another, they tipped their glasses without clinking and downed them in one shot.

Laura felt the alcohol burn her throat, liquid fire rushing through her veins. She set the empty glass down on a table nearby. Turning back to Kayne, she delicately placed her hands on his upper body, looking up to gauge his reaction. No help would be found there. Though his eyes tracked her every move, his expression remained inscrutable. With shaky fingers, she played with the buttons of his shirt. She could feel his chest rise and fall with the ragged breaths that tickled her neck, yet he remained phlegmatic. Her moves uncertain, she slowly pulled his jacket off his shoulders.

With a restrained smirk, Kayne patiently waited as she got to his belt, furrowing her brows as she struggled with the buckle. He stood still, charmed by her wonder and trembling fingers as she unbuttoned his trousers. She met his gaze, pulling his briefs down and over his growing erection. With a soft sensuality emanating from her, she lowered herself to the floor.

Engrossed in his overwhelming masculinity, Laura leaned in and, with luscious eyes meeting his, took him in her mouth. She wet the skin first, covering her teeth with her lips, and wrapped her hand around him, slowly taking his whole length.

A rough groan escaped his lips. He brought his hands down on her shoulders and closed his eyes, consumed in the moment. But it wouldn't take long for his nature to break the spell, forbidding him a pleasure he did not control. Kayne's hands suddenly wrapped around her wrists, pulling them apart and away from him.

Laura quickly looked up, inquisitive and anxious. But he gently pulled her to her feet, reassuring her with a sweet caress. His smile slowly turned predatory, and he circled around her with a voracious stare, once again reminding her of a tiger on the prowl.

"You know what you've married, Mrs. Malkin. Do you really want to play with monsters?"

"Only mine." She gently turned her head back to him.

His hands grabbed her hips, and he pulled her back against him. He placed a soft kiss on her bare shoulder and proceeded to unlace her gown. Once she was left in her undergarment, he scooped her up in his arms. "Let's play, then," he told her with a sinful grin, and carried her to bed.

Laura felt her stomach knot and her heart fluttering in her chest, trying to anticipate his next move. The eyes that fixed Kayne as he removed her corset and used her garter to tie her wrists above her head were not those of a loving bride. They belonged to fearful prey, carefully tracking their predator's movements.

Kayne smirked at Laura, at her nervousness and the desire he knew overpowered her apprehension. How he missed their old games. Tonight, lion and lamb would meet again. He removed his clothes and climbed by her side, returning her vulnerable stare with unabashed hunger.

His fingers glided on her soft skin. "So on edge…" He shook his head with sadistic pleasure. "Why do you keep doing this to yourself?" he asked, nibbling on her ear in a voice husky with carnal desire. His hand kept slipping downward, and he began applying pressure on her pulsating nerves. "Which is it, Laura? Do you fear me, hate me, or want me most?"

Her panting increased, and all her senses awakened at once, but she didn't answer. How could she be so naïve and envision him making sweet love to her on their wedding night? He had before. Why not again? But affection with Kayne was never freely offered. It only came as a remedy for the damages incurred.

She would get her bliss if she was willing to pay. She closed her eyes, understanding she always would be. No matter how high. No price was too great. She would not only accept the cost but also chase the dealer for more, regardless of the tears, fears, and pain that inevitably came with it.

"Tell me, Laura. Tell me which is it," he insisted in a warm whisper, his nose and lips tracing every line of her face.

"Each adds to the other," she confessed, finally meeting his gaze. In a perverse way, she thought, weren't they perfect for each other? Who else but her Monster could truly understand her broken soul, meet her in her madness, find her in the depth of her despair, and somehow alleviate her from it all?

"Don't you realize how easily I can crush you? Why do you come back to me?"

"Because you've seen my darkness and stayed. Sometimes, that's all you need. Someone who can understand your pain. Even if it is the Big Bad Wolf." Laura bore her all, releasing the monsters under her bed to the only one she knew could fight them off.

Kayne stared intently at her face, aware he was walking the secret path to the darkest recesses of Laura Spencer's soul. He continued playing with her, keeping the rhythm slow and steady.

Laura was nearing the edge, giving in to the unwholesome pleasure. The high was more potent than any drug, the euphoria more addictive. And she cried as her body shattered in a mind-numbing orgasm. But Kayne did not smirk as usual, when he'd make her come on his twisted terms.

His eyes, dark and intense, rested on her drained body. He kissed her with the hopeless passion of a cursed lover. Wordlessly, he willed her to understand what his guarded heart wouldn't allow him to betray. Kayne pulled and tugged at her, possessively manipulating her body to quench his thirst for her. With a guttural sound, he collapsed on top of her. He then pulled her close and stroked the side of her face, watching her eyes close serenely under his touch.

Laura then raised her hand, wanting to return the caress but clasped her fingers shut, reconsidering at the last second. "Do you not like it when I touch you?" she softly asked, lowering her gaze to his chest.

He sighed. "Of course I do."

"So why did you stop me... *earlier*... was I not... doing a good... *job*?"

He shook his head, sensing the hurt in her innocent question. "Because I'm a fool."

A sad smile formed on her lips. "You... killed... Tanya?"

With neither his features nor his voice betraying any emotion, Kayne provided his remorseless answer. "Yes."

"Why?" Laura asked in a whisper, imagining his response. *For you, because of you, because she hurt you, because... I love you.*

"She betrayed me."

Feeling foolish, the young bride closed her eyes with a bitter smile. "Did you love her?"

Kayne considered her question. Of all people, how could *she* think that? How to make her understand what he couldn't bring himself to admit? He waited for her to meet his gaze. "No, Laura. I didn't love her."

"She loved you," she replied, her face hardening at the plethora of poisonous memories associated with the fallen temptress.

"Love with no loyalty means nothing," Kayne automatically repeated his father's words.

Laura considered him. "Natasha knew about her... and Dimitri," she went on, "she befriended her. She told me... she... befriended her husband's mistresses." She looked up at him, pain twisting her features. "I could *never* do that."

Kayne kept watching her, sharing in her pain, knowing he was the cause of it, knowing he couldn't put an end to it. Once again, the path ahead of the young couple led to a dead-end. Dimitri had spoken to him at the party earlier. He'd promoted him; a wedding gift, he'd called it. Kayne was now to overlook all aspects of the operation and act as his primary counselor. He knew Dimitri too well to be honored. It was a test, a chance for him to prove his loyalty and that his marriage would not be a threat to his involvement with the Organization.

He could no longer benefit from being the lone wolf; he would now be directly responsible for all aspects of the trade, including the prostitution rings and sex trafficking. The implication was way beyond his participation in some morally questionable parties. What an ingenious way, Kayne thought with bitterness, to drive a rift in their fragile bond.

"I'm not Dimitri," Kayne tried to reassure her in a reductive answer.

"What does that mean? No mistresses? Because there *will* be parties and whores, won't there?"

How could he explain it to her? How to break this new reality to her? Tomorrow he would tell her, Kayne decided. Tomorrow he would step in as the underboss. Tonight, he just wanted to be her husband.

Facing his silence, a silence more revealing than any answer, Laura turned on her back, staring vacantly at the ceiling. There was no answer he could give to appease her and remain truthful. Kayne Malkin didn't lie, so he'd remained silent in the face of her despair. He had no intention of ever altering his lifestyle. Kayne Malkin came with heartbreak and the sound of clicking heels. *Why delay the inevitable?*

"You should get back to your party," she offhandedly declared, feeling her broken heart hardening, and she turned away from him.

His eyes narrowed. Did she think she was the only one to suffer? That her pain allowed her to dismiss him as he did his whores? He wanted to strike her, to strangle her and holler his own torment. But Kayne swallowed his anger and simply nodded. Without a word, he got off the bed and picked up the pants and shirt thrown carelessly on the floor, not bothering with the jacket. He was still buttoning up when he calmly closed the door behind him.

Laura regretted her words the moment she felt his weight shift on the mattress, the emptiness of him heavier and more tangible than any other truth. She wanted to throw her naked body in his way to stop him. Instead, she watched him leave, pinned to the bed, and trapped in her oppressing solitude. Why *not* delay the inevitable? Why had she forbidden herself this one night with him, their wedding night? Tomorrow, he could have his whores. Tomorrow, he could slaughter and destroy. She would even wave him off and send kisses from the port. Just let her have him for this one night. She prayed with all she had, to heaven and hell, to whoever would answer first. She would trade it all for this one night.

She jumped off the bed and, frantically reaching for the discarded wedding dress, hastily pulled it over her shoulders. Her bare back fully exposed, she rushed to the door. Maybe it wasn't too late. Maybe she could still find him. Maybe, there was still hope. Never had a word held a soul's fate so irrevocably.

She swung the door open and stopped right in her tracks, feeling her nerves shatter and her chest collapse. Kayne was there, leaning against the wall facing the door. He just stood there watching her, his face impenetrable.

"Kayne…" she cried, relieved and crazed. "Kayne… Kayne…" she repeated his name, over and over, as though uttering an arcane prayer. "Forgive me… forgive me…" she threw herself in his arms and softly pleaded, her face buried in his chest.

"No. Forgive *me*." Kayne tightened his hold on her.

He was apologizing for it all. For everything he had already put her through. For everything he would still put her through. Knowing he was too selfish, too rotten, to ever push her away. Knowing she would always come back to him, no matter what he did. And that he would always be there, waiting to collect all the pieces of her and put her back together again, until the next time she broke apart in his hands.

Their lips frantically sought each other, their tongues mingling with desperate hunger. Kayne dragged Laura back into the room and kicked the door shut behind them. He slammed her bare back against the wall and felt her cry out in pain in his mouth. Lifting the skirt of her dress, he wrapped her legs around his and penetrated her with all the raw emotion he felt: anger and passion, lust and regret. With the animalistic hunger she ignited in him and the cursed desire afflicting him.

They fell asleep clinging to one another, every inch of their bodies touching, with no other words needing to be exchanged. Come morning, he was gone.

DAY-76

KAYNE LEFT BEFORE SUNRISE, reluctantly stepping out on his slumbering bride. He kissed her forehead and saw her smile in her sleep. He could never face Laura following these stolen moments of intimacy. The man who fell asleep in her arms was not the one who awoke by her side.

He'd been at peace with himself before Laura. Now the wild wolf within bared its teeth to the emerging dog tempted by domestication. The fight was unbalanced, raging on the wolf's long-established territory. Like in Laura's beloved book, Kayne Malkin could never fully embrace his conflicting sides. Every token of affection, every step toward reconciliation, would inevitably be followed by his retreat into the wilderness, back to his domain. Kayne belonged to the Organization, not in a loving home. And yet, the crux of his dreams and desires revolved around a life with Laura.

He asked Lucas to drive his new bride home and stayed behind at the Drugov residence, as instructed; Dimitri was throwing him a party at the second mansion to celebrate his official promotion.

★ ★ ★

Laura felt a pang at waking alone and looked, without conviction, for a love note she didn't find. She spent the day with Natasha, who informed her early on that Kayne was busy with Dimitri but offered no further detail.

It was well into the evening when Lucas pulled into the Malkin residence. Heading inside, it wasn't lost on Laura how the security guards, who'd always ignored her, now bowed their heads in respect.

The house inside lay dormant, the moon shining down the forbidden twin stairs. Their mystery called out to her, the quiet and darkness in collusion to provide the perfect cover. Could she? Lucas's words came back to mind; she was Mrs. Kayne Malkin, after all. *Who would stop her?* Her eyes burning with a conqueror's determination, Laura set forward.

Her heart sank with every step she climbed, but she continued her journey, her head held high. As a true Malkin, she would not let her fear show, even with no witnesses around.

There were only two doors, one on each side. She tried the left first to no avail. Her chest pounding, she turned around and felt the handle give way. For all the ways he had invaded her life, body, and mind, Laura would finally penetrate Kayne's inner and most private sanctuary. It lifted the hairs on her skin, and she stepped inside, feeling as though she violated a sacred temple.

Kayne's bedroom reflected him in every way; no woman had left her mark, no other being had left a trace. From texture to color, to style and composition, it mixed the bold with the chic, adding a classic touch to the modern feel. Laura swirled, her arms open wide and her head tilted back. She could sense and smell it all around her: Kayne's essence. It would be the only unguarded version of him she would ever encounter.

She pulled the drapes open, exposing the ceiling to floor glass walls. Behind them, a sleeping world bathed in the moon's silvery glow. Laura looked up and smiled; it was a wolf's moon, the benevolent light in their darkness.

She looked around. With hesitant fingers, she opened the first drawer and found everything neatly folded and color-coordinated. The walk-in closet itself could contain a small-sized room, and turning on the spotlights, she saw rows upon rows of suits and other items she recollected seeing him in. Her fingers lovingly glided down the material of his clothes, lifting some sleeves to her nose so she could breathe in his scent. When she reached his bed, she warily opened the end table, expecting all sorts of sordid paraphernalia. But she found only one item: a worn-out first edition of *The Little Prince*.

With solemn deference, she pulled it out and opened the cover. On the first page, she found a note in elegant cursive.

Dearest Lena,

Our meeting was written in the stars. Our love, inevitable. Let me gaze upon your eyes until my last breath, and I will die a happy man.

Lev M.

Laura turned the pages carefully, understanding the value of what she held in her hands. Pieces of paper were inserted throughout the manuscript, and she smiled when randomly landing on one with a transcribed quote. *"What makes the desert beautiful,"* says the little prince, *"is that somewhere it hides a well."*

And just like that, another piece of Kayne Malkin was revealed. His favorite book had been his mother's. She closed her eyes and kissed the cover. She would not give up. Her desert, too, contained a well. She knew this with certainty, from the elusive kindness she'd seen in his eyes to his all-consuming caresses when words failed him. How could she not believe in the well, having tasted its water?

In a world that was all Kayne and in desperate hunger for him, she removed her clothes and put on one of his shirts. Still cradling the book against her chest, she fell asleep on the mattress, feeling warm and safe.

★ ★ ★

Kayne returned home very late, his eyes shining with the too many beverages in his system. He considered meeting Laura in bed and hesitated behind her closed door but thought better of it; his demons came out to play so easily in his current state.

With his thoughts on his bride, he pushed his bedroom door open, the light bleeding in gradually to reveal the sleeping lump on his bed. He stood in the doorway, unsure how to process that information, his inner tumult narrowing his eyes. Laura's first act as his wife had been to break his rules and invade his privacy. Goldilocks sure seemed comfortable, asleep in his clothes and on his bed. That's what he got for being soft with her, he thought with a reproachful sneer. He sat in the black leather club chair facing the bed and, in the darkness, watched her.

Laura's sleep became agitated under his gaze, and her eyes slowly blinked open. She raised herself on her elbows and smiled tentatively at the stormy figure in the shadows. "You're back…"

"Come here." He pulled out his arm to her, his voice low and gruff.

It wasn't the sensual call of a lover; the very air around her felt heavy with accusation, and she stiffened, sensing his brooding mood. Laura gingerly obeyed, recognizing from childhood the eerie calm that inevitably preceded devastating storms.

Kayne sat her on his lap. "It suits you," he said, playing with the cuff of his shirt, his soft voice contrasted with his forbidding expression.

"Are you mad?" she breathed.

He exhaled deeply, then tucked a strand of hair behind her ear. "Had you asked, I would've said yes."

Laura could sense the water retreating around her feet, the sea pulling back only to unleash its fury in a monstrous tsunami.

"But… I'm your wife," she uttered, her voice cracking.

"And that entitles you to openly disobey me?"

She dipped her chin, shaking her head despondently.

"Get up," he calmly instructed, tapping softly on her leg.

She stood up and quietly took his hand, sheepishly following him out of the room. Laura walked with her tail tucked in, feeling like a dog getting kicked off his Master's bed and being led back to his kennel.

But Kayne turned into the western wing once they reached the ground floor and headed to the study leading to the private basement.

"Kayne... no. I'm sorry... I didn't think," Laura tried to reason with him, her eyes increasingly chaotic as the spiraling stairs came into view.

"You did think, Laura. You just didn't care. You're right. You *are* the lady of the house. But I'm the Master. You should never forget that," he said with quiet anger, pulling her forward.

Laura bowed her head. He was right; she hadn't cared. And truth be told, she would do it all over again. She didn't want permission to enter his bedroom, nor a separate bedroom for her own.

"Are you going to whip me?" she whispered, her bitter eyes avoiding his.

Kayne lifted her chin, shook his head, and saw a lonely tear roll down her face.

"Don't you trust me, Laura?"

"I didn't do anything wrong," she blurted out through gritted teeth, angrily wiping off the two additional drops spilling over.

Though the smirk he gave her brimmed with unholy promise, he placed a soft kiss on her lips. He then retook her hand and led her into the dungeon. He abandoned her at the entrance and went to sit in a big leather chair, eying her with devilish amusement.

"Get on your knees."

Her jaw tightened, but Laura obeyed nonetheless.

"Crawl to me."

Her eyes grew round with bewilderment. She hesitated but lowered herself to hands and knees, meeting his sadistic stare with venomous resentment. Slowly, painfully, she crawled to him.

The shirt lifted on her body, revealing its most exquisite parts with every step. *What a delicious punishment*, he grinned. He could see the silent but determined rage in her. It was one intent on being swallowed only momentarily, set on avenging its wronged host. Kayne smiled; his beautiful bride, how far she'd come, how far she'd descended. What kind of monster celebrated the fall of an angel? He wondered for a split second, then immediately shook it off. He looked at her with pride. He still remembered the terrified girl in the purple dress he'd first kissed at the party. Laura Spencer had not only survived her environment but also adapted to it, Laura Malkin emerging from the cocoon. *Laura, his purple butterfly.*

Perhaps that was the source of her power, he thought. Laura would always bend but never break. She would rise and rise again, transformed into a version befitting her circumstances. As a child, she'd learned the subtle art of walking the shadows in the face of the storm. As a young adult, she'd channeled carefree youth, showing the world an agreeable face she hoped it would accept. Caught in the beast's lair, it was a meek prisoner that had appealed to his humanity, as would a lost puppy in the snow.

It was hard to conceive that deep within the Russian doll were the seeds of the enticing woman facing him. *Laura.* He could spend his life pushing her over the edge and watching her transform, always rising from her ashes. She would lose countless battles. But never the war.

His eyes alight with wickedness, he stared her down as she reached him. "Kiss my feet."

"*What*," she hissed through gritted teeth, instantly standing upright.

Kayne cocked his head to the side and, with a mock sorry expression, shook it disapprovingly. "Tsk-tsk-tsk."

"You're fucking out of your mind if you think I'm going to do that."

A spine-tingling chuckle escaped his lips. He lifted her to her feet and pulled her backward with a devilish grin. He lifted her arms and bound each to a metal ring dangling from the ceiling. He then walked back to his leather chair and casually sat back down.

It seemed too easy, she thought, but soon enough, her muscles began to cramp. Her discomfort increased with each passing minute, and she cursed the man quietly watching her from his cozy seat, a knowing smile etched on his face.

But Laura would not beg or plead, willing to pay a hefty price to hold her ground. He could whip her if he wanted, but kissing his feet? *Never*. Beyond the revolting act itself, it was the meaning it carried. It was deeper than submission, infinitely worse than woe or wound. It was humiliation. Scars on her back would heal. Her broken heart could mend. Humiliation, however, was a different beast. It eroded the soul, deviously smuggling in her twin sister: shame, darkness's whisperer.

Laura had lain awake too many nights in her short life, reliving past indignities and reviling herself. So many hours spent fantasizing about different versions of the events: endless self-soothing retellings where she had had the spine to stand up for herself. The outcome of the reimagined altercations didn't matter. The point was never to win. It was to fight back. Laura had understood then that the most excruciating torment from the abuse was her complicit silence. Remaining calm and complaisant, ignoring nature's primordial call to take up arms, and dressing up that cowardice as reason. Laura painfully recalled her younger self, crawling of her own volition into the cage and hoping her dutiful compliance would yield a milder verdict. Never again, she had vowed later on, would she partake in her own degradation. *For both heaven and hell may await you, when you look into the mirror.*

"The pain will only get worse," Kayne informed her, stretching his arms and readjusting his position to maximize comfort.

Laura remained quiet, her eyes set with a determination that fascinated him.

"You know… some women would be glad to please their Master. Whatever way he wanted."

"Great. Have one of them lick your dirty feet, then," she spat back without thinking.

He considered her for a moment, then licked his lips as if in response to his thoughts. His eyes boring into hers, he slowly nodded and, taking out his cell phone, called a number on speed dial.

He saw the dread creeping in her features break her childish stubbornness. He waited for her to speak up, willing her to stop him as the call connected. She didn't. She just stared in horror as he spoke into the phone. "*Ten minutes*," was all he said before hanging up.

The elapsing seconds hung heavily in the air, each waiting for the other to stop the monstrosity about to unfold. Their staring contest ended with the sound of clicking heels.

Laura watched in disbelief as a beautiful blonde entered the dungeon. She displayed no reaction at seeing Laura tied up and quietly removed her trench coat, revealing all-black lingerie, stiletto heels, and a choker. Without being told, she got down in a kneeling pose and, with her head bowed, calmly waited.

Kayne tracked Laura's facial expressions down to her blinks and grasped the horror in her gaze. *Apologize*, he willed her. *Say something. Anything. Just make a sound.* And he would send his submissive away.

But Laura was not attuned to his intent; her attention was on the thunder-stealing vixen. She stared wide-eyed, transfixed, repulsed, and silent.

Kayne inhaled deeply. *So be it.* He turned to the unwelcome guest. "Come here, Pet."

The luscious blonde gracefully abided, her crawl feline and sensual. When she reached him, Kayne looked at Laura in a devilish taunt, his window of mercy sealing shut.

Laura met his gaze, her breathing heavy. But her eyes, though appalled, did not supplicate.

"Kiss my feet," he purred to the woman kneeling beside him.

With deference, she removed his shoes and socks, placing them carefully one beside the other, then proceeded with no shame. The blond beauty seemed perfectly at ease performing the task Laura had deemed so demeaning. It seemed that even the nature of the offensive lay in the eyes of the beholder, Laura noted with slight astonishment.

Kayne commanded his submissive to stop and raise herself. He smiled at her, brushing her cheek with his thumb as he cradled the side of her face in his palm. "What do you want, my Pet?"

She rubbed her face on his hand, seeking her Master's touch. "I just want to please you, Master."

Kayne's eyes turned to Laura, dissecting her fragile stoicism, and then returned to the sultry siren at his feet. "Please me with your mouth."

He felt his growing erection as she took him in, lathering him with her expert tongue. He grabbed her hair and held her head down, all the while watching Laura; his trapped butterfly, helplessly watching as another woman pleasured him. It struck a deep nerve in Kayne, the perversion of it enticing his most sadistic demons.

Laura both despised and pitied her rival. And though she recoiled from the twisted spectacle, she did not turn away, allowing the flames of jealousy to engulf her.

His eyes boring into Laura's, Kayne came with an imperceptible groan. And after a few ragged breaths, he released the blond hair from his hold.

"Leave us," he instructed his submissive in a low tone, slightly bending to her ear.

Kayne slowly got off his chair and, zipping up his pants, languidly walked up to Laura. Her eyes tracked his every movement, following his hands as he let the tip of his fingers glide down her side. She shivered at the contact and ground her teeth but remained silent.

He sneered, moving in even closer, and towered over her. He brought his face to hers, his hand nesting between her thighs. Slowly, it went up to the sound of Laura's rapid and labored breathing. "Bet you miss the whip now..." he huskily whispered with a sinister chuckle.

He heard her gasp when his index and middle finger found her engorged flesh. Kayne hardened instantly at finding her wet and, licking his lips, stared her in the eye. Laura. His perfect woman. His Goddess. He wanted to worship at her altar and degrade her in his dungeon. He fell to his knees and forced her legs apart. Her body twisted and turned in his grip, but he held on firmly, bringing his lips to her wet core.

A strangled cry escaped her lips, the world around her subsiding after the storm. Kayne knelt before her, his every touch and caress tailor-made to appease and soothe.

Her pained moans only increased his hunger, and Kayne licked, kissed, and teased until he pushed her over the edge. Her orgasm came out in a long, wounded, and guttural sound, and she broke into a hysterical sob. Her whole body gave out as he unbound her. And though only held up by his arms, Laura rained her fists down on him the instant they were freed. She hit him on the chest, over and over again, howling her pain and fury.

Kayne stood still as she expelled her poison, accepting his penance. Keeping her in his arms, he let her hit him until she had no strength left and lowered to the ground with her. Laura sniffled on the floor, and every now and then, she would hit him again. A few times, she'd tried pushing him away, but he'd refused to let go and sensed her relief. He would take as long as needed for her to understand: he would never abandon her. He would stay and hold her. Forever and ever.

Laura had fallen silent, staring up at the ceiling with Kayne still at her side. With her eyes now dry and her breathing even, she sat up. "I'm going to bed," she flatly said, standing up on her own. She didn't want his help, his pretense at chivalry, romance, or kindness. Regardless of how desperately she craved them. She felt him grab her arm and, turning around, found him standing behind her.

With a subdued smile, he offered his hand and, sensing her hesitation, took the lead and grabbed hers. He gently led her up the stairs and all the way to his room. Kayne had never brought anyone before, and he kept looking back at Laura, wondering what was on her mind. This calm and collected version disgruntled him. He felt their bond so fragile, hanging by a thread pulled so tight the slightest exertion would break it.

It was so bittersweet: invited into his room at last. Her heart wouldn't let her walk away. Its fresh wounds wouldn't let her savor the moment. When he pulled the covers open, Laura got inside alone, avoiding his touch whenever possible.

The entire night, he remained at a respectful distance, even though she could feel, in his deep breathing, his urge to reach for her.

Kayne fell asleep thinking of the woman lying next to him. He woke up not long after, feeling uneasy, and immediately looked to his left and found her side empty. He snapped up and, scanning the room, saw her huddled on the floor in a corner. Laura hugged her legs, staring straight ahead.

The moment his feet touched the ground, he felt her body tense and saw the panic in her eyes. It twisted like a blade in his heart, but he understood. He wouldn't go to her. The Laura he now faced was wild. He would have to tame her all over again, earn her trust, and, for once, hope to be worthy. Holding up his open palms in a reassuring gesture, he slid himself to the floor and leaned his back against the bed. He made no more moves toward her, consciously maintaining the distance she had deemed safe. Noticing her shiver in his shirt, he slowly reached for the cover and, with cautious moves, slid it over to her. Watching him like a hawk, Laura tentatively reached for it, covered her legs, and returned to surveillance. Kayne stared back at her through heavy eyelids, never shifting from his uncomfortable position.

The sun crept up as they maintained their standstill, exhausted on the floor. Laura feared closing her eyes and allowing him to break their established boundary. Kayne feared closing his and enabling her to pull away even further from him.

DAY-77

THEY WERE AWAKENED BY the buzzing of Kayne's mobile vibrating on the end table. They stared wide-eyed at one another, both surprised at having fallen asleep, both relieved at finding the other exactly where they were. Kayne tiredly reached for the phone, rubbing his eyes as he picked up and exited the room to take the call. When he returned, Laura was gone.

★ ★ ★

It was well into the afternoon when Laura quietly snuck out of Kayne's room. She had not been able to find sleep at his side, constantly wanting to go to him and feeling the burn when she tried. She had wanted to go back to her room in the middle of the night but had only found the will to crawl ten feet away. Even at that moment, she had found comfort in his presence. How she wished he had whipped her instead. Physical pain could be contained. What she felt was pure chaos; her heart, a burning city, her mind, the mad king, her soul, the sizzling amber left behind.

She got ready for supper in a trance, unconsciously reaching for a black dress befitting her mood. Laura smiled back at her glamorous reflection, her hair and makeup fixed as if for a night out. She had never been one to pride herself on her looks or invest the time and effort required to enhance them. Hiding her frailty behind smoky eyeshadow, she finally understood the motivations behind the art of esthetics. Beauty was a beguiling mask and powerful ally: the magician's assistant, diverting the audience's attention away from the hollow trick. Laura stood up and lifted her chin, steadying her nerves for the tête-a-tête she was not ready to face.

* * *

Kayne awaited Laura in a formal black suit, his somber state mirroring hers. He slowly nodded in greeting, scrutinizing her every tell, from the fluidity of her moves to her choice of attire and makeup.

"Good evening," she said in a deep voice and pulled out her chair.

Though their eyes spoke volumes, they fell into a heavy silence for the remainder of the meal.

"I'll be leaving for a while." He dropped the bomb after finishing his plate. They hadn't yet exchanged a single smile.

Though Laura's heart clamped and her chest tightened, she did not ask him for how long or where he would be. Even as she felt her insides rip to shreds, she did not ask why he had to go or if it was his choice. She simply looked up at him with curiosity as he stood up and went to her side, placing a few items on the table by her plate.

"A bank account has been opened under your name. Credit card. Cell phone. Lucas is coming with me. You can go to Kiev for anything you need. He will take care of you."

For a second, Kayne seemed to be reaching for her shoulder. And though he lingered halfway, he brought his arm down, tapping his fingers on the table. Laura slowly nodded with a thin-lipped smile. Was that it? Was that all he had to say? Her blood boiled. "Well… Bon voyage," she said, her voice betraying no emotion.

Kayne opened his mouth and shut it right back, assessing the precarious situation. He deeply inhaled. "While I'm away, you may go wherever you like. Inside the house… or out. All I ask is that you take Kiev with you when you leave the premises."

A jaded smile crossed her lips. *Take Kiev with you*; her newly earned freedom was only extended insofar as she was supervised at all times. Laura barely nodded in acknowledgment.

She watched him leave. The man, she realized with a twist in her heart, she had fallen in love with. The man who'd ripped her world apart. And yet, it was he who didn't trust her—she, who had never wronged him. A guilty heart, it seemed, could never learn to trust.

Her eyes followed Kayne's footsteps until he became nothing more than a little black speck disappearing into the night. She swallowed the desperate scream calling out to him. Instead, she silently prayed for his return.

DAY-126

KAYNE FACED THE GLASS wall of his fancy hotel suite. He had a view of the entire city and stood with a whiskey in hand, staring at the full moon. It made him think of Laura. It had been almost two months since he'd last laid eyes on her or even heard her voice. He'd traveled to many countries, meeting with business associates from all walks of life; endless nights he barely remembered spent at underground parties and shows. He had all types of orders carried out, left countless bodies behind, and had more women than he could account for. And yet, the moment he was alone, his mind unfailingly revisited Laura.

When Dimitri had called him, advising him of the travel, he'd been reluctant to leave the way things were. He'd realized with a sting that she, however, was only too glad to be rid of him. *Well… Bon voyage.* He could still hear the light timbre of her voice, recalling her relaxed eyebrows and cool eyes. He feared he'd lost her forever. Though he hadn't reached out directly, he'd made sure to program his number into her mobile. But her name never flashed on his screen.

Sometimes, when he lay alone in bed, especially on nights like these when the moon shone exceptionally bright, he would think of an old Russian folktale Olga used to read to him as a child. He would imagine Laura and himself as Alexei and Aniska, the two of them against the whole world, two parts of an unbreakable whole.

But that couldn't be further from the truth, and reality always reared its ugly head. Laura had her Alexei—he'd taken him from her. How he wanted to be her Great White Wolf. But he knew himself to be the villain.

Kayne was and would always remain the *dreaded monster, the tyrant that sheds innocent blood.*

* * *

Emptiness. It filled Laura's world. It was not the type that left you bedridden, depressed, and alone, seeking solitude and afflicted by it. It was the loneliness of a clown hiding behind fun and spectacle. Laura Malkin didn't sulk. She hired an entire staff to fill the house with life and went out as often as possible, spending her days shopping away and her nights hosting endless gatherings. She dressed in the finest gowns, laughed the loudest, and danced the night away. She was always the last one standing, pushing out the inevitable lonely nights as far as possible. For all the things she bought and the people she surrounded herself with, nothing could fill the void Kayne's absence left.

Every once in a while, the moon would call to her. She would slip upstairs into his room and, wearing his shirt, would fall asleep on his bed. On those nights, he invaded her dreams. The following mornings were always the hardest.

* * *

Kiev had helped hire the new staff through an agency approved by the Organization. Olga was very grateful for the help and the company. Most were of Russian origin except for the two youngest. Barely in their twenties, French Canadians Louis Lavallé and Geneviève Roy were as thick as thieves, always giggling together in the corners of the house. Olga felt wary of the young blond beauty and, even more so, of the protective way Louis always eyed her. She wondered why Mrs. Malkin had accepted to hire her. *Why invite trouble within your home?* She didn't like the defiant way Geneviève took orders from the women, saving her sweet façade for the men on whom she perfected her flirting techniques. But Olga knew her place. She didn't breathe a word of her concern to the lady of the house, but she kept a close watch on the French Lolita.

DAY-145

LAURA HAD JUST RECEIVED the news. *Master Kayne* was coming home. She could barely contain herself and, pacing around all day, decided to shop for a new outfit. A violet dress called out to her. It reminded her of their beginnings: the night the barrier was first broken. Kayne had planted the seeds of the woman she'd become with a single kiss, all the madness of that evening eclipsed by the memory of his soft lips.

She carefully laid out her new dress on the bed with a smile. Then getting self-conscious, she would wonder, what if he no longer cared? It seemed ages had passed. She'd resisted calling a few times. What would she say? What could she say? Did he even want her call, or had he only left his number on a "for emergencies" basis? Was their disastrous last night together a factor in his hurried departure?

Her prayers had been answered, she reminded herself. Kayne was coming home. It was perhaps their chance to start things anew, to go back to the night of the purple dress and take a different path. Arming her heart with courage, Laura took the first step toward reconciliation and enlisted Olga to help prepare his favorite foods. They spent the day in the kitchen, Laura laughing heartily at Olga's resigned headshake following her third burned batch of knish and kalduny, Russian versions of dumplings.

She set the table all done up and sat down, patiently waiting with an expectant smile. Hours passed under Laura's close supervision, and she finally fell asleep, her head resting in her palm. She woke to the clock striking midnight, an untouched meal, waning candles, and no Kayne in sight. With a bitter taste in her mouth, she smiled coolly back at the empty room and, lifting her chin, headed to her bedroom, her dress unseen.

★ ★ ★

Kayne had delayed his return as much as he could, extending the hours with the help of a bottle. He'd fantasized about their reunion for so long; now that it was here, he felt apprehensive about facing the reality of Laura's welcome. The sun was rising when he stumbled home with Lucas holding him up. He was greeted by a sexy young blonde who introduced herself as Geneviève, boldly looking him in the eye with a seductive smile. She was putting away a cold meal he assumed Olga had prepared for him and smiled dejectedly upon recognizing all his childhood favorites.

Walking into his empty bedroom, he realized he'd hoped to find Laura asleep there. And climbing on his mattress, he thought he recognized her scent on his pillow. He passed out fully clothed and with Laura on his mind.

DAY-146

LAURA HAD QUIETLY SNUCK out at the crack of dawn and stayed out past store closings and the hospitality industry evening rushes. She'd sheepishly hoped her mobile would ring, that an infuriated voice would beckon her home, but her phone had remained silent.

She had fantasized of so many romantic date nights with Kayne out and about in the city: taking a stroll up Saint-Laurent boulevard, evenings sipping wine on Saint-Denis terraces, and late nights at jazz clubs, swaying their head to live music. How she loved her hometown. Montreal, there was no place like it. She'd only discovered other worlds on paper and screen, but she knew in her heart that none would match its quaint charm. Montreal didn't fan her feathers for the world to see. She was no star next to the likes of New York and Paris. She was a jewel to be discovered, only delighting eyes that recognized beauty in its simplest form. Was there any feeling like walking down the cobble streets of Old Port on a warm summer night? Its packed restaurants announcing the end of the long winter, and its ever-present artists offering you back a piece of your lost childhood? It was Laura's gate 9 ¾, her portal to all the magic and wonder she would ever need. But even Montreal couldn't dazzle her out of her lonely truth. Crossing Pont Jacques-Cartier to the night skyline, Laura could only offer Kiev a brittle smile.

She had been initially disappointed with her assigned escort, having preferred Lucas to the taciturn older man. Lucas would have found a way to make her laugh and see things in a different light. But Kiev had proved himself a loyal companion, and she'd learned to lean on his quiet strength, finding comfort in his morally blind devotion.

★ ★ ★

Louis had been tracking the interactions between the newly arrived Master and Geneviève. All day, he'd caught sideway glances and sly smiles. Geneviève was a flirt. He'd learned to accept that in his best friend. He knew her every move, from the subtle way her hand lingered after a friendly hug to her fingers unnecessarily brushing your back when passing by in a cramped space. Her touch, although seeming innocent, was anything but. He should know; she had honed her seduction skills on him from the first kiss she'd given him back when they were only ten. They grew up neighbors, often mistaken for twins with their matching blue eyes and sun-kissed hair.

Louis was in awe of her. While he was just a shy little boy afraid of his own shadow, Geneviève was strong-minded and outgoing. He had no friends; she had the entire third grade at her feet. Of all the boys pining over her and the girls competing for her friendship, she had picked him. They'd been inseparable ever since.

He had followed her to summer camps, had taken up smoking with her, and had even dropped out of high school to remain at her side. While their former classmates celebrated prom night at the fancy hotel, they'd spent it in the backseat of his mother's car, getting drunk off a stolen bottle of cheap champagne. They'd lost their virginity to each other. He'd thought they would be together forever. She'd told him he was the best friend she'd ever had. Louis had worn the badge with honor, regardless of the heartbreak that followed her every conquest.

He'd spent years grateful just to exist in her shadow, dismissing his suffering heart's pleas for distance and healing. Geneviève was wild and unpredictable, and every moment shared with her turned into adventure and excitement.

When things got out of hand, and he couldn't save her from her hell, he'd followed her into it. They had all given up on her, thinking she was beyond the point of no return. It was he, and no one else, who was able to convince her to go through rehabilitation. She had cried in his arms, sweaty, feverish, and covered in vomit. She'd told him that she loved him, that he was the only one for her. He'd thought he was the luckiest person in the world. When she felt better, Geneviève never mentioned the *incident* again. And Louis knew better than to bring it up and face her cruel laughter.

When two short months ago, she had mentioned a job her friend had told her about, he knew it was bad news from the get-go. He didn't like that particular friend of hers, one of her many conquests. He was ignorant, arrogant, and heavily into drugs, with a violent streak and mafia aspirations. Louis couldn't get her to change her mind: the money was good. There was no way Geneviève would ever accept her résumé's restrictive opportunities. She would be caught dead before working the counter at a fast-food joint. Geneviève Roy liked the shady aspect of the job; she reveled in danger.

She knew she would be safe. She knew Louis would come along and stand guard over her.

DAY-147

LAURA'S LOOSE CREAM SHIRT kept sliding down her shoulder, and she fixed it again with mild annoyance as she sorted through her purse. Just like he had that first night at the club, Kayne watched her from the corner of the entrance hall, silently willing her to turn around. He barely recognized the distinguished lady facing him, the sun coloring her dainty features.

The air changed around her, and she felt a tingle down her neck. Slowly, she turned her head, only her head, sensing his presence before her eyes could confirm it. Her face lit up momentarily but, landing on his sardonic smirk, quieted to a grey canvas.

"You're back…" she said, deadpan.

"You're leaving," he observed with amused nonchalance.

Laura's heart pounded in her chest. She had prayed for his return. She'd even pleasured herself with his face in her mind. Now that he was here in the flesh, she froze. She would have forgiven him all and would've gladly run to meet him, if it was her Kayne who had returned. But it was the other: the one who'd stared her in the eye as she was being shackled and hurt. The one who'd repeatedly forced her down the winding stairs to worsening nightmares. The one who seduced and tortured her. But through him, her Kayne found his way to her. Would he ever exist on his own, or was the path through hell unavoidable to reach him? Her Kayne, she was powerless against. This one taught her the lessons she would use against him.

"Well... I'll see you around, I guess," she broke the strenuous silence, casually lifting her shoulders.

Kayne's mouth quirked up. "I'll see you *tonight*. For supper. Seven sharp."

"Oh... I'm sorry. I can't... I have plans." Laura held his narrowing eyes and smiled back at the fury dancing in them.

Kayne licked his lips, his predatory instincts kicking in. "Cancel them," he commanded with a restrained voice, his gaze swaying between threatening and entertained.

"It's with Natasha—"

"She'll understand," he interrupted with decisive calm.

They stared in silence, each studying the other as would adversaries before a battle. Kayne caught up to Laura in a few strides and saw her fear mixing with excitement. She didn't fool him. Behind her proud stance and daring eyes, he could still see his little girl. He could still bring her out with one touch.

His Laura, his purple butterfly. He would move the earth for her. Raze the world to the ground, if she asked, and spend eternity rebuilding it, should she remain in it. Never had a woman stirred his Monster so deeply she uncovered another layer. How he wanted to be her savior. But it was the villain in him who always dragged her to bed, kicking and screaming until she moaned and gasped, powerless in his grasp.

But his very ability to manipulate her into wanting him at any cost held a darker truth: she would never love him. He could twist, bend, please, and break her body. But he could never reach her heart; not through the strings he'd skillfully attached to her and constantly pulled to his selfish designs. He felt a stab at the thought and instantly shook it off. Bringing his face closer, he gave Laura a smug look. "Anything you want to add?"

She exhaled slowly and lifted icy eyes to his. "No, Master. Your wish is my command."

Her heart had skipped a beat when he'd approached her, and she'd unconsciously held her breath, feeling his on her face. She had counted the days down to the seconds until she would see him again. He, on the other hand, had preferred spending the night out, presumably in the company of other women. She knew he'd been with many others during his travels, but his choosing to extend his time away from her once he'd returned home cut right through her. That was the injury. The insult came in the form of a cool and seductive Kayne, beckoning her to make herself available the moment it suited his mood, as one would expect of a toy. She could've rebelled but aimed at indifferent submission, hoping to sting his pride. But even then, her heart fluttered at the prospect of an evening with him.

★ ★ ★

Kayne had kept busy all day, catching himself with increasing irritation looking at his watch. By seven o'clock, he was already seated, the rhythm of his tapping fingers intensifying with the passing minutes.

When the pendulum on the wall marked the closing of half an hour, Kayne stood up, his rage turning to frost; the injury, Laura's rejection, the insult, her disobedience. He retreated to the reception hall and poured himself a whiskey, drank it too fast, and refilled another. By the fifth glass, he could barely stand his reflection in the mirror.

He resented Laura for turning his world upside down and despised himself for wanting her so desperately. But most of all, he hated the Monster within that would never allow him to ever be worthy of her love. In blind fury, he punched through the mirror, annihilating his tormentor.

Geneviève, lurking nearby, jumped at the sound of shattering glass. For two days, she had shadowed her new employer and shamelessly flirted, fantasizing remorselessly about the married older man. Guys her age fell to her feet effortlessly, each more of a disappointment than the previous. The first man who'd ever understood her needs and hadn't melted like putty in her hands was twice her age, married, rich, and very handsome. He'd used and discarded her. Geneviève had longed and grieved for him, understanding these feelings as love.

Her therapist had called her *a classic case of father abandonment issues*. She had a difficult relationship with a pious mother she disdained, struggled to maintain friendships with other girls, and treated men as pawns or kings.

The only person in the world to ever see through her thorns, to see goodness in her and care for her, was Louis. Sometimes, she thought him a fool; other times, his optimistic view of the world rubbed off on her. And though she teased him relentlessly, she never hesitated to bring out her claws when suspecting anyone of approaching him with ill intent.

Geneviève cautiously opened the door, finding a handsome figure looming in the dark, surrounded by shards of broken glass. Kayne stared at his bleeding hand, his fragmented reflection on the wall beastly looking.

"Sir, are you all right?" she asked in her soft voice, her French accent pronounced.

He turned to her, his hollow stare sending shivers down her spine. She cleared her throat and walked toward him. "I'll clean the mess. Can I see your hand?" She was by his side before he could answer, and meeting his eyes, she lifted his arm with a gentle touch.

"What's your name again?" he asked, his curiosity piqued.

"Geneviève… at your service, *Sir*," she added coyly. "If you allow me, I could bandage it for you."

"There's no need. I'm fine. Thank you, Geneviève."

Though her feminine attention appeased his bruised ego, his thoughts were elsewhere. Another fifteen minutes had passed. But he refused to call Laura and hound her as would a forlorn husband.

"But, Sir, it is my job. To take care of you... To see to all your needs..."

He chuckled, amused by the amateur seduction. "How old are you, Geneviève?"

"Old enough." She grinned.

"Answer me."

"Twenty."

"Twenty..." He shook his head. "You don't even *know* how to see to my needs..." he finished, turning away from her.

"With all due respect, *Sir*, you grossly underestimate me."

"Do I?" Why hold on to a grudge when such a delectable little thing tried so earnestly to divert him? "All right. Get me hard without touching me, and I'll graciously recant. You have five minutes." Kayne gave her a devilish smile.

"I do love a challenge." She met his luscious gaze, putting one heel before the other. Sitting down, she slowly undid the top button of her tight uniform, exposing a black lace bra. Her eyes filled with longing, and she seductively swayed her legs sideways, revealing black nylons held up by matching garters. She then brought her fingers to her glossy lips and began sucking her manicured thumb.

"Four minutes," he called and grinned at the nervousness creeping in her eyes.

"You think I'm just a kid." She brought her hand to her neck and down her chest, caressing the inside of her breast down her belly. "I've wanted you since the moment I saw you. I know you want me too." She began touching herself and, pushing her thong to the side, widened her slim legs further apart.

It was enough to hold his attention. Remaining silent, he sat facing her, encouraging her to go on.

"Don't you want to fuck me? Make me your little slut? I've been such a bad girl." She slid a finger in and began rocking herself against her hand. "I want you to make me come so bad. I'll be a good little fuck-toy, I promise."

With less than a minute on the clock, Kayne's demons answered the call. He would recant. *Graciously.* "Don't come."

She stopped moving, immediately removing her hand.

"Did I say to stop touching yourself?" he asked, a wicked grin on his face.

"Sir..." She brought her fingers back, cautiously rubbing her engorged flesh. "Will you make me come?"

★ ★ ★

It was well past eight when Laura hurried back in. She'd stayed out for as long as she could, preferring the dreamy loneliness of her solitude to the grim reality of his presence. She had aimed for fashionably late and had waved off Kiev's warning to leave downtown before rush hour. As a result, she'd spent the last two hours fretting in the backseat, nervously consulting her watch in bumper-to-bumper traffic.

Standing in the hallway, she fixed a few rogue strands of hair and readjusted her blouse, taking a few deep breaths in front of the mirror before making her entrance. With a meek smile, she walked into the empty dining room. She wasn't surprised to note Kayne Malkin had not patiently waited for her. She wondered where he was and what consequences there would be. Facing his underwhelming return, she had acted out as a neglected child, choosing reprisal over indifference.

She searched for him through the house, cool dread trickling down her spine, and heard moans from the reception hall. She recalled, reviving spent venom, walking in on him and Tanya, a woman between his legs.

With narrowing eyes, Laura pushed open the door and looked on with disdain as Geneviève lay flat on her stomach, bent over a high table. Pinning her hands down her back, Kayne leisurely thrust himself in and out of her. At the interruption, he calmly slowed to a halt. Geneviève lifted her head and, seeing the Missus, flashed her a supercilious sneer.

Laura walked in with her chin up, taking measured and deliberate steps. She then bent down to meet the young girl at eye level. "Geneviève, sweetheart. Would you kindly get off my husband's dick? I would like a word."

The young hire stumbled to her feet, thrown off by the intimidating Mrs. Malkin. She quickly glanced at Kayne, looking for guidance and some reassurance. But the Master of the house only had eyes for his beautiful wife. With a half-smirk creeping on his face, he lazily pulled his zipper up. He turned to Geneviève as if in afterthought and nudged his head toward the door, his attention impulsively returning to the elegant lady facing him.

Geneviève scurried out of the room. She'd dealt with complacent partners before. In fact, she quite enjoyed facing the cuckolded lover. Even the most tolerant ones always lost their cool when facing her. Geneviève prided herself on being the mistress, the one men jeopardized everything for. Her sense of worth inflated in direct correlation with the depth of the betrayal. She'd learned this in childhood, earning her father's scarce attention when teaming up with him against her mother. They would roll their eyes and giggle behind her back as she lovingly slaved away in the kitchen, preparing favorite meals. In her teens, she'd adapted this dynamic to her relationships. She'd come to believe her value could only be acquired at the expense of another woman, defined in a zero-sum game arbitrated by the object of her affection.

It had felt very different this time. She was not the accomplice and keeper of the sinful secret, elevating her status above that of the deceived and long-suffering spouse. It was clear from the moment Mrs. Malkin had walked into the room that she commanded her husband's attention with a mere look. Geneviève wasn't a threat, merely a distraction, easily discarded without a second thought. Once the trio faced, it was she who felt like the odd one out, the clueless player to the true rules of the game. For the first time, she admired her rival. For the first time, she hated *the wife*.

⋆ ⋆ ⋆

Laura held Kayne's stare. "Really, Kayne... The help? How appallingly cliché," she noted in a steady and velvety voice, not an inch of emotion disturbing her marble face.

He hated her cool composure, her serene features in the face of his tactless infidelity. It only strengthened his crushing suspicion: if she once cared, she no longer did.

He smiled. "My apologies. Should I get creative, then? Perhaps make you choose your own punishment. Which will it be, Laura, the cage, the whip, or the whore? Your pick," he asked, desperate to stir anything in her and get under her skin.

He got the reaction he wanted, and she turned to him, her eyes round with shock. With her expression horrified, she exhaled as if punched in the gut. Kayne could almost hear her say the words again and smirked.

You're a monster. But she remained quiet, turning away with disgust before resuming her walk.

"Where the fuck do you think you're going?" he called out, his voice booming in the room.

Laura picked up her pace, desperate to reach the door and flee the web forming around her. But Kayne caught up to her in an instant and, pulling her arm, turned her around. She vainly wrestled from his hold, turning her head to conceal her bubbling emotions.

He pinned her down and lifted her chin. And forcing her glistening eyes to meet his, he immediately softened. This Laura, he couldn't hurt. *She still cared.* He exhaled deeply. "Why were you late?"

"Why were you fucking the maid?" she snapped back.

A subdued snort escaped his lips, sad and jaded at the same time. "Answer me."

Laura shrugged her shoulders. "I was caught in traffic… Why do you care? You don't even care."

"I don't care… Is that what you think?" he asked, his voice, though guarded, vibrating with restrained emotion. "I married you. I killed for you. I risked *everything. For you.* I checked in on you while I was away… It seems you were doing great. Shopping away and throwing parties… Having quite a blast." Bitterness came through the cracks in his mask. "Did you think of me even once? Or were you too busy showing off your new wardrobe for other men to gawk at?"

Laura had felt her heart skip a beat at the beginning of his confession and, for a naïve moment, had thought Kayne would pave the way for her to surrender her heart. But today would not be the day. "Don't worry, Kayne. I thought of you. I thought of all the women you were fucking. Of all the men you were hurting. I thought of all the lives you continually destroyed. Beginning with Peter's and my own."

Kayne let go of his grip, looking her up and down as if studying a rare specimen behaving unexpectedly. Laura. She'd come into his life as prey he stalked for the Organization. He should have realized from that very first night, escorting her back to safety on his arm, the power held in her soft magic. She'd insidiously invaded every aspect of his life, from his home to his mind, sprinkling traces of herself all over his dreary existence.

He raged at her unwillingness to have more reasonable expectations of him and accept their way of life, as had Natasha. However, he felt a visceral response to the idea of Laura sharing him unbothered. Wasn't it precisely her inability to dilute her feelings, whether for her brother or her stories, whether in passion, curiosity, or anger, that had beguiled him so? His Laura wanted him, all of him, Monster and all. And she wanted him all for herself. He understood then that he wouldn't have loved her any other way. The thought resonated within him, coming as a revelation. He loved her.

"Laura…" he softly spoke her name.

His tone reached deep into her, and her heart swelled, recognizing the voice of her Kayne. She looked up at him, her sad eyes expectant.

But the words choked in his throat. The Monster tightened his hold on the reins, ensuring Kayne remained mute. The Monster had always had one purpose: keep the wounded boy locked deep within and out of reach so he may never suffer again. And the Monster had pursued this aim with a one-track mind, oblivious to the destruction he left all around the very boy he sought to protect.

Laura could see him clearly now, her Kayne. And she offered him a broken smile in acknowledgment of his failed efforts to extend an olive branch. Her Kayne always came too late, standing with a warm and tender gaze in the rubble of their love.

They stared at one another, understanding the poignant truth that remained once wounds and masks had been peeled off: they both suffered, they both cared, knew it to be hopeless, and hoped nonetheless.

★ ★ ★

Hoping to eavesdrop, Geneviève had lingered behind the door in the aftermath of the interruption. She had anticipated the lady of the house to show her true colors once she faced her husband alone. To be reduced to a nervous heap of tears and insecurity; for him to reassure her half-heartedly, apologize insincerely, and give concessions begrudgingly.

But it wasn't a hysterical high tone she had overheard but a deep and incendiary one. Why would the cheater lash out? She had wondered. It unnerved her, solidifying her growing suspicion: there was something about Mrs. Malkin. She guessed she was barely a few years older than herself. And yet, she seemed ageless, like she'd lived and seen it all. Someone you could no longer surprise and catch off guard. Geneviève hadn't paid much attention to it before.

She was lost in her bubble when Louis tugged her arm late into the evening. He began phrases and abruptly changed subjects, jumping randomly from one topic to another as he always did when feeling anxious. But that night, Geneviève was in no mood to gently coax him into spilling the source of his distress. She couldn't get the Malkins off her mind.

Seeing Louis walk away, burdened and miserable, she felt a tinge of remorse. Geneviève was well aware of her selfish nature and considered it one of her most valuable assets. She saw how the selfless were marked for exploitation; how the most devoted were also the most likely to settle for crumbs. Geneviève would never beg for love. She would choose herself over all others—every time.

She had come to this conclusion at quite a young age, watching her mother stop at nothing to save her marriage. But her father had grown increasingly distant the more ardent his wife's efforts became. He ended up leaving when Geneviève was still a child. She lived for the much-awaited getaways he would promise. They would often get canceled at the last minute for a game of golf or whatever activity better suited his mood that day. Geneviève blamed and resented the mother who'd always remained at her side. The father who'd spoiled and abandoned her was seen as grand and above reproach.

DAY-148

GENEVIÈVE WAS DISTRACTED THROUGHOUT the morning, trying to anticipate the Malkins' next move. Would they terminate her contract? Would a reason be given to the agency? Mrs. Malkin most certainly didn't seem the type to forgive and forget. Geneviève hadn't seen either of them since locking eyes with the wife, the husband inside her. She felt tingly all over, revisiting the feeling.

Kiev, whom she mockingly called *Le Grognon*, came to fetch her sometime in the late afternoon. "*Boss wants to see you*," was all he said. Was Mr. Malkin hoping to resume their activities before sending her off? Or would he deliver the news with affected formality, acting as a mouthpiece to a script clearly dictated by an indignant ghostwriter? In her experience, it was always one or the other; genuine remorse, she'd never seen. If she had to place a bet, she'd surmise Mr. Malkin wasn't the type to grudgingly take orders from a nagging wife. She glanced quickly in the mirror and, pleased with her reflection, followed Kiev down the corridor.

Being led to the reception hall, she grinned: *pick up exactly where they left off*, then. She played with her hair, adding a little pop to her hips, but her face immediately dropped upon stepping into the room.

Laura flashed Geneviève a radiant smile. "Geneviève. Come in. Please, have a seat."

The blond beauty swallowed her saliva, unnerved and on high alert. She obeyed instructions, fidgeting on the chair under her employer's patient stare.

"May I get you anything to drink?" Laura, always the gracious hostess, asked the young girl once she had settled.

"No… thank you," stammered Geneviève, highly uncomfortable in these unknown waters. She looked around, waiting for the Master to jump out of the shadows. She'd come across women that had demanded a seat to her beheading, mainly to ensure their husband wouldn't stray from the carefully prepared speech. But they would hang back, in silence and with a petty smile, half-hiding behind the man doing their bidding. And all the while, their husbands stole lingering glances between parroted *gross misunderstandings* and *with deep regrets*. Never had a wife taken charge and confronted her on her own, let alone with such calm and composure.

"Tea, coffee, juice… water? Nothing at all?" Laura insisted in a pleasant tone.

"Coffee… Let me get it. *It's my job*," Geneviève replied with bitterness at her rank in the hierarchy. "What would you like, Mrs. Malkin?"

Laura chuckled, waving her off. "Nonsense. Kiev, please bring us two coffees. Milk and sugar on the side."

She turned her attention back to Geneviève once they were alone. Crossing her legs, she slightly dusted off the top of her knee and then placed one hand on top of another. She gave her guest a little sigh. "So, Geneviève. Do you know why I hired you?"

The French Lolita hated the grounds she found herself standing on. She was off her game, playing against the home team at a severe disadvantage. So she did the only thing she knew: she played dirty. "Your husband asked?" She leaned back with regained confidence and a smirk, pleased with her offensive strike.

Though demons flashed in Laura's eyes, her smile remained undisturbed. "You enjoy seducing married men. Don't you?"

"Look. He came on to me. Okay?"

"How *awful*. And you seem like such a *sweet, innocent* girl…" Laura responded in a soft sarcastic tone.

"What do you want, Mrs. Malkin?" Geneviève put an end to the jabs and perverse foreplay. She hadn't heard Kiev return and looked over her shoulder as Laura waved him in. Mrs. Malkin gratefully thanked him as he handed her a mug. She then turned to Geneviève and ensured her coffee was to her satisfaction before resuming their conversation.

"I'm afraid there's nothing I need from you anymore, Geneviève. You've served your purpose."

"You hired me to sleep with your husband?" Geneviève asked in disbelief. "I think you're *firing* me because of it."

"Oh no. You're not fired." Laura's honeyed reply was instant. The student had learned well from her Master, her eyes gleaming with the same wickedness endured, internalized, and now unleashed.

Laura considered her young rival. From the moment she had laid eyes on her at the interview, she'd recognized the Jezebel in her, a Tanya Malone in the making. Her first instinct had been to rip her application to shreds. *Would he?* Laura then wondered. Would he disgrace his Missus in their own home? He hadn't hesitated before. Would their marriage change anything? As she had done time and time again, Laura lifted once more the cover to Pandora's box. She preferred facing the most devastating answers to the torment of feeding the dimmest and most unlikely hope in vain. She needed to know: was there a line Kayne Malkin wouldn't cross?

After he'd crossed it, came the even more harrowing question: was there no line he could cross that she wouldn't forgive?

The broken mirror, half-empty bottle, and bleeding hand were not lost on her, however. Late at night, she'd tossed and turned in bed, replaying his words over and over again. *I married you. I killed for you. I risked everything. For you.* For all his remorseless cruelty and stoic composure, Kayne buried, deep within the beast's fortress, a human and fragile heart. Though unreachable behind its impregnable walls, it had somehow become entangled in the finest thread. She slowly came to realize that its extremities, though invisible and feather-light, were held in her hands. Was there anything grander and more terrible than holding sway over a monster?

But what to do with the young Jezebel, she had pondered. The morbid response formulated in her mind went unchallenged by her heart and soul, surprising even Laura herself.

She recalled her discussion with Natasha about playing the long game with Dimitri's mistresses. Even then, she had had the same outlook. *Keep Kayne's whores around? They wouldn't survive the day.* But it was one thing to decree "Off with their heads" to faceless and hypothetical rivals, and quite another to stare a twenty-year-old in the face and still coolly arrive at the same consensus.

"Mrs. Malkin? So you're *not* firing me?" Geneviève asked tentatively, snapping Laura out of her haze.

With her eyes spewing venom, Laura shook her head, her acquired facade faltering. "No. There won't be need for that."

"Je ne comprends pas... Qu'est-ce qui se passe..." Geneviève mumbled, her eyelids drooping. The room began spinning before her, and feeling a bout of nausea, she collapsed on the ground.

"Bonne nuit, Geneviève." Laura stood up, her hard face matching her icy tone.

"Have you decided, Boss?" Kiev approached and picked up the limp body.

She nodded. She'd considered having her sold, putting her seductive skills to good use. But even the scorned woman in her couldn't reach that far down such a dark path. "Make it quick. And painless."

* * *

It was late into the evening. Laura sat at her vanity in a long and backless midnight blue nightgown, absentmindedly brushing the same handful of hair. Upon hearing a gentle knock at her door, she lowered her silver hairbrush with a deep breath and looked into the mirror, as if hoping to gain courage from her seductive and amoral doppelganger.

Without awaiting permission, Kayne entered her room.

"Hello…" she murmured in a deep and controlled voice, meeting his gaze in the looking glass.

He nodded, his expression enigmatic.

"And to what do I owe the honor?" She turned to him with a hair flip before resuming her nighttime routine, straining to project nonchalance.

"Laura… what have you done with Geneviève?"

His face was serious, his tone grave, yet she knew in her heart that he both knew and approved of the answer. "Tell me, Kayne. What would *you* have done had you walked in on me fucking another man in your house?"

He bowed his head in concession, a hint of gained respect on his features. "Kiev?"

She gave a quick nod.

"He should've come to me first." He shook his head. "She was just a kid."

"Funny… Didn't seem to have stopped you… But do tell me, Kayne. Had Kiev sought your approval, would you have overturned my directive?" she challenged him with belligerent eyes and an icy smile.

Kayne responded with a devilish smirk, impressed with his reluctant but gifted protégée. Mrs. Malkin was not one to be easily crossed. "Her friend, the blond one. He won't believe she just upped and quit without a word. He's been badgering Olga all day. She just came to see me about it."

Laura looked away, shrugging her shoulders. "Does it matter?"

"Yes, Laura, it matters. What do you think happens to those who sniff too close? No loose ends. Remember? They can't all be exceptions like you."

Laura met his stare. "I see. So he must die. Because of… us."

"Yes."

Her eyes dropped to the ground, and she hunched her shoulders, breathing uneasily as she began to grasp the magnitude of her actions. "I hadn't thought of him. I've seen him around. He's a good kid." She gasped for air. "I was just… so caught up in it… I had someone killed. And now someone completely innocent has to die because of it… I've become a monster." Laura's soft voice sounded eerie.

Kayne was at her side instantly, grabbing her shoulders on a bent knee. "You did what any true Malkin would have done. It's on me. Do you understand?"

She nodded feebly. "Is there no other way? I just can't see him being a real threat," she pleaded his cause with no conviction.

"Don't worry, Laura. I'll handle it," he closed the discussion, standing back up. Kayne would pay the retributions for her actions. The woman he'd helped create and mold, leading her down the path of darkness after ensuring all others had been cut off.

The Laura he'd met should have been spending her weekends at the municipal library, not at parties and dungeons. He recalled her enthusiasm on one of their first evenings, sharing her impressions of *The Usual Suspects*, her eyes sparkling excitedly. Or the time she went on a surprisingly passionate monologue culminating in an apologia for one of her dearest anti-heroes: Professor Severus Snape.

He'd put her through hell and back, forcing her into a corner: she only did what was needed to survive. A vision of the Winter Witch came to him. *All hardens and darkens, that which must endure.* But the Evil Queen had not always been so. *Once upon a time, my heart beat true like yours*, she had warned the young Aniska. Now Laura believed she'd herself become *the dreaded Monster*. Like him. Because of him.

He would not allow it. Kayne looked his wife in the eye, asserting his undying devotion. So her white-gloved hands remained unsullied, he'd slaughter lion and lamb alike and let their blood rain down on him. From the underworld, his laughter would echo all the way to the heavens he would have secured for his Malkin Queen.

Kayne would handle it. Laura nodded heavily at the implication. When was it exactly? At which point had she consciously bartered her soul and crossed the gates of Hades just to rendezvous with her Monster in Tartarus?

"All this trouble, just to make a point." Kayne shook his head, his expression turning wicked. Reaching for her arm, he pulled her up and leaned in. "You do realize I still have to punish you for your little tantrum."

Laura jumped out of his embrace. Murder, he would stand by. Tardiness, however, would cost her. "You're joking."

"Did you think for a second you'd pull all this shit and walk away scot-free?"

How he loved toying with her. How he loved that feral look she'd get, her eyes wide with alarm, tracking his every move. The sweet surrender he would inevitably extract from her would quiet his own chaos. Only his Laura could bring him peace with her submission, ground him with her sweet touch, and bind him with her soft kiss.

She stepped back as he approached her, holding his stare as she cautiously circled around him and stepped toward the door.

It amused him. "Really, Laura… You're gonna make me chase you? How *appallingly* childish."

Her eyes narrowed, but she kept quiet, walking backward and away from him.

He chuckled. "Fine. Have it your way. I'll even give you a five-second head start. Don't let me catch you," he warned seductively.

She hadn't meant to run. She'd wanted nothing more than to stand and face him, fearless and defiant. But the moment she'd heard him count up, her legs snapped on their own accord. Before she knew it, she sprinted down the hall and felt him catching up too soon.

She turned into the kitchen, panting and breathless behind the island. Kayne faced her with his hands in his pockets and cocked his head at her disheveled state. Laura could see from his posture, his predatory stare and sadistic grin, how the chase had only further ignited his animal instincts.

"Kayne…" she pleaded. "Please, don't do this. I'm begging you." It hurt to beg. It hurt to run. It hurt to fear so deeply the man you loved.

He smiled, entertained. For him, it was all part of the game.

"Please, *Master*… I'm begging you. I don't think I can handle it."

"You don't give yourself enough credit, *baby*," he replied in a sinister tone.

"Kayne. I'm begging you! Haven't you tortured me enough?" she wailed, her hands gripping the counter so tightly that her knuckles turned white.

His expression changed, his smirk disappearing as his eyes studied her. He was calm when he addressed her, his voice soft. "Laura... This is who I am. You know this. This is it. This is what you'll get from me. Always. Or are you still hoping I will magically morph into the man of your dreams?"

Her whole world came crashing down. It was his voice, *her* Kayne, who had shattered the illusion that had kept her going in the dark. There were no two Kaynes. No Dr. Jekyll and Mr. Hide. During the worst of it, her Kayne hadn't been locked away by his evil twin. No, he was there in the shadows, nodding approvingly as she endured and prayed for him. Her guiding light was nothing more than a mirage.

"Kayne, please. Stay away." Laura reciprocated each of Kayne's sidesteps with its opposite. He stared at her, a certain tenderness softening his gaze; it melted her broken heart. "Stay away..." her voice cracked with emotion.

He took another step.

Laura reached for the first weapon at her disposal and grabbed a butcher knife off the counter. With shaky hands, she held it with arms stretched out in front of her. "I'm not fucking around, Kayne. Please, stay away."

He smirked and rounded the corner, coming over to her side. "What do you plan on doing with this, exactly?"

She stepped back. "I'm not going down there with you. Okay?" she tried to command but pleaded instead.

He cocked his head to the side. "You didn't answer my question."

"Listen to me, Kayne. I'm not doing this tonight. Okay? I'm not going in no fucking cage, getting fucking whipped, or watch you fuck some fucking bitch. Do you hear me?" She gripped the knife tighter, her tone going up and down along her faltering nerves.

Kayne closed the remaining distance in one swift move and, grabbing her hands, brought the blade to his throat. "You still haven't answered *my* fucking question," he replied in a gruff voice. He pulled her into him and felt the metal pierce his skin. He didn't care. His eyes boring into hers, he leaned in and kissed her, blood dripping down his neck.

Laura's weapon fell from her lax hands, her head lulling back as Kayne took her into his mouth, prying her lips open with his tongue. Her body didn't resist the intrusion, and she obeyed like a rag doll when he brought her arms around his neck and pulled her waist against his. He kissed her with the built-up passion brewing in his blood for over two months. Laura. His favorite toy. His one obsession.

Wedging his knee between her thighs, he forced her legs apart and broke the kiss. But the dim grey eyes that returned his stare housed no conflict or burning lust.

"I... can't," Laura said, paining to get each word out. "I can't... do this anymore." She looked down. "You were right. I did hope. And I did dream. I kept thinking... if I could just... find a way. If only I was just a bit tougher, or *more feminine*... I... I *murdered* someone," her voice cracked. "I sold my soul, Kayne. For you. Because of you." She looked him in the eye, weary and defeated. "I will never know peace again. I've lost everything. To you. And all I'll ever get from you is more torment, scar tissue, and humiliation."

Kayne let go of Laura, his eyes burning with intensity as he stepped back. He nodded slowly, turned around, and exited the room.

How long she stayed by herself staring at the abandoned knife on the floor, she didn't know. She returned to her room, and for the first time in months, she reached for the grey yoga pants and purple hoodie that had once been her daily uniform.

Buried in her clothes, she curled into a ball and stared at the heavy rain tapping against the foggy windows. Laura tried and reverted to old tricks: escaping into her mind. Hypnotized by the sliding and amalgamating droplets, she tried to predict future paths and fusions. But every now and then, Geneviève's face appeared in the mist, wronged and vengeful, and Laura would squeeze her eyes shut in a wince.

Images of recent events would replay one after another. The knife with Kayne's blood lying on the floor. Kayne standing behind Geneviève at the desk. Geneviève lying unconscious. Kayne chasing her. Kayne kissing her. Kayne walking away. The knife with Kayne's blood lying on the floor...

Kayne would never change. He'd told her himself early on, his actions reinforcing his warnings. What had enabled her to fantasize still, Laura probed the highs and lows of their journey. What had she realistically hoped for? How achingly little was she prepared to accept? And even that was denied to her.

Would her heart ever rise against its ruler and banish Kayne Malkin? Or was it cursed to forever remain his prisoner, wherever she walked the earth?

Bits and parts of their story flashed again before her eyes, each pulling different emotions out of her. *Do you trust me?* he'd asked her in the backseat of the Audi on their way to the Party after making her strip down to her underwear. *Would you stop me? Would you consent?* he'd whispered in her ear, pinning her down on the sofa. *If you only knew... what your Monster would do for you*, he'd asserted in the bedroom, his forehead resting against hers.

She'd seen in his eyes a glimpse of what lay beyond the gates. But every time she'd tried to find her way through, barbed wires had ripped her to shreds. Kayne Malkin would never love her, not the way she needed. Whatever he felt for her came wrapped in thorns.

Laura thought of another one of Olga's stories. About two young porcupines in love, lost in the merciless Russian wilderness on the coldest night of the year. Having learned all about porcupine safety, they knew better than to get too close. But the further they stayed apart, the harsher the cool winds whipped their claws at them. And when they tried to embrace, their spines pierced and bled them. All night long, they fought for survival, constantly adjusting and readjusting to one another. By the crack of dawn, a little farmer girl found two porcupines peacefully asleep: just close enough to create their own warmth, just far enough to protect each other from their quills.

Was there no stretch in the universe that could contain the Monster and the Dreamer? Laura sat up in bed, her eyes set with resolve. She would find it. She would tear through the fabric of space and time to create it. A place where her love would dull his blades, and his monstrosity kept all other beasts at bay.

★ ★ ★

Kayne sat on his bed with his eyes closed and his back against the headboard. Was history doomed to repeat itself? Dimitri had cautioned him about pursuing Laura, using the tragic outcome of his father's stubborn love as a lesson to be learned from.

Laura. The kind-hearted bookworm with disarming innocence, a vestige of man's lost grace. How ironic, he thought, that he'd fallen for the replica of his mother's ghost, a soothing image fashioned in childhood from snippets of hushed conversations. The small and lonely boy, however, had been severely reprimanded over memorializing the Malkin Judas.

Laura, too, now revolted at a reality presented to her from the beginning. Hadn't she baptized him the Monster on the very first night? She'd answered the beast's call regardless, giving him dominion over her body. He'd understood in the kitchen that the peace her submission nurtured in him was being drained from her. Whatever she felt for him was filled with loss and grief. Kayne felt a wave of sorrow and bowed his head. One day or another, she would either leave him, or her conscience would get the best of her, leading her to a police station. Lucas would be sent to retrieve her. *Are you going to kill me?* he heard her ask again. *Only if you make me... Don't worry, I won't let you,* he'd replied.

The softest knock snapped his eyes open, and fully alert, he fixed the door.

With sneaking glances, Laura entered the room and slowly approached the foot of his bed. She offered him a regretful smile he didn't return and felt her chest tighten. "I'm sorry." The whispered words flew from her mouth without intent. So often, she'd begged forgiveness from a father for reasons unknown; trying to soothe angry storms had become an ingrained mechanism.

Kayne almost winced at her words. Laura offered the olive branch he'd failed to deliver, tending to his wounds before hers. He resisted the urge to go to her, to kiss and carry her to bed. "You should leave," he said quietly, turning his head to the window.

"No," she softly replied, with no defiance, remorse, or regret. And she took a cautious step closer. Stopping at the foot of the bed, she hesitantly reached for the bottom of her hoodie, then the top of her pants, a primal emotion shining in her eyes.

Kayne gave a subdued chuckle, remembering her reaction the first time he'd made her play with the hem of her clothes. *Take off your clothes, Laura*, he'd instructed, the wetness on her face both contradicting and enriching the one betraying her body.

He wanted nothing more than to play along and wash away the bitter truth of her earlier words. But Kayne remained silent. For the first time, the jaded lover in him overpowered the insatiable sadist. "Get the fuck out, Laura," he said in a low and gruff voice, keeping his gaze downcast.

"Is this what you want, Kayne?" Laura asked, open and vulnerable.

A desperate dog howled inside him, reaching with all its might toward his loving mistress. To him, there were no unforgivable scars, no unavoidable dead ends. Only a beloved body within reach and the promise of a touch long yearned for. Kayne deeply exhaled. What could he respond? That he wanted to tie her to the bed and convince her over and over why she should never abandon or betray him? That the very reason he loved her so desperately would likely turn her against him one day? That even in the best-case scenario, the wisest bet would still be for her to flee from him to the end of the earth? And that even then, he didn't trust himself to stay away?

Nothing. Silence. Rejection. It was cancer to a man's soul but death to a woman's. Laura narrowed her eyes and lowered her head, somewhere between a nod and a bow out. "Your wish is my command, Master." She then lifted her chin with regal dignity and, turning around, slowly walked out of the room.

Kayne watched her leave somehow in disbelief, considering stopping her long after the echo of her footsteps had dissipated into the void. But he'd remained immobile, pointlessly looking out his glass wall. The waning moon in the dark skies retreated, both mourning and condemning Laura's departure. He doubted himself. Was it truly altruism that had made him push her away, or a terrified and wounded beast that feared the light?

Ominous clouds claimed the night, and a flash of lightning illuminated his room, a deluge ensuing. Kayne felt release at the fury unleashed around him, the violent banging against the glass drowning out his inner chaos. For a moment too quick to truly grasp, he believed Mother Nature held her arms out to him, crying the tears he'd never be able to shed.

Thunder boomed in the electric sky, and Kayne wondered where his wife had sought refuge. Was she safe? Was she inside? Was she already and unknowingly on her way to the arms of another man?

He calmly reached for his cell phone, lingered over Laura's name but pressed the name below. "Lucas, can you see her?"

"Yes, Sir. She's… in the middle of nowhere," Lucas answered, perplexed. "She's… in the woods."

Kayne shut his eyes and flared his nostrils. He'd driven her straight into danger when all he'd ever aimed for was to protect her however he could. *You will take care of her?* he heard Peter again. *You have my word.*

"Keep tracking. I'm going after her," Kayne said into the receiver and stormed into the tempestuous night.

★ ★ ★

Dripping wet, Laura walked pointlessly into the woods. She'd strayed off the beaten path of the civilized world. She was no longer part of it. She was no longer part of anything. Once she had been a sister. It had defined her identity and given her the strength to go on. But that was taken from her. She became a prisoner and remolded her entire being to survive her new cage, forsaking all for her captor. Then the jailor she'd grown dependent on set her free, opening the door and walking away. She could acknowledge the frightening gash in her heart oozing blood and yet, march on, desensitized to the pain.

She no longer felt complex emotions, instinctively returning to the wilderness as an abandoned animal in the wake of the lethal injury.

Crouching on the earth, she hugged her knees and rocked herself, humming a familiar tune whose origin was lost to her. In the numbing cold engulfing her, Laura longed to see her brother again. Would he greet her at the gates, liberated from his demons at last? Would he have forgiven her betrayal? She then thought of Kayne, of the madness and tragedy of their love. As she often had as a child, she told herself a bedtime story: the tale of a monster and his captive, of Beauty and the Beast.

She pictured a young Laura listening, enraptured, her expressive face at times terrified, enthralled at others. A serene smile softened her features. It was better to have loved and lost. Not all fairy tales were meant to end well. She could feel the cold permeate through her wet clothes and flesh, right down to her bones. But Laura didn't fight the slumber invading her limbs. As she drifted to the realm of the wise and silent, she wondered if Kayne looked for her. If his kiss held the sorcery to wake her.

★ ★ ★

Kayne had abandoned the Audi on the side of the road. With Lucas on the phone directing him, he dove deeper into the foreboding woods. Under vehement thunders, he screamed her name, beating away the sinister-looking branches blocking his path. In the dark of the night, the Beast bargained with a God it didn't believe in.

★ ★ ★

It seemed as if it came from another world, and Laura tried to ignore the incessant call driving the peaceful shore away. She thought she heard her name and, in her remerging consciousness, felt the comforting warm glow retreat back into the void. She thought she recognized the strained voice invoking her name, louder and closer, piercing through the veil to bring her back to the living.

By the time she blinked awake, she felt his hand on her cheek and could see the beloved features facing her. He seemed tired, his face dripping, his hair unruly. Her Kayne. He was there, his eyes boring into her.

"How did you find me?" she asked, still dazed, struggling to force a sound out of her hibernating body.

Kayne lowered his head, bringing their foreheads together as he deeply exhaled, relief softening his features. "Oh, Laura." His smile was brittle as he reached for her sleeve and crooked the bracelet with his finger.

"I don't understand…"

He turned the bracelet around, showing her the engraving. "For as long as I'm your Monster, I will always find you."

He helped her to her feet and removed his jacket, draping it around her shoulders.

"Let's go home." He grabbed her hand and started walking away. But the small fingers slipped from his hold, and turning around, he found Laura standing still.

"Laura. We have to go," Kayne warned, looking up apprehensively at the angry skies.

But Laura only shook her head. She could feel the strings pulling her to him. Never had a man looked so devastatingly beautiful. Never had a monster been so unconditionally loved. She didn't want to return to her ivory tower. She would cast away its safety and solitude to perish in the dark forest, devoured by her beast.

"We're going to die out here! Is this what you want?"

"YES!" Her scream was long and pained.

Kayne considered her for a moment. "So be it."

He captured her in his arms as the world growled around them. His elusive prey. His lips met hers with ferocious lust under the illuminated sky. He didn't care. If lying in her arms was his last deed in this wretched life, he would meet his end with a smile. The Monster and his captive, they were never meant for a happy ending. Their story had claimed too much blood. Their happily-ever-after would await them in the underworld.

He laid her on the muddy earth, pulling off her wet clothes in a frantic kiss as she ripped his shirt open. With the bundled hoodie around her wrists, he held her down with one hand, and with the other, he pulled her pants down to her knees. He didn't take the time to tease and seduce. Driven by his desperate need, he unzipped his jeans and penetrated her, taking her savagely on the ground.

"Enough of this," he panted, delirious at finding her willing body instinctively opening to him. "Enough, Laura. Say you'll never stray... Say... you'll never leave," he growled, in between a threat and a plea.

With a raspy voice and her lids half closed, Laura voiced the truth she long felt and, even longer, resisted. "I'll be yours until the end of time."

DAY-149

IT WAS NEARING DAWN when Kayne led Laura back to the car under clear blue skies, birds chirping in the distance. On the ride home, he left his hand on her thigh and would give it a gentle squeeze every now and then, offering her a weary but grateful smile.

When they reached the house, he led her to his bedroom and ran a bath. Laura instinctively lifted her arms when he reached for her shirt, and she stood comfortably passive as he removed her clothes. She took his offered arm with ease and, getting into the tub, nuzzled between his legs. She let him bathe her body and brush her hair and, for the first time, found serenity in her surrender. Calm and quiet extinguished the restlessness that had shadowed her since the first steps she'd taken as a toddler. She closed her eyes as he dried her off and grinned when he reached for one of his T-shirts, pulling it over her head. Once he'd brought her to bed, he caged her body with his legs, keeping her locked in his arms. She felt his kiss on her temple right before she drifted off. At this moment, she didn't understand why it couldn't always be that way. In her last waking thought, she murmured *thank you* to whatever had her lying in his bed again, building a home in his embrace and feeling his even breathing on the back of her neck.

That night, she had the most peculiar dream. She was having brunch at a fancy country club on a warm summer day in an elegant black dress with matching long gloves and stilettos, a veiled hat pinned over a low bun. She first noticed the deafening silence and, looking around, realized under darkening skies that she was all alone. A white stork appeared as if from nowhere, strutting by her table, and Laura followed it against roaring winds to an abandoned stage at the back. At its center lay a gigantic prop of a baby book. In the gathering storm, Laura's hat flew away, her hair blowing wildly around her face. "I… can't… have… babies," Laura tried to explain, shouting against the wind in slow motion. She opened the make-believe book regardless and gasped with horror when a scorpion emerged from it. She stumbled backward and, feeling betrayed, looked for the white bird. But it was no longer there. Instead, she noticed a small black crow perched on a nearby pole. It just stood there watching her, its clear blue eyes strangely human.

It was well into the afternoon, the setting sun leaving a pinkish hue behind, when Laura awoke with a start, sweaty and troubled. She let her fingers trail along the empty space by her side, her dread lingering as she traced the indented body in the folds.

★ ★ ★

As the silent hours trickled by, Louis's panicked thoughts grew increasingly louder. He spent the day obsessively calling Geneviève's mobile and filling her voicemail with unanswered messages, ranging from lightheartedly reproachful to alarmed outrage.

He refused to believe she would abandon him like this. But Louis didn't fool himself as to the reasons why. It wasn't out of love or a sense of duty. Geneviève was simply far too self-serving to relinquish such a faithful and accommodating companion. His reward for his loyal years of service was his irrevocable place in her life. He'd earned it with his sweat and tears and wasn't about to let it go without a fight.

Torn between worry for her well-being and anxiety over his status in her social hierarchy, he'd reached out to all their acquaintances. No one had heard a word. He'd lowered himself further and began calling her most recent lovers. If she lay in their bed, they'd remained silent about it, some even laughing in his face before hanging up. As desperate as he was to find her, he couldn't shake the tiniest relief he felt at each negative response. *He hadn't been replaced after all.*

In only two days, Geneviève Roy seemed to have vanished off the earth's surface. Something was wrong. He could feel it in the eerie calm and peacefulness her absence left. For the second day in a row, Louis went to the nearest bar and got as drunk as his wallet permitted. He replayed the discussion he had with the Master of the house. He had demanded to see him and did not lower his gaze when questioning him. Kayne Malkin had remained calm and patient, even tolerant, facing the inflamed young man. Louis hadn't fallen for any of it. If anything, it strengthened his suspicions. Only the guilty could display such nobility and indulgence in the face of monstrous accusations. Something bad happened to her. And the Malkins were behind it.

From his early years as a scrawny and soft-spoken dreamer, he'd learned to sniff out predators. Some waited after school, pushed and shoved, and bruised and broke, laughing like brainless ghouls. Some tore sketchbooks and pulled down pants, smiling angelically at the dean afterward. There were different types of wickedness; the worst kinds were always the best concealed.

But his days of getting picked on had ended once Geneviève arrived in town, stepping in and taking him under her wing. Life was never the same after that. He owed her everything. He owed her his happy childhood filled with laughter and misadventures.

At the bar, he ran into Carlyle, the beat-up thug who'd told her about the job. He was massive with disproportionate features. Geneviève sure hadn't picked him for his looks, Louis suspected. It must have been the air of danger that surrounded him and his connections to a shady world that had lured her to him.

Louis marched forward with all of his one hundred and fifty pounds. With the determination and courage found at the bottom of a bottle, he confronted the gold-toothed sneer of the behemoth awaiting him.

"Have you seen her?" Louis spat at him, stumbling closer.

"Gen? That your girl, ain't it?" Carlyle responded with malevolent calm.

"Answer me!" he shouted with bloodshot eyes.

"Nah, man…. Haven't seen her face in a month. Saw her back though… last week in the backseat of my car." He broke off snickering. A few thug-attired look-alikes laughed along, looking at one another for cues.

Louis reddened. Further words were exchanged. He was not even sure who threw the first punch. He only remembered being pulled away and thrown out of the bar. He recalled a blonde policewoman, short and mean. The policeman with her was kinder, patiently nudging him into the back of the cruiser.

Louis hated the police. He had been part of too many peaceful protests ending in indiscriminate pepper spraying and mass arrests to see them as anything but government lapdogs. He suspected a disquietingly high majority to consist of short-minded, inadequate-feeling, and perfectly mediocre people desperately seeking a taste of power. Rather than serve and protect, these despicable posers abused their bestowed authority. So high off their own importance, it was impossible to reason with them. The others, he believed, had sold out to the Mafia instead. Those, he actually preferred. They had enough on their mind and tended to leave you alone. But Louis prided himself in his unfailing optimism, which he reluctantly extended to law and order. He reckoned there had to be a few decent men or women out there for the right reasons. But that was the thing with power: it attracted the worst humanity had to offer. Those deserving of it too often wanted nothing to do with it. His mind returned to Geneviève, to all their philosophical debates over shared joints in the woods. She would be so proud to see him getting arrested over an actual fight for once, and not his *hippie shit*. Louis cackled alone at the thought, resting his forehead on the cool window.

He was still drunk when the officers interrogated him. He was barely coherent but managed to shout out, "The Malkins! It was them! They did it! The Malkins!"

He was ushered out with eye-rolling and more force than necessary and then placed in a holding cell for the night with a homeless man. He made for a strange cellmate, with rotten teeth and matted hair but a soft demeanor and a kind smile. Every now and then, he approached Louis, insistent on offering him the same suspicious-looking banana, his one belonging. Louis graciously declined each time, considering the lost young man. He didn't seem much older than him. Geneviève had ventured close to the edge of addiction herself. A few different choices, and who knew, they could've also ended up roaming the streets at night. At least they would've been together, a deep voice echoed within.

Anything but her absence. If the Malkins truly did hurt her, there would be nowhere to turn to for help. No one would take him seriously. He hadn't expected the cops to believe him either. No, he was alone in this.

If the Malkins truly did hurt her, he would make them pay. Even if it was the last thing he did.

One second, he had blood on his mind. The other, he looked forward to laughing with Geneviève about the simple and logical explanation for her disappearance that had just slipped his mind. With sweet thoughts of revenge, and sweeter thoughts of a miraculous return and passionate reunion, Louis fell asleep with a dreamy smile.

DAY-150

KAYNE HAD SPENT THE day with Dimitri revising logistics for the scheduled cargo shipment. The old patriarch was known for his hands-on approach. Though a man of vision and great ambition, he'd always kept his feet firmly on the ground, continually studying his environment to turn it to his advantage. Dimitri Drugov was born to lead the Organization. His every trait served this purpose, from his charm to his ruthlessness, to his business savvy and his flair for reading people.

When he'd inherited the leadership, the Quebec branch was disorganized, with big tempers, bigger egos, and little result. With Lev by his side, they'd expanded and diversified, uniting previously warring factions under one banner. Kayne could only recall one occasion of raised voices between the two. He'd later understood it was about his mother.

He was driving home and ground his teeth upon seeing Maxwell's name blink on the screen.

"Maxwell," he curtly greeted him.

"Kayne," Maxwell responded, gravity injected in his honeyed tone. "Louis Lavallé. He's one of yours, isn't he?"

"What about him?"

"He's a problem."

"I'm aware."

"Good, good. Are you also aware that he spent the night in lockup? Riley got hold of the report… your name was in it. Something about a missing girl?"

Kayne exhaled with frustration. He knew Maxwell reveled at the opportunity to have one up on him, sweeping in as the fixer in a messy situation caused by the Malkin household.

Kayne Malkin and Maxwell Bane. Their mutual aversion to one another had been almost instant. He reminded Kayne of something reptilian, spineless, and deceitful. He'd seen in his eyes a level of sadism that had left even his Monster on guard. Maxwell had come out of nowhere, slithering his way up the Organization to become the highest-ranking foreigner. He'd left behind a young wife and son in Europe he barely visited. He'd even missed the birth of his child to partake in a mission crucial to his ascension. Kayne had had a few conversations with Dimitri about him. But the old man had brushed him off. He could see right through him, he'd assured Kayne. Was opportunism really an undesirable trait? Dimitri had countered. He rather appreciated the up-and-comer's duplicitous mind and could empathize with his cruel streak. Maxwell's unparalleled intelligence and lack of conscience made him a force to be reckoned with and an invaluable asset to the Organization.

Among his most notable triumphs was securing Officer Thomas Riley's allegiance. A respected member of the force and beloved by his community, his word was law. No one would ever doubt anything he'd stamped.

Riley was a man of values, forged in an unyielding character guarding a gentle heart. He'd joined the police force as if admitted into a sacred order, with deference and aspirations to make the world a better place. Atop his towering height and massive build, he'd never looked down on anyone, serving his neighborhood with diligence and a warm smile. Unlike some of his coworkers, he didn't regard beggars, streetwalkers, and drug addicts as a nuisance but rather as lost souls who'd suffered enough and needed more than anyone else a dose of kindness.

Late at night, after all the lights at the station had been turned off, he'd stay behind at his desk. Rather than booking the latest batch of lawbreakers for minor misdemeanors, he would reach out to local charities, trying to get them the help they needed. He'd look at the pinned pictures in his cubicle and feel pride. He did it all for them, his two greatest loves. One of them, he'd yet to meet. The other sent him off with loving kisses and hot coffee every morning, rubbing her growing belly with a serene smile.

Seventeen years later, the only difference he'd made was to destroy his marriage and alienate his beloved daughter. To this day, he still badgered his ex-wife with impassioned calls placed during lonely and liquor-filled nights. In the shameful mornings that followed his cries of despair, he would reach out again, his tail tucked between his legs. She always forgave him, interrupting his profuse apologies to patiently reassure him before rushing off the line, turning her attention back to her new family.

His little princess, however, hadn't shown her mother's clemency. She'd already raged as a child at his absence on birthdays and recitals. What kind of father chooses strangers over his own family? Why should they pay the price for others' misfortunes? Was he truly out to save the world, or had he just become addicted to the validation and accolades? She'd later accused him.

As a teenager in a blended family, she begrudged the whole world and blamed him for it all. Worse than the void his workaholism had left in her childhood was how powerless she'd felt, tending to her fragile mother in her never-ending cycle of hope and heartbreak. While the publicly lauded figure pursued naïve and heroic dreams, he'd left a depressive and neglected lover at home with an anxious child unable to soothe her caregiver's distress. Upon the divorce, she'd dropped his last name and cut him out of her life.

A year ago, he'd finally received a call from her. His elation, however, was short-lived. She was in the bad kind of trouble, with the worst kind of people. He had run to her side, fixed the problem, and paid off her debt with money he didn't have. For the first time, he'd noted gratitude, even tenderness, in her eyes. She didn't see a corrupt cop or a failed missionary. She'd hugged him tight, like she never had before, clinging to the father she'd always craved. He'd sold his soul for his daughter, bribed in the currency of her love; he'd never regretted it. He'd been Maxwell's man ever since. Maxwell, who, unbeknownst to Riley, had specifically targeted his offspring, understanding it was the only way to get to him.

Kayne considered the new information and the implication it carried. He remembered seeing Louis pacing around the house. He'd barely paid him any attention. His mind was on the sleeping body that had unconsciously resisted when he'd carefully removed his arm.

"Understood. Thank you, Maxwell. I'll handle it." It was all the gratitude Kayne would impart.

"Kayne, I will be at the cabin with Carlo. Some other business… You already have enough on your plate with the shipments and all. Not to mention your beautiful bride."

Kayne's hands tightened on the wheel, picturing his toothy sneer. How he hated hearing any reference to Laura from his mouth.

"Just get him here. I'll take care of him for you. Tell him we have his girl. He'll believe you. He so desperately wants to," Maxwell added with eerie playfulness.

Kayne might have considered it, but he knew better than ever to accept Maxwell's helping hand and be in his debt. The underhanded leech would use it at every turn to smear the Malkin name. He would position himself as the savior in an explosive domestic situation, consciously stirring the pot to revive the ripples his marriage to Laura Spencer had caused in the Organization.

The Lavallé boy needed to be dealt with. Once upon a time, he wouldn't have cared about innocent blood being shed. This time, however, he felt a twist in the gut. He sympathized with the boy. Not so long ago, he'd stood against Dimitri for Laura. What was a man, if not the last wall defending his tribe? Louis, barely old enough to drive, was stepping in as Geneviève's protector, and he now had to pay the ultimate price for his honorable pursuit. Kayne lowered weary eyes, again finding himself in the villain's shoes. He could not spare the boy's life. He would at least ensure him a quick death. He knew Maxwell too well to expect him to handle the matter efficiently and not prolong his twisted pleasures. "I'll bring the boy. I'll handle him myself. Take care of the scene and clean up."

"Very well," Maxwell conceded with bitterness to the higher-ranking Kayne.

★ ★ ★

Louis had returned to the Malkin residence in the early morning, disheveled and visibly upset. He'd mainly kept to himself all day, his eyes down and his movements agitated. Seeing him constantly checking his phone, Laura felt a pinch, realizing with a guilty conscience the futility of it. His presence became intolerable to her, his anguish a constant thorn in her side. She'd intended to stay and wait for Kayne, but her remorse vanquished her yearning. She made herself small and, acknowledging her cowardice, flew the scene of her crime.

★ ★ ★

Louis fidgeted nervously on the couch in the reception hall. Obediently, he awaited Mr. Malkin as instructed by the head of security. It seemed to him like hours had passed until the door finally swayed open, Mr. Malkin walking in with Mr. Belfort behind, their mood somber.

"Louis. Thank you for waiting." Kayne approached him.

The young man jumped to his feet and nodded, wiping his clammy hand on his jeans before shaking his employer's.

"We have information about Geneviève," Kayne paused.

"Yes?" Louis responded apprehensively, his mouth unconsciously twitching.

"We know where she is."

"Where?" he almost screamed, his voice scratchy with emotion.

Kayne nodded his head somewhat compassionately. "I'll take you to her." The words carefully chosen only alluded to the boy's death sentence. It was his one ethical code. Through this one trait, he'd achieved notoriety and bought himself some resemblance of morality. Covered in blood atop a pile of skeletons and dirty money, he'd held on to this one mantra: he was no liar.

"Is she okay?" Louis asked without conviction, his strained features reflecting his awareness of the grim answer awaiting.

"No."

The blond youngster defensively turned away, blinking his eyes dry. When he faced him again, his stare was hateful and filled with unspoken accusations.

"Let's go," Kayne commanded in a grave tone to the hostile face. He maintained eye contact until Louis folded and lowered his gaze to the floor. His head bowed, the young boy silently followed Kayne to meet his fate.

★ ★ ★

The trap was set. Maxwell would be awaiting them at the cabin with Carlo. Kayne would proceed with the interrogation alone, retracing all the different paths that the boys' inflammatory words could have taken. He would be shot in the temple using an unmarked firearm, and his body placed in a manner to suggest suicide. The case would be overseen and ultimately signed off by Officer Riley.

The drive was long and eerily silent under a moonless sky. At last, Kayne turned into a gravel road and drove deeper into the wilderness, pulling up to a cozy-looking log wood cottage.

"Ready?" he asked with a grave expression.

Louis looked around suspiciously but voiced no concern at the unusual meeting point. He nodded, rubbed his sweaty palms on his lap, and reached for the handle.

Once out of the car, Kayne purposely took the lead, walking ahead of the boy and leaving his back unguarded to suggest a climate of trust. They walked in through the back door and straight into the kitchen area.

Maxwell, conversing with Carlo, turned to greet them, twisting his slimy features into a smile. Kayne walked up to him and, reaching out his hand, nodded in complicit silence.

"And this is Mr. Lavallé, I presume?" Maxwell bent his body sideways to look at the restless boy hanging behind.

"Everything is ready?" Kayne leaned in, inquiring in a hushed tone.

"Most certainly. Everything is ready for you," Maxwell responded louder than expected, ablaze with malevolent delight.

Kayne's eyes grew round with bewilderment. By the time he heard the gun cock behind him, he understood, too late, that it was he who had walked into the trap.

Louis Lavallé, the invisible boy. Even within his family. His parents, always fawning over his athletic and extraverted older brother, often overlooked his agreeable and sensitive sibling. Geneviève, the first person to ever give him importance, had breathed life into him. There was nothing before her. There would be nothing after her.

He'd sensed she was no more from the moment she'd disappeared. The world had turned grey again. The Monster and his Babylonian Whore were behind it. He'd known this as well without a shred of evidence. He'd felt it in his gut, as a woman recognized a rival when all others saw charming innocence. As a mother sniffed out and loathed her child's foe before they'd even wronged them.

Laughed off as a conspiracy theorist, he'd refused to wallow in despair while in lockup and vowed he would not let the Malkins get away with it. His prayers were answered in the form of his bail being miraculously posted for and an auspicious black Lexus awaiting him upon his release. It seemed the Monster had made more than one enemy, even within his clan.

A short man in a pinstripe suit had greeted him in the backseat. He knew a lot about Louis and didn't waste time before delivering the devastating news. He'd spoken with Kayne, confirming Louis's suspicions. He'd asked him if given a chance to avenge her, would he take it, and responded with a toothy sneer at the darkness in Louis's eyes.

Patiently, he'd gone over the details, asking him to repeat each step to ensure the flawless execution of his Machiavellian plan. Louis had been initially terrified, but the balding stocky man had given him a pill to help him relax when the time came.

Louis was to return to the Malkin residence and avoid all interaction while awaiting his call. Maxwell would speak to Kayne, luring him to the cabin. Once confirmed, he would give Louis the go-ahead, setting in motion the orchestration of Kayne Malkin's assassination.

All day, Louis had paced around, anxious for the signal and constantly pulling his phone out of his pocket under the inquisitive eyes of Mrs. Malkin. All evening, he'd resisted the urge to confront the Monster.

At last, Louis's phone vibrated with the awaited number. As instructed by Mr. Bane, he requested a meeting with the Master of the house. Under no circumstance was he to show suspicion and inquire about Geneviève's situation. But he couldn't help asking one question and test the Monster's famed honesty. Kayne Malkin had remained true to his reputation.

The conversation had gone precisely as per Mr. Bane's prediction. He'd followed the Monster into the cabin in the woods and found the gun hidden behind the flowerpot, as advised. He would get his vengeance, as promised.

He waited for Kayne to turn around; this part was crucial, and he pulled the trigger with shaky fingers. "She's dead! She's dead!" Louis screamed hysterically.

Kayne winced and, looking down at his chest, saw his white shirt turning crimson. When he raised his face again, his eyes seemed as old as time, a crooked and pained smile curving his lips.

"You killed her! She was everything! Everything! You used her as a whore! And you killed her!" Louis yelled, his sweet face distorted into that of a manic clown.

Kayne growled at the sharp burning, feeling his own body turn on him, fluids rising in his chest and choking him. He struggled to breathe, and coughing blood with each breath he drew, he slowly fell to the ground.

A part of him felt at peace, knowing this was the only end befitting a monster. He felt no resentment toward the boy. In his shoes, he would've done the same. Hell, he would've tortured him for days and laughed at his pleas for death. He would have brought him back to life just so he could do it all over again.

"She was everything…." Louis's voice cracked, his fury dissipating and abandoning him to his unbearable pain. He was about to speak again when another bullet was fired. The shot was precise and aimed right between the eyes, taking Louis Lavallé down in one fell swoop.

"How could I resist? Bringing the two lovebirds together… Ah! I'm just a hopeless romantic." Maxwell smirked and, pulling a chair to face Kayne, sat down with glee.

Kayne coughed again, remaining silent as blood pooled around him.

"You know…" Maxwell carried on conversationally, "I do owe sweet little Laura my gratitude. She's the reason you had the poor girl taken out, isn't she? I barely had to convince the boy. He was ready to take on the both of you on his own. You have to admire youth's fervor…" He shook his head with a chuckle.

Kayne's eyes narrowed with murderous threat, his menacing air broken as he heaved on the floor.

"Shall I get you some water?" Maxwell asked with mock concern and broke into a chortle. "Oh well… I think it's rather poetic, wouldn't you agree? So much blood spilled. Not for money. Not for glory. But all in the name of *love*. I've been dreaming of this for so long." He grinned. "I just had to wait for you to slip up. It is you who handed me the perfect opportunity on a silver platter. You've been off your game lately. What's the matter, Kayne? Too preoccupied with the lovely Miss Spencer? Or should I say Mrs. Malkin, now? She's been playing with your head since the night you brought her to me. So sad she will be the end of you."

Maxwell sneered, his unadulterated hatred blazing through. "You may think that I've been planning this for years, that there is nothing I wouldn't do to get ahead. You would be correct. However, as I look at you, pathetically drained of your own blood, do you know what I'm thinking of? *Who* I'm thinking of? A goddess. A goddess with fiery hair and emerald eyes. She is worth murder and betrayal. She is worth eternal damnation. You've killed her for the woman you love. You will now die for killing the woman *I* loved. You know what's the best part of this? When my time comes, I will be reunited with my Tanya. Your sweet little Laura, you will never see again. Not where you're going."

Kayne lay immobile on the ground. It was a funny feeling to be on the receiving end of a death sentence. He thought of the fallen scarlet siren. From beyond the grave, she'd thrown her last arrow straight into his chest. He smiled with resigned calm, accepting his fate: it was a good fight. He would make sure and shake her hand in the lands below.

But his last thoughts were with his beautiful captive. He deserved to die. He wasn't sorry for himself. The unrest he felt as his vision darkened was for Laura. He'd failed her, as her lover, as her Master, and as her Monster.

How would Dimitri react to his passing? Kayne wondered with dread what his stance on the young widow would be. He'd tried with all his might to shield her from the darkness he'd introduced her to. But he could no longer protect her. Her only hope was to now fully embrace the demons she'd been trying to outrun her entire life. To emerge as a monster in the dog-eat-dog world he'd abandoned her in. Lucas and Kiev would remain loyal. Olga had already claimed her as her own. Natasha, too, could most likely be counted on to lean in her favor. Laura would be safe, he reassured himself.

Laura. He'd met her as a child of light so pure even his Monster struggled to snuff it out in her. And yet, she'd risen to the occasion time and time again, transforming under his very eyes from white dove to purple monarch.

How different would his life have been had he never met her? How heartbreakingly different would hers have been? But then Mrs. Malkin would have never been born. He smiled; he did not regret a thing. It was better to have loved and lost. His Laura. He'd loved her with ferocious protectiveness. He'd loved her with desperate passion and depraved, insatiable lust. He'd loved her with tenderness and the humility to want to become worthy of her. But she would never know. She would never hear it from him. And as his heart bled out, that one regret consumed it.

Maxwell could have never guessed the heart-wrenching thoughts ripping his victim apart. Gathering his remaining strength to spit his last words, Kayne looked victorious.

"Where I'm going, I'll make your goddess my bitch."

Maxwell's fury turned his cheeks beet red. He raised his arm to strike him but restrained himself. He had to wait for Kayne to stop laughing and oozing blood. He had to wait for the last painful breath to leave his body. The scene had to remain intact.

* * *

Laura had returned home around midnight and felt her chest tighten at Kayne's absence. It was not unusual for him to come home in the wee hours of the morning, and she felt at a loss to explain the uneasy feeling gnawing at her. Unable to sleep, think, or sit still, she roamed the lonely corridors, not knowing what to do with herself.

* * *

It was past two in the morning, and still no word from Kayne. Lucas had repeatedly attempted to reach him with no success. He had reassured Laura unconvincingly before retreating to the office. Kayne had asked him to oversee some of the preparation for the expected shipment while he handled the Louis issue. With such important business looming, there was no way Kayne would go rogue, thought Lucas with increasing concern.

★ ★ ★

Maxwell looked with loathing at the inert body at his feet. He had expected the long-awaited victory to drown his senses with euphoria and for the sustained nirvana to last for days. He'd fantasized of a pitiful Kayne groveling before him. *Where I'm going, I'll make your goddess my bitch*. Kayne had once again robbed him of a well-earned denouement. *Curse him*, he thought, grounding his teeth.

Maxwell Bane had detested the Malkin heir upon their first meeting, just as he had despised all the other Kaynes before him. He knew his sort all too well. Born under a lucky star. Blessed with looks. Showered with money. Gifted with charm and confidence. The Kaynes of the world were made aware of their elite status since childhood, moving through the world expectant of the best it had to offer.

The Maxwells of the world, however, were cursed with an uninviting form and no social skills. They were the black sheep within the community and even within their own family, either shunned or invisible. They pined after the girls the Kaynes took carelessly and dismissed ungratefully. They worked twice as hard for half the payoff and none of the recognition.

The Maxwells of the world were thought of with scorn and called snakes for simply trying to even the skewed balance. What others called *fair* were just rules favoring the stronger adversary. Virtue was a luxury afforded only to the powerful. Deceit was the only defense of the weak.

When all others had recoiled from his so-called sadism and devious thinking, Tanya had smirked at him. Only she had ever truly understood him, appreciating the twisted mind created by the twisted face. Tanya Malone, his bloodthirsty goddess. She would've not died in vain.

He reached for his cell phone. "Mr. Drugov. I apologize for disturbing you so late."

"Maxwell?" Dimitri's voice was alert, even when dragged from sleep.

"Something has happened."

"Speak."

"Kayne. Kayne Malkin is dead," he announced in a somber voice.

"*What*," Dimitri raised his tone, incredulous.

"He was shot in the chest. Louis Lavallé, this insignificant servant boy. Kayne had his girlfriend taken out, and he was running his mouth. Kayne was supposed to bring him up to the cabin to deal with it. He wanted to go alone, but I insisted on meeting them. It seems the boy was able to slip a gun past him."

"How could this have even happened?" Dimitri growled on the other end.

"He'd been quite distracted lately... Thankfully Carlo and I were there. Took down the boy in one shot."

"Have you touched anything?" Dimitri asked, still processing the news.

"No, Sir."

"Don't. I'm on my way," Dimitri commanded and disconnected the line.

Maxwell knew his word wouldn't be enough. Not when it came to Golden Boy's head. He admired his latest masterpiece, the concocted story the two silenced men would tell.

Carlo came in behind him. "Is it over, Boss?"

The trap had been set. And it had perfectly played out. Dimitri would come and confirm the story himself. Maxwell's gun would then be placed in Kayne's hands. An anonymous call would be made in the morning to the police. They would find two armed bodies positioned as to suggest a shoot-out. The case would be overseen and ultimately signed off by Officer Riley.

"Yes. It's all over."

DAY-151

LAURA HADN'T SHUT AN eye. All night, she'd paced around Kayne's room with ever-increasing angst. Like the madwoman in the attic, she could be heard below, an unsettling presence lurking in the shadows.

By the time the sun had risen, Laura's deep-seated unrest had spread throughout the Malkin Mansion. Olga rushed through her tasks, distracted and on edge, with a tense smile under dark circles. Kiev sat alone in the solarium, quiet and brooding, an untouched glass of vodka on the table before him. For his part, Lucas gated his inner turmoil even from himself, only allowing through rational thought. He strived to remain cool-headed, the pillar the Malkins could unfailingly rely on.

★ ★ ★

Laura was still in her nightgown, lying on the covers, when she heard a tap at her door.

"Yes…" Her voice came out strained, unrecognizable even to herself.

"It's Lucas. May I come in?"

"Lucas… Please."

He stepped inside the bedroom, gently shutting the door behind him. "I've just got off the phone with Dimitri. Natasha wanted to speak with you. I preferred telling you myself… Kayne has been shot."

"He's dead," she put in words the felt horror her heart was attuned to, but that her conscious mind had concealed into a vague dread, unable to fathom this cruel fate.

"I'm so sorry, Laura." Lucas lowered his eyes, swallowing the tremor in his voice. He quickly composed himself, however, and proceeded to summarize his conversation with the Mafia Boss.

"He's dead," she repeated with a deadened voice at the close of the explanation, still processing the impact of these words. "And Maxwell was there..."

"Maxwell was there." Lucas returned her stare, an unspoken emotion burning in both their eyes.

"The boy was just his pawn."

"My thoughts exactly."

"We must find the link, Lucas. We must find the link. And make him pay."

Lucas bowed his head, resolute, and took his leave.

She remained still until the door closed behind him, then collapsed on the ground. She didn't cry. She didn't make a sound. She stared ahead, wondering if she was losing her mind. Kayne Malkin couldn't possibly be dead. She'd just slept in his arms... was it last night or the night before? She couldn't tell anymore. She'd whispered I love you... Was it *I love you*... or *Thank you?* Why couldn't she remember? Kayne Malkin. Dead. How to even conceive of a world he would no longer shape? How to process that she would never be able to profess her love?

Had she stayed and waited for his return as planned, she could have had the opportunity. Instead, she'd missed that last chance due to remorse over that human stain of a boy, who, in the meantime, plotted

Kayne's murder. She clenched her fists at the thought, narrowing her eyes to villainous slits. An intense impulse for destruction took hold of her. Laura wanted to set the world on fire and watch it burn with everything in it.

Kayne Malkin. Gone. She looked at the radiant day and wondered, *hadn't the sun heard?*

First Peter, and now Kayne. Her two greatest loves had snuck out of her life through the back door like thieves in the night. She looked at her bracelet and let her index trail over the engraving. Her Monster, who'd promised to always find her, had gone where she could no longer follow. Unconsciously, her thumb found the scar on her wrist, and she felt the old itch again. Laura Spencer would have done it. Life was not for the faint of heart. Mrs. Malkin, however, would rise. She would be worthy of her Master. Mrs. Kayne Malkin would dedicate the rest of her life to avenging her teacher. She would meet her cursed life in her best attire, with her eyes dry and her hair perfectly set. Laura Spencer writhed deep within, unable to sustain the latest blow, inflicted while she still struggled to stand on broken knees. Mrs. Malkin reached in and lovingly cradled the fading soul in her arms. She caressed her hair and made shushing sounds, soothing her like the doting mother figure she'd always craved. "He will pay... We will make him pay," Laura repeated over and over as she hugged herself and rocked on the floor, an unholy spark filling the cracks in her shattered eyes.

She received the official visit from two courteous investigators not long after. Once again, she was subjected to the gruesome details, though she did note the slight but telling differences of the official report. When questioned about Kayne's line of work, she played blissful ignorance to perfection. When asked about their marriage, however, she let her genuine emotions show. If not Kayne, someone should bear witness to the depth of her love. When they left, she knew she had cried her last tears.

* * *

Laura sat with her back straight on the highchair in the reception hall. She was dipped in black from head to toe, somehow coming across as more retro chic than in mourning. Lucas had called earlier to summon her and Kiev. The two soon arrived dressed in formal black suits, not unusual for Lucas, an appreciated gesture from Kiev.

"We were right. Maxwell must have masterminded the hit," Lucas began.

Laura's eyes glinted with sinister intent.

"We'd been tracking him. We had a chip in his car..."

She looked down at her bracelet. "Like this one?" she asked, lifting her wrist.

"Similar," Lucas conceded, slightly uncomfortable. "It was an earring made by the same jeweler... We've dealt a lot with him. Maxwell even knows him... Kaminski. He's old as a mummy but silent as a tomb."

"And Maxwell wasn't suspicious of receiving earrings from Kayne?" Laura inquired with sarcasm.

Lucas cleared his throat. "They were Tanya's. She was working with Kayne... spying on Maxwell. She hid them there."

"I see." Laura felt a sting hearing her name. Even from the grave, Tanya still managed to rub her closeness with Kayne in her face. The crimson temptress had never been a burden to him, a damsel in distress in dire need of his protection. She was an ally, a respected equal entrusted with secret missions. "Please go on," Laura calmly instructed, her icy features giving no clue to the harsh thoughts ripping her insides apart.

"Maxwell was at the police station sometime late at night yesterday. His man, Thomas Riley, was on duty that night, so that's not that suspicious. But... Louis Lavallé was also there... spent the night in lockup. The chip shows Maxwell driving around until dawn.... And then awfully close to here... about two streets down... sometime in the early morning... Not long before Louis came home..."

Kiev shook his head. "It's not enough. We can't go to Dimitri with that. He checked out the scene himself, you say?"

"We won't go to him with that," Laura said in a cool tone. "Maxwell Bane...." She looked above and around her as if tossing a pleasant idea in her head. "He's married... with an adorable little boy, isn't he?"

Lucas nodded.

"You're right, Kiev. What we have is not enough. We'll need to get our confession straight from the horse's mouth before we go to Dimitri. Let's see how *he* holds up in interrogation... We need to find his wife and son. We'll use them as leverage."

Lucas looked at her, seeing a glimpse of a woman he could follow, one worthy of the memory of his best friend.

"I hear they're in Europe?"

"Yes. I don't think they've ever stepped foot in North America. It's always Maxwell who goes to them. He seldom does, mind you," Lucas said.

"Kiev, how would you like to visit the Eiffel Tower... or the Big Ben?" Laura smiled with all the hatred in her heart.

"My lifelong dream, Boss." Kiev returned her vicious sneer.

"Take the men you need. Find the wife and child. Lucas, keep your eyes on Maxwell. Once we've secured the family, we strike."

Kiev and Lucas exchanged a stare, but she didn't see them. She was lost in a bloodthirsty vision involving the torture and demise of a bald-headed snake.

"That will be all. Thank you, gentlemen."

The two men nodded in unison, turned around, and left the room.

She watched them leave and, once alone, returned to her morbid fantasy. Maxwell had stolen her Master away and any chance she ever had to prove her love. His grotesque and mutilated body would be her shrine for her Monster. The horror she would inflict on him would be heard of by gods and demons alike. Little children all over the world would tremble in their beds at night, having heard the tale of the Monster's wife and the aftermath of her broken heart. And Kayne, wherever he dwelled, would know how helplessly Laura Spencer loved her Monster.

Laura stood up with her head held high. She would step in her Monster's shoes. Wasn't it how all monsters were created, through fire and brimstone? She thought of the tale of Alexei and Aniska. She'd related so strongly to the twin sister, believing their fates intertwined. She now understood she was always destined to become the Winter Witch. Or perhaps they were one and the same, two sides of a coin; *'Tis but a series of choices that turns the lamb into a fiend.*

* * *

Kiev and Lucas walked side by side in the great hall, their walk resolute and their faces bleak.

"The King is dead," Lucas muttered, mostly to himself.

"Long live the Queen," Kiev completed.

They stopped and looked at each other. After a long pause, they nodded, bowing their head to one another in quiet complicity. Their allegiance was pledged.

Out into the beautiful sunny day, two grim reapers set out on their macabre mission. Up in the clear blue sky, a crow circling overhead cawed along. It followed the two men as they headed to the awaiting black cars and then returned to the Malkin mansion. Atop the iron *M* crest, it perched itself and watched the front gates open, its clear blue eyes strangely human.

★ ★ ★

One for the witch,
Two for the boy,
Three for the wolf and the wood-chipped toy,
Four for the brother,
Five for the sister,
Six for the children that were kissed by Mother,
Seven for the light,
Eight for the strife,
Nine for the flame that brings eternal life...